PYGMALION'S RECKONING

QUINTIN VARGAS

Novels by Quintin Vargas:

IBERIAN TIES

THE UNRAVELING

PYGMALION'S RECKONING

ISBN: 978-1-7337028-6-7 (paperback)

*In memory of my first, and best,
teacher—my dad, Quintin Vargas II.*

*Also, in tribute to all loving mothers—in particular,
Esperanza Vargas and Wanda Kellam—and
others, some departed, others not. Because of their
selfless dedication, like Miriam Epstein, a character
in this trilogy, their memories live on.*

Western Mediterranean Coastline

PART ONE

THE DROWNING

"How people die remains in the memory of those who live on."

DAME CICELY SAUNDERS

CHAPTER ONE

[Chicago; November 2021]

Commander Rob Rivers of the Chicago PD's Twentieth District was clear: "Either you get your choppers and their strobes to stop flashing their lights on us, or you and the rest of your crew will be cleared out." In a loud voice, Rivers addressed Horace Rosenberg, rising star reporter for the *Chicago Tribune* and chronicler of the Shelley-Epstein family escapades for several years. "And, Rosie, you know the drill—stay behind the yellow barricade tape."

Rosie pulled up his jacket collar and with a nod acknowledged the Chicago PD commander. The pine-scented chill of the Lake Michigan shoreline was typical for a Midwestern fall. As two choppers circled and the strobes took a southwestern approach, they cast shadows of the enormous white pines of the park on the lakeshore. Against the soft light of the half moon, the bright lights cast a spectral, almost unearthly image on the outline of the moored sloop anchored fifty yards from the lake's shoreline.

The chopper's lights focused on the pier, extending its reach toward the boat. Next to and under the wooden pier, two bodies had floated toward the shore, and more than a dozen newshounds fought for a closer look at the victims. Adding to the strobe lights of the choppers, the flashes of the photojournalists created an unwelcome mayhem that Rivers would soon put to an end.

Although he directed his aggravation at Rosenberg, Commander Rivers carefully studied the gaggle of reporters and their cameramen who followed Rosie around. Rivers now flashed his own LED flashlight onto Rosenberg's face. The cold November darkness had not kept a dozen TV, print, and radio reporters from arriving almost immediately after Rivers's crew. In fact, the CNBS chopper had arrived at the scene before Rivers.

As usual, the cub reporters from the area's news networks followed Rosie's lead. Rosie had a reputation, a good one, which had been earned during his short tenure at the *Tribune*. Investigative reporting at its best—in the old-school kind of way. Well-earned respect. The chopper that hovered above clearly identified itself by its CNBS logo, but Commander Rivers could count on Rosenberg to take the lead in controlling the various ambulance-chasing journalists and their breathless reportage.

Without acknowledging the airborne scandalmongers above, Rosie raised his right arm and made a circular whirling motion. More than once in the past, CNBS had attempted to disregard the Chicago District Commander, and each time they had come to regret doing so. Rivers never used empty threats. He meant what he said, and he said what he meant. This time, however, before swooping away immediately, the chopper hovered over the lakeshore area, floodlighting the distinctive outline of two casualties floating a few feet from shore. Later that night, the image would flood every television network station across the country.

• • •

Horace (Rosie) Rosenberg quickly jotted his notes regarding the scene: *Two bodies found floating near a sloop by the name of* The Black Pearl. In his notes, Rosie placed an asterisk before jotting down the next fact. It was a reminder to himself that he should mention in his article as a footnote that "twenty months ago, two charred bodies had been found aboard *The Black Pearl* and a renowned psychiatrist, his wife, and daughter had been rescued after a failed attempt on their lives". Rosie carefully put brackets on the footnote and continued with his report.

Now, floating toward the shore of Lake Michigan by Belmont Harbor, the bodies of two young men—children, really; they could not have been more than fifteen years old—*not yet decomposing, but grotesquely covered in mud, slime, and pine needles, bobbed in the water and drifted toward the frigid lakeshore.* Rosie's asterisked notes estimated the bodies had been in the water maybe twenty-four to forty hours, certainly fewer than three days.

Commander Rivers's LED flashlight found Rey Gund as he attempted to move toward the bodies, camera at the ready to take close-ups of the two corpses. His leather shoes sank into the mud, and he lost his balance when the commander flashed his light on him.

Since Gund was Rosenberg's photographer, Rosie called out, "The chief means business, Rey. Stay behind the yellow tape or you'll find yourself behind bars, and I don't have the money to bail you out."

From twenty feet away, another reporter exclaimed, "Commander, do you think these deaths are related to the burned bodies found on *The Black Pearl* in the spring of last year?" It was the tinny, piercing voice of the Univision TV reporter, whose image appeared in the Southwest Chicago billboards that proclaimed bold and unfiltered reporting. As it swooped away from the Lake Michigan scene, the helicopter's yellow beacons lit the night sky with a festive glow. Commander Rivers' crew, who had resorted to the use of megaphones to keep the reporters away from the medical examiners, hurried about helping medical personnel and chasing the reporters from the shore. The scene resembled an eerie mud wrestling competition gone amok.

"Were they burned like the other victims aboard *The Black Pearl?*" inquired Univision's newsperson. Her rubber boots were muddied, indicating that she had gone undetected as she got closer to the floating bodies.

The CNBS reporter, not a favorite of Rivers, asked, "Have you figured out who they are? Since they appear to be minorities, can we assume that it'll take months for your department to identify them?" She aimed her microphone at Rivers, hoping to get an incriminating response.

Agitated, Rivers just rolled his eyes without responding to the comment. "Okay, that's it! We're expanding our perimeter and we'll cordon off the barricade. For now, the scene is blocked off from any further investigation from non-essential personnel. All members of the press leave—right now."

"You—Rosenberg—come here. I want you to know that there is no evidence of foul play; obviously, we haven't identified the two male casualties, and we have no idea if these deaths are related to previous ones—got it?"

"Thanks, Commander," said Rosenberg. As he turned to leave, the fully expanded EMT gurneys almost ran him over as they slushed toward the shore. While he waited for his photographer, Rey Gund, to join him in his Toyota Corolla, Rosie scribbled a note to himself to call his friend "Mad Max" Kempball to bring him up to date on the latest murders related to *The Black Pearl*. His friend would be interested. Max's half-sister, Miró Epstein-Shelley, her husband, and their daughter had survived last year's massacre that had taken place aboard the infamous sloop.

Originally from Austin, Max Kempball had relocated to Chicago to help solve the attempted murder of his relatives. Smiling, Rosenberg could just hear Max saying, "Y'all Midwesterners sure do like to make a big splash when you're up to no-good, Rosie. The murderer, he probably left a few clues behind—perps always do." Still, after having known Max for a few years, Rosie could not get used to his friend's easy Texas drawl and his propensity to using an unnecessary pronoun after introducing a subject. "By the way, my dad," Max would say, "he sure would like to see you."

Gund sprinted to the compact car and tossed his equipment into the back seat. Rosenberg started the engine and drove to his *Tribune* office to finish writing his article regarding *The Black Pearl's* most recent deaths.

CHAPTER TWO

[Skokie and Winnetka, IL; November 2021]

=MAX=

Rob Rivers, he called me at 2:00 a.m. A courtesy call from a good friend who attends the Evanston Vineyard Christian Church— you know, the church I'm part of. We're members of the same men's group and often start our Wednesdays with 7:00 morning prayers and Bible study at our favorite coffee dive, the Backlot Coffee Shop. Rob simply said, "Forgive the late call, but we've got a crime scene at Belmont Harbor. I thought you might be interested." He was right. I was interested. I rushed over to the scene of the tragedy.

My full name is Maximillian Kempball. I go by "Max." I'm a private investigator from Austin, Texas, but I've been living in the Chicago area with my dad for the last couple of years. My half-sister, Professor Miró Epstein-Shelley, is married to a big-shot psychiatrist, Dr. Nathaniel—Nate—Shelley. Miró has a sixteen-year-old daughter, Minnie, from a previous marriage. After my sister and Nate got married, he adopted Minnie—or "Minerva," her given name—as she prefers to be called now.

The reason my buddy from the Chicago PD thought I'd be interested in the crime scene at Belmont Harbor off Lake Michigan is that twenty months ago, Nate, Miró, and Minerva escaped being executed aboard *The Black Pearl*, which is moored at Belmont Harbor in the Lincoln Park area. The harbor is home to numerous upscale sailboats and small yachts and sloops. By November, many of the vessels had already been placed in dry dock in preparation for winter and a frozen Lake Michigan. The crime that occurred at the dock twenty months ago is part of the reason I've remained in Chicago. Since my relatives feel their lives are still in danger, I've offered to dedicate my private investigator skills to help apprehend the creeps responsible.

My buddy, Commander Rob Rivers, is a precinct commander at the Chicago PD. He and his men had just fished out of Lake Michigan two teenage bodies that were found floating close to *The Black Pearl.* When I arrived at the scene, Rivers and his men had sent the reporters away and eliminated what he described as a "circus atmosphere" created by the hovering helicopters and the gaggle of "gossip peddlers." Though respectful of serious journalists, Rivers does not tolerate any disrespect for victims' privacy or their loved ones. He informed me that he believed the young victims were two Winnetka teenagers who'd been missing barely twenty-four hours. Winnetka is a small, upper-middle class community sixteen miles north of downtown Chicago.

Rivers had spoken to his counterpart at the Winnetka PD and had received the okay to notify the next-of-kin if his suspicions proved correct. The Chicago PD coroner would take less than six hours to verify the kids' identities. Only then would the difficult part begin—notifying loved ones.

After spending three hours checking out the crime scene with Rivers, I returned to my apartment and tried going back to sleep. However, I kept remembering Rivers's last words, "A desperate single mom from Winnetka by the name of Rosales reported her kids missing, and so far, the kids' bodies fit her description."

Could it be that there's a connection with the seasoned criminals involved with my niece's—Minerva's—disappearance twenty months ago? Prior to an attempted execution aboard *The Black Pearl,* Minerva had been kidnapped. Pedro and Macario Rosales were identified as my niece's kidnappers. Shortly thereafter the brothers had been murdered on the same day—March 13, 2020. In fact, Macario, one of the kidnappers, had died on the deck of *The Black Pearl.*

Shortly before noon, I received the second call from Rivers. The bodies of the fifteen-year-old kids had been identified. The distraught mom had reacted hysterically when she saw her sons' decaying bodies. It was obvious that the teenagers had been hog-tied and gagged. Although there was no indication they had been shot, stabbed, or tortured, it was clear that the cause of death had been drowning. They were indeed the twin sons of Raquel Rosales, widow of the kidnapper Macario Rosales. And the connection with my half-sister, Miró, and her husband, Nate, was obvious. I pleaded with Rob Rivers to allow me to tag along to interview the mother. Rivers didn't think it was a good idea, but he promised to involve me as soon as it became permissible.

The following morning Rosie Rosenberg and I invited Rob Rivers to breakfast. I wanted to clarify my family's connection to the international criminal responsible for *The Black Pearl* massacre, which had occurred in March 2020. Since Rivers had not worked the case, he was unaware of important details. As Rosie stood in line to order our coffee, Rivers arrived and apologized for his delay. He'd received updates regarding the twins' drowning, which he promised to share later.

"Okay, Max—I know you and Rosie have been dealing with these matters for some time. I need some background," said Commander Rivers.

Knowing that we were all short on time, I got to the point. "This story began in 2016. It's about a family feud, a deed of ownership, and revenge."

My buddy Rob Rivers laughed. "Okay, Max. I did *not* ask for a bedtime story."

"Well, Rob, I was trying to summarize."

Rosie approached the table with coffees in hand. "Commander, first of all thanks for showing up although you knew that a member of the press was going to accompany your friend, 'Mad Max', here."

Nodding, Rob Rivers said, "All I ask is that you be respectful of everything that is shared here. I know that you're responsible and honorable. But I do need to remind you that everything I say here is off the record."

"By all means," said Rosie. Turning to me, he asked, "Max, please go on. Just wanted to thank the Commander for joining us."

"Y'all know that, at the request of my dad, I moved here from Austin roughly two years ago to help my sister and her family out. Although their troubles began in 2016 when they traveled to the Canary Islands, the threats to their lives continued after they returned home to Chicago. Their principal nemesis is Diego Montemayor, an international drug lord—perhaps, the most wanted international criminal in the world. He is the person responsible for the original *Black Pearl* massacre."

"And," said Rivers, "the person that we presume is behind the latest murder of the Rosales kids we found two nights ago."

By the way, I ordered some breakfast tacos for us," said Rosie. "Max, why don't you give Commander Rivers the historical—by that I mean, the genealogical—perspective?"

"Ooh. That may be hard to do, but since we do not have my dad, the genealogist, present, I'll give it a stab." Clearing my throat, I continued: "In the late 1600s the Spanish Crown gave a certain Spanish conquistador an enormous land grant in New Spain."

"New Spain being what we now know as Mexico?" Rob was asking.

"Exactly," I said. "This parcel of land comprised one-fourth of what is present-day Texas. The conquistador, he became the governor of this vast piece of real estate."

Since I noticed that Rob's eyes were glazed over, I interrupted myself and said, "Here come the long-awaited breakfast tacos." I took my first bite, and although Rosie had highly recommended the restaurant, I was disappointed that Chicago had not caught up with the true Tex-Mex art of breakfast tacos. I decided to keep it to myself.

"Sorry, Max, but why is this history lesson necessary?" Rob asked.

"Hold your horses. I'll make the connection. Since the conquistador was childless, he groomed a nephew to succeed him as governor. This nephew went against tradition and deeded his land to a daughter. This daughter married and had two children, Eliza and José Antonio. Eliza became the great-grandmother to Miró, my sister."

"Okay, I cannot say that I'm riveted to your story, Max, but I see the connection," said Rob.

Rosie Rosenberg valiantly jumped in, "Stay with us here, Commander, because the serendipitous link becomes fascinating. In a tragic fire, José Antonio—Eliza's brother—died as a young man, but his wife left the New World and settled in the Canary Islands with a newborn child."

"And, since land could not be passed on to anyone but a direct family member, the widow inherited nothing," I said. "That widow became Yael Vidaurri Montemayor's great-grandmother."

"And was Yael Montemayor Diego Montemayor's wife?" Rob asked.

"The same one," Rosie Rosenberg said. "However, do not fail to note that Yael's maiden name was Vidaurri—the same maiden name of Miró's mom.

"As far as I remember my history, neither Miró's family nor Yael's kept the property, did they?" asked Rob.

"No, of course not," Rosie said. "But since this gargantuan land grant the size of Rhode Island stayed in the Vidaurri family until the second half of the nineteenth century, Yael assumed that the side of the Vidaurri family who stayed behind in the New World sold the land for a fortune. The truth is that some newcomers to Texas—in one of the most audacious swindles in history— 'purchased' the land for a pittance from a local rancher who claimed to own it."

I finished Rosie's thought. "And so Yael Montemayor until her dying day assumed that her family in Spain had been cheated out of the ownership of a grand piece of real estate in the US."

"Now I see the genealogical connection," Rob said.

"And," I added, "do you now see why I initially stated that the story began with three elements: a family feud, a deed of ownership, and revenge?"

"I do indeed," said my buddy, the Commander.

• • •

After our breakfast, I called my brother-in-law Nate to give him an update, but the call went to voicemail. I chose not to leave a message because the unfolding mystery had taken an unpredictably promising twist, and I didn't want to arouse any false hopes over the phone. *Could this tragedy become a lead to the capture of the person, or persons, responsible for so much crime and bloodshed?* I was hopeful but not optimistic.

The international drug lord, Diego Montemayor, had disappeared soon after the March 13, 2020, massacre—as the newspapers called it. I was certain the news media would speculate on the likely connection to the recent murders. The journalists would do anything to glamorize the violence, the downtown explosion, and Lake Michigan murders from 2020. A repetition of the cries for crime control and violence would again capture the attention of a horrified public and the media would be more than glad to contribute to the hysteria.

Per FBI investigations on *The Black Pearl* massacre, the European drug lord—now missing for almost two years—was believed to be responsible for the death of five federal agents, one police officer, a federal informant, my stepmother, and two of his own associates, Macario and Pedro Rosales. After the murders, American authorities believed that the evasive Diego Montemayor had escaped to Europe. I considered but quickly dismissed the possibility that Diego had returned stateside. A powerful man like Diego would simply order someone else to conduct a hit without putting himself at risk.

Although Commander Rivers of the Chicago PD enjoyed an excellent relationship with most of the chiefs in the Northshore area, it was highly unusual that a precinct commander from Chicago would be allowed to conduct interrogations outside his jurisdiction. However, he was a respected professional and a man of integrity who never hesitated to cooperate with his colleagues, and when possible, he went out of his way to give others the credit for successful outcomes. Because the crime had been committed in Chicago, he asked the Winnetka police chief for permission to interrogate family members of the deceased. Rivers's colleague in Winnetka offered his full cooperation and even suggested that Rob Rivers be the one to take the lead in informing Raquel Rosales of the death of her twin sons.

Per Rivers, when the grieving mother traveled to the medical examiner's lab to identify the bodies, she did not take the tragedy well. After all, she had lost her husband less than two years before. Now she had lost her "only joys," her two strapping sons. Rivers made an appointment to see Mrs. Rosales three days later to question her about the disappearance of her sons. To Rivers's surprise, she called him the following day to say that she was ready to answer any questions he might have. Immediately after receiving her call, Rivers reached out to me asking if I'd like to join him. I agreed, and we drove to her home early the next afternoon.

CHAPTER THREE

[Winnetka, IL; November 2021]

=MAX=

During my time in Chicagoland, I had not explored the North Shore area, nor was I familiar with the communities along the vertical Lake Michigan shoreline. As Rob and I headed toward the Rosales residence, I discovered that Winnetka was an extremely well-to-do community, a village dotted with soaring fall vegetation in the many parks and bike trails that contrasted with Chicago's downtown commercial district. Though the skies were overcast, down the main thoroughfare, Sheridan Road, the orange, yellow, and red foliage seemed to brighten the day. The wall of vegetation shielded passersby from the pastoral setting of the enormous mini and not-so-mini mansions deep in their properties.

Yet nothing could have prepared me for the extravagance of Raquel Rosales's estate. As Rivers continued northward on this principal boulevard, he was instructed by his GPS to turn east to approach Mrs. Rosales's home. It appeared to me that we almost reached the shore of Lake Michigan. As we neared the estate along a fifty-yard asphalt road bordered by tall evergreen hedges, a massive black wrought-iron gate blocked our entrance. Standing guard at each end were two bald eagles perched atop nine-foot white brick pillars. The bald eagles, sculpted in bronze, matched the round initials "R.D." on the center of the gate's entrance. A four-foot white-brick pillar housed a digitally controlled screen and voice-activated microphone, which instructed visitors to identify themselves. Rob Rivers did as he was told, and five seconds later the electronic gates swung open from the middle.

We drove on the red cobblestone driveway for approximately fifteen yards and a sign instructed us to circle to the right. At the base of the turnaround, we could see that the driveway was circular, and it created a three-hundred-sixty-degree path to direct guests in and out of the estate. In the center of the circular driveway was an enormous fountain, about fifteen feet tall and at least twenty feet in diameter. Later, I learned from Mrs. Rosales that it was a two-tiered fountain done in patina bronze. Undoubtedly, my jaw dropped when I goosenecked from the passenger seat to admire this magnificent fountain as Rivers circled the driveway toward the front of the manor house entrance. The first tier of the fountain was adorned with four females in Roman robes playing different instruments—two of them playing lutes and the other two playing harps. Above, the second tier of the fountain supported three wild horses facing outward and standing on their hind legs. At the top of the structure was a fierce lion, also standing on its hind legs. Water spewed out of its roaring mouth. The fountain was lit and fully operational. A pedestal that supported the fountain stood on a natural stone pool that held the cascading water.

As Rob opened the driver's side door, he chuckled again. "Hey, Max—you look like a kid on his first visit to the zoo. We've arrived. Let's go up to the front door."

I admitted that I was overwhelmed. Turning to the front entrance, I almost gasped. If I thought the gated entrance and the fountain were impressive, the front of the manor house, which had been hidden from view, took my breath away. I'd never been to Linderhof Palace, but I'd read about it. This was the closest I could envision. Of course, the front entrance to the manor was not as enormous, but the symmetry of the boxwood hedges and the plantings on either side of the entrance reminded me of that kind of grandeur. The front plantings were manicured in geometric shapes and laid out in symmetrical patterns. The boxwood hedges, which extended from the front entrance to the edge of the driveway fanned out from the entrance to the two stone parapets upon which lay two adult bronze lions. Thirteen gradual steps guided visitors to the front door. The different levels of the front garden were united by the harmony and order of the cascading beds of greenery on both sides. When I thought about the owner of this property, I could only think of this structure being a manifestation of self-glorification and power.

"Wow, Rob—let's ascend to the shrine."

Rob merely smiled.

Walking side by side along the wide entrance, I realized two others could have joined us. If I've ever been intimidated by architecture, this was my introduction. All I could imagine was a property owner conveying dominance, status, and influence.

Halfway up the steps, I stopped to take in the front of the façade. It appeared that the imposing stone structure had four floors, and like the gardens, the building was perfectly symmetrical. On either side of the main entrance were two round towers with conical roofs. The rest of the building's roof was steeply pitched, and on either side of the round towers two massive chimneys adorned the roof line. Several dormers, which I didn't stop to count, also dotted the roof line.

Since I imagine I must have been gawking as I took each step, Rob reached the top step and stood waiting for me at the front entrance. The enormous wooden doors had rounded arches.

Upon entering, I expected to be greeted by a tuxedoed butler, but the massive black doors opened automatically. The entry foyer was not carpeted, so each of our steps created a hollow echo. As we walked through the immaculate, white-marbled entrance, a computer-generated voice instructed us to continue toward the "rear exit" and follow the path to the north "cottage." Since it appeared that we were stepping into a medium-sized mall, with opened areas on both sides, neither Rob nor I had a clue as to where to proceed. To our right, we ambled past a huge living area furnished with armchairs of plush brocade fabrics and velveted jacquard. All the furnishings were in cornflower blue, which contrasted with the rich mahogany hardwood floors. Adorning the walls of the corridor, Old World Mediterranean tapestries competed with sixteenth-century masterpieces that graced the numerous French gilded frames. The orange-reds and corn-silk yellows of the rugs seemed to cushion our footsteps as we walked toward one of the towering rear doors. On the way, Rob and I approached partially drawn double doors on the left. Like a kid in a video arcade, I had to peek inside. Jaw undoubtedly dropping, I motioned to Rob to follow me inside this enormous library, which could have housed the entire collection of the Library of Congress. The dark cherry shelving and multiple tables on the auditorium-like space thankfully had their own lighting, which helped us find our way back out to the hallway.

As Rob and I finally found the rear exit, another computer-generated set of instructions told us to walk out onto the terrace, "which overlooks the estate," then proceed down to the lower level of the gardens. From the top of the terrace, it was obvious that trees were planted in straight lines and carefully trimmed to a certain height. All vegetation seemed constrained and uniform. We chose the circular steps to the left. Across from the slate stairs was its twin set of steps also leading down to a path of red crushed granite.

Rob Rivers and I walked down to a park-like setting. In front of us was a ten-foot-wide path of crushed red granite that led to the left, northward. The far end of the curbed path was shielded by a row of enormous Italian cypresses, probably a freeze-tolerant variety that I had not seen in the Chicago area. From behind the tall row of trees, we heard a friendly human voice telling us to proceed to the left and follow the curve of the path for another thirty yards. Rob and I looked at each other, speechless, I'm sure, for various reasons.

We had not quite walked the entire distance of the granite path when a svelte woman dressed in a two-piece, pink jogging suit approached us. Wearing athletic sneakers, she rounded the end of the tall Italian cypresses and waved. Smiling broadly, but with a certain melancholia in her eyes, Raquel Rosales shook our hands and welcomed us to her home. At this point, the path was bordered by pretty flower beds and a manicured lawn. When she pointed to our left, we realized that she was leading us not to the structure from which we'd come, but to a different building that appeared to be her home. Although somewhat smaller than the grandiose structure through which we entered, this charming "cottage" was a two-story limestone building at least six thousand square feet in size.

"May I invite you to my home for some coffee maybe?" said our cordial hostess.

"At the risk of giving away my humble status in life and my country-boy culture, could I first ask—what is beyond the Italian cypresses?" I said.

"I am so sorry for being such a poor hostess. I should have offered you a walk around the property, or at least a visual tour of it," Raquel Rosales said. "Please follow me." She walked back to the foot of the tall hedges, and there before us stood the rest of the property in all its splendor. At the far end of our view was the second "cottage," the "south cottage." Like its north version, it stood perpendicular to the wide main structure through which we had entered. So the estate appeared to have three structures forming a giant "U." Although I knew better, the distance between the two "cottages" that faced each other could have been a mile. (Later in the conversation, Mrs. Rosales stated there was a three-hundred-fifty-yard distance between the two cottages.)

The stadium-like area that stood between the north and south "cottages" caused me to gawk shamelessly. Between the two structures stood a huge athletic field—a one-hundred-yard football field—sodded professionally. Giant sprinkler heads irrigated the central football field. Surrounding the football field was a professionally covered track. In my mind, most university field and track meets would have salivated at hosting their competitions in such elaborate and up-to-date facilities. Not only was the full-sized oval track surrounding the football field marked by white lines for each lane, but its surface was covered with synthetic rubber over an asphalt base. The sodded field was in immaculate condition, complete with opposing team benches, goal posts, stadium lighting, and very likely accommodated with showers and lockers in an enormous adjoining clubhouse. The glass dome at the far end of the field suggested that an indoor swimming pool was housed in the adjacent structure.

"The owner built this field and clubhouse 'cause he saw the athletic potential of my kids," said Raquel. Smiling, she added, "I resorted to using a golf cart to summon my kids to dinner at times."

Probably embarrassed by my awkward silence, Rob Rivers interrupted the tour. "This is Max Kempball, Mrs. Rosales. He's a private investigator, and I hope you don't mind, I've enlisted his help."

"No, of course not," said Raquel Rosales.

I extended my hand again in greeting. I thanked her for her hospitality and apologized for being awestruck. Mrs. Rosales was gracious, and she urged me not to be apologetic about my curiosity. It was, she claimed, the way she had first reacted when she first saw the property.

A strikingly beautiful woman in her early 30s, Raquel Rosales was approximately five-foot-seven inches tall with jet-black hair and fine features. Although she was clearly Hispanic, my guess (albeit the source is a country boy from Austin) is that she was not Mexican American, but if so, not of a mestizo heritage. More than likely her blood line extended to Iberian roots. Of course, I realize that in these times such an assumption will be considered "racist," "prejudiced," and "unwoke."

What I should add in my defense is that the descriptions of her late husband did not fit the wife. While the deceased Rosales brothers had been described as Chicago Hispanics raised by poorly educated, first-generation Mexican immigrants, Raquel Rosales had the bearings of an upper-middle-class, almost aristocratic environment. Her lithe and graceful movements suggested a well-to-do upbringing, perhaps as someone trained in ballet or maybe even as a professional model. Her speech was measured, and her dark eyes expressed a tranquil gaze, albeit a sorrowful one. I had to remind myself that she'd recently lost a husband and two sons.

As I was making mental notes regarding Raquel Rosales, she invited us inside her impressive home. I noticed as we approached the so-called cottage that we were following the flagstone entrance to the rear of the structure. *The front of the cottage*, I thought, *must be on the opposite side.*

The sizable backyard was fenced with whitewashed concrete. The white gate through which we entered opened to a placid scene of a Japanese-style rock-and-sand garden that was meticulously raked. The garden was lined with a few shrubs and medium-sized trees for accenting purposes. Beyond that garden was a small square plat of a three-hole putting green, which I presumed the twins had insisted on. Since the back of the house was situated on a small hill, the area approaching the entrance to her den was marked by rock ledges that led visitors to a slight incline that brought them to a redwood deck. The entire back wall of the den consisted of floor-to-ceiling windows.

The landscaping on our right side as we walked toward Mrs. Rosales's home had an Asian theme, with a babbling brook on the opposite side of the rock-and-sand garden. The brook, which had its origin somewhere else, was bordered by large, rough-hewn rocks. She pointed out a koi pond on the far side that had been constructed entirely "by her boys." On the closest side of the main walkway was a multi-terraced rock bed with white flowering shrubs and plants. Walking up the easy flagstone incline, we stepped through a wooden archway onto a large redwood deck furnished with comfortable outdoor wooden pieces.

As we reached the deck, we saw that the entire far wall was covered with medium-sized bamboo trees potted in large containers along a white stuccoed surface. On the near wall on the right, colorful pillows on a white wooden sofa sat on concrete blocks. White plant boxes, on either side of the sofa, also contained winter-hardy flowering plants. The plant boxes were built into the wall.

As we stepped onto the wooden deck, we noticed that the same dark rock that accentuated the multi-terraced flower bed below lined a narrow brook against the slate background that formed the right side of the patio wall. The brook flowed to the garden below. The slate wall and the far one formed the corner, which encased the visual centerpiece of the deck. A rock mini-waterfall created a cascading sound from the top of the patio walls and dropped into a small pool. The brook flowed to the garden below. The whole visual effect was one of a Zen-like sanctuary of serenity and peace.

We entered through the glass sliding doors to her den, which was at the same level as the deck. Mrs. Rosales invited us to sit in two plush armchairs. Between Rivers's chair and mine stood a pedestal with two empty coffee cups and a carafe. After we were seated, Raquel Rosales served us the coffee and filled her own cup.

I noted that the furniture in the vast room, what catalogs would describe as "contemporary Mediterranean," contrasted with the Asian theme outside. It appeared that Mrs. Rosales, who sat opposite us on the center of a large sofa, was comfortable in eclectic settings. Between the three of us, a photograph album sat on a contemporary wrought-iron coffee table with a glass top. Mrs. Rosales placed her coffee on it. On each side of the sofa were two expensive-looking table lamps that sat on two end tables that matched her coffee table. (After researching some of the décor, I can now label the lamps as "Castile" lamps, which according to catalogs, cost over $1500 each.) I noticed that matching sconces adorned the two inner walls. A floor lamp of similar pedigree stood unlit behind Commander Rivers's easy chair and mine.

I was clearly overwhelmed, but I remembered my manners and exclaimed, "Your home, Mrs. Rosales, is not only tasteful, but frankly—well, it's frankly elegant. Truly overwhelmingly beautiful."

Raquel Rosales seemed amused. "I would reserve the word *overwhelming* for the building you just left."

I nodded and acknowledged, "I stand corrected."

"Yes, your own décor and all the furnishings are magnificent," said Rivers. "Without forgetting the business at hand, however, could we ask you some personal questions?"

"Of course," said Mrs. Rosales.

"How would you describe your deceased husband's work?" Rivers asked. Like me, he was probably wondering how they'd come across such wealth. Like me, he also could guess.

After taking a sip of coffee, she held on to the cup tightly and answered, "My husband's employer, whom I only know as 'Rodrigo,' owns a large corporation. I believe it involves shipping, the import-export of pharmaceutical goods, something to that effect. My husband never specifically described his work."

Noting that Mrs. Rosales wringed her hands and avoided Rob's look, I attempted to break the ice. "I'm truly enjoying your coffee. Could I freshen your cup?" Without waiting for an answer, I stood up and poured her another cup. I then continued: "It's difficult for me to be nonchalant about the extravagance of the compound. I must ask, Mrs. Rosales, have y'all ever hosted any school athletic events?"

She was clearly amused, smiled, but did not answer the question. Acting as if she appreciated the distraction, she set her cup and saucer down and said, "I gave you a brief tour of the outside, and I foolishly ignored the inside. Would you like to see the main floor?" She guided us through the first level of her home, came back, took another sip of her coffee, and sat down in a more relaxed state. She explained, almost apologetically, how her husband and brother-in-law were associates of a wealthy man who ran a worldwide corporation of mysterious origins.

"At first I was embarrassed about living in such surroundings. Frankly, we, the family, were discouraged from asking too many questions. My husband's employer provided these living quarters for our two families—us and my husband's twin brother's family."

"That sounds extremely generous," I said.

"Since our husbands' deaths, my sister-in-law, Rosa María, and I have made a few changes to suit our needs and tastes, but most of the estate remains the same. Most of the furnishings came from him. But the Asian landscaping was more my twin boys' idea, for example. I suppose I feel more at home now that Rodrigo—my husband's boss—is gone."

Rob Rivers asked, "After he left, has he allowed you to stay—rent free? Has your husband's boss paid all expenses?"

"Yes, Commander. My boys and I occupy this residence, and Rosa María and her children live in the south building, or 'cottage.' Our privileges are many. We do not pay a penny. We have two separate homes, plus the main building." Raquel Rosales paused, then continued. "My husband's employer, whom as I previously said we know only as 'Rodrigo,' occupied the main building."

"Hold on, Mrs. Rosales," said Rivers. "Are you saying that your husbands did not live with you?—but this Rodrigo person lived in the main building of the compound?"

Clearly embarrassed, Raquel Rosales lowered her gaze and turned away. "That's right. Before their deaths, our husbands lived in a separate property close by in Winnetka, but we were forbidden from having any contact. Toward the end—before their deaths—we were not even allowed to communicate by Internet, phone, or anything."

"Were you allowed to venture out on your own?" I asked.

"No. We were prisoners in our own homes. I understand that our husbands were not allowed any freedom either," Raquel Rosales said.

"Did Rodrigo have contact with you and your husbands?"

The awkward silence that ensued lasted several seconds. Like me, Rivers was probably wondering the extent of Rodrigo's "privileges." Neither he nor I broached the delicate subject.

I should state, however, that shortly after the crime spree in March 2020, tabloids printed excerpts of the transcripts of interviews of the Rosales widows. Known for their sensationalist reportage, the Rosales widows had been "kept in a Winnetka compound by the villainous Diego Montemayor (aka as "Rodrigo Díaz") and had been forced at gunpoint to serve as his sex slaves." Rosie, who had full access to the transcripts, indicated to me that although some references had been made to Diego's suggestive advances, nothing in the transcripts convinced him that any sexual favors were granted. Therefore, "Rosie" Rosenberg had refused to print anything that could cast disfavor upon the two families and their children.

CHAPTER FOUR

[Skokie and Winnetka, IL; November 2021]

=MAX=

Yes, Macario's employer had contact with us," said Raquel Rosales. "For the most part, he kept us informed about them, but it was minimal information that he provided. Don't get me wrong. He provided private tutoring for all our children and—all the comforts of our home. He amply provided for our needs. He fed us, clothed us, and even transported—well, he *had* us transported—to medical and dental visits. He paid all our bills."

"Were you transported to the mall, or other stores, to buy your clothes?" I asked.

"We ordered all our clothes online," said the widow. "Of course, his assistant, Estevan, had to approve all our purchases. They didn't care about the cost; they were just concerned about keeping us from communicating with the outside world."

"How about your husbands? Did he also provide for them?" I asked.

"He certainly did. I understand that the home he provided for them was well furnished, and he provided for all their needs," said Raquel. "I never visited—nor do I want to."

There was a long pause, and Raquel rose from the sofa to offer us more coffee. "Macario was a loving husband and father, but I could tell from his communications during the last year that he was depressed and very worried about us."

"Describe how your husband—and his brother—assisted Rodrigo. What was their role in the corporation?" asked Rivers.

"Like I mentioned, I was never sure," Raquel said. "Both Macario and his brother Pedro traveled a lot. They did a lot of work from home, and Macario arranged deals and contracts online. Although my husband was not formally educated, he was an exceptionally talented IT person. He taught me—and the boys—a lot."

"Did your husband have enemies? Were you ever in danger?" I asked.

"Yes, throughout the years we learned that Macario and his brother made dangerous enemies. In fact, before going to work for Rodrigo, they worked for a powerful drug lord—also from Mexico. Since Macario and his brother's testimony brought down their former boss's entire organization, their lives were constantly threatened. They testified against him, and the Mexican drug lord by the name of Gómez was convicted."

"Wait a minute," said Rivers. "You're not referring to the celebrated case of El Chato Gómez, are you?"

I quickly interrupted. "Rob, I believe I can fill you in on those details. I'll also share the *Tribune*'s series published after the murders. Please, Mrs. Rosales—go on."

In my previous investigations of my own sister's disappearance, and the kidnapping of my niece and her grandmother, I'd learned of the lengthy history of the Rosaleses' involvement in the drug trade and human smuggling. I was familiar with their past and that same evening Rob Rivers and I reviewed the details after arriving at his office. In addition, I shared the extra copy of Rosie's newspaper series for which he won several journalistic awards. After that evening's conversation, Rivers had a better understanding of Raquel's husband and his brother.

"So, Mr. Kendall, you know about my husband's history?" She seemed surprised.

"Only what I've read about that particular case," I replied, lying. "And, if I can add, my last name is Kempball."

"Oh, I'm terribly sorry. I apologize. I do hate it when people mispronounce my name. I won't make that mistake again."

"Don't worry. No offense taken."

"Immediately after the Chato Gómez trial, all of us were given US federal protection. There were several contracts out on their lives—ours too, I suppose—but the feds were good to us. Then, their new employer—the Spaniard we know as Rodrigo— "rescued" us from the feds, as my husband phrased it. Rodrigo provided all the protection we needed. In many ways, he protected us better than the US government."

"Please let me interrupt you," said Rivers. "Their new boss, Rodrigo, why do you say he protected you better than the feds?"

"Well, my husband's enemies seemed to 'disappear.' Macario and Pedro told us that Rodrigo 'took care' of all their enemies—the Mexican mafia as well as other foreign dealers," said Raquel Rosales.

"By that," I asked, "did they mean that Rodrigo—what—threatened them? Eliminated them, what?"

"We learned not to ask, Mr. Kempball. You know, our husbands were no angels, and in their line of business they dealt with many shady characters. Sometimes violence was used, and we preferred not to be informed."

"You keep saying 'we,'" I said, interrupting. "Are you referring to you and your boys, your sons?"

"No, no. Because Macario and his twin brother, Pedro, were inseparable, our families also grew close. We practically raised our children together, constantly visiting each other. Pedro's children were constantly with us, and vice-versa. It seems like Rosa María, Pedro's wife—his widow—and I raised our five kids together. But Rosa María and I tried to shelter our kids from as much of the violence as we could."

"Five kids?" I asked.

"Yes, Pedro and Rosa María had three—one boy and two girls. Macario and I only had our twins, Pablo and Mateo. After the first year of tutoring here at home, we enrolled them in a Catholic private school, Notre Dame High. Kids there called them 'Paul' and 'Matt,' so they became Paul and Matt."

"Isn't that school in Evanston?" I asked.

"It is, yes. Do you know it?" asked Raquel.

"My niece attends Ursuline Academy in Evanston, and I think Notre Dame High is like their sibling school—the all-boy Catholic counterpart."

"Then you can probably understand," said Raquel, "that their friends Anglicized their names and my boys accepted it."

"Mrs. Rosales, could I ask us to come back to the issue of—uh—possible enemies? Do you have any idea who would want to hurt your twin boys? And why?" asked Rivers.

"Of course, Mr. Rivers. At first, I suppose, it seemed like all of Macario's, and Pedro's, enemies had disappeared, literally disappeared, according to my husband. But then…"

"Then what?" Rivers pressed.

"For some strange reason, it seemed like they started to fear Rodrigo. They must have done something to enrage him."

"Why do you say that?" I asked.

"At the end of 2019, Rodrigo's behavior toward Macario and Pedro drastically changed. Let me give you an example. In December of that year, Rodrigo paid for a wonderful Christmas and New Year's celebration—which involved all of us—in his beautiful estate in Mazatlán. That was such a joyful celebration, the last one we had together."

Rob and I waited for her to continue.

"After the two-week celebration in Mazatlán, Rodrigo moved us—wives and kids—to Winnetka. Mind you, we had our own homes in the South Side of Chicago, but he displaced us from our homes. Rodrigo flew us from Mexico, and he moved us directly to Winnetka, to this compound. But Pedro and Macario were forced to stay behind in Mexico."

"Hmm," Rob Rivers mused. He gave Mrs. Rosales a curious look.

"We were clueless, confused," said Raquel. "We were angry—and scared."

Rivers asked, "How long did Rodrigo keep your husbands in Mexico?"

"He kept them for almost a month longer. Late in January, the following year, Rodrigo brought my husband and his brother back to Chicago, but he prevented us from being together."

"What do you mean 'prevented' you?" I asked.

"Exactly that, Mr. Kempball. It's like we were prisoners. He moved us here to this estate, this enormous mansion, but we were not allowed to go anywhere without his—or his assistant's—permission. We were not even allowed to communicate with our husbands."

"And your husband and his brother?" asked Rivers. "Where did they live after they returned to Chicago?"

"They stayed in our homes in Chicago briefly, but then Rodrigo moved them to another property here in Winnetka, close by. But we could not see them, nor could we communicate. Don't get me wrong. These surroundings are beautiful, and Rodrigo provided for every single need. Even the kids' medical and dental needs were provided. Their educational needs were taken care of—everything. But…"

"But you couldn't see your husbands." I completed her thought. "I'm assuming the kids couldn't see their fathers either—am I correct?"

"You are. None, no contact whatsoever. At first, Mateo and Pablo were angry—rebellious, antagonistic against Rodrigo and his assistant, Estevan. The more they rebelled the more that their father suffered. Every time my kids failed to obey orders, their dad suffered punishment."

"So they felt they had to comply," I said.

"Exactly. Then we get the terrible news that Pedro was killed in an explosion and that Macario, my husband, was burned—horribly burned—aboard the that horrible ship— *The Black Pearl*—docked in Lake Michigan. This happened on the same day in March of 2020."

"Were your families provided any information on the circumstances of their deaths?"

"Commander Rivers, in many ways we didn't want details. When our husbands chose their lives—their lifestyles—we, their spouses, also reached an understanding of the many dangers and sometimes the so-called benefits of such lifestyles. The good and the bad. It's not easy to explain."

"I think we understand," said Rivers. "On the day your husband and his brother were murdered, Rodrigo left the country. Have you heard from him since?"

"Not at all. What I do know, however, is that I will never forgive Rodrigo. Because I hold him responsible for their deaths."

"Yet you're here. Living under his roof, living in a compound owned by Rodrigo. Could you explain that to us?" I asked.

"I believe that Macario and Pedro gave their lives in exchange for our safety. There is no other way to explain it," said Raquel Rosales.

"Could you expound on that, Mrs. Rosales?" asked Rivers.

"Well, what I think happened was that Rodrigo wanted a job done, and our husbands agreed to do it—conditionally. I'm guessing, but they probably agreed to risk their lives only if Rodrigo promised to take care of us."

"So do you believe that you are protected by Rodrigo even now? Are you certain you have no form of contact with him?"

"We have no idea where Rodrigo is. But how else can you explain that a trust has been set up in our children's names; or that the deed to this compound has been given to us? The property is ours, no questions asked," said Raquel. "He takes care of the upkeep of the property. Plus, we receive a stipend—like clockwork on the first of each month."

"Does your sister-in-law own part of this compound?" I asked.

"I own this enormous building. The one across the football field belongs to Rosa María. The main building—the largest—is communal property," said Raquel. "I'd gladly give all of it up if I could get my family back."

"I know this interrogation can be painful, Mrs. Rosales. Are you certain that you want to continue, because we can come back later to inquire about the more immediate loss of your sons?" Rob Rivers used a warm and considerate voice. Though his manner is mild and compassionate, his presence is imposing. He's probably two inches taller than me and his large frame suggests a strength worthy of respect. Probably most suspects whom he apprehends think twice before resisting arrest.

"I would like to continue, Commander Rivers. But let's take a break. I can bring out some pound cake that Rosa María brought me earlier this morning. She knows I'm staying away from carbs, but she knew

I'd have company today. She's thoughtful like that." Raquel Rosales got up from the sofa and slipped into the large kitchen. From there she announced that she would not be joining us for cake, since she was on the keto diet. She proudly announced that she'd lost the extra twelve pounds that she'd gained since the loss of her husband. "My grieving unfortunately included careless eating and gloomy behavior twenty-four/seven," she said. "I'm taking control—of my weight, at least. Now, with the loss of my kids—well, I don't know."

CHAPTER FIVE

[Skokie and Winnetka, IL; November 2021]

=MAX=

Obviously Raquel Rosales was a remarkably strong individual. She regained her composure and returned to the den. Setting down a tray with the pound cake, she said, "I met Macario when I was in high school. Though my parents could afford private schools, they wanted me to remember my roots—actually, they drilled into me that I must not forget my heritage—so they gave me a good public-school education."

Rob Rivers commented, "It's unusual for parents with means to choose a Chicago public school."

"They thought about sending me to a private school, but my mom was the principal at the first public school in Chicago that offered bilingual education. In that way, my parents held on to a pretext of providing a respect for our heritage. I suspect the true reason was that Mom wanted to keep an eye on me and keep me from joining the wrong crowd."

Raquel Rosales, instead of sitting back down, walked to look out onto the deck through the back windows. I had to admire the elegance with which she carried herself. Wearing the pink jogging suit—which I realized now was no ordinary exercise outfit, since it appeared to be made of a cashmere blend—she stood a moment too long at the glass doors, as if expecting to see her twins return home. She held herself perfectly straight, but she had the forlorn look of an expectant medieval princess looking out her castle window.

She regained her composure as if her concentration had been broken. "They were so disappointed when I started dating Macario. Eventually, I introduced my cousin, Rosa María, to Macario's brother Pedro; so, we double-dated. Both my parents thought—or hoped— it was a passing attraction. It was not. The twins were…you know, undesirable. They belonged to gangs, both were into drugs, and pushing grass—losers, per my parents."

"It seems your parents tried to raise you correctly. What attracted you to the Rosales twins?" Rivers's curiosity was growing.

"They were sweet boys, kind, funny, and—handsome. They may not have been nerds, but they treated us—my cousin and me—like queens. They bought us gifts, expensive gifts that other boys couldn't afford." She gazed out the windows, as if trying to recollect the innocence of youth.

"What do you mean?" asked Rivers.

"Oh, nothing big, not jewelry or anything. Macario bought me the latest video games, phones—you know, techie stuff."

"So your parents couldn't keep you from seeing the twins?"

"They tried, but it was too late. Too little, too late. Macario and I fell in love—and eventually we sort of eloped." Raquel Rosales's voice broke. "My parents were so disappointed."

"In what way?" asked Rob Rivers as he rose from his seat and walked in her direction.

"I'm okay, Commander. Please have a seat." Raquel Rosales stepped back to the sofa, trying to force herself into the gist of the conversation. "They had saved for my college education, my career. During my junior year in high school, they took me on a tour of ivy league schools. Their dream was that I graduate from one of the "Seven Sisters." I applied and got into Radcliffe."

"Wow! Radcliffe—that's an elite school," I said. "Did you finish there?"

"No. By that time Macario and I were in love, and we eloped at the end of my second year." Again, Raquel Rosales looked away.

Rivers broke the silence. "You mentioned your mom was an educator. What did your dad do for a living?"

"He was an accountant, a CPA. Some of his clients, per my husband, were not the 'straightest arrows.' He said they were with the mob or connected with them in some way."

"How did Macario find that out?" I asked.

"Macario said he had connections."

"Years later when I asked my mom, she didn't exactly deny it. She did say, however, that my dad had made some mistakes as a young man, and that's why he wanted to shield me from all the corruption around us."

"Were you the oldest in your family?"

"I'm an only child."

"Your parents deceased?" Rivers asked.

"My mom still lives in the family home in Chicago. My dad passed away when my kids were two years old. The twins don't remember him—sorry, I still can't accept that my boys are gone. I meant to say, they *didn't* remember him." Mrs. Rosales looked away.

Rob Rivers leaned over in her direction. Lowering his voice almost to a whisper, he said, "We know it's difficult for you to speak about your family, but if at any time you feel like we're overstepping our bounds, please let us know."

I could tell Raquel was having trouble concentrating. She forced herself to look our way. "Like I said, I don't mind. I want you to find whoever is responsible. Personally, I believe Rodrigo is guilty. If he didn't commit the act, he had someone else do it." There was a lengthy pause, then as she teared up, she added, "I'm not sure you'll be able to do anything about it, though."

"Why do you say that?" asked Rivers. The expression on Rob's face indicated he was stepping outside his objective investigator role. I believe he was eager to pursue any lead to help the grieving mother, and widow, to the fullest.

"Please understand. I want to trust you," said Mrs. Rosales. "But Rodrigo is a very powerful man. According to my husband, Rodrigo paid off numerous law enforcement people," said Raquel. Then with uncharacteristic contempt, she added, "A lot of them."

"If he was involved in shipping or the export business, why would he need to pay off law enforcement agents?" Rivers asked. Before my eyes, I could tell that Rob Rivers was realizing the scope of this case.

"In the words of my husband, Officer Rivers, in business 'you have to grease a few palms.' It's the cost of doing business."

"Hmm," Rivers could not help shaking his head.

"Up to now, Commander—and Mr. Kempball—I've been afraid of discussing Rodrigo and his evil ways for fear of offending your profession. By that I mean that most people don't believe that those in law enforcement can be bribed or bought. I know better."

I got up to inspect some family photos on the mantel above the fireplace. I picked up a framed photo of the twins practicing their putting on the green outside the den. After putting down the framed photo, I approached the glass trophy case on the adjacent wall. The trophies included not only sports paraphernalia but academic awards as well. "Why do you think he went after your sons?" I asked. "Rodrigo, this powerful criminal, why would he order the killings of two fifteen-year-olds?"

"I…don't…know," said Raquel. "It doesn't make sense." She turned to look at me with tearful eyes. Why *would* he kill my sons? What could he gain from that?" She grabbed a tissue from a dispenser near her and tried to continue.

I approached her, but she gestured that she was fine.

Regaining her composure but with her voice still cracking, she said, "This monster, Rodrigo, the only time he showed some tenderness was when he warmed up to the boys. At first Paul, my son, was the rebellious one, so he and Rodrigo exchanged some cross words. Eventually fences were mended, and—although I hesitate to say this—it even seemed that Rodrigo treated them as his nephews, or close relatives."

"I would tend to agree. Why would an uncle figure order the murder of his 'adopted nephews'?" I said, almost to myself.

Raquel Rosales completely disregarded the question, but she added, "My husband said that many law enforcement people were in their payroll. In fact, he personally sent checks to several Chicago policemen and more than a few federal agents in Washington, DC."

"Did he ever mention any names?" I asked.

"Of course not. However, if word gets out that I'm bad-mouthing Rodrigo, I know he—or they—will come after me," she said.

"Mrs. Rosales, if you feel your life is in danger, or if you feel our presence here is putting you in danger, we will gladly leave. We would provide protection, of course," said Rivers. "However, please understand that neither Mr. Kempball nor I will rest until we find the person responsible for the death of your sons."

"Thank you, but—please continue. If I can help you incarcerate that monster, I'll cooperate."

"Fine." Rivers hesitated before continuing. "So how did your boys end up at Belmont Harbor? Do you know?"

"The only thing I know is that I agreed to have the twins transported to our church's *Día de los Muertos* celebration."

Rivers asked, "The...what...celebration?"

"For several years, instead of Halloween being celebrated, our church community, which is primarily Hispanic, has sponsored a jamboree of sorts—we call it a *jamaica*—to celebrate All Saints' and All Souls' Day. We celebrate on November 1 and 2. That's how we remember friends and family who have died."

"Yeah," I said, "I remember living in Austin, people parading in weird costumes, wearing grotesque masks, skeletons, and zombie-like makeup. But I never knew it was connected to All Saints' Day."

"Mrs. Rosales," Commander Rivers asked, "you said you had the twins 'transported.' Did you not drive the twins, Paul and Matt, to the celebration?"

"Father Morgan Rowstone, our pastor at St. Nicholas Church in Evanston, offered them a ride, and I agreed," Mrs. Rosales said. "He was helpful when Rosa Maria and I grieved for our husbands. He became a friend to the entire family. Father Rowstone picked the twins up at exactly 7:00 p.m., and he told me he would return them promptly by 10:30. I got worried at 11:15, so I dialed Fr. Morgan directly. When he failed to answer after several tries, I started calling everyone—the church's main number, the police, even the local hospitals. All day, the following day, I was panicked. I reported my boys missing. Rosa María and even her kids helped me call hospitals, called the church dozens of times, called the police every half hour. I even called the football coach. Nobody could help us."

"When did you realize? When did you hear the bad news?" Rob asked.

The following night—I watched the horrible news on CNBS. They spoke of two boys who drowned in Lake Michigan, and I knew…I knew it was…my boys. They showed pictures. Horrible photographs. The clothes matched what my twins were wearing." Raquel Rosales broke down for the first time.

"We're very sorry, Mrs. Rosales," said Rivers. "We usually try to prevent that kind of reporting, but unfortunately the media…" Rob apologized.

"I understand. It was beyond your control," said the grieving mom. "I'm okay. I think I'm numb—disembodied. I'm not trying to be weird, nor spiritual, or anything. I'm not into new age hocus-pocus either. I'm just saying I feel like I'm caught up in a dream—a nightmare that started with the death of my husband and now continues with Paul and Matt."

"Please don't apologize. However, I need to ask this, Mrs. Rosales," I said. "Have you had any thoughts of hurting yourself?"

She promptly responded, "No, no. Nothing like that. I have trouble sleeping, sure. And I get depressed, but I'm determined to live long enough—to see justice done. That monster responsible for the death of my loved ones has to pay." Not knowing what to do with her hands, she reached for another napkin and rubbed the palms of her hands. "Even Father Rowstone is missing. He's been missing since the church celebration."

"Um hmm," said Rivers. "Are you protected, Mrs. Rosales? Do you own a gun?"

"Yes, I think so. Macario owned at least one gun. He even got me a small-caliber pistol for my protection, and he taught me how to use it. But he didn't want the boys around any kind of weapons."

"Could you show us your pistol?" said Rivers.

As she left the room to retrieve the weapon, I asked Rivers if he thought the Catholic priest was involved. I also asked if Mrs. Rosales should be in protective custody, or if personnel should be posted at the estate.

Raquel Rosales returned before Rivers could respond. Rivers looked at the Walther PDP handgun and handed it to me for my inspection. He turned to Mrs. Rosales, who remained standing, and said, "I suggest you keep your pistol loaded and within reach."

I added, "Mrs. Rosales is the compound's gate locked, or can any visitor enter as we did?"

"Yes, yes. We keep the entrance gates locked at night. During the day, if we're expecting deliveries or visitors, we activate the visual and voice monitors to allow them in. Do you think we should keep them locked twenty-four/seven?"

"Yes, but all of it can be temporary," said Rivers. "With your permission, I'd also like to provide law enforcement protection. Like I said, for only a few days."

Raquel swallowed hard. She looked away, then said, "I'm not delusional. My husband was involved in shady dealings. I learned that several years ago when he and his brother Pedro testified in federal court against El Chato Gómez. I know they had plenty of enemies. Yes, I'll gladly accept your offer of protection, Commander Rivers. Thank you."

Raquel Rosales walked us back to the cavernous and empty main building and out the front door. On my way out, I couldn't help staring at the museum-like extravagance of the furnishings. Outside I shivered. I was not ready for the sudden drop in temperature. As we drove away from the estate, a frigid, light drizzle came in from the lake.

"It's become obvious, Rob, that my sister's family may still be in need for much prayer. If this international criminal is still causing local trouble, it means he will continue to come after my family. Let's accelerate our prayers, not only for them, but also for the Rosales family and the missing Catholic priest."

"You can count on it, my brother," said Rivers as he drove back toward Chicago. "By the way, I've looked into Father Rowstone's background. His credentials are intact. He's served the church faithfully without even a trace of complaint of misconduct. In my opinion, he was collateral damage. I hope his body doesn't turn up somewhere."

CHAPTER SIX

[Evanston, IL; November 2021]

=MAX=

Arriving at his office that evening, I mentioned to Rob Rivers that I would give Nate and my sister a call to inform them of our visit to the Rosales estate. I also gave Rob as much information as I could regarding the history of the Rosales family's involvement with my own. I promised that the following day I'd deliver the *Chronicle's* series of articles written by Rosenberg.

"Tell me more about your brother-in-law, the psychiatrist," said Rob.

"He spent a year away from his family working as a profiler for Interpol to help the international authorities capture the fugitive Diego Montemayor, or "Rodrigo," as Raquel Rosales knew him. He was briefly headquartered in Lyon, France."

"But you mentioned he's back in Chicago, right?" asked Rob.

"Yeah, he felt he, or they—Interpol and the various countries involved—were making little progress, if any. Nate hinted that his efforts were re-directed to examine anti-terrorism," I said.

Although Rivers knew basic facts about *The Black Pearl* murders, he had not been involved in the investigations. So he wanted me to give him my insider's perspective. Although I trusted Rob completely, for some reason, I'd refrained from bringing in my family during weekly prayer meetings. I decided to change that and explain that

Nate had visited various Interpol sites throughout Western Europe at the behest of Gabriel Picard, his direct supervisor. I told him Nate had spent time in Israel, investigating the Middle Eastern Peace Studies Center, headed by a celebrated scholar by the name of Ari Weiss.

"So did Nate come up with any information that got him or Interpol closer to finding Diego Montemayor?" Rivers asked.

"Unfortunately, Rob, Nate returned to Chicago somewhat disillusioned after seeing the complex dynamics of world politics and international intelligence networks. Though he uncovered potentially helpful information regarding Diego Montemayor, he returned to his practice in Chicago a little disappointed."

"Too bad."

"Yeah, Diego is so well insulated by powerful politicians that Nate doubts whether Diego will ever get caught."

"Let me ask," said Rivers. "Are you as disillusioned as Nate?"

"No, I'm not. I should add, though, that my sister Miró gave Nate an ultimatum of sorts. She agreed to grant him twelve months away from home, but if no credible leads could be uncovered, she insisted that he return to his family. Nate agreed. Without any worthwhile leads, Nate honored his promise and returned to Chicago four months ago."

Rob Rivers dropped me off at the Evanston Vineyard Christian Church parking lot. I thanked him for the opportunity to meet with Raquel Rosales. I drove directly to Nate and Miró's, hoping to catch them at home.

Nate received me at the door. As soon as he opened the door, I felt the warmth of the fireplace. "Wow—it feels good to be indoors. It's providential that I found y'all here. You'll never guess where I've been."

As I walked toward the hearth, I realized that the fireplace was not affecting the chill in the family's discussion. Miró, not sitting in her usual place, was sitting stiffly at the sofa, her hands on her lap. She did not smile. Nate attempted to break the ice: "Max, come in and join us. Miró and I were speaking to Minnie about—"

"Hold on, Bro. Doesn't Minnie want to be called 'Minerva' now?"

"Yes, I keep forgetting. All her friends call her 'Minerva' because they think 'Minnie' is too infantile. I'm not certain I can get used to it," said Nate.

"Sorry I interrupted you. You started to say you were talking to her about something or other."

"Yes," said Nate. "Miró and I learned from our daughter that she has some details that can help. By that I mean information regarding the meeting you had with Raquel Rosales."

"How did you learn that I was interviewing Macario Rosales's widow? I just returned from her home in Winnetka," said Max.

"A certain Natalie, whom I understand is close to you, told Minerva that you were excited to join Commander Rivers on his visit," said Nate. "There are no secrets nowadays." Nate chuckled. Miró did not. She ignored the statement.

"I believe it," I said, smiling.

Standing next to me by the fireplace, Nate explained, "Minnie—er, Minerva—told her grandfather. And he called us and brought us up to date regarding your collaboration with Commander Rivers from the Chicago PD."

"Max," said Miró from her perch in the Shelley den, "join us for some pre-Thanksgiving cheer, if we can call it such."

I was uncertain how to interpret my half-sister's comment. Though she tried to smile, a scowl masked her face. The slight squint in her eyes indicated that she was studying the matter at hand. As I moved in her direction, Miró rose from the sofa and moved in the direction of the kitchen. "Would you care for something to drink?" she asked no one in particular.

I responded, "I'm perfectly fine, sis."

I moved toward Minerva, who was standing in the middle of the room. I noticed she was almost in tears. I hugged her, then proceeded to embrace Miró, who'd left the kitchen empty-handed. She accepted the hug and sat back on the sofa.

"Minnie is telling us, Max, that—"

"Mom, everyone except you and dad calls me 'Minerva.' For your information, Minerva was the Roman goddess of wisdom. Do you mind?"

"Okay, Minerva, Minerva, Minerva. I'll get it right eventually. You've always been our 'Minnie'—that's why I'm having so much trouble."

Miró addressed me. "Anyway, Max, Minerva tells us that while she was at the *Día de los Muertos* celebration at St. Nicholas she might have seen something that may interest you, and the rest of us, of course. Although she'd never learned the last names of the kids found in Lake Michigan, she knew them as Matt and Paul. Evidently, Paul was the jock who 'stole' the starting quarterback job from Minerva's boyfriend."

Minerva, who'd been standing, moved to her mom's favorite piece of furniture and sat. "Mom, I never said that Paul stole it from Cal. I just said that the coach hated Cal's dad, and he might have taken it out on Cal by giving the starting job to Paul."

"Whoa," I said. "Wait a minute. I know that Calvin quarterbacked his high school's team last year. Was Paul Rosales—the dead twin—your boyfriend's back-up last year?"

"No, Paul is—or up to recently was—a freshman. Though he was new at the school this year, he competed for the position and took the job from Cal," said Minerva. "Cal thinks there's a lot of favoritism because his dad is not the most popular guy in town. It wasn't until this whole drowning thing hit the papers that I learned Paul's last name, Uncle Max. And I'm learning from Mom and Dad that Paul's dad was the person who kidnapped Grandma and me a couple of years ago."

"Is Cal Steele's dad the city councilman, Jim Steele? The 'de-fund the police' guy?" I asked.

"Yep."

"So what happened that I need to know about?" I asked. "You were at the Day of the Dead celebration, then what? Did you see Paul and his brother Matt before they disappeared?"

"Not only did I see them, but Paul and my boyfriend had a little disagreement at the celebration," said Minerva.

Miró interrupted. "It was more than a disagreement, Max. Evidently, Paul bloodied Cal's nose. Also, and this is something that

Minnie—uh, Minerva—admitted: Cal and his friends ambushed the twins and started shoving and pushing them. Not Cal, but one of his friends hurled a racial epitaph at Matt Rosales, and his twin brother turned to swing at Cal's friend. Unfortunately, Cal was in the way, and he caught the blow. Minnie thinks Cal's nose is broken."

I was now standing where Minerva had stood. Nate stood next to me, holding his eyeglasses and pinching the bridge of his nose. "What happened then?" I asked.

Miró responded, "Well, supposedly it's fuzzy to Minnie, but she doesn't remember seeing the twins again until they boarded the church van with a costumed driver. They think the driver is the church priest. The twins left the celebration in the van."

"Yeah, Uncle Max, practically everyone was wearing a costume, so it didn't seem strange for the driver to be wearing a costume and a mask."

"Do you remember the time, Minerva?" I asked.

"Not really, but it was about half an hour, or maybe forty minutes, before Dad picked me up."

Nodding his head, Nate agreed. "And that was at exactly 11:00 p.m. I picked up Minerva and two other friends at 11:00. After we dropped them off, we came straight home."

"However, we didn't find out about the whole incident—Cal's and Paul's little scuffle—until today," said Miró. Addressing Minerva, she added, "Which is very disappointing, Mi'jita."

Miró was upset, but Minerva was in tears.

"I'm sorry, Mom and Dad…I suppose I didn't think it was that big a deal."

51

CHAPTER SEVEN

[Evanston, IL; November 2021]

=MAX=

My niece, Minerva, is not used to disappointing her parents. In fact, I believe that throughout her life she's been a model child. During the years that I've known her, she's been honest, diligent in her studies, and well spoken. No profanity, no sneaking around, and as far as I know, she's never disobeyed her parents. A surprisingly good record for a sixteen-year-old. So seeing the disappointment in my half-sister's face and listening to her verbal reprimand deeply affected her. She ran upstairs to her bedroom and locked herself in.

After an awkward silence, I asked, "What is it, sis, that displeased you so much about Minerva?" I wondered if I was missing some pieces of information.

Miró, sitting with crossed arms in her favorite spot, was staring off in the distance. Clearly she was disappointed with her daughter. "I suppose what bothers me the most is Cal's use of racial slurs. To know that my daughter tolerates that behavior—in her own boyfriend—saddens me," Miró said.

"Whoa—wait one minute," I said. "What I heard you say was that one of Cal's friends used those words, not Cal. And even if it had been Cal using such language, it seems you are blaming your daughter."

Nate jumped in. "That's exactly what I told Miró, Max, but she came down on Minnie—on Minerva—as if it had been our poor daughter using that language." Nate turned to Miró and said, "'Critical race theory' aside, I believe we're being a bit harsh on our daughter."

"Let's not engage in that discussion again," said Miró. Crossing her arms, she mumbled, almost to herself, "Dad has always said, '*Díme con quien andas, y te diré quien eres.*'"

"Sorry, sis. I need some translation for that one," I said.

Miró got up and walked to the kitchen. On her way, she said, "It's the Spanish version of 'Birds of a feather flock together.' Literally translated, my dad's version is quite clear: 'Tell me who your friends are, and I'll tell you who you are'." Miró rose and walked away.

I followed Miró into the kitchen, and I reasoned with her: "Even Dad would probably say that your interpretation in this case is a little extreme. Please let me go up to Minerva's room to try to get her out of her funk."

"I think Nate is already up there, Max. When I made my way into the kitchen, he snuck up to speak to her," said Miró. She opened the fridge and offered me a beer. "No, thanks. I should be counting my carbs." To my surprise, my sister took one out and took a swig of beer.

"Hey, sis—since when have you started drinking those? I've never seen you drink a beer."

"I was seventeen when I had my first—and last—beer," said Miró. "But you know what? This isn't so bad. What is it?"

"It's a Mexican ale called *Negra Modelo*. It's the beer that Nate keeps in your fridge for my visits."

"I've never paid attention." Miró took a tall glass and poured her beer. She walked back to the den."You know, Max, as a parent you never know how well you've raised your child—until something like this pops up." She took another drink, which she seemed to enjoy. "I mean, I'm a Mexican-American born in South Texas. Both my parents are first-generation Americans since their parents were born in Mexico. Well, you know that. Dad never hid his ethnicity from your mom, right?"

"Not at all, sis. In fact, Mom said that as an undergraduate, Dad had a sizable chip on his shoulder. He was proud of his heritage, and I believe that's one of the main things that attracted her to him."

Miró took a bar stool and plopped down. Visibly with less tension on her facial expression, she asked, "Surely, you don't think Minnie—don't correct me, Max; I'll do it on my own—*Minerva* has concealed her ethnicity from her friends, do you?"

I tried to reassure my sister. "No, I don't. But even if she had, it would not be the greatest offense in my book. Look—she's a great kid, and you should count your blessings for having such a special child." In my book, I've never met a teenager as responsible and respectful as my own niece. I know that I'm somewhat biased, but I consider her a model child.

Miró nodded her head and changed position on the stool. Still squirming on her seat, she added, "You and Nate are probably right. I overreacted. It's simply that I would hate to find out that my daughter is hanging around a bunch of ignorant, narrow-minded, and hate-filled racists. I would be so disappointed…"

"I understand, sis. But don't you think that Minerva deserves a little more trust from you? She probably thinks—" I stopped mid-sentence. Miró also froze when she heard Minerva's door open.

Nate, accompanied by Minerva, was walking down the stairs. "Miró," he called out, "I believe Minerva has something to say!"

I interrupted Nate. "Listen—I should be getting back to—"

"No, no," said Nate. "Max, you're part of the family, and there's no reason you can't be a part of this family talk."

"Yes, Uncle Max. I'd also like you to stay," said Minerva. Though the reddening around her eyes indicated she'd been weeping, she bravely continued: "Mom, Dad explained to me a perspective that I was totally unaware of. I was looking at everything selfishly. I was thinking how unfair this whole thing was. I couldn't see how you could possibly lose your faith in me. How you two didn't trust my judgment—you know, regarding Cal. Now I see that both of you, you can also go through your own doubts—as parents, I mean. I want you to know you haven't failed me. It's probably the other way around."

"Oh, my sweet, sweet Minerva," said Miró. I could see that my sister was trying to regain her composure. "You're an amazing young lady, and in truth, you are being much more mature than your mom.

I should've allowed you to describe the entire situation without jumping to conclusions. Please forgive me."

Miró got up from her bar stool and took her daughter in her arms. Since losing her own mom, Miró appeared to be stricter, more demanding of Minerva. I wondered if Miriam's absence was imposing a larger responsibility on Miró to assume the exclusive role of disciplinarian and loving mom.

"Oh, Mom," Minnie sobbed. Neither mother nor daughter could break their embrace. I glanced at Nate, and he also had tears in his eyes.

Finally Minerva said, "First of all, let me tell you how proud I am of my best friend, Cal. He may not be the best football player in the world, but he stood up for his principles."

"What do you mean, his principles?" asked Miró.

"I didn't want you to think I run around with a bunch of Neanderthals or tools, Mom, but Cal did get into a big fight. His nose *was* broken, but he tried to make things right."

"Explain," Miró said. "What's a 'tool'?"

"You know, just someone that's willing to go along, or someone who can be used by others. When Cal realized why Paul Rosales had taken a swing at him, he turned to his friends and asked who'd insulted Paul. Realizing it was one of his buddies, Chip Maris, Cal grabbed him by the shirt and head-butted him. Cal, bloodied nose and all, then turned to all his friends and told them that I had a Mexican heritage. So he may not have stood up for the twins, but he stood up for his principles."

"Sounds to me like he was standing up for *you*, Minerva," I said. "But as I heard it, the security guards had to intervene to restore some order."

"Yeah, well, after being head-butted, Chip hit Cal and it was then that Cal's nose was broken. Several other kids joined in, took different sides, and the fight was on. Unfortunately, the sides were divided by racial, or ethnic, lines."

"Where were the twins—the Rosales twins—in all this?" asked Nate.

"I don't know, Dad. Not in the fight, as far as I can tell. I didn't see them until they got in the van to leave the church grounds," said Minerva.

"And you? I hope you…" Miró was at a loss for words.

"No, Mom, I did not get involved. My friends and I watched from a distance, and I actually ran to the entrance gate to inform the security guards about the fight."

"Where *was* the fight?" I asked Minerva.

"Behind the gym. When the guards arrived, Cal was the first one to be held because he was bleeding and kneeling on his best friend's chest. He was about to punch him. The guards called the parents; they also called for backups."

. . .

CHAPTER EIGHT

[Evanston, IL; November 2021]

Thank God that you didn't get involved," Miró said. "You deserve a huge apology from me. I jumped to irrational conclusions."

"That's not all," said Minerva. "Before you start apologizing or thinking that I completely excuse Cal's behavior, you need to know that Cal is grounded by his parents. We both realize there are consequences to our actions. Thank God, though, that he wasn't arrested or suspended from school."

"You said that was not all," said Nate. "Tell us what else we should know." Nate, who had been standing, sat next to Miró.

"It's so silly, Dad. Apparently, my boyfriend, Cal, found out that I'd been messaging, or responding to messages from, a Snap Chat friend. You could call him a 'secret admirer' because at first I didn't know his name. All I knew was that he attended Notre Dame High."

Nate asked, "How did Cal find out?"

"He borrowed my phone to call his dad, and he must've seen my messages," said Minerva.

Miró immediately said, "That doesn't sound very respectful. I mean, doesn't he respect your privacy?"

"I've never had a reason to hide anything, Mom. And, besides, this other person is just an online friend."

"Let me ask you a question," said Nate. "Have you ever met this friend in person?"

"S-o-r-t of…" Uncharacteristically, Minerva stretched the word *sort*, indicating some ambiguity.

"Minerva, what does that mean? Either you've met him or not," said Miró.

Minerva's eyes started to water. She swallowed hard and continued. "Mom, I'm trying to clarify things as best I can. While my friends and I were at the coffee shop, I got this message from my mystery friend." Minerva made air quotation marks. "I responded with a 'Hi,' and he asked if he could treat me to the drink that I was about to order. I asked how he knew where I was, and it turned out that he was standing behind me—in line, behind me. We chatted for maybe five minutes. He only told me his first name, Matt, and I thanked him for the drink. That was it."

Max invited Minerva to sit next to him on the couch. Though she sat next to Max, she said from the edge of her seat. "Well, everyone, it's all a big mess. Cal is depressed. He's jealous. His dad is livid. And his mom refuses to talk to her husband—the whole thing over at the Steele home is a powder keg ready to explode."

A contrite Miró said, "Oh, *Mi'jita*, I'm sorry to hear this. Sometimes these things set off an emotional chain reaction."

Max jumped in. "When you say that Cal is depressed, is it because he's jealous that you're communicating with someone else on your phone? Because he lost his quarterback position, because of the death of the twins, or because of the fight itself?"

Always a thoughtful young lady, Minerva took a while to respond. "I suppose the same answer to those four questions is yes. Right now Cal and I aren't allowed to communicate, but even before the jamboree, Cal was upset. He hates his dad. There's a lot he's not sharing with me, but at times he can't stand his dad."

"This must be difficult for you," said Nate. "On the one hand, you're juggling our own family dynamics and you're also trying to help Cal with his. On top of it all, you don't have all the facts to help Cal. What do you think Cal is keeping from you?"

"I'm not sure. But I think it was more than the racial slurs that started the fight, or the loss of Cal's starting role as the team's quarterback."

Nate nodded. "Go on."

"At the jamboree—the *Día de los Muertos* celebration—Cal accused me of betraying him with his rival's brother."

"Explain, *Mi'jita*. What did he mean?" asked Miró.

"Mom, the Matt that was messaging me was one of the Rosales twins, Matt Rosales, the brother of the kid who took over the starting quarterback position."

"Oh, my goodness!" Miró turned to Nate as if asking for help.

"Thank you for unraveling this mess for us," said Nate. "You're a very responsible young lady, and I know that you're doing the best to help Cal. Our hearts go out to him because right now, the poor kid is overwhelmed with so many struggles. He needs much prayer."

"That's right, Dad. Thank God you're all so understanding—most of the time." Pausing, Minerva continued: "Cal is doubting me, and he doesn't know to whom he should turn." A tear trickled down Minerva's face. "He believes that his dad is upset, not so much because of the fight but because of the way that it reflects on his political career. Cal says that his dad is afraid it will affect his standing as a village council member and his plans to run for mayor."

"Hmm. I'd forgotten that Jim Steele is a member of the city council, or the 'village council,' as Winnetka calls it."

The wind was causing serious rustling of the fall leaves on the Shelleys' patio. With the darkening of the skies, the windows appeared to freeze over. It was obvious that the rain would soon turn to a few inches of snow, which would stick to the ground.

"Plus, Cal is dealing with an icy-cold home environment where his parents don't talk to each other. They shut the kids out of the family problems. He doesn't tell me, but I think his parents are headed for a divorce."

Taking the bar stool next to Miró, Nate asked, "Why do you say that?"

Minerva stood closer to the granite kitchen island. "You know how it is. People talk. Around school we hear rumors."

Miró asked, "What kinds of rumors?"

Minerva rested her elbows on the island. "Oh, Mom, it's so hard for me. I always feel that if I repeat the horrible things that people say, I'm just spreading gossip. Plus, I don't know for a fact that any of the things I hear are true."

Nate reassured his daughter, "You are not obligated to share any idle talk or tittle tattle. On the other hand, if any of this gossip is affecting Cal, then a strong effort must be made by those supporting him to boost his confidence. At some point or another, we all must face false accusations and vicious slander. And the maturation process is all about deciding when it's best to confront the attacks and when to simply ignore them."

"Thank you, Dad. I guess I just don't know how to help Cal," said Minerva.

"So you feel helpless." Nate could not help himself. He tried not to inject his professional techniques into his family life, but at times it was necessary. He repeated his effort to reflect his daughter's feelings: "You feel like you are incapable of helping Cal?"

"Exactly."

After a long pause, Minerva asked, "Can you all help me decide what's best?"

"Of course, *Mi'jita*," said Miró. "Forgive me, though, but is your Uncle Max influencing your speech patterns? Did I hear you say, 'y'all'?"

"Oh, Mom I said, 'you all,' not 'y'all.' But it's funny that you mention that because my friends tell me the same thing."

"It's about time that y'all learn proper English," quipped Max.

While the four shared a laugh, Miró took out from the pantry the cookies that Max had baked earlier in the day. He brought the entire batch and bragged that he'd used his step-mom's, Miriam's, recipe for oatmeal raisin cookies.

Savoring the first bite, Miró said, "I must admit that they're almost as good as Mom's. You even used her secret ingredient, Max."

"Hush, sis. I promised never to divulge the secret," said Max. "Would anyone care for some milk?"

"Before I was rudely interrupted," joked Minerva as she picked up the loose crumbs on the granite island. "If anyone is still interested in my dilemma, I asked you to help me. This is the situation that Cal is facing. We already know that Cal lost his starting quarterback spot to Paul Rosales. That was bad enough to send Cal into the dumps; however, to top it off—according to hearsay—when Cal's dad saw the twins standing in line waiting for their drinks at the coffee shop, he assaulted Paul and his brother. This supposedly happened on the Saturday before the church jamboree."

Max was coming back to the den with a glass of milk. "You're telling me that Jim Steele, esteemed member of the Winnetka Village Council, a thirty-something grown man, hit two teenagers because his son Cal lost his starting quarterback position to one of them?"

"Uncle Max, I don't know if he hit either one, but apparently he shoved them against a wall and used abusive language against them. Some kids caught that on camera. I've refused to see the video."

"Prince of a guy," said Max. Assuming the persona of Peter Sellers's version of Inspector Jacques Clouseau, Max took center stage and stated, "Let us examine this case." In sotto voce and starting the count with his right thumb, he continued—"FACT: Paul Rosales took Cal's position as high school quarterback." He continued enumerating with his forefinger—"FACT: Cal's dad confronted Paul at the Holy Grounds, the local coffee shop hangout." Max used the middle finger to enumerate the third point—"FACT: Cal's mom wants a divorce…"

Even Minerva laughed at Max's memorized dialogue from *The Pink Panther* movies, a family favorite. Nate, however, admonished, "As Minerva says, Max, we don't know all the facts."

"If it was caught on camera," said Miró, "there's not much to doubt about the assault of the twins at the coffee shop."

Minerva added, "I'm sure that Cal saw the video. By Monday, the day of the church jamboree, it had gone viral. Cal was furious at his dad. Mostly embarrassed, I guess. Cal even apologized to me. I pled ignorance and told him I hadn't seen any video, which was true."

"Sorry to interject," said her mom, "but an aspiring writer should know it's preferable to use 'pleaded.'"

"Oh, thanks for the correction, Mom. That is now in my memory bank."

"You did the right thing," said Nate, "…regarding the video matter."

"There's more, Mom and Dad."

Nate added, "Minerva, remember that this is not an interrogation. And I don't want you to feel that you're obligated to share personal details if your safety is being compromised. Whenever you feel you're stepping into gossip territory, use your judgment."

"It's okay, Dad. I'll try to draw the lines. Although this goes into— as you would say, Mom— 'unsubstantiated allegations,' some of Cal's own friends have told him that 'the entire village of Winnetka' knows that his mom is seeing another man. In fact, the night of the jamboree, Cal's best friend, Chip, told him that after dropping Cal off at the church grounds, his mom had met this other guy and they drove off in the direction of Lake Michigan."

"Oh, dear!" Miró put her cookie down. "Did Chip actually see this?"

"Supposedly."

"Wait—back up," said Max. "When did this Chip guy tell your boyfriend that he'd seen Cal's mom with another guy? Before or after the fight?"

"Well before the fight, Uncle Max. But just to be clear, I don't know if Chip's story is true or not. I just know that he told Cal, and I know that it bothered Cal all night long."

Nate asked, "Is this friend of Cal's, Chip Maris, the same person who used the racial slurs against the twins?"

"Yup. The same one."

"No wonder Cal later punched him," said Max.

"That's why I call it such a mess," said Minerva. "I don't know how to help him."

Instinctively, Nate realized that he needed to break the ice. Minerva was feeling overwhelmed with her impossible challenge, and no amount of advice or recommendations would serve any purpose. He suggested that they all congregate around the breakfast table and enjoy the delicious oatmeal cookies that Max had brought.

"I've already had two," Max confessed.

Miró was about to bite into hers but changed her mind. Exercising her self-discipline, she said, "I'll save this one for later."

"If y'all don't help me consume those babies, I'll return home with them and devour the whole batch."

Minerva was the first one to jump at the offer. She exclaimed that it had been so long since having "Grandma's cookies," she would claim a half-dozen. "Mom, did you buy me some almond milk?"

"Not only that, but she also bought the Mexican chocolate that you love so much, the one you like for your midnight snacks on cold winter nights," said Nate. "It looks like this will be a good night to start your winter indulgence."

Minerva smiled. "If I'm not mistaken, you probably love it more than I do. Would you like to join me?"

CHAPTER NINE

[Evanston, IL; November 2021]

For the next twenty minutes the four enjoyed each other's company, reminiscing about the various favorite recipes that Miriam Epstein had perfected. They were astonished at how many dishes they considered "favorites."

"I think we could come up with enough recipes to fill a respectable cookbook. I may put my mind to it someday," said Max.

"Well, I know who would be the first one in line to buy the book," said Minerva.

"Oh, yeah. Who?"

"Horace Rosenberg," said Minerva. "I remember he became part of the family simply because he loved Grandma's cooking so much."

"Which reminds me that I should call Rosie," said Max. "I bet he's come up with valuable information that we could use in this whole investigation regarding the twins' abduction and murder."

"You're absolutely right," said Nate. "We should invite him to dinner soon."

"Uncle Max—" Minerva blurted out, then held her tongue. "I better not say anything. It'll only get us back to the whole mess trying to differentiate between gossip and fact."

"Gladly, that used to be the job of good journalists," said Nate. "They saw their job as investigating allegations and sniffing out the truth. Now they simply print stuff whether or not it's been substantiated."

"Or worse," said Max. "Some simply make up the allegations and print them as truths."

"Here we go again," said Miró. "Just don't get me started on politics."

"Miró, that's right. We really don't need to delve into polemics," said Nate. "What impresses me about Rosie is that he maintains standards. He's responsible about differentiating between fact and hearsay. And that, my dearest daughter, is what you're doing. I respect that. You want to be responsible about resisting gossip."

"It's sometimes hard, Dad. What I was about to say is that regarding the twins' death, several people, including Cal and me, saw the twins leave the jamboree by boarding the church van driven by Father Rowstone. Or, at least, we *think* it was him. The driver of the van was dressed in a skeleton costume just like the one that Father Rowstone wore earlier that night."

"And the twins never made it back home," said Max. "Nor Rowstone, for that matter."

"Right, Uncle Max. But what I refrained from sharing was that several friends have told me that they saw Cal's mom, Gail Steele, being dropped off a block away from the church grounds before she picked up Cal. She then picked up Cal at the church grounds just a couple of minutes after the twins left with Father Rowstone, or whoever was driving the church van."

Nate asked, "Why do you think that's important?"

After a brief pause Minerva said, "Okay, I've given this some thought. On the way out, three cars, two white ones and a black one, followed behind the church van. The one in back, the one Cal was in, was the vehicle driven by Cal's mom. It's a white Audi minivan. In front of the Audi, a white or silver Range Rover was driven by Bud Milton. The front vehicle in the caravan was apparently speeding to catch up with the church van, and it was described as an American-made black panel van."

Unable to resist her teaching instinct, Miró corrected her daughter: "The vehicle *in which* Cal was riding. If you want to make a living as a writer, you must learn proper grammar, or at least satisfy stuffy librarians who made up the rule."

"Yes, Mom. As soon as I said it, I knew you'd correct my misplaced preposition."

"Okay, back to your account of the different people leaving the church grounds. I still don't see what you're getting at," said Nate. "Why do you think describing the caravan is significant?"

"That's just it. I have no idea if it's significant, but if that black van—the one in front of the three-car caravan—was following Fr. Rowstone, then the driver of the white Range Rover may have additional information about the route taken by the mysterious black van."

"I see your point," said Nate.

"Of course, that information may go nowhere, but isn't it worth investigating? Since those drivers may be the last ones to have seen the vehicle that the twins were riding in—oops, I did it again—I know, Mom, I know. I'll re-phrase to '*in which* the twins were riding.'"

Miró smiled.

"That's true," said Max. "This Bud Milton, the driver of the Range Rover, was he also picking up one of his kids at the church?"

"No, Uncle Max. Bud Milton doesn't have any kids. The kids gossiping about Cal's mom said the bachelor Bud Milton is the person who dropped her off a block away from the church grounds. He was the driver right behind the black van."

· · ·

CHAPTER TEN

[Evanston, IL; November 2021]

=MAX=

My niece Minerva, she is a bright young lady. Without any doubt, she was on to something the other day. I spoke to my buddy Rob Rivers, and we both agreed that her lead was invaluable. Even as an eleven-year-old, Minerva had surprised her parents with her own observations and helpful insights regarding their troubles in the Canary Islands. Despite being kidnapped at that age, her intrepid approach to obstacles was obvious to the family. *Where did this courage come from?*

Shortly after our Bible study on Wednesday, Rob Rivers and I loitered in the Evanston parking lot, where I gave Rob a summary of Minerva's dilemma. I told Rob how my niece was so reluctant to share rumors and hearsay. Rob understood. "That's a rare breed, my brother, because most teenagers thrive on juicy gossip, especially when it involves their acquaintances."

Rob followed up on the information I provided. I was careful not to violate my niece's cautious descriptions. I explained to Rob that Minerva was careful not to present any of the rumors as fact. Following the lead, Rob proceeded with caution.

As he visited Minerva's boyfriend, Rob confirmed that Cal was nursing a broken nose and a serious shiner that was turning purple. To his credit, Cal did not deny that he was at the center of the fight in the church grounds. He asked if Commander Rivers was there to arrest him. Rob reassured the dejected teenager who'd lost his starting quarterback position to Paul Rosales that he was not in trouble. He explained that he was merely following up on an official report filed by the St. Nicholas Catholic Church security guard. Per Rivers, Minerva's boyfriend answered all questions in a respectful and cooperative manner.

In his phone chat with me, Rob added, "He's a nice kid, a little too full of himself, but he's trying to do the right thing. I don't think you need to worry about your niece. She chose well."

Although I had confidence in my niece's opinion of Cal, I was glad to hear my buddy's reassurance.

"If anything, the loss of his quarterback standing and the whole mess with his own friends may help him grow up," said Rob. "It may also bring some needed humility."

"Explain what you mean," I said.

"Well, his dad's narcissism may have rubbed off on Cal. The kid is surprised that his so-called friends have abandoned him since the jamboree, the Day of the Dead celebration. He's also embarrassed that his friends not only used racial epitaphs against the Rosales twins but also bullied them. He acknowledged that he hated Paul Rosales for taking over the quarterback slot, but Cal understands that when one of the twins threw the punch that landed on him, the twin was merely standing up for himself—and his twin brother."

"That's impressive. Glad to hear that."

Rob continued: "And, speaking of bullying, he's also ashamed of his own dad bullying the twins at the coffee shop. He can't believe that his dad got away with the assault without any consequences. Just to show you how much Cal may be growing up faster than his dad, he went on to share an even more shameful development. His dad is suing the parents of the kids who posted the online video—the video which clearly shows the councilman shoving and pushing the twins against the wall of the coffee shop!"

"Did he tell you all this?"

"Yes, without any prompting. Cal is ashamed of both his parents.

And he's also upset that they're punishing him without owning up to their 'hypocrisy,' as he calls it."

"Tell me, Rob—did you tip-toe into the whole infidelity thing? Did you ask him if his parents were having marital problems?"

"I didn't have to. Cal brought it up himself. He confronted his mom about the whole thing because his dad is in denial. Apparently his mom wants a divorce, but the councilman won't give her a divorce until the next election is over. Per Cal, that's all his dad cares about—his political career."

"You mean that Cal knows about the affair?'

"I don't think he knows details, but Cal's buddies—former buddies, I should say—have given him enough gossip. His mom is completely disconnected from the marriage, and from what I can tell, she has one foot out the door."

I said, "Did you ask if he was able to see the route taken by the church van the night of the Day of the Dead celebration?"

"As you know, when you exit the Evanston church grounds, the road leading east toward Sheridan Road is roughly a mile and a half of unlit and undeveloped land. Cal remembers all three vehicles following the church van and proceeding eastward toward the lake, but upon reaching Sheridan, Gail Steele, Cal's mom, turned north and the other three vehicles turned right, or south toward Lincoln Park."

"Did he identify the people in the two vehicles ahead of them?"

"He clearly said that the Range Rover in front of them was driven by a 'moron' by the name of Bud Milton. He had no idea who was driving the vehicle behind the church van. He said that second vehicle was a black Ford cargo van with heavily tinted windows."

"So just to confirm, four vehicles drove out of the church grounds. The church van was leading the impromptu caravan. Following the church van were three vehicles—a black Ford cargo van, the white Range Rover, and Gail Steele's Audi minivan. Is that right?"

"Yes, and the Range Rover, per Cal, is silver, not white."

"Great. So did you get anything else?"

"Oh, yes—much more," said Rob Rivers.

• • •

Without my prompting, Rob continued. "I visited Cal's dad at his office to interview him, but he refused to speak to me. He referred me to his lawyer, who refused to return my calls."

I asked Rob, "That's curious. Did he think you were there to bring charges against him?"

"I don't know, but he's a strange one. After assaulting those teenagers, Cal's dad correctly assumes that things might get messy, especially for someone hoping for a political career."

I wondered why Rob had assured me he had obtained "much more" information, since Jim Steele, Cal's dad, had been so guarded. So I waited for him to elaborate.

Rob evidently had been handed a note from his assistant. "Sorry for the interruption, Max. When I spoke to Gail Steele, however, that was a different story. It even seemed to me she was eager to unload on anyone who would ask. She explained how difficult it was not to share with her own kids the miserable life she'd had with Jim, her husband. According to her, throughout their nineteen years of marriage, Jim Steele had proved to be the most selfish, the most egotistical, and the most inconsiderate person she'd ever known. It was as if he'd been transformed the day they got married. He would often travel to D. C. without her and return home more distant than ever. He'd gamble, and he'd drink—a lot. Furthermore, before she moved out of their bedroom, he had struck her more than once. However, she never pressed charges."

"I'm amazed they're still together," I said.

"According to her, Jim would not give her a divorce because it would ruin his political career. His plan was to run for the state legislature, then go to Washington after that. None of his plans took her or the kids into consideration. She was sure of his unfaithfulness. Now she too had found someone who 'understood' her, a considerate and kind man whom she met many years ago when they lived in Knoxville. She'd met this guy at Knoxville High School."

"You mean they went to school together?"

"Not exactly. She was a high school biology teacher, and he was her student. She tried hard to explain that she'd just graduated from college and that the age difference was not that great. Her student was a high school senior."

"Wow!" I said. "So now teacher and student get reacquainted? Or had they been involved before?"

"That wasn't clear, but she did say that even before—in high school—they had 'been fond' of each other."

"Um, hmm. So—what? Did they get reacquainted by accident, or was it planned?"

Rob continued: "She claims it was coincidental, but he ended up working for State Farm and relocated here. When they met at a council meeting, she knew that it was meant to be. The two would like to get married, but Jim Steele refuses to grant her a divorce. According to Gail Steele, they're both devout Catholics, so…"

"Yeah, I get it. But she wants a divorce."

"She claims she can get her marriage annulled."

I laughed. "Good luck with that one. With three kids and a nineteen-year-old marriage, that'll be hard to do."

"Anyway, the relationship is a mess," Rob said. "And everyone in the family is unhappy."

"Did you interview Bud Milton, the insurance agent?"

"Yes, I asked him to meet me in my office, and he agreed. But once he realized that I'd be asking about Gail Steele, he got tight-lipped. He refused to acknowledge that there's an affair. He claimed it's a platonic friendship and that he wants the best for Gail. When I informed him that there are eyewitnesses of his dropping off Mrs. Steele at the church celebration, he got quiet and said he needed to talk to his lawyer."

I interrupted Rob. "Did you explain that we're investigating something else entirely?"

"Yes, I explained that his relationship with Gail Steele was not our concern. I explained we were investigating the murder of two teenagers, but he clearly would not even acknowledge he was at the church grounds the night of the disappearance. At this point, he's panicked.

He mumbled something about fearing that Jim Steele will accuse him of 'alienation of affection' or something to that effect. He just left my office, saying he had no information for us."

CHAPTER ELEVEN

[Chicago; November 2021]

Several days after the discovery of the twins' bodies, Commander Rob Rivers was grateful for the first break in the case. On a regular patrol of Lincoln Park, one of his officers picked up a disoriented and confused man wandering around the park. The roaming individual, suffering from hypothermia, was dazed—probably drugged—dehydrated, and virtually naked. His feet were shod with worn sneakers that were too large, and he covered himself with a thin wool blanket. Heavily bruised and blistered, the man was not being described as a vagrant, nor did he appear to be violent. The helpless man was immediately taken to a local hospital where he was being treated, fed, and held for observation.

After being fingerprinted and submitting to a psychological evaluation, the victim said he was robbed, beaten, and left to die by the shores of Lake Michigan. Allegedly he had been injected with unknown drugs. Unable to regain full consciousness until days following the assault, the white male in his late forties remembered wearing a costume at his church's celebration of All Saints Day. Upon reading the police report, Commander Rivers immediately drove to the hospital to join the interrogation.

Upon arrival, Rivers went to his bedside and recorded his interview. "My name is Commander Rob Rivers of the 20th District of the Chicago PD. Can you remember your name?"

"Yes, I believe that I can…now. My name is Morgan Rowstone,

Father Morgan Rowstone. I am pastor at a church…St. Nicholas… in Evanston. St. Nicholas Catholic Church. Although I'm not clear on too many details, I remember that I was assaulted by two men. They hit me—took away my van keys, forced me to…to disrobe, and tied me up and threw me in the back of a black van. They also gagged and blindfolded me."

"What happened then?"

"At one point they injected me with…something powerful…a very powerful drug. I lost consciousness. Though, wait—before that I do remember something else…. I remember they drove away with my church van. But the black van without windows followed them."

"The one you were in?"

"Yes."

"How do you know? You said you were blindfolded," Rivers asked.

"Well, after they took my keys, my costume, and my clothes, they threw me in the back of the black van. I was not blindfolded then. Afterward—I don't know when—they must have blindfolded me. I remember bouncing around in the back of the van…and by that time I was blindfolded."

"Wait," said Rivers. "You can't remember when exactly they gagged you and blindfolded you?"

"After they threw me in the back of the van."

"Okay, then someone drove off with your church van. And the black van that you were in followed the church van. Am I understanding you?" Rivers asked.

Rowstone blinked hard and tried to concentrate. "Yes. The van I was in did not have a carpet, mat, or anything…just a plain metal floor. I remember being cold and the two men—the one driving and a passenger—kept complaining in Spanish that the church van in front was driving too fast. They didn't want to bring attention to themselves or to be caught speeding."

"You a Spanish speaker?" asked Rivers.

"I understand some—we have many parishioners who are Hispanic," said Rowstone.

"So let me get this straight. You were beaten by how many men?"

"Only two men approached me. After we exchanged a bit of information, one of them struck me in the back of the head and I blacked out. Later—I don't know how much later—two or three men beat me—while they laughed—and took my keys and my clothes, along with my costume. Then they threw me in the back of the van. I believe I vomited after they hit me."

"Where did this happen? Was there no one else around to see all this happening? Were you in church when the two men approached you?" asked Rivers.

"We had a celebration at the church grounds, a jamboree to celebrate All Saints and All Souls Day," said Rowstone. "I was wearing a traditional costume over my clothes. I stepped outside the grounds to smoke—a nasty habit of mine—and since I don't want to be a bad influence on kids, I prefer not to smoke in front of them."

"How did you end up in Lincoln Park?" Rivers asked.

"I don't remember. All I know is that after I was drugged, I woke up in this strange place—your officers have told me I was in a remote part of Lincoln Park."

"The celebration was almost a week ago. What happened between that night and now?" Rivers asked.

Morgan Rowstone appeared to tear up. He was frightened and confused. "I'm afraid...I'm afraid I can't offer much information in that regard, Commander Rivers."

Rivers pressed on. "Father Rowstone, can you remember anything else? You see, we have reason to believe that the suspects may have used your van to commit at least one other crime. Any other details will be very helpful for our investigation."

Rowstone apologized, "Oh, dear...I'm very sorry." He was silent for a long while, but Rivers also kept silent. Then Rowstone added, "My mind is still foggy. I seem to have lost track of time, and I'm confused."

"Do you remember what your assailants looked like?"

"Why, yes, now that you mention it." Rowstone paused, struggling for details. "The taller one, in his late thirties, was about five-foot-eleven and white. He was of medium build, and he had an Australian accent—very thin, light brown hair, and balding. Although it was dark where they approached me, I could tell he had light-colored eyes—green, maybe blue. The other one had a darker complexion and was mostly silent. He was dressed in cowboy clothes, hat, dark mustache, and no more than five-foot-six in height. I believe he looked Hispanic."

"And you say that the taller man was Australian. Are you sure he was not British?"

"I'm Irish, Commander, and I'm certain he was not a Brit," said Fr. Rowstone. "I can tell the difference between the two accents."

"Of course," said Rivers. "Since he obviously spoke more, do you remember anything he may have said? Or did he give you any other information?"

Father Rowstone smiled and began to nod. "As I talk about it, some of it's coming back. The Aussie approached me and asked for a light. I remember that before I was hit on the head, we were standing outside the church grounds smoking and watching the jamboree full of teenagers through a chain-link fence. The Aussie asked me a strange question."

"What question?" Rivers asked.

"He asked me to identify the football team's starting quarterback at Notre Dame High School."

Rivers asked, "What did you do?"

"I told him how proud I was to know the fine young man. I even said that I'd be taking Paul and his brother home in exactly thirty minutes."

"Then?"

"Then," said Rowstone, "I pointed to Paul Rosales standing next to his brother, Matt. The next thing I know, he hit me on the head."

• • •

=MAX=

On our following Wednesday breakfast meeting, Rob Rivers shared the latest information on the Rosales twins' murder. "Although Father

Rowstone's information brings us some clarity, we have zilch on motive, and even less on the identity of Rowstone's assailants, who more than likely committed the murder. Who are these two perps, and why did they target the Rosales twins?"

"Have you spoken to Special Agent Ram Edmunds of the FBI?" I asked. "I bet these two suspects are somehow connected to Diego Montemayor."

"Max, I've given that some thought, but things don't fit. When we spoke to the twins' mother, she made it clear that Diego had handed over the deed to their property. Remember the trust fund? Diego was providing for the kids' needs, their education. It just doesn't make sense for him to turn around and order the hit."

I agreed with Rob. The whole investigation was missing important information. After a few cups of coffee, we both agreed that we'd enlist the help of Ram Edmunds from the FBI. Perhaps he could shed light on this puzzle.

Ram Edmunds agreed to see us early Saturday morning. I'd forgotten that Ram's work week extended to six days. Fighting traffic to downtown Chicago on a Saturday morning was relatively easier. Wearing sportier weekend attire, Ram had skipped the tie and the vest. He still wore a two-piece gray suit. Rivers and I showed up wearing dockers and cotton sweaters.

Ram invited us into his conference room. I was impressed. His "war room"—a large conference setting with a long board room table equipped with the latest technology—was replete with files, diagrams, and photos of the various cases he was investigating. The main wall, however, was reserved for Diego Montemayor's organization. Evidently, Ram Edmunds's priorities had not changed in the last three years. I reminded myself that Diego, after all, was the unacknowledged son of his ex-partner, Angelo Calabrese—the most elusive criminal in the Western world. He was reputed to oversee at least eighty percent of the world's drug, arms, and human trafficking. In collusion with the Chinese Communist Party, he also controlled the activities of much of America's political system.

Rob spent thirty minutes catching Ram up on the latest findings.

He even shared Father Rowstone's interview, but we both commented on the confusing bits of information. We posed our doubts to Edmunds.

"If Diego Montemayor was involved in the latest *Black Pearl* murders, why were the young twins targeted?" Rob asked.

"Please understand," said Edmunds as he looked at Rivers, "until there's a connection with Diego Montemayor, this case remains a local issue with jurisdiction in your court."

"We respect that, Ram. However, couldn't you inquire from people in your custody if they have any information regarding this crime?" I asked.

"What are you asking, Max?" Ram had taken off his suit jacket, and he walked over to his expansive picture window overlooking Roosevelt Road. Looking out at the cloudless skies, he hooked his thumbs on his scarlet suspenders and added, "Other than Dr. Ivo Wu, the plastic surgeon, we have no one else in custody who is remotely associated with Diego Montemayor. Most of the information he has given us has been useless."

I explained to Ram how close we were to linking Diego to the latest crime, but we needed just one tiny piece to the puzzle. It was worth our while to at least ask Dr. Wu about any Aussies in Diego's organization.

"It may take a few days, since Wu is in a minimum-security facility outside the city," Ram said.

"Fine. Do you mind if we're present while you interrogate your person in custody?" I asked.

"I'll do better than that," said Ram. "If the three of us are present, both of you can ask questions."

On the following Monday at 4:00 p.m., Dr. Ivo Wu was brought into the federal building. As soon as he was made comfortable, Wu relaxed, smiled, and optimistically asked if he was being granted a reduction in sentence. Ram Edmunds smiled and suggested that every consideration would be made when conditions were met. Then Ram introduced Commander Rob Rivers and Private Inspector Max Kempball, yours truly.

Interlocking his fingers on his generous paunch, Wu sat in his armchair with a complacent smile. He asked for a cup of "that Jamaican brew" for which Ram had become known. Ram obliged and first served the rest of us.

After some routine questioning by Ram Edmunds, he asked Rivers if he had any questions to ask Dr. Ivo Wu. Rivers quickly responded, "Only a couple of questions, Dr. Wu." Then Rob Rivers proceeded to ask about Wu's familiarity with the Rosales family, Diego Montemayor's safe houses, whether he had visited the estates in Winnetka, and whether he had met other "associates" in Diego's organization.

To our surprise, Wu was amiable, contrite, and humble. Later in private, Rivers was amazed at how Dr. Wu had sung "like a canary." Previously, Wu had failed to disclose any connections between Diego and his Mazatlán associates.

When Rob Rivers asked directly whether he knew of an Aussie working for Diego Montemayor, Wu nodded and said he knew him well. As he took his last sip of coffee, he extended his empty mug to request from Ram another serving. Addressing Rob Rivers, Wu mentioned that the Aussie Lucas Williams was employed by Diego and, in fact, had become an invaluable member of Diego's inner circle. Furthermore, Lucas had recently been appointed Diego's lieutenant in charge of the Mazatlán compound. Wu offered his opinion that soon Lucas could be put in charge of Diego's "North American division."

As a follow-up, I described a Hispanic with a dark mustache, slightly overweight, and about five-foot-six in height. "Did you meet any such person in Mazatlán?" I asked.

Dr. Wu laughed and said that I had described about eighty-five percent of Diego's employees at the Mazatlán compound.

At the end of the two-hour interrogation, Special Agent Edmunds informed Dr. Wu that he would be detained at a local facility because additional questioning would be necessary. Wu was summarily dismissed. Dr. Wu quickly slurped his last sip of Ram's specialty coffee brew.

After the physician was escorted out of Ram's office, I said, "Wu's information will be helpful. If I can make a request?"

"No need," said Edmunds. "We have enough evidence to put in a request for Mexico to extradite Lucas Williams from Mazatlán—ASAP."

The *federales*' response from Mexico was unusually prompt. Perhaps in their eagerness to gain favor with President Spanner's new American administration, not only did Mexico extradite Lucas Williams in record time, but the authorities also transported Williams directly to Chicago. He was accompanied by three burly *federales* wearing white guayaberas. Lucas Williams was quickly arraigned in the Illinois federal court for murder, kidnapping, and theft.

With the Mexican *federales* considering him an "undesirable" and with a positive identification from Father Rowstone, Lucas Williams pleaded guilty. Joined by Dr. Ivo Wu, he quickly negotiated a plea deal with the FBI that would eventually help in the hunt for Diego Montemayor. When faced with the alternative of a death sentence or Edmunds's promise of partial immunity and federal protection, Lucas opted for the Americans' offer. He knew that Diego's wrath would entail a much more ruthless end.

In their formal deposition, Lucas Williams and Ivo Wu not only directly named members of the Mazatlán organization but also implicated the deputy director of the FBI, Jacoby Homely, as a known "friend" of Diego's cabal. Furthermore, Williams freely produced deposit slips for generous monthly "contributions" made to Homely's bank account in Grand Cayman, voice recordings of communications to Homely's private mobile phone, as well as photographs of the deputy director in compromising romantic entanglements with underage females in Diego's Mazatlán compound. The various pieces of evidence would be enough to convict the average citizen to life imprisonment.

CHAPTER TWELVE

[Evanston, IL; late November 2021–January 2022]

=MAX=

Throughout Wu's and Williams's depositions, I observed my friend Ram Edmunds fall into a profound depression. He became quiet and withdrawn. Though his colleague Jacoby Homely had not been supportive of Ram, my friend was deeply loyal to his own. The FBI was his life, and he would support it to his utmost. I could see him enduring a heartbreaking disappointment in Homely's lack of honor, a superior's obvious moral failures, and his complete lack of integrity. Although he had been at the receiving end of Homely's sacrosanct preaching and his unfavorable decisions, Edmunds could not accept that the office of the Deputy Director of the FBI was being sullied. Even after listening to the recordings presented by Lucas Williams and reviewing the records that clearly indicated Homely's guilt, he sought to protect his superior's innocence.

During one of our meetings, as if trying to convince himself, Ram insisted, "You both know that Diego's electronic surveillance and his technological skills are far superior to anything that we have. Who knows? They can frame anyone they want." He attempted to convince Rivers and me that Deputy Director Homely was still innocent "until proven guilty."

After a long silence, I responded, "It seems to me, Ram, that the proof has been submitted to us. The question is how we'll proceed."

Commander Rivers, fellow member of the brotherhood of law enforcement, could just say, "Ram, we can only do our job. We must follow the process."

For the next two months Special Agent Edmunds presented his findings to the Department of Justice. After six weeks of stonewalling most of the evidence, President Willy Spanner's new appointee to head the Department of Justice was forced to respond to a series of articles first published by Horace Rosenberg of the *Chicago Tribune*. Unable to get open cooperation from Ram Edmunds, Rosie had simply interviewed Commander Rivers, who shared only the evidence that appeared on his desk. Once the information on the deputy director of the FBI became a topic of discussion on most social media sites, the DOJ could not simply dismiss it as a foolish conspiracy.

On the morning when the first articles appeared, Ram called me. "Tell me the truth, Max. Did you leak the story to Horace Rosenberg?"

"Rather than lie to you, I will simply say that I cannot respond truthfully. If I do," I said, "I will remove your ability to claim plausible deniability."

Ram Edmunds chuckled and ended the call.

As an interesting addition to the case being made by Chicago's PD Commander Rob Rivers, the depositions of Lucas Williams and secondary depositions of Dr. Ivo Wu unveiled details about another local political career that was quickly becoming derailed. Lucas Williams in his deposition stated that FBI Deputy Director Homely leaked information to the press about a local Winnetka politician. Apparently, Jim Steele's addiction to pornography and his "fascination" with pedophilia was given to the local press. Though few in the news media picked up the information—since Steele was such a small, insignificant fish—Steele's own family, namely his wife, was made aware of the leaks.

When Ram shared the depositions with the DOJ, Homely, upon questioning, indicated that he had facilitated "a few encounters" for Steele with underage prostitutes in the D. C. area. Although Lucas Williams could not produce any evidence of the encounters, Homely himself had sent videos to Gail Steele of her husband *au flagrante* in numerous encounters. Inadvertently, the deputy director incriminated himself every step of the way. Of course, Gail Steele filed for divorce after receiving the videos of her husband's indiscretions. Shortly afterward, she began her affair with Bud Milton.

Furthermore, Lucas Williams indicated that Homely regularly used the same tactics to blackmail hundreds of politicians across the nation. "It was his M.O. He's got thousands of files on hundreds, perhaps thousands, of politicians throughout the country," said Williams.

"Homely controls these politicians by seeking favorable legislation from them at the local, state, and federal levels. Those politicians who cooperate are granted political favors as well as generous 'foundation donations' toward their campaigns," stated Williams under oath. "Often, through Estevan Chengfu, Diego's assistant, Homely would ask me for special favors."

"Such as?" Edmunds asked in the deposition.

"Estevan was not pleased with recent intrusions of the Winnetka's local police on Diego's estate," stated Williams.

"What kinds of intrusions?"

"You know, mate, extreme curiosity from some local cops. For example, they wanted to know what went on in Diego's safe houses, so they snooped around," Williams said. "They asked local business owners to report any strange behaviors coming from the two Winnetka compounds."

"And what about Jim Steele? What kinds of demands were imposed on Jim Steele?" asked Edmunds.

"You need to understand, mate—I had no direct contact with these characters," said Lucas Williams. "I got all my communications from Estevan Chengfu. All I know is that Homely wanted a 'defund the police' campaign launched in Winnetka and Jim Steele complained that he was not in favor, nor would any member of the village council agree to such a campaign."

"I don't know, Lucas—as I recall, Jim Steele was the one who championed the cause to defund cops. I don't think he needed to be persuaded," said Edmunds.

Lucas Williams laughed. "That's because Homely applied the

screws. To 'persuade' Jim Steele, Homely leaked evidence of Steele's porno addiction. When that didn't work, Homely ordered a hit on Jim Steele's son, Calvin Steele, his pride and joy. That's where I came in."

"Do you mean that Homely ordered you directly to kill Cal Steele? I thought your organization pulled the strings on Homely."

"No, no. I never communicated with Homely," said Williams. "I don't work for him. Homely must have asked Estevan to order me to get the job done. I received my orders for the hit from Estevan."

"But you killed the wrong kids," said Edmunds. "Why did you end up killing the Rosales twins?"

"Look, mate. It was a mix-up, okay? Estevan asked me to 'rub out' Jim Steele's son. I did not get names, and I told Estevan I had no idea who the Steeles were. Estevan said to ask around for the Notre Dame High School quarterback."

"And you did," said Edmunds.

Lucas Williams nodded. "Estevan provided information on the church celebration. He said the kid would be there, that it would be simple. That night when I asked Father Rowstone to identify the high school quarterback, he pointed out one of the twins. How was I to know that Paul Rosales had replaced Jim Steele's son as the school's quarterback? I'd never met the kids."

"So you're telling me that the killing of the Rosales twins was a case of mistaken identity?"

"That's exactly what I'm saying. I'm not saying it makes it right—in fact, it got me into hot water with Estevan, but it was his fault that he did not give me the name of Jim Steele's son. Estevan simply said, 'We've put a hit on the high school quarterback.'"

. . .

=MAX=

This year's Thanksgiving and Christmas holidays were about the same as last year's. My stepmom, Miriam Epstein, had been killed on that fateful day of March 13, 2020, the day of *The Black Pearl* massacre. I remember that last year valiant efforts were made by the family to celebrate both holidays without her, and despite the resilience of my dad, my sister, and her family, they were unable to pull off the genuine gratitude and cheer that I had witnessed before.

To his credit, Dad instructed me on the third week of November of last year to help him host Thanksgiving dinner at his home. Miró and I prepared a festive turkey dinner with all the trimmings. Even Horace Rosenberg joined us. And on the 25th of December, Miró hosted our Christmas dinner at their home with several friends from outside the family joining us. Minerva's boyfriend, Cal Steele, joined us briefly before returning home to celebrate with his family. After each celebration, my dad, Abraham, spent hours in his bedroom reviewing family photographs, videos, and listening to Miriam's favorite music.

This year Dad even hired a professional decorator to create a Hanukkah/Christmas celebratory environment for the Epstein-Shelley family—a celebration of Jewish and Christmas traditions for the Judeo-Christian family that we are. Since Miró hosted Thanksgiving dinner, Dad and I hosted our Christmas/Hanukkah celebrations, starting on the 28th of November, including the gifting of gelt coins, dreidels, and handwritten blessings for each member of the family. On Christmas Day the gift jar's festive blue and silver ribbons were changed to red, green, and white. Although we commemorated Miriam's presence in our lives, the celebrations were less mournful.

Perhaps the most significant event of our holiday celebrations this year was Minerva's statement on Christmas Day that she and Cal Steele would make two announcements. As the adults in the room held our breath, wondering what momentous news would be reported, Minerva cheerfully said, "I'll make the first announcement, and Cal will help me make our second declaration."

There was nervous laughter among the group, but I detected a stunned silence in my sister. Then Minerva stated, "Cal and I are planning to graduate from high school at least one semester earlier than anticipated." Probably more to break the anxiety of the group, I cheered loudly and applauded. Applause from the group followed.

Then Dad asked, "And for the second announcement, what do you have to share along with Cal?"

"Minerva and I have been dating for years now, and I believe that our relationship is better than ever," said Cal Steele.

"However, we have decided," Minerva said, "that neither one of us is prepared to proceed to any future commitments. We have decided that over the next year or so, we will concentrate on our studies and prepare for our next phase of education. Cal will be applying to West Point, and I—well, I have several fine universities that I'm considering. As you all know, I want the best education to become a full-time writer."

"Well, congratulations to you both," Miró said, perhaps with a bit too much enthusiasm. I'm certain that Miró was holding her breath anticipating that Minerva and Cal were about to announce their engagement. And knowing her, I'm sure she was relieved to find out that was not the case.

CHAPTER THIRTEEN

[Isle of Corsica, France; late January 2022]

sabella had just tidied up Diego's bedroom suite when she heard the shattering of silver platters and cups on her master's private garden. As she walked out, Diego hurled a large French Press at Estevan. With a single movement, the mute *consigliere* deftly sidestepped the flying container and walked up to Diego. He stood in his face and with a fierce glare signed slowly, *You…do not…want to do that.* With a firm left grip he held Diego's right wrist. Diego dropped the silver creamer in his hand and it bounced several times, clattering on the pink granite of the patio floor.

Checking his tirade, Diego turned and paced in the opposite direction. He stood beneath a tall Italian cypress at the edge of his manicured turf and screamed, "What do you mean Lucas Williams is in American custody? Since when?"

Estevan signed in rapid fashion. *I just learned it myself. When the Mexican president, attempted to cooperate with the new Spanner administration, he agreed to extradite Lucas. The* federales *contacted me. The president ordered his troops to storm the Mazatlán compound…*

"Okay, Estevan—stop. Call Isabella in so she can interpret for me." Diego was still pacing. Isabella rushed to the garden, making sure she did not step on several shards of glass at her feet. She interpreted Estevan's signing.

"He say that Lucas Williams was…how do you say…sent…*estradato* to the USA. He say that the Mexican president attempted to take over your place in Mazatlán. He, the Mexican president, coop-erates with the new American president, Spanner. And the *federales*… how do you say…backed down…when our own Mazatlán men cap-tured and tortured four of the *federales*. The four dead Mexican *fede-rales* are hanging from a bridge in downtown Mazatlán. The Mexican president is no longer making trouble. We sent him a nice present."

Turning to Estevan, Diego asked, "What did the Americans charge Lucas with?"

Estevan signed, *Murder.*

Diego continued: "If Lucas is in custody, who's running the com-pound right now?"

Estevan signed, *Lucas's second-in-command, Lorenzo McAbbee.*

Failing to understand, Diego looked at Isabella, "Who?"

Isabella spelled it out: "M-c-A-b-b-e-e."

"Who the devil is Lorenzo McAbbee? I never appointed anyone as second-in-command to Lucas."

He came highly recommended by your Washington friend, Jacoby Homely.

"And I suppose you approved it." Diego was asking a question. He turned and glared at Estevan.

Averting Diego's face, Estevan turned to Isabella and signed, *Remind Diego that he gave me authority to help run the Mazatlán compound after we left Mexico. With Lucas gone, we needed someone to run the compound in Mazatlán.*

Holding up his hands to Isabella, Diego interrupted. "Never mind. I understood Estevan."

"Have you communicated with Lucas?" Diego asked Estevan.

He hasn't answered my encrypted emails, Estevan signed.

"Can't Jacoby Homely help?" Diego asked.

Homely also is being investigated by the DOJ. He may be in trou-ble, said Estevan.

"*Dios mío. ¡Me rodean puros idiotas!*" exclaimed Diego to the sky. Pacing and flailing his arms, he continued to pace. "Why exactly is Lucas in custody? Did he get careless in Mexico? Did he kill a friend of a friend? Did he fail to pay off our friends…what?"

Apparently he murdered the Rosales twins in Evanston, signed Estevan.

Using his iPad, which was still on the garden's bistro table, Diego grabbed it by its edge and lunged at Estevan as if to smash it on his head. He stopped in his tracks and instead smashed the device on the granite flooring. He screamed again, "*¿Qué? ¿Qué? ¿Mató a Mateo y a Pablo? ¿Porqué, diablos?*" To no one in particular, he exclaimed, "*¡Me persiguen los demonios!*"

As she held Diego, Isabella intervened, "*È stato un errore*—it was mistake."

Turning to Estevan, Diego screamed, "How can you kill two innocent teenagers by mistake? Explain to me, Estevan. How?"

Estevan slowly offered Diego the padded wrought-iron chair that had been overturned, and he signed, *Like Isabella said, it was in error. Lucas had received orders.*

Now seated, Diego stared at Estevan, hunched his shoulders, and raised his forearms from the elbows with his palms up. Without verbalizing anything, he mouthed inaudible mumblings. He looked about in disbelief. He stood up again, and massaging his temples, Diego looked straight at Estevan and tried to calmly ask, "Who… gave…the orders?"

For the first time, Estevan hesitated and signed, *The request came from Jacoby Homely, but I gave the order.*

Turning to Isabella, Diego instructed her to leave them to speak in private. Isabella rushed inside and shut the sliding doors.

. . .

For the next two hours Estevan informed Diego about Lucas's botched murder of the Rosales twins. When he attempted to explain how Lucas Williams had mistaken the twins for the son of an insignificant local politician, Estevan indicated that he was following practices that Diego himself had used in the past.

Estevan signed, *You have always said that in America the only thing that matters is the political party in power. And to control the levers of government, not only should we grease the wheels, but also we must comply with friends' requests.*

"So Jacoby Homely wanted the twins killed? For what reason?" asked a confused Diego.

Estevan continued signing. *Not exactly. Homely controls many politicians at every level. He was attempting to strong-arm a politician from Winnetka, so he wanted the politician's son hurt. Homely told me the politician's son was the high school quarterback, so that's what I told Lucas.*

"So?"

So...since Pablo...or Paul...Rosales had become the high school quarterback, Lucas killed the wrong kid.

"And Mateo, his twin brother?" asked Diego.

Diego, they were twins, they were together, so Lucas took care of both. A case of mistaken identity, Estevan signed.

For the first time in his life, Estevan saw his boss weep. Diego wept silently for several minutes. Perhaps in anger, perhaps in frustration or grief, Estevan did not know, but Diego tossed his small glass of sherry against his office's limestone wall.

Estevan left Diego sitting dejected in his garden. He wondered if it was time for him to take greater control of matters.

• • •

[Washington DC; late January 2022]

As soon as the director of the FBI summoned Deputy Director Jacoby Homely for an important private meeting, Homely telephoned Diego Montemayor's assistant, Estevan Chengfu. Homely wanted to inform Estevan that he had received advance warnings from several agents in the American intelligence community that incriminating evidence had been presented to the DOJ and the FBI Director. The evidence clearly pointed to a connection between his own office and Diego's cartel. Estevan failed to return his call.

When Homely first heard the incriminating rumors, his first reaction was to immediately suspend the special agent in charge of the

Chicago office of the FBI, Ram Edmunds, for insubordination and misconduct. It was at that point that Homely realized his enormous power within the FBI was in jeopardy. Apparently the director of the FBI himself had intercepted Homely's communication with the Chicago office and called him in for questioning. When Homely showed up for his meeting with the director, he was informed that he had temporarily been stripped of his authority and was being placed on administrative leave.

To Homely's worst humiliation, he was escorted out of the FBI headquarters by two federal agents. Somehow the press had been tipped off, and a gaggle of photographers were there to record the event. The following day, all his office's personal belongings were sent to his home via Federal Express.

Countless calls that Homely placed to Estevan were ignored. His email service returned his communications to Estevan; they were labeled with an "unknown recipient" marker. Unable to communicate directly with Diego Montemayor, Jacoby Homely resorted to a risky and dangerous effort to telephone Lucas Williams directly. Of course, Homely was not aware that Lucas Williams was in federal custody, nor was he aware of the plea deal that Williams had made with Special Agent Ram Edmunds. Homely's first call to Lucas was intercepted by Agent Edmunds, who proceeded to record Homely's desperate cry for help. It was this fatal mistake that served as the nail on Homely's proverbial coffin.

When Homely walked into the FBI director's D. C. office for the second time, Director Wren played the recording of Homely's call to Lucas Williams. Without saying a word, Wren handed his deputy director a written statement indicating that Homely was forthwith on administrative leave.

On the third day of Jacoby Homely's administrative leave, the same federal agents who had escorted him out of his office appeared at his home's front door with a search warrant to confiscate all equipment and information they saw fit for seizure.

On the fourth day of his administrative leave, the agents returned at 10:20 at night. When they rang the doorbell to his home, they heard a single gunshot. The agents broke down the door. Jacoby Homely had committed suicide. In a note, Homely provided one piece of information: "To the best of my knowledge, Diego Montemayor is in Bonifacio on the French island of Corsica." It was signed, "J. H."

PART TWO

THE QUEST

> *"…it is not the intellectual who finds Him,*
> *but He who finds the intellectual."*
>
> CRISS JAMI

CHAPTER FOURTEEN

[Israel; ten months before the twins' drowning]
(February 2021)

Nate landed in Tel Aviv. His flight from Lyon to Frankfurt had been an interminable bore. He'd had an insufferable conversation with a young New York City family physician who had the window seat next to him. Dr. Anthony Falsey prided himself as "well-rounded" and "well-read," and one would assume, eminently qualified to pontificate about science, the pandemic, and everything that could be considered "woke" in the current parlance. Dr. Falsey was a slight, short man, but he was a giant in his own mind. His face was rodent-like, and his voice was raspy and measured. It gave him an air of self-importance. After ordering his second gin and tonic, Falsey commandeered the conversation to lecture Nate about the dangers of faith.

After clearing his throat, he extended his short neck outward and upward—as if the Supreme Being had anointed him to be the oracle for all humanity. "Men like you and me, Dr. Shelley, must resist the temptation to indulge in religion, or anything spiritual. Science—that's our religion!"

Seeking a break in the present conversation, Nate ordered a tonic water, not finding any wine in the airline's offerings that suited him. In the hopes of getting a conversational rescue, he asked the flight attendant if she was based in Frankfurt. Unfortunately, she simply smiled and added, "No, my husband and I live in Manhattan." She quickly returned to her duties.

Dr. Anthony Falsey continued. "For men like us, Dr. Shelley, it is incumbent upon us to maintain the standards of objectivity. And God's existence—or his non-existence—must remain a question that only science can answer. And because in my humble estimation we will never be able to ultimately confirm his existence, we must uphold objectivity and the human intellect as our official response to the masses."

Nate fell for the bait and finally asked, "But what about great minds like Einstein, C. S. Lewis, and so many others who were great apologists and firm believers in the existence of an Almighty who is involved in the human drama?"

"Oh, come, come, Dr. Shelley. You know that sometimes we who are enlightened must succumb to more pedestrian exchanges, just to pacify dangerous efforts of the masses. In our station in life, we must give people what they want—for the moment."

Nate was experienced at intellectual jousting and cocktail party twaddle. However, he was tired and had no desire to entertain this educated buffoon. He excused himself, took out his sleep mask and summoned the flight attendant for extra pillows.

Thankfully, upon arrival at the Frankfurt Airport, Falsey deplaned and exclaimed to Nate how much he had enjoyed "their dialogue." The rest of the trip from Frankfurt to Tel Aviv was a restful flight aboard Lufthansa's Airbus A320. For many years Nate had wanted to experience what other "believers" had felt when they'd set foot in the Holy Land. But as much as Nate wanted to dispel his faithlessness, he only hoped for a mere resolution to his ambivalence. He also felt guilty about his antipathy toward "holy rollers" and superspiritual individuals who claimed to have "intimate conversations" with the Almighty.

Nate did not consider himself an atheist; however, he could not claim to be a committed believer either. Since Miró insisted on it, he attended Catholic church services on a regular basis for the sake of family unity. Although Miró's parents were Jewish, Miró had attended

Catholic schools and felt more comfortable attending mass on Sundays. Plus, growing up in South Texas, she experienced much humiliation for being the child of "Hebrews." Also, Nate had accepted a few invitations from Max, his brother-in-law, to attend "non-denominational" services. However, their contemporary music and production-level entertainment was somewhat radical for his tastes.

Compared to his brother-in-law, Nate was a heathen. And his father-in-law, although Jewish, had accepted that the Messiah, for whom he'd been waiting all his life, was most assuredly Jesus, or "Yeshua." Max called Abraham a "Messianic Jew", whatever that was. At this juncture, Nate was clueless—clueless but hopeful. *Will my trip to the Holy Land enable me to resolve my spiritual ambivalence?*

It was specifically this ambivalence that bothered Nate the most. He absolutely detested the quasi-intellectual drivel of agnostics—such as the one to which he'd been subjected in his flight to Frankfurt. His own social circle was replete with such nonsensical discussions. In fact, to his own dismay, he sometimes joined in and even tacitly agreed. Yet when threatened by things beyond his control, he often prayed. *What was that about?* Still, he could not come to a firm belief in God.

When Nate confided to a colleague that he was looking forward to his trip to Israel, she sheepishly confided that her own trip to the Holy Land had transformed her life. Although a closet believer, she did confide to Nate that she was a devout Catholic. The colleague preferred to "keep her religious beliefs" private, she said, because she preferred not to engage in controversial discussions with her peers.

"Nate, when I landed in Tel Aviv, it was as if God changed me instantly. All the teachings of my parents, all the teachings of the church, all my catechism classes invaded my mind and removed all my doubts. I felt like I was walking the streets where Jesus had lived and died on the cross." His Catholic friend seemed content and convinced. What confused Nate was why, if Dr. Julie O'Malley had been truly transformed, she would want to keep her faith a secret.

Nate's arrival in Tel Aviv was uneventful. No, Nate did not fall on his knees to kiss the ground at Ben Gurion Airport, nor did he hear angelic harps playing. Upon arrival, Nate was escorted beyond the customs station to a separate room where he was politely questioned regarding the reason for his trip to Israel. Nate was surprised by the ubiquitous presence of Israel's armed military, both young men and young women who seemed to be barely out of high school. He remembered reading that Israel required all high school graduates to serve two years in the military after completing their secondary education. The weaponry appeared to be the most advanced and latest-developed equipment available. After the brief interrogation and thorough review of his passport, his escort met him at the exit toward the parking lot. As promised, Professor Ari Weiss himself was there to receive him.

Wearing a gray tweed sport jacket and khaki pants, Dr. Weiss conformed to the typical scholar's wardrobe, one who happened to be out and about. In his mid-sixties—suggested by the gray shock of curly hair—he still had a powerful and square body with the onset of a slight paunch. His wire-rimmed glasses and brown walking shoes completed the academic stereotype. In a joyful embrace, Professor Weiss exclaimed, "I finally get to meet you, Dr. Shelley."

"Likewise, Professor Weiss. I've read all of your writings," said Nate. Although the professor's writings focused on international relations and the politics of the Middle East, Nate realized that Weiss was considered the most respected authority in his field. After joining Interpol and learning of his assignment to interview the professor and his Center, Nate had brushed up on Weiss's publications.

Driving out of the airport, Nate couldn't help noticing how much the Israeli countryside resembled some areas of the American Southwest—rolling hills with a preponderance of stones, rocky soil, and cacti for miles and miles. Unlike the American Southwest, however, olive trees dotted the landscape. In his mind, Nate acknowledged that he'd been wrong to anticipate a peel of thunder to greet him. *I suppose that is not how one spiritually develops, eh, God?*

"So tell me. Your first trip to Israel, is it, Dr. Shelley?" asked Professor Weiss.

"I'm sorry, Dr. Weiss, but I was distracted. What was your question?"

"I was merely asking if this is your first trip to Israel. Your facial expression tells me it is, and it also indicates disappointment." Professor Weiss was smiling. He had the wise and temperate countenance of an unassuming intellectual, which is a rare breed in academia.

"No, no—I'm not disappointed," said Nate. "And yes, it is my first trip to Israel. I suppose that my emotions are catching up with my anticipation. You see, I expected…"

The stocky, bespectacled legend of the Middle Eastern academic world was playing the role of Nate's chauffer, and this also was making Nate uncomfortable. Dr. Weiss injected, "Like many other people, Dr. Shelley, you may have anticipated a supernatural event upon landing. Reading so many passages of Scripture, one anticipates a holier moment, an impact that only spiritual experiences can give you."

"You are quite perceptive. I suppose you get that from many visitors," said Nate.

"Most," said the professor. "But one's spiritual journey is not merely impacted by the places one visits—it's the visits one experiences at each step."

Nate was not certain he understood, but he nodded anyway. "Where are you taking me, by the way? Are we on our way to the institute, the center?"

"We call it the Center for Middle Eastern Peace Studies, Dr. Shelley. And we are honored to have you visit with us," said the professor. "But first I'd like you to have a brief tour of our home—our land, I mean. I know you are very well read, and you must know much about Israel, but there is nothing like a guided tour."

"I can't agree more, but for you to dedicate such valuable time to merely entertaining me is unthinkable. It is I who is in awe of you and all your many accomplishments, Professor Weiss. In fact, I feel extremely awkward that you are driving me. I should be your chauffeur."

"Nonsense," said the professor with a smile. "You are probably the youngest psychotherapist to assume the role of president of the World Psychiatric Organization. And you have done it with great efficacy. My only curiosity is why a man of your stature is serving as a so-called 'profiler' for Interpol?"

"That, my dear professor, will take at least two glasses of wine to discuss."

Again, with a twinkle in his eyes, Professor Weiss smiled and said, "A man after my own heart. I may just know the place for us to relax."

"But we are driving northward, Professor. I thought we would be headed toward Jerusalem."

"Haifa is just ninety kilometers, fifty miles, from Tel Aviv. I know the perfect place," said the professor, "where you can relax and 'unwind,' as you Americans say."

In less than forty minutes they arrived at the Wine Bar by Andre Suidan. It was a cozy, intimate bar where guests immediately felt welcomed and appreciated. Despite the bright sun outside, the dim lighting in the bar created a welcoming and restful respite for Nate. The red comfortable leather seating of the circular booth embraced him to the point that Nate felt an immediate decrease in muscle tension and heart rate. Even his respiration rate slowed down.

The professor was an acquaintance of Andre, so they were given treatment fit for royalty. "There are other very good wine bars, but some of them serve only Israeli wines, and I do not believe you should be limited in that way on your first day here," said the professor. He hand-combed his shock of gray hair after being seated and asked Andre for the menu. They exchanged a greeting in Hebrew. Then the owner whispered in the professor's ear and turned to leave. Andre returned without a menu, but he brought with him two bottles of wine—one white and one red.

"Andre brought a white wine from a mountainous region in Italy that he suspects you will love." Ari Weiss said, "He's asked me if you will allow him to serve you a taste."

Intrigued, Nate asked, "Yes, of course, but tell me, Professor Weiss, is it customary for Andre to predict customers' taste in wines by just looking at them?"

"Not always, but often." As they watched Andre, without hesitating he poured the professor a glass of red wine; then he poured two ounces of the white wine for Nate.

As Nate proceeded to taste the opened bottle of a white wine produced in Sicily called "Etna Bianco," he held up the glass to the light and noted it had a bright straw-yellow color with a few golden streaks. He first looked straight down into the glass. Then he tilted his glass and allowed the wine to roll toward the edges, noting that the golden color remained in the center while its full range of pale-yellow danced around the edges. After swirling the small amount of the libation in his glass and allowing some air to mix in with it, he brought it up to his nose and sniffed it. The momentary impression gave him a fresh hint of earthy minerality and white peaches mixed with orange blossoms. The bouquet brought to mind a previous visit to Spain. Now with a smile on his face, again he gave the glass a good swirl. He brought the liquid up to his lips. Nate took his first sip and attempted to take in some air without making a sucking sound.

"You're among friends, my friend," said the professor. "Go ahead and take in the air, aerate your wine, and circulate it throughout your mouth."

Nate thanked him. He swirled it in his mouth to invite his taste buds to compare with the aromas he'd sniffed. The Etna Bianco was bone dry. Yet it was balanced with an explosion of flavors. *What a perfect blend of minerality, floral, and fruity tastes!* thought Nate. The wine was bright and zippy, with a pleasant acidity and volcanic minerality that frankly reminded him of his favorite Spanish wine. Nate shared with Professor Weiss, "Either this man is a savant, or he got some advance information regarding my taste in wines. Please tell him that my favorite wine is a wine produced in the Canary Islands, which I have trouble finding in the US. Although Italian, this wine is similar."

Ari Weiss turned to Andre to pass on the information. Andre smiled and asked if Nate's favorite wine came from Lanzarrote.

Without waiting for a translation, Nate answered him directly. "I believe I understand. Yes, the wine is produced in Lanzarrote." Turning to the professor, Nate asked, "Please ask Andre how he knew."

"Andre said the Etna Bianco comes from the *carricante* grape and it is produced on the slopes of the Mount Etna volcano in Sicily. No wonder it is like the wine from Lanzarrote," said Ari Weiss. "He said you probably enjoy the volcanic taste suggested by the grape."

Obviously, Andre was quite pleased and attempted to use English. "I leave the bottle, yes? Compliments of the house, I bring appetizers."

* * *

Andre returned with a sizable platter of an assortment of different canapes and hors d'oeuvres, which, of course, suggested a thoroughly Mediterranean presentation. Again, Andre whispered in the professor's ear. According to Professor Weiss's translation, the bite-sized bread cutouts of the canapes each contained different spreads. Some contained smoked salmon, pate de *fois gras*, or lobster. Others contained cheeses with minced onions, chives, or caviar. "Oh, and the base of the bread cutouts," said the professor, "has been spread with a thin film of flavored butters."

"Interesting," said Nate, "For added flavoring?"

"Actually, the flavored butters not only accentuate the taste, but also prevent the canapes from becoming soggy," said Professor Weiss.

"Allow me to comment on the garnishing," said Weiss. "Andre takes great care in the presentation of every single plate, whether large or small. He would be delighted if you noticed the little touches like the colorful and dainty garnishes that are presented in harmony with the spread of each canape. For example, Andre does not allow his chefs to cut the tiny leaflets of parsley or watercress. They should always be placed in their natural form. The pimentos, the green and red sweet peppers, the paper-thin carrots are all carefully arranged."

"Wow!" said Nate. "My dearly-departed mother-in-law would truly appreciate—much more than I—Andre's talents. She was a wonderful chef herself."

"I'm afraid my culinary knowledge does not do justice to Andre's talents," said Professor Weiss.

"Please give him my compliments, and apologize to him, because I'm about to devour this platter and destroy the presentation," said Nate.

"Andre will consider it the greatest compliment! His supreme joy is seeing his guests enjoy his food."

As Nate reached for his glass to take his third sip, Andre approached the table to fill it once again. Nate acknowledged his gesture and thanked him.

"Let us turn our attention to your visit," said Professor Weiss. "Tell me why you're actually here, Dr. Shelley."

CHAPTER FIFTEEN

[Israel; ten months before the twins' drowning]
(February 2021)

After Nate Shelley and Professor Ari Weiss consumed the exquisite canapes, Andre approached the table with a more substantial serving of hors d'oeuvres. The tray contained hot offerings of meatballs, fish balls, and stuffed mushrooms. In the center was an elaborate centerpiece of fruits and vegetables. Professor Weiss ignored the artfully prepared tray and repeated his question: "I know that Interpol did not send you to Israel merely to consult with me regarding peace efforts in the Middle East. Why are you truly here, my friend?"

"I have known Gabriel Picard, the deputy secretary general of Interpol, for several years, Professor Weiss. After facing false accusations of crimes that I didn't commit in Spain, my entire family received help from the Spanish authorities and Interpol. He became a family friend of sorts."

"I understand," said the professor.

"Do you know him well?" Nate asked.

"I've never met the man, no."

"Well, to summarize my involvement with Interpol," said Nate, "I must explain that the person responsible for committing the crimes for which I was accused is intent on killing my family. He is a cartel leader who blames me—and my entire family, I may add—for the death of his wife. He has since gone underground. Picard has offered to help us find this criminal if I will serve as an advisor, or profiler, for Interpol."

"But you have a successful practice in Chicago. You're an eminent psychiatrist. Why would you abandon your practice to serve as a consultant to Interpol?"

"Professor Weiss, my family and I have lived in fear for more than five years because this drug lord and cartel leader has haunted and pursued us to see us all die—by his hand, I must add. A year ago he murdered my mother-in-law. You probably don't know that feeling."

Professor Weiss had to chuckle. "My friend, forgive my levity, but since Israel's inception, all of us have been haunted—and hunted— by our enemies every day of our existence. We know and have experienced the hatred of our enemies. I *do* know the feeling."

"I forget myself—and where I am, Professor Weiss."

"No need to apologize."

Nate was grateful because he had not intended to offend the professor. "So I agreed to join forces with Interpol in the hope that we can apprehend—or eliminate—Diego Montemayor, our nemesis." After a brief pause, Nate added, "I realized that we could not rest while Diego Montemayor was free. Every day of our recent lives we have felt like his prey."

"Um hmm. Now I know why you joined Interpol…. On the other hand, Dr. Shelley, you have not explained why you are here. What does Diego Montemayor have to do with Israel or the Center for Middle Eastern Peace Studies?"

Being the consummate professional that Nate could not help being, he forced himself to follow the "party line" and respond with vagueness and generalities. Not wanting to betray Interpol, Nate took a sip of the Mount Etna wine and thoughtfully said, "Well, Professor, I do have my assigned duties as 'profiler' and consultant to Interpol. I did agree to serve the agency in matters other than the ones directly related to the apprehension of Diego Montemayor."

"Please do not think I'm being indelicate or that I'm doubting your word, but it's entirely unclear to me why Interpol wants to interrogate me regarding the activities of the center…or my research."

Although Picard had not fully clarified to Nate the purpose of his visit, Nate had discovered that the agency's brass—and perhaps Picard himself—suspected that the Center for Middle Eastern Peace Studies was surreptitiously aiding right-wing extremists who sought to overthrow the present American administration. In fact, there was talk of prominent American Christian leaders who were seeking an alliance with "Zionists," radical Jewish militants, to foment violence against a more liberal global agenda. Although Interpol itself, Picard argued, must maintain a neutral stance, it certainly must not allow "insurrectionist movements" of any sort.

Nate privately agreed that Gabriel Picard had not presented a clear justification for sending someone to interrogate Professor Ari Weiss. Nor had Picard given Nate a clear set of objectives for his visit.

"Yes. I understand your concern, Professor Weiss. However, I can assure you that I was not given any hidden agenda, nor was I instructed to spy on you to ferret out any undue political motivations."

Professor Weiss paused; then he added with a smile, "I am a good judge of character, Dr. Shelley. So I believe you. Nonetheless, I think that neither you nor I have a clear notion of the purpose of your visit. Let us proceed with such an assumption if you don't mind. In the meantime, let us enjoy your visit."

"Thank you, Professor." Nate lifted his glass, swirled it, and took in a deep breath as he savored the remaining wine.

"By the way, Dr. Shelley, do you know it's after nine at night? We have some traveling to do tomorrow, so I suggest we turn in. There's a place here in Haifa that I know where you will have a restful night. We'll be staying at the Santa Maria Guest House. It is owned by a very nice lady who takes pride in accommodating her guests. The prices are reasonable, and the accommodations are fit for kings."

Upon their arrival, a smiling guest house owner received them at the entrance. She welcomed them as if they were family, describing all the amenities available. She informed them about the various restaurants available within walking distance. Taking advantage of the owner's English fluency, Nate asked if the magnificent gardens adjacent to the guest house were part of the hotel. She laughed and simply stated that the Bahia Gardens that led up to the domed Bahai shrine on the peak of the mountain were not hers.

Nate said, "Those must be the most stunning gardens I've ever seen. Although it's dark, even with the dim street lighting I can tell there are multiple tiers of flowering plants at each level. How many tiers lead up to the shrine?"

Although the guest house owner shrugged in embarrassment, indicating she'd never counted them, Professor Weiss intervened, "There are nineteen terraces, Dr. Shelley, leading all the way up to peak of Mt. Carmel."

"Are you saying that is *the* Mt. Carmel, where the prophet Elijah challenged the prophets of Baal?"

Again the professor responded, "The same one, Dr. Shelley."

"But how would Israel allow the Bahá'í faith to erect a shrine in such an important Jewish location?"

Obviously bemused, Ari Weiss said, "It is one of the ironies that few Americans realize what kind of democracy exists in the state of Israel. If Israel is so intolerant of other faiths—as our Palestinian brethren claim—how can this tiny nation function with so many religious differences allowed to interact within it?"

Nate had to admit, "I had no idea."

. . .

The following morning Nate awoke full of energy. He was well rested and felt a need to stroll outside the guest house to admire the flora of the adjacent gardens. The clear blue skies invited Nate to take photos. Taking his first step out, he was assaulted with the sweetest, most fragrant aromas of countless blossoms. Torpedoing his senses, an explosion of colors from flowering succulents and multi-colored bougainvillea caused Nate to surrender in awe and simply smile at the majesty of the garden's Creator. Several species of palm trees, plus yellow, purple, and magenta ground cover that carpeted each of the nineteen terraces, invited him to stroll barefooted for hours in the grounds. Variegated species of plants that hung from each level made it impossible to capture in a single photo the beauty with his tiny iPhone. Nate immediately sent his photos to Miró, but he explained that no photo could capture this enchanting visual orgy.

Before he realized it, Professor Weiss was standing next to him. "To think that these gardens pale in comparison to Solomon's gardens, according to the Hebrew Scriptures."

"That is too difficult to imagine, Professor Weiss," said Nate.

The professor took Nate's elbow. "Given our banter yesterday and the delectable morsels we both enjoyed in each other's company, can we dispense with titles? Why can't you simply call me 'Ari'?"

Nate smiled. "The truth is that I am honored to be in your presence. You have sustained your academic reputation—and integrity—through so many years and so many assaults on your scholarship. Yet here you are, still considered the preeminent scholar of Middle Eastern studies. Heads of state heed your counsel, Dr. Weiss. Heck, truth be told, *I* welcome your counsel."

"Nonsense. I am Ari and that's all that needs to be said."

"Fine—then please call me 'Nate.'"

"We have an agreement, Nate. And since I promised a tour of my country," said Professor Weiss, "after a light breakfast, I suggest we start our journey. Although we could stroll these grounds for hours, since we can dedicate only two days to our trip, we must move on to the rest of our travels to give you a taste of Israel."

"What a shame!" said Nate. "Frankly, Ari, in addition to Jerusalem, I'd hoped to get a chance to visit Bethlehem, the Jordan River, the Sea of Galilee, and without offending your Jewish faith, I'd hoped to visit Golgotha, where Jesus was crucified and walked the Via Dolorosa… but…"

"Yes, yes, Nate. We can do all that. And by the way, you need not be apologetic about your Christianity. We share the same faith," said the professor.

Nate listened intently and digested two important revelations. First, Ari Weiss intended to give him a whirlwind tour, and he stated they could traverse the entire country of Israel in two days. Nate did not look forward to a rushed, "drive-by" tour of countless locations.

Second, Ari Weiss—the preeminent Jewish scholar—had made a comment about sharing "the same faith." Hesitant to seek clarification without sitting down for a discussion, Nate decided to hold his tongue. He also wanted to avoid his own lukewarm approach to Christianity.

They returned to the Santa Maria Café, had some delicious Arabian coffee, and rich breakfast pastries that neither one could resist.

"I promise you that we will eat a healthier meal on the road trip," said Ari Weiss. "In the meantime, I'll order a small assortment of *bourekas*."

As he ordered his second cup of coffee, Nate tiptoed into his questions. "Professor...uh, sorry...Ari...as I remember, we are in the northern part of Israel, and you intend to show me your entire country's main sites in two days. If you don't mind my asking, when do you intend for us to sleep? Or do you have a private jet?"

Ari Weiss was amused. "Ha—last night you told me how you would often visit the state of Texas with your wife, Miró. It took you more than ten hours to drive from the northern tip of Texas to her hometown on the Mexican border. You must realize, my friend, that Israel is tiny in comparison. For example, if we were to drive nonstop from Tiberias, on the northern section of Israel, to Jerusalem, it would take us approximately two hours."

"Wow! That truly puts into perspective the size comparisons!" exclaimed Nate. He looked out onto the cloudless sky beyond the café's patio. Although he was curious about the professor's statement about a shared faith, he decided to wait. "So what's our itinerary for today?"

The professor offered the first *boureka* to Nate. The attentive waiter explained to Ari that the pastries were freshly baked. "Let me suggest this particular one," said Ari, "which will give you some sustenance. It is filled with lamb mixed with pine nuts and almonds, Israeli feta cheese, mashed potatoes, and spinach."

Since the puffy pastry seemed to be made of a buttered phyllo dough, Nate was expecting it to taste like a croissant. When the professor described the filling, Nate reacted with some skepticism. Biting into the triangular *boureka*, however, Nate closed his eyes with a wistful desire to memorize the flavor. The buttery aroma and the warm ingredients melted in his mouth. "I was not expecting that, Ari. This is delicious."

Nate signaled to the waiter for another cup of coffee, but the professor recommended that he switch to a cappuccino, since his next *boureka* would be sweet. He helpfully pointed out the next morsel of thin, flaky dough. "That one is beckoning," said Ari.

Nate waited for the waiter to sweeten his cappuccino. Only afterward did the waiter artfully craft the frothy design of a menorah. Hating to destroy the foamy design floating in his cup, Nate took his first sip. His hot coffee was rich and flavorful. The aroma reminded him of his first visit to Rome, where he'd learned to appreciate strong coffee. To prepare his palate for the switch to a sweet pastry, Nate took a healthy drink of mineral water. He turned his attention to his second *boureka*, which he noticed had a paper-thin, flakier dough. He bit into it, not knowing what to expect. So far he had not been disappointed. The filling that he withheld from his soft palate had a fruitiness with a touch of honey. He wanted to breathe in its flavor using his sense of taste as well as his olfactory ability. In his imagination he was already constructing a text to describe to Miró this heavenly parcel of blueberry delight. "Please, Ari—rescue me from this indulgence. This is rich. I will gain twenty pounds in two days if we keep this up."

"Ah, don't worry. We shall be walking quite a bit," said Ari. "And the Mediterranean diet will be good for you. In a few minutes we'll drive to Nazareth, then on to Tiberias and the Sea of Galilee, then retrace our steps to the Mediterranean coast to stop at Caesarea. If we're fortunate, we'll end our day in Jerusalem. If not, we'll stop for the night en route."

CHAPTER SIXTEEN

[Israel; ten months before the twins' drowning]
(February 2021)

As Ari Weiss started his drive, he steered south along the Mediterranean seacoast, retracing the route they had taken to Haifa. "I've made a slight adjustment. Instead of driving toward Nazareth, we're headed to Caesarea, using Highway 2, the motorway."

They drove in the Toyota Highlander with windows rolled down, allowing the invigorating sea breeze to chill them along the way. Clear skies and the salty smell in the air brought pleasant memories to Nate, reminiscent of his summer vacations with his own parents in the California Bay Area.

"This drive reminds me of a drive south from San Francisco on Highway 1," said Nate.

"Yes, I've driven that route, but the California coastline has many more curves," said Ari.

The professor stopped in Caesarea to give Nate an opportunity to witness the still-standing Roman influence upon the Israeli landscape. Nate was only vaguely familiar with the significance of Caesarea or its relevance to Israeli history. When Ari stopped at the magnificent aqueducts, Nate was struck by the solid Roman structure and its survival through millennia. The enormity of the sandstone blocks used in their architecture did not escape Nate's attention. Standing at one end, Nate could imagine the arches of the aqueduct extending for miles. The aqueducts looked like an enormous bridge that could stand another thousand years. From the aqueducts, Ari drove to the Roman amphitheater, which was still standing in testimony to ancient structural engineering. The ruins of the Roman construction were now only one fourth of its original splendor, but the amphitheater survived as more powerful evidence of skilled architecture. After the short walk to the partially standing remains, Nate sat high on the steps of the theater and looked down to its main level where Ari had remained to respond to an incoming call on his cellular. He realized that while sitting halfway up the bowled structure, the amazing acoustics of the amphitheater enabled him to hear part of the telephone conversation that Ari was conducting down below at the center floor.

Anticipating Nate's questions, in a normal voice Ari called out from the flat stage below, "Caesarea is where Pontius Pilate governed during the time of Jesus," said Ari. "It was the seat of Roman power. It is also where Paul was imprisoned for two years because of his belief in Jesus, the Christ."

Although Nate remained quiet, he suddenly realized that the occasional lessons he received in Sunday school had some historical relevance and that events that occurred in ancient Israel impacted real people. Although Nate was snapping pictures of the ancient structure, his mind was struggling to absorb an impact not experienced before.

In a clear message to Nate that their journey was just beginning, Ari started walking back to their vehicle, which was parked one quarter of a mile down the unpaved paths. Nate descended the steps, one step at a time, delaying unnecessarily to savor the moment.

"I promised not to make your tour a whirlwind drive-by," said the professor. "However, this is merely a taste of other things to come." Ari Weiss smiled and pointed out that although his trajectory might appear somewhat circuitous, there was "method to his madness."

"We will drive back in a northeasterly direction toward Nazareth. Allow me to point out the various *minarets*, the tallest points of the Islamic mosques, from where early calls to prayer are announced to the faithful Muslim world.

"Does that mean that we're entering Palestinian territory?" Nate asked.

Ari was quick to respond, "Not at all. It is simply evidence that Israel has always made allowances for varying expressions of worship—not always broadcast by anti-Semitic propaganda."

Nate said, "I was hoping we could dedicate some valuable time to our visit in Nazareth. After all, if I recall from my Sunday school teachings, Jesus grew up there, didn't he?"

"Indeed, he did grow up in Nazareth. There Jesus performed his first miracle, converting water into wine at the Cana wedding. It is also believed that Mary was visited by the angel Gabriel in Nazareth to announce the virgin pregnancy."

"Therefore, I believe this may be one of our tour's highlights, don't you think?" Nate asked.

The bespectacled professor turned to Nate as he started their vehicle's descent toward Nazareth. In the barren distance, Nate could see a small basin surrounded by various hills. "I'll let you be the judge of that."

Nate said, "I'd like to see the specific places where Jesus may have grown up and where Mary may have lived."

Ari parked his SUV and both men walked through a busy marketplace. It was the only location where crowded activity seemed to be taking place. As they walked, there was a lengthy pause. An apologetic Professor Weiss said, "We may be able to visit a few shrines dedicated to Mary and the Annunciation, where Mary was told that she would give birth to our Messiah, Jesus. However, there is no archeological evidence of the actual site."

Nate's facial expression may have shown his disappointment because Ari added, "The truth is that the Gospel of Luke reveals that Jesus himself stated that 'no one is prophet in his own land.' He was referring to Nazareth, and it appears that this place was not very receptive to Jesus's ministry."

"So is that why you did not consider Nazareth a focal point of our tour?"

"The truth is that Nazareth is most famous for its *shuk*, Arabic for 'market,' and many people from the area come to this market for its Arabic produce. That was the bustling center of activity that we crossed when we first parked. But let me suggest that our next stop may satisfy your need to experience Jesus's impact."

"What is our next stop?" Nate asked.

"Our next stop is Tiberias, which is thirty-one kilometers from here, or less than twenty miles by car. However," said Ari, "we'll take almost forty minutes to get there because the Sea of Tiberias, or Galilee, as you know it, is surrounded by mountains. We may stop by the side of the road on the way there because you will be able to take some magnificent photos to send to your wife."

It was clear to the professor that Nate thoroughly enjoyed the ascent up to Mounts Tabor and Meron. Though it became increasingly chilly on their drive, Nate breathed in the fresh air and smiled as he said, "Incredibly amazing scenery, Ari." He asked for a five-minute stop to capture the experience on his digital camera.

When Nate finally returned to the parked Toyota Highlander, Ari was snacking on a protein bar. "My wife, Gilah, always packs these for me when I'm out. She's concerned about my hypoglycemia. Please have one."

"I'll pass for now, Professor—I mean, Ari. I didn't know you had low blood sugar."

"It's controlled and not a huge issue. Changing the subject now, on to Tiberias," Ari said. "You know, of course, that the Sea of Tiberias is technically a lake. It is fed by the Jordan River and at the southern edge the sea drains into the Jordan. It is approximately thirteen miles from north to south, and about seven miles from east to west."

"I must admit that I was ignorant of those facts," said Nate. "I'm not much of a Bible scholar." Nate hesitated before he made the following request. "Ari, I do not mean to be disrespectful, but I have an urge to use my ear pods in order to listen to my favorite piece of music. This impressive approach to the Sea of Galilee calls for it."

"What is it, may I ask?"

"It's Bach's violin concerto in D minor, the Stern and Perlman rendition," said Nate.

"If it's the concerto for two violins, count me in," said Ari. "Skip the ear pods. We can pair your iPhone to the vehicle's speakers." For the next few minutes, as they descended toward Tiberias, the two men seemed to be transfixed by the scenery's beauty and the melancholic second movement of Bach's masterpiece. In the distance Nate could see on a plateau the water surrounded by steep slopes from three directions. It was a dramatic setting, with the hills falling abruptly to the water's edge. Neither man spoke a word as they enjoyed the stunning views leading to the sea.

Before parking at the shores of the lake, Ari said, "I could not have thought of a better accompaniment to this approach. It was the perfect musical piece to prepare us for this momentous occasion. We will board a large fishing boat, like the one probably used by Jesus and his disciples and sail to the north end. There we can stop at the Church of the Beatitudes."

"Why there?" asked Nate.

"It is where Jesus delivered the Sermon on the Mount and where he taught the Lord's Prayer," said Ari.

"Isn't that where Jesus was reputed to have performed the multiplication of the fish to feed a thousand people?" asked Nate.

"It was the feeding of five thousand, my friend. They brought Jesus five loaves and two fish, and he fed them all."

"Hmm."

Ari smiled. "You seem skeptical."

"Aren't you?" asked Nate. "Certainly, Ari, you're a Jewish scholar, and you cannot believe the literal translation of those accounts, can you?"

"Ahh, my friend—we have much to discuss on our way south toward Jerusalem. But first, let's enjoy your tour."

. . .

CHAPTER SEVENTEEN

[Israel; ten months before the twins' drowning] (February 2021)

For the next hour Nate and Ari Weiss strolled the Mount of Beatitudes. It was breezy, but the sunshine made for a pleasant early afternoon. As they walked, Ari Weiss spoke of his own conversion. He described the difficulties of an orthodox Jewish believer who had come to accept Jesus as the Messiah for whom his people still waited. "The more I studied Scripture and the many prophecies that foretold His arrival, the more I became convinced that the ancient prophets were speaking of Jesus of Nazareth. I am now called a Messianic Jew, just like your father-in-law," said the professor. "There are—relatively speaking—very few of us. And I'm afraid this fact alone has also invited additional detractors to my efforts."

"So was it your Scriptural studies that led to the conversion?" Nate asked.

"Not exclusively. The truth is that I experienced more than an intellectual understanding," said Ari.

"That is extremely difficult for me to accept, Professor. Your academic credentials and your intellectual prowess are beyond reproach. Yet do you speak of something beyond the convictions of the mind?"

"A brief reminder, my friend. You promised to call me Ari—you also promised to drop titles. Let me also remind you that we both experienced something when we listened to Bach's violin concerto for two violins. Would you call that experience an intellectual one?"

"Hmm…I suppose I would…to a certain extent. One needs to appreciate the singular excellence of the intricate composition of the composer," Nate said.

"Wouldn't you also say that the music stirred some emotions in you?" asked Ari.

"Well, yes," said Nate. "But with all due respect, Ari, when I eat a delectable pastry, like I did this morning, that experience evoked pleasant memories, perhaps specific emotions that bring joy, or comfort, or happiness. What's your point?"

"Eating a piece of lemon meringue pie—or a *boureka*—may satisfy a human appetite and bring joy, but it hardly engages your intellect, like a fine piece of music does." Ari continued: "When we listened to Bach's violin concerto, our human senses *and* our intellect were engaged, were they not?"

Nate nodded. "I see your point. You're saying that listening to a fine piece of music transcends the experience of simply eating a fine dessert."

Forcefully nodding and making his wild, curly gray hair fall over his forehead, Ari said, "Exactly. We both experienced a thing of beauty, not merely a sensual experience. What I'm saying is that people can have a wonderful intellectual experience when they solve a mathematical problem, but certainly that is different from listening to a musical masterpiece. It is also different from the experience of eating a piece of pie. Solving a math problem does not engage my emotions. And eating a piece of pie fails to stimulate my intellect."

Nate said, "Your point is that an intellectual experience—like solving a math problem—does not engage my emotions. In other words," Nate asked, "are you saying that the two are different because experiencing beauty—such as listening to good music or seeing a beautiful painting—engages both the intellect and the senses of the body, or our emotions?"

"Yes," said Ari. "A spiritual experience is like that, but much deeper because it brings in the third dimension of the spirit. A spiritual awakening is what Christians refer to as being 'born again.' The Bible says that the human spirit must be awakened."

Ari had hit a nerve. Nate normally responded to such a statement with extreme skepticism. Individuals who claimed to be "born again"—whatever that meant—always came across to Nate as claiming to be morally and "spiritually superior"—and a little unhinged. "Super-Christians," he called them—boorish people who claimed to speak to God on a daily, or even a minute-by-minute basis. Nate stopped in his tracks, and he abruptly changed the subject.

"Ari, are you hungry?"

"I was thinking the same thing," said Ari. "Let's board the fishing boat and head back to the opposite shore."

On the way back, Ari pointed to the approximate spot where Jesus more than likely walked on water, according to the New Testament. Nate acknowledged the statement, but he did not respond.

Ari Weiss said, "Nate, I sincerely hope that you're enjoying this tour." He went on to describe where he planned to stop for their midday meal. He recommended that for the sake of the restaurant's specialty, Nate try the dish called "fish of St. Peter." Ari added that it was fresh fish caught right in the Sea of Tiberias.

Nate and Ari had a relaxed meal. A traditional Mediterranean offering of fresh fish (branzino and cod), salmon patties, cucumber salads, broccoli rice, and hummus or *baba ganouj* was served buffet style. Later, two waiters approached them with a selection of multiple kinds of whole fish, freshly caught in the waters of the Sea of Galilee, and grilled.

Surprisingly, Nate looked out onto the lake and said, "To think that Jesus and his disciples might have enjoyed the same types of fish, freshly grilled in the same fashion."

Ari decided it was the better part of wisdom not to inject his own thoughts.

. . .

Ari Weiss drove in a southwesterly direction. "Although our trip to Jerusalem would be more direct and shorter if we traveled directly south," said Ari, "we will circumvent that area since Israel has given over large areas of the West Bank to the Palestinians. The shame is that we will not be able to stop at Nablus and Jericho."

"Hmm," said Nate. "I refreshed my biblical knowledge by reading about Joshua's conquest of Jericho last night, but I'm not certain I know very much about Nablus."

"Nablus appears as 'Shechem' in the Bible, Nate. It was the home of Jacob and where Joseph was buried. Although Bethlehem is also in the West Bank, we will approach it from Jerusalem, where it's safer."

For the next two hours Nate was pensive and relatively quiet. At one point Nate asked about the professor's spiritual conversion and wanted to know if Ari had abandoned his Jewish beliefs.

"On the contrary, my friend—I sincerely believe that I am a better Jew now that I've accepted that Jesus is the Messiah. Every prophecy of the Old Testament was confirmed by the person I considered to be a mere prophet. I am a Jew who believes in Jesus."

Ari could sense Nate's skepticism and curiosity. On their drive to Jerusalem, Ari spoke of his quest for truth, his own skepticism regarding Christianity's claims, and his discoveries along the way.

"Professor...okay, Ari...I have deep respect for your scholarship. And believe me—I envy your spiritual convictions. Yet I cannot simply ignore the intellectual doubts that I have regarding the authenticity of the Scriptures."

"I completely understand. I also tried," said Ari.

"You did?" For a scholar to swallow some biblical claims, in Nate's mind, it would require the suspension of intellectual curiosity, an abandonment of logical and scientific reasoning. Yet here was a scholar of impeccable pedigree saying that he believed in the authenticity of the Scriptures.

"Yes!" Ari exclaimed. Smiling broadly, he adjusted his wire-rimmed glasses and added, "My mistake was attempting to turn off a switch. I genuinely thought that I would need to force myself to discount my intellect, believing that I needed to put my intellect aside to 'believe.' How foolish I was!"

"I'm afraid I don't follow," Nate said.

"In the end, I could not ignore what was happening to me. Like

Saul, I was being visited, as if a powerful force was knocking at my door. Believers in Christ accept that when Jesus departed this world, the Father sent Jesus's Holy Spirit to serve as Counselor, Consoler, and Confidante. To believers, the Holy Spirit—that third element of the tripartite deity—is a real presence who beckons us to Jesus's words."

Nate said, "You mean the third element of the Holy Trinity—the Father, Son, and Holy Ghost?"

"Ha. That's a curious word for the Holy Spirit, but yes, that's exactly what I mean. I believe that just like Saul, who persecuted Christians more viciously than other sacrosanct Jewish scholars, I had scoffed and ridiculed Bible scholars who strayed from the Old Testament. I spent years dispelling Christian scholarship, but like Saul I was figuratively thrown off my horse and struck blind for a season, while my Messiah—Jesus—converted me. Now that my spiritual questions are resolved, I can fulfill my academic mission."

"Which is?" asked Nate.

"Not only to pray for, but to help bring peace to Jerusalem," said Ari Weiss.

Is there a place where we can stop to have a glass of wine, Ari? I'm full of questions for you, but I'm not certain that I can unload my doubts while traveling at high speeds down Route 1."

"Not that I want to be insensitive, my friend, but let's wait until we get to Jerusalem and the King David Hotel for that glass of wine. I can guarantee that you will be able to rest from the trip and be ready to 'unwind' in a more suitable manner. It should take us another hour approximately."

Nate reluctantly acquiesced. He had so many questions for his new friend. For the next fifty-five minutes, Nate pretended to nap. In truth, he intended to merely lean into the passenger window and meditate on Ari's words.

CHAPTER EIGHTEEN

[Israel; ten months before the twins' drowning]
(February 2021)

The two men drove in silence along the Mediterranean coast-line. Despite his efforts to contemplate, a light slumber overtook Nate. In a dream he ran toward a distant and invisible destination. He was barefoot, running in a meadow in a definite trajectory. He wore white linen clothing. No one had given him directions, but he followed a defined route. Along the way, he caught up with several loved ones, first his parents, then Miró, hand-in-hand with Minerva. Up ahead were two men, who turned to face him as they kept run-ning forward. They urged him to catch up, but none of his efforts enabled him to do so. Finally both men, who were a fair distance ahead, briefly stopped to lend a hand. It was Abraham, his father-in-law, accompanied by Miró's half-brother, Max. Sweating profusely, Max suggested to Abraham to let Nate rest.

"He will be fine, Dad. Let's go."

To Nate's dismay, he was left behind while both men strived to fin-ish the race, to reach the prize at the end of the destination. Fatigued to the point of exhaustion, Nate was unable to go on. He hated him-self for quitting, but he could not help it. In his nap he heard a dis-tant voice. The voice was calling his name.

"Nate we're approaching Mt. Zion," said Ari. "I thought you might want to know."

It was Ari's voice, and Nate recognized that he had been awakened. He thanked Ari. When he opened his eyes, there it was. It was as if the scene to which he awoke was the continuity of his dream. Without lifting a finger or resuming the run in his dream, Nate—as a passenger in Ari's SUV—now had a view of the ultimate destination. He knew that on top of that mountain—Mt. Zion—was the prize he was attempting to attain. Following the road, Ari circled the circumference of the mount. The road gradually ascended the majestically forested mountain. However, despite the treed landscape, Nate did not lose sight of the peak. *Was this still part of his dream?*

Nate blinked as a huge yellow moth flew into the Toyota Highlander's windshield and left a smudge that served as the only blemish on the spotless glass protector, which Ari wiped at every pit stop. *No, I'm no longer dreaming.*

Without realizing what was happening, Nate felt the tears streaming down his face. He wiped them off without use of a handkerchief, but the tears kept coming. He faintly heard Ari ask him a question, but Nate could not respond. He was transfixed by the sight. Utterly unaware of the reason for his weeping, Nate felt embarrassed. He took a handkerchief and again wiped his tears. Nate accepted the moment, without being able to give a cogent explanation for his reaction. Ascending via three more circuitous times around Mt. Zion, they came upon the City of David and beyond. Ari mentioned something regarding the spot where David probably spotted Bathsheba as she languished after her grooming. But Nate was still engrossed with his own emotions, or were they feelings at all? Frankly, Nate could not care less. He only knew that the experience was totally his. He finally turned to Ari, as he continued driving in silence. Ari had a smile on his face.

Sensing the moment, Ari remained quiet. Nate smiled and looked ahead. As they drove on silently on their way to the King David Hotel, Nate asked, "Is this what you meant when you said that it is not about how many places you visit, but how many visits you experience?"

"I have no idea what you are talking about, my friend," Ari said with a smile on his face.

. . .

The wise old scholar had a motivation for delaying the ascent to Jerusalem. After checking into the luxurious King David Hotel, Ari stated, "My friend, I suggest we not get used to these accommodations. This will be a rare treat. The King David is a world-class hotel, and we academic types get to experience this only occasionally. Let's unpack, freshen up, and meet downstairs at the bar for a glass of wine. Then you will be able to ask all the questions you want."

Nate quickly showered and wondered what had occurred. He was still clueless about his weeping as they had ascended toward Jerusalem. *Was it a late onset of jetlag? Was I emotionally exhausted and perhaps experiencing sensory overload?* He walked toward the ceiling-to-floor double-hung windows and opened them for what the professor had said would be a magnificent view of the walled Old City of Jerusalem. *Was I experiencing an allergic reaction to Jerusalem's vegetation?* Oddly, he could see several minarets from his window, something he did not expect. *What a beautiful scene!* he exclaimed to himself. *Miró and Minerva must join me here soon.* For some reason he was talking to himself, but he was whispering.

He was startled by a ring of the hotel's telephone. It was Ari saying he was waiting for him at the bar. "You will find me sitting in a plush royal purple armchair. I've ordered you a glass of wine."

. . .

Nate joined Ari at the opulent bar done tastefully in royal purple colors. The drapery provided an ambiance of a plush private country club reserved for elite heads of state. Nate felt underdressed wearing his Dockers. He noticed that Ari, still wearing his khakis and sports jacket, had added a gray tie to his wardrobe. Behind Ari, he had a view of the golden Dome of the Rock. Greeting each other, both men toasted their arrival in Jerusalem.

"They had the same wine you had in Haifa, so I ordered you a glass," said Ari Weiss. For the next few moments, they enjoyed their respective drinks in silence. Nate crossed and uncrossed his legs.

Finally Nate leaned over and said almost in a whisper, "Ari, in our ascent toward Mt. Zion—toward Jerusalem—I felt like I had arrived. Like I had finally arrived—at my destination."

Then Nate explained to Ari how he'd been dreaming before Ari announced their approach to Jerusalem. He described how in his dream he'd met loved ones along the race and how he was pursuing an unknown destination. "But when I saw the peak of Mt. Zion—as we approached Jerusalem—I knew I was at my destination, the one I was trying to reach in my dream. I was finally home…I simply cannot understand what happened to me…I was in tears."

The professor looked at him and just smiled.

Nate pleaded, "Ari, please—I need for you to help me understand. What happened? Is this what you call being 'born again'?"

"Not at all, my friend," said Ari. "You had a powerful spiritual experience. I believe that you are being asked to open some doors."

"Ari, please don't provide riddles for me at this point. Please clarify some things for me," Nate said.

"Scripture tells us that to be born again, you must declare that Jesus is your Savior—and your Lord—out loud, with your mouth. God wants all of you, not merely your emotions, your tears, or your repentance. He wants your intellect also. That is why you must acknowledge by uttering that confession."

"And then what, Ari? I suppose I need to promise that I'll not go astray anymore. That I won't sin anymore?"

"When you declare that you're willing to make Him Lord of your life, the Scriptures say that he will deposit his Spirit in your human spirit and that he will take care of the rest. Sanctification becomes a process. He wants you as you are; he'll do the rest."

As Nate formed air quotation marks, he asked, "But who is this 'he'?"

"The Holy Spirit in you. We believers consider him a person—a radical bunch we are, I admit. But we're not devoid of reason."

"What if the 'Holy Spirit' tells me to do something contrary to the words of Jesus?" Nate asked.

"Can't happen. You are confusing the Holy Spirit with your conscience, my friend," said Ari. "Your own spirit—which is separate from your conscience—has always been a part of you, but it was not alive. When your human spirit comes alive, God's Holy Spirit will be deposited in that part of you that was dead. He will be in you and counsel you consistent with the words of Jesus."

"Whoa! That is a tall order, Ari. I don't think I'm ready to go that far," said Nate.

"No one is rushing you, my friend. I'm certainly not. I believe there is a time for each one of us. Of course, that calling may come, and you will always have your free will to reject it."

"Hmm." Nate finished his glass of wine, and he suggested they go into the dining room for dinner.

. . .

CHAPTER NINETEEN

[Skokie, IL; four months before the twins' drowning]
(Late July 2021)

=MAX=

When Nate returned to Chicago after being in Europe for a year, he was different. He'd been back almost three weeks, and we had not visited. We'd spoken briefly during various phone calls, but since he immediately wanted to reopen his practice, he dedicated most of his time to that effort. So my dad, Abraham, and I allowed him some breathing room. The difference in his demeanor, however, was noticeable. I casually asked Dad if he'd noticed anything different about Nate, and he said, "My son-in-law had a spiritual conversion. It's written all over him."

I objected. "You know, I had the same vibe and thought there might be a peace about him. However, he hasn't shared any kind of spiritual awakening with me. He seems surer of himself, more steadfast in his manner…Yet…why hasn't he mentioned anything? When I had my encounter with Christ, I couldn't stop talking about it. In Nate's case, it seems he's embarrassed…hesitant to admit anything."

Abraham smiled. "Like most highly educated people, Nate is timid about proclaiming his newfound faith. It's not that he's embarrassed about his conversion; he simply doesn't know if he can live up to it."

"Up to what?"

"He's still not convinced that he's finally arrived because he did not have to work for his spiritual awakening. In his life he's had to earn every accomplishment. In this case, his salvation was freely given—he can't be convinced it can be that easy."

Abraham Epstein, my dad, and I share the same beliefs. He has always been a God-loving orthodox Jew. Since I was raised by my single mom, who was a rock-solid atheist, I grew up non-religious. My maternal grandparents, however, are strong Christians and they were a great influence. As an adult, I accepted Christ as my Savior. Recently, after I moved to Chicago and after my stepmom's murder, my dad accepted that Yeshua, the Jewish name for Jesus, was indeed the Messiah for whom he'd been waiting all his life. So now he's considered a Messianic Jew.

I asked Dad, "When you accepted Yeshua as the Savior, the Messiah, did you have similar difficulties?"

"For me," said Abraham, "it was entirely different. My colleagues at the hospital, other cardiologists around me, all know me as a devout Jew. A profound adjustment to my Jewish faith notwithstanding, my secular friends could not appreciate the distinction between a Messianic Jew and an orthodox one. To them it makes no outward difference."

"And for Nate," I said, "the difference between being a 'respectable intellectual heretic' and a Christian believer is huge. Is that what you're saying?"

"Exactly." Abraham thought for a moment. "I should mention one thing, however. In the couple of weeks that Nate's been back in the States, he's mentioned a recurring dream that he's had since returning from Europe… come to think of it, he always says, 'since returning from Israel.'"

I smiled. "That's odd. You think his conversion has anything to do with his visiting Israel? And are you saying that his dreams have a spiritual connection?"

"I'm certain of it," Dad said.

I asked, "Has he described the dreams?"

"Very vaguely. He's mentioned re-reading a work by George Bernard Shaw. Shaw's work seems to come up in his dreams."

"That author was not the most exemplary Christian around, as

I recall. He wasn't converted or anything toward the end of his life, was he?" I asked.

"On the contrary, he scorned religious arguments," Abraham said. "But Nate says that his recurring dream sometimes keeps him awake for hours during the night."

"Is it nightmares that he's having?"

"Not at all—more of a leading, a puzzle of sorts. Nate seems to think he is being led to investigate something more fully, but he doesn't know what."

"Dad, I think we must resume our Sunday evening family meals. We don't want to lose touch with a member of the family. Is it okay if we invite them over?"

"Sure. I was giving Nate and the family some adjustment time, but I agree that it's time to reconnect with those three."

. . .

I was in the kitchen preparing my osso buco specialty when Nate and Miró rang the doorbell. I could hear from the kitchen that Dad had greeted them at the door. When Miró walked into the kitchen to put a few things in Dad's fridge, I told her I was preparing osso buco. Nate called out from the hallway, "My favorite!" Of course, I was aware of his fondness for the dish. It was the reason that I'd prepared it.

Still at the entrance, Dad asked, "Where is my granddaughter? Has she decided to ignore her Gramps?"

"Well, Dad, your granddaughter Minerva is out on a date with Calvin. And the answer to your second question is 'definitely not.' She asked me to give you a special hug."

While Dad and Miró were discussing Minerva, I asked Nate if he would like a glass of *Bermejo Seco*, which he quickly accepted.

Taking his first sip of wine, Nate said, "To me, our daughter is growing up too rapidly. I'd like to keep her right at fifteen, but I need to remind myself she just turned sixteen in May. Yet she can't wait to go off to college and embark on her writing career."

"I have a feeling that we will be seeing less of Minerva now that she's a teenager," I said. "I'd set the table for five—sure was looking forward to seeing my niece."

"She's on a date with Cal, and they did say that they might drop by after a movie and a burger," Miró said.

After Abraham prepared a Bellini for Miró, they walked into the den. Then he asked, "Nate, you haven't spoken much about your trip to Jerusalem. I thought you'd be eager to share."

"Truth is that I believe I had a life-changing experience, but at this point...I don't know..."

"Whoa, Bro!" I called out from the kitchen. "If you're gonna talk about life-changing experiences, this osso buco can wait. I intend to hear that." Drying my hands on the Longhorn apron that I customarily wore around the kitchen, I took a stool from the bar and rushed into the den.

Nate continued: "That's just it. I had a powerful spiritual experience in Jerusalem...and before I left, this friend of mine, Ari Weiss, took me through a prayer of salvation."

With a big smile on my face, I said, "So what's unclear? You just said, 'I don't know,' as if you're uncertain about something."

"Frankly, Max, I don't know if I can cut it. All my life I've heard how perfect Christ's life was when he lived here on earth...how we should learn to live like him," Nate said as he sat on the couch next to Miró. Nate's pregnant thought hung in the air. Abraham and Miró sipped their drinks. Calmly, Abraham got up from his easy chair and handed them two coasters.

Nate continued, "On my last day in Jerusalem, Ari and I were at the Ben Gurion Airport, and I asked Professor Ari Weiss to lead me through a 'prayer of salvation,' but since my return home, I'm not sure if I'm doing it right."

"Doing *what* right?" asked Abraham.

Nate scratched his head and bit his lower lip. "You know, trying to live like Christ. Trying to imitate Christ. Drinking wine, for example—is that acceptable?"

Dad said, "If Professor Weiss were here, Nate, he would tell you that when you accepted God's lordship in your life, it was settled. You are accepted before him. No one can live the kind of life you're talking about. It's impossible. Only Christ can. He simply wants you to allow him to lead you."

"Yeah, Bro—welcome to the fold." I walked over to Nate and hugged him. "As for now, let me get back to the osso buco. I'll listen from there."

From the kitchen I heard only silence from Nate. I assumed he was in deep thought trying to understand Abraham's comments. He then cleared his throat. "That sounds pretty simple, Abraham. I just don't know what that means…how do I allow God to lead me?"

"Hey, guys, raise your voices," I asked. "I need to hear your comments."

Using an unnecessarily loud voice, Abraham said, "All right, Chef, we'll shout!" Then as he addressed Nate, I could hear Dad chuckle and say, "Son, relax. What I meant is exactly that. There is a time to sit, a time to stand, and a time to walk. Right now, for you it is time to sit and allow the Lord to lead you."

"Abraham, can you say a bit more about that?" Nate asked.

I could hear Dad continue: "Son, when you prayed the prayer of salvation, you didn't merely trust Jesus to take you to heaven when you die. It meant that you chose to allow God to come from heaven to live *in* you."

"Yeah, Dad," said Miró. "What Nate means is that he's unsure what it means to allow Jesus to live in him or to guide him. In other words, when people say that special prayer, does it mean that they now magically have a direct line to God?"

Although I wanted to jump in and forget about the preparation of my special dish, I decided to allow Dad to handle Nate and Miró. In fact, he could do a better job than I could.

"Yeah, Abraham—I've never been a fan of fantasy," said Nate. "Your explanation sounds too supernatural, and I don't know what it means. Give me more practical explanations."

I could hear Abraham return to his favorite easy chair and set his crystal wine glass down on the pedestal next to his chair. "Okay, Nate.

It took a certain amount of faith to pray the prayer of salvation. By that I mean that you got out of your purely rational self to trust that when you accepted Christ into your life, you would be 'saved' from eternal damnation."

It sounded like Nate had gotten up to pace the floor. "I suppose that's right…. No, I know that's right…I resisted for several days until I realized that there was something in me compelling me to ask Professor Weiss to lead me in the prayer."

"But there's more to it than that, Nate," Abraham said. "When you allowed Christ into your life, you must also understand his total love and acceptance of you. You can't grow to love God if you think you must run away from him because you can't live up to his expectations."

"Okay, are you now saying that I must develop a better self-image?" Nate asked.

"On the contrary," said Abraham. "It is not that you need to think more highly of yourself. The gospel you chose to believe in is in direct contrast to the prevailing philosophies of the world. When the apostles talk about our identity in Christ, they didn't speak about 'loving ourselves more.' Instead, they spoke of loving God's character living in us…his identity, not ours."

Nate pulled the kitchen bar stool that I had left behind and dragged it across the wooden floor closer to where Abraham sat. "Professor Weiss spoke of my spiritual awakening as if a part of me had to be 'born again.' In the past, when I heard you and Max talking about such things, I considered it hocus-pocus, outlandish, somewhat naïve, to tell you the truth. Now you seem to be saying the same thing, that my 'spirit' came alive."

"I understand," Abraham said. "We don't need to engage in super-spiritual matters at this point. Let's simply say that I don't believe you need a 'good self-image.' Instead, you need a proper self-image, an identity based on truth. It is an understanding of yourself in the correct perspective with God. While Paul the apostle warns us against 'thinking more highly of ourselves than we ought,' we realize that the new identity given to us by the grace of God is more wonderful than we could ever imagine. You have become a child of God, absolutely loved, and totally acceptable in His sight."

Nate asked, "If the apostle Paul told us not to think more highly of ourselves than we should, doesn't that contradict what you're saying about our total acceptance from God?"

"When we rest on God's assurance of His total acceptance of us, we also learn to love and accept others as they are. You see," Dad said, "God knows that we will treat others in the same way we think God treats us."

Wow! Dad was preaching better than I'd heard in a long time.

"Hmm." Nate remained quiet until Abraham suggested they all move to the patio.

CHAPTER TWENTY

[Skokie, IL; four months before the twins' drowning]
(Late July 2021)

=MAX=

Since I'd brought my osso buco to a simmer and added the wine before putting in the veal shanks in the oven, I left the kitchen to join everyone on the patio. Although it was still summer, the evening air outside was remarkably cool. I still could not get used to summers in the Midwest. Back in Austin, in late July people do not enjoy an early evening out in their backyards unless they have plenty of shade and beverages. And sunscreen is a must. In my dad's Skokie backyard patio, however, I unrolled my long sleeves, and before the evening was over, I'd retrieved my windbreaker from my closet. As I walked onto the decking, I breathed in the smell of pinecones and I realized that if I ever moved back to Texas, I'd probably miss the invigorating breezes of the Chicagoland summer.

I sat on my favorite cushioned swivel lawn chair—the one with extra burnt orange cushions. Dad's seat matched mine. Nate sat on his blue cushioned lawn chair with maize-colored pillows, and Miró had recently replaced her Harvard crimson cushions with the Northwestern purple ones, since she'd accepted her new job at the local university.

Nate held the floor, speaking freely about his experiences at Interpol and the Center for Middle Eastern Peace Studies in Jerusalem.

He seemed to be in a more relaxed mood. Now on his third glass of Bermejo, he expounded on his long days at the center.

"For some reason, when I arrived at the Jerusalem Center for Middle Eastern Studies," said Nate, "the rest of the staff were waiting for me as if a dignitary had arrived. Professor Weiss introduced me as a dear friend and a respected scholar in my own field. In addition to the four or five graduate student research assistants who stood toward the back of the conference room, the three principal scholars in residence were front and center."

Nate described his audience as being "almost humorous," but I could tell that he was flattered by the attention he received. He even jokingly mentioned how he wished his own colleagues at the World Psychiatric Association would treat him with the same adulation.

Nate continued: "These three scholars who assist Professor Weiss are all in their thirties. Brilliant people. They prepare the first drafts of articles and other documents and manuscripts that serve as the archives for the world's most prestigious source of peace efforts in the Middle East."

"If they're based in Israel," I asked, "do people elsewhere doubt the documents' objectivity? In other words, don't they assume that all the research is one-sided, pro-Israel?"

Nate said, "Not really, Max. I thought the same thing. But when I realized that world leaders, journalists, and academics from the entire world—even anti-Semites—recognize the center as the repository for all things Middle East, you can't help but be impressed. Much of it is due to Professor Weiss's scholarship, which is, according to experts, beyond reproach."

Miró asked, "Is the staff diverse? By that I mean does he employ researchers from different backgrounds?"

"The professor demands that his research associates be objective, excellent scholars, and good writers. Otherwise, he ensures that various backgrounds be represented. His three scholars in residence are Mustafa Yavuz, a Turkish political economist; Sanura Gamal, an Egyptian political analyst; and Yosef Peretz, a brilliant Israeli historian and computer analyst. I worked an extra ten days in Jerusalem, and I got to know them all."

"Forgive me for asking a silly question," said Abraham, "but I thought you agreed to serve as 'profiler' for Interpol because you wanted to help apprehend Diego Montemayor. How does your interview of the center's staff help anyone get closer to Diego's cartel?"

"It's complicated," said Nate. "For many years, Professor Ari Weiss's Center for Middle Eastern Peace Studies generated the most accurate archives of the region *vis à vis* Russia, China, and the US. The professor's meticulous guidance of the center became the source of information for much of what happens in international affairs throughout the world—until recently."

Abraham leaned forward. "What does that mean?"

Miró interrupted. "That's exactly what I asked, Dad."

"What it means, Abraham, is that someone in the current American administration believes that Professor Ari Weiss is aiding and abetting right-wing extremists—connected to some Christian leaders—in the overthrow of the American president."

"And you," said Abraham, completing Nate's thought, "were sent there to find out if it's true. Am I right?"

Grimacing as he pursed his lips, Nate only nodded his head.

"So, then, my dear brother-in-law, what did you find out?" I asked.

"I submitted a thorough report. I found no evidence of any collusion with right-wing extremists. Nonetheless, I found out after I returned to my office in Lyon that Interpol is petitioning the various funding sources of the center to cancel most of their grants." Nate paused to shake his head. "They want the center to be de-funded. I was about to travel for another similar mission when I told Gabriel Picard that it was time for me to return to the US."

Abraham interrupted. "Do you mean that Gabriel Picard asked you to return to the center in Jerusalem to dig for more incriminating evidence against Professor Weiss?"

"No, no," said Nate. "He asked me to 'interview' another individual who was considered a right-wing extremist—a 'troublemaker,' according to the current American administration and the Vatican."

"Also Israeli?" asked Abraham.

Nate chuckled. "Actually, no. A certain Catholic archbishop who opposes Pope Francis and has been in hiding for some time. He served as the former Papal nuncio to the US."

At this point confused, I asked, "If he's in hiding, how on earth would you be able to interview him?"

"Sorry, Max. I should've explained that Interpol believes that they know where the archbishop is hiding. He would first be apprehended; then I would be assigned the job of investigating his political affiliations and his potential for inciting violence," said Nate.

Abraham chuckled. "This gets more convoluted by the minute. Wouldn't this take you totally away from the original purpose of finding Diego Montemayor?"

"Possibly," said Nate. "Gabriel Picard claims that religious extremists are funding these conspiracies."

I had to jump into the discussion. "I remind you that Diego's former right-hand man, Tío Dante, claimed the opposite. He claimed the Cue-Anon conspiracy theorists were trying to expose Diego's enormous influence on world politics. Tío Dante claimed that Diego was at the center of Deep State efforts in this country and abroad."

"Oh, I agree, Max. When I telephoned Miró and shared what Interpol was doing, we both agreed that it was time for me to return to my practice here," said Nate.

"I hope you have not broken off communication with Interpol," said Abraham. "Did you leave in Picard's good graces?"

"Oh, Picard and I have no issues to resolve," said Nate. "In fact, I agreed to continue to serve in an advisory capacity to Interpol—in a more limited role, of course. I may still help them from a distance."

"After your return, do you now consider your one-year stint at Interpol to have been a waste of time?" I asked.

"Not at all. I discovered that an Asian shipping company funded terrorist activities conducted by the PLO and even the Iranian government. In fact, those same shipping magnates leaked the rumors that led Interpol to investigate the Center for Middle Eastern Studies."

"Yeah," I said, "but that still has zero to do with Diego's cartel."

"I'm not so sure, Max." Nate stood up, rubbing his hands and grabbing his empty glass to walk back into the den. "The same shipping company shares Diego Montemayor's business interests. They're involved in human, weapon, and drug trafficking. They too have a keen interest in bribing American politicians."

"And," said Abraham as he opened the sliding doors, "let's not forget the monumental spiritual blessing Nate experienced. He accepted Jesus the Christ into his life. I would not call his stint at Interpol a waste of time."

· · ·

It was good to escape the evening chill. Plus, the osso buco was two minutes away from being ready. I served everyone a glass of our favorite Barolo and placed the goblets on the dining room table. When I brought out the main dish, even I was impressed by the delicious aromas. In my mind I congratulated myself for coming very close to Miriam's original recipe.

Over the next ninety minutes we enjoyed each other's company and caught up with the latest happenings. Miró was thrilled with her new job as dean of the Northwestern School of Social Sciences and Humanities. She was thankful for the supportive faculty and staff. Also, she was pleasantly surprised by the mentoring she received from the outgoing dean, who had stepped down in order to teach.

When Abraham asked about Minerva's ongoing relationship with Cal Steele, Miró beamed with pride. She acknowledged how she had seen her daughter mature beautifully into a fine young lady, and she also mentioned how Cal, her boyfriend, seemed to be a responsible young man. Excellent teachers at Ursuline Academy were also providing her a number of valuable connections to creative writing programs throughout the country.

When we finally got around to having coffee with our cannoli, the conversation turned to Nate's recent series of dreams. He explained to us that for some reason, George Bernard Shaw's writings had become central to his dreams. Shaw, not one of Nate's favorite authors, kept popping up. His first dreams, said Nate, revolved around an eccentric celebrity. This character appeared as a rabid and persistent opponent of vaccines. Nate's sleep was interrupted by these dreams, and he woke up during his first week back from Europe, wondering what it meant. Of course, an ongoing battle in the US medical community was raging regarding the COVID-19 vaccines, but it was not a battle that Nate had an interest in fighting. Later in his series of dreams, the celebrity in his dreams turned out to be Shaw.

"My dreams during the next week turned to a concentration on eugenics, an abominable topic that I would not consider even discussing in polite company. In truth, it confused me because even now I have no idea if I'm being led spiritually in any fashion," said Nate. "I have no interest in any kind of discussion of either topic—eugenics or vaccinations."

"Forgive my ignorance," I said, "but how is George Bernard Shaw connected to this topic?"

Abraham jumped in. "I believe that Shaw was opposed to vaccines and was also a proponent of eugenics in real life."

"Exactly," said Nate. "Don't feel bad, Max. I had no idea either, but I researched Shaw's life, and I found that out."

"But that's not all," said Miró. "Nate's latest dreams are even more confusing." Turning to Nate, she said, "Tell them, honey, the subject of your latest dreams."

"Pygmalion. I keep dreaming of this sculptor—a deranged one—who falls in love with a work of art he created. Bernard Shaw appears in my dreams, and he explains to me that this Greek sculptor fell in love with his own creation. Of course, after waking up, I realized that the story is the subject of Shaw's play *Pygmalion.*"

Miró must have noticed my confused look, because she added, "You probably know it, little brother, as *My Fair Lady.* Although the modern version does not mention sculpture, it's an adaptation of Shaw's original."

"You mean the movie and the stage production?" I asked.

"The same one," said Abraham. "Julie Andrews did the stage production on Broadway and Audrey Hepburn did a magnificent job in the movie playing Eliza Doolittle."

"And Rex Harrison did a fabulous job at playing Professor Higgins in both stage and film," said Miró.

Over dessert and two servings of coffee, we all had a good laugh and suggested to Nate that it would all be clarified somehow. Nate assured us that he was not conflicted about the dreams anymore. However, he was as perplexed about their meaning as he had been from the start.

. . .

PART THREE

THE RUSE

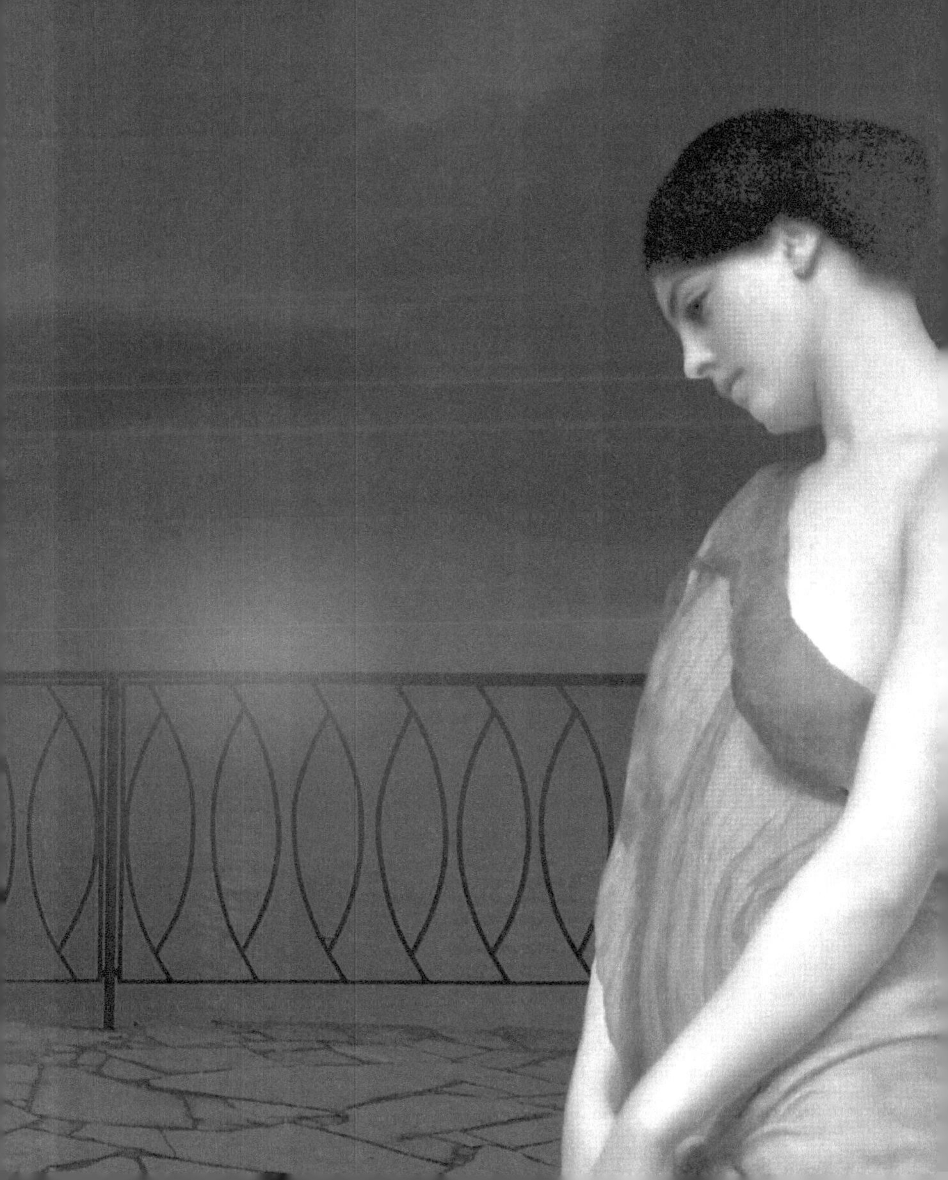

"It's easier to fool people than it is to convince them that they have been fooled."

MARK TWAIN

CHAPTER TWENTY-ONE

[Chicago; three months after the twins' drowning]
(February 2022)

=MAX=

Six months after Nate's return from Europe, I visited Special Agent Ram Edmunds. As special agent in charge of the FBI's Chicago Field Office, he was a busy man. So I hesitated to interrupt his schedule often. Plus, rumors abounded regarding his future promotion to deputy director of the FBI. Evidently the new American administration was grateful for Ram's careful handling of the bureau's indiscretions and ordered the DOJ to "amply recognize" his accomplishments. To his credit, Ram had not once given the press a single criticism of his former colleague, Jacoby Homely. On its own, the press had crucified Homely without mercy.

Yet I considered that since Ram had been involved in the entire investigation of Diego Montemayor's vendetta against Nate, Miró, and Minerva, I should keep him updated regarding our family's ongoing saga. I called early on a Monday morning and asked for a personal meeting that same day. His office manager, Laurie Martin, she knew my voice and despite Ram's loaded schedule, she accommodated my request for a face-to-face meeting with him. I left Dad's Skokie home early at 6:30 thinking that I would avoid the rush hour, but it still took almost ninety minutes to arrive at the Medical District, where Ram's office was located. I parked on Roosevelt Road and arrived ten minutes early.

I didn't have a long wait. After greeting me with the initial pleasantries, Ram asked, "The last time I spoke to Nate, he was ready to accept Gabriel Picard's offer to become an Interpol profiler. Has Nate moved his entire family to Europe?"

Surprised that they had not spoken since Nate's return, I informed him that Nate was back in the States. Without getting into specifics, I responded with vagueness, thinking that Nate could explain to Ram if he chose to do so. "No, Ram—I thought you knew. The original plan was for Nate to move first to Lyon; then he would find a home for the family. My sister Miró gave him so much flack that he came back home."

Ram smiled. "Miró can be quite persuasive when she wants to."

"From what I know, when Nate notified Picard that he'd return to the US, he reached an agreement with Interpol to cooperate in some fashion—long distance, you could say."

"I wondered why I hadn't heard from Nate," said Ram. "So is he working for Interpol full time from Chicago, or is he still doing psychotherapy?"

"Still a growing practice after the temporary lull." Since I felt awkward speaking for Nate, I quickly changed the subject.

"Ram, let me ask you a delicate question."

"Shoot." Always gracious in his manner, Ram Edmunds stood up and opened the door to the secretarial pool outside his office. He summoned Laurie to request some beverages for his guest. Ram was wearing his customary gray three-piece suit, without his jacket, which was hanging on the mahogany coat rack at the entrance to the conference room. As always, his black Allen Edmonds wing-tip Oxfords were freshly shined. Though I was wearing a conservative sport jacket and my best loafers, I still felt underdressed—as I always did around Ram. I was tieless.

I opened the conversation. "Most of the public became aware of the details of *The Black Pearl* murders in March of 2020. Newspapers throughout the country picked up on Horace Rosenberg's series of articles, and some sensitive facts even became known. But I'm still missing a very important detail."

Ram Edmunds folded his hands on his buttoned vest. "You probably know as much as I do, Max. What are you missing?"

"After the murders, Diego Montemayor went into hiding and presumably returned to Europe. Now, according to the suicide note left by Jacoby Homely, we assume he may be in Corsica. Have you followed up on that possibility?"

"We've reached out to Interpol, Max, but…" Clearing his throat, Ram continued: "It's a delicate subject."

I explained to Ram that I understood and that I didn't want to put him in a spot. I also went on to say that I was there on a totally different matter. "My other question relates to a mysterious note that Tío Dante, Diego's right-hand man, left for Nate and Miró—the one he asked you to deliver post-mortem."

"Yes, Max, that sure was a bizarre note. What about it?" Ram asked.

"Nate and Miró have refused to discuss it. All I got from them was that Tío revealed the identity of Diego Montemayor's 'handler.' However, they're both tight-lipped—they evade the question each time I ask them to share the name."

"Yeah," said Ram with a wide grin, "that one was a doozy. Tío claimed something so outlandish that even Nate and Miró realized the note must have been a hoax. At my request, they agreed they would not share the note's content."

For a year I'd wondered why Nate and Miró had not shared Tío's note with anyone—not Abraham, not me, and certainly not our reporter friend, Horace Rosenberg. Ram's response confused me even more. *Why would Tío lie about something like that?*

Ram must have noticed the confusion on my face because he added, "Let's just say that in my fact-checking, I came up with some inaccuracies that Tío passed on to me. It became obvious that he seemed to inflate his self-importance in Diego Montemayor's organization."

I responded with unintended skepticism. "Hmm. Do you have any examples you can share?"

Ram Edmunds quickly responded, "Well, here's one. Do you remember when Tío followed me into the Marriott at the end of his deposition? At the time, you were parked a few feet away listening with your high-tech devices."

"Of course. That happened just minutes before the explosion that killed him. I was recording from a distance. You even indicated that Tío warned you about Diego's cabal—and that even you could be in danger."

"What I did not mention, Max, is that he told me that his last project for Diego Montemayor was to develop a software program called 'RULE.' According to Tío, the software was sold to some clients in Venezuela. Get a load of this one: the software"—at this point Ram again chuckled—"would ensure that every election in the civilized world could be controlled and manipulated."

I asked, "Well, did you discover that was false?"

"Without question that was fiction, Max. There is no such software. The civilized world has gotten too sophisticated. With so much legal monitoring and supervision, elections can no longer be fixed—not even in Third World countries."

I had to shake my head. "I wouldn't be so sure, Ram."

Eager to convince me, Ram added, "Another doozy. Tío claimed that there was an 'underground railroad'—underneath major American cities—that was used to hide children and women for the purpose of human trafficking and enslavement. One of the major tunnels, per Tío, was beneath DC." Ram paused and laughed. "Beneath our nation's capital, Max! That Tío could spin some tall tales."

I forced myself to acknowledge that some of those claims appeared rather far-fetched. However, I'd come to know Tío, and he convinced me that his only interest was to expose Diego's organization. Since he'd betrayed his boss, he might have been motivated by self-preservation. However, he knew that Diego Montemayor would need to be brought down if he had any chance of survival.

"Ram, I simply cannot believe that Tío would lie to us."

"In the end, Max, Tío was as much a criminal as his boss, Diego Montemayor. He was also a blowhard."

"Ram, why do you consider Tío Dante's claims so incredible?"

Ram laughed again. "Tío was given to hyperbole. He even claimed

Diego Montemayor's handler was the future Secretary General of the United Nations."

"You mean the former US president?" I asked.

"Yep. Archie Washington himself," said Ram. "Now, I don't care if someone is a critic of the man himself, but I respect the office of the Presidency of the United States. And if that does not convince you that Tío Dante could spin yarns, nothing will."

I could see that our conversation was leading nowhere, so I redirected our attention to Nate's involvement with Interpol. I explained to Ram that Nate had agreed to provide input to Interpol regarding some Middle Eastern individuals seeking political asylum in the US.

"I would think that would be the job of the Citizenship and Immigration Services," said Ram.

"Yes, except that these refugees appear to be wanted by Interpol."

"Ah, therefore Picard's interest in having Nate involved," Ram said as he got up for his second cup of coffee. "That could get sticky, Max, since it may be difficult for Nate to circumvent our own federal guidelines." Before taking his seat once again, he reached over to refill my cup.

Taking in the rich aroma, I said, "Always appreciate your taste in coffee, Ram. As for Nate, he's been in contact with the Center for Middle Eastern Peace Studies. He says they've been extremely helpful."

Still standing, Ram raised his eyebrows. "Wow. If I'm not mistaken, the center's director is a certain Professor Weiss, and he has not endeared himself with our new administration. In fact, he's a *persona non grata* in DC." Ram made air quotation marks. "Tell Nate to tread carefully."

CHAPTER TWENTY-TWO

[Chicago; three months after the twins' drowning]
(Late February 2022)

=MAX=

Twice I had informed Nate about my meeting with Ram Edmunds after Nate's return from Europe. In a telephone call, I suggested to Nate that he should reach out to Special Agent Edmunds before he became "Deputy Director Edmunds."

Nate chuckled, "You think those rumors are valid?"

"Not sure, but it wouldn't hurt to make contact. I'm certain he wants to bring you up to date and you could do the same," I said. "You know how much he respects you, Nate, so he'd like to see you. I did mention that you were extremely busy trying to get your private practice back in shape."

"Good," said Nate. Then he went into a lengthy silence, and I thought we'd lost the connection. "Nate, are you still there...can you hear me?"

"Sorry...yes, I'm still here, Max. It occurred to me that this may be a perfect opportunity for us to finally accomplish our goals."

"Okay, Nate—you've lost me. We just spoke about putting you back in touch with an old friend, and you say it's our opportunity to reach our goals. Help me here. I'm not connecting the dots."

Without explaining, Nate invited me to visit him immediately. He was home nursing a cold, but he said he would keep his distance.

When I arrived, Nate met me at the door fully masked. He led me to the den, where we sat twelve feet apart.

During the phone conversation, Nate had sounded distracted. Now, in his home, Nate couldn't sit still. He paced up and down the den. His comments came in rapid-fire fashion. "Max, listen to me. There's much that I cannot share right now, but I see an opportunity. When it comes to Diego Montemayor, we're following rabbit trails. Yet we've got obvious answers in front of us. We—Commander Rivers, Ram, you, and even I to an extent—are still following leads on Gail Steele's lover, trying to make connections between Jim Steele and Diego's organization, and generally—just chasing our tails. I'm not faulting law enforcement officials—and least of all your friend Rob Rivers—but it's time we get down to business."

"In all fairness," I said, "if Bud Milton could confirm the kinds of things we learned from Lucas Williams, then we could present a tighter case. Right now, Williams claims he got his order to 'rub out' Steele's son Cal from Estevan Chengfu. Our job is to pin the responsibility on Estevan's boss, Diego Montemayor. You know that Estevan won't make a move without Diego's orders."

Nate was hardly listening to my objections. He continued making his case. "Who cares? Estevan, Diego's assistant, or the man on the moon. You're right. Everyone knows who calls the shots...we know Diego Montemayor is responsible. We're in obvious agreement."

"Maybe," I said, "but you and I are following gut instincts."

"Very reasonable instincts."

I reminded Nate. "You know our legal system will require a motive. All they have is Lucas Williams's confession. And he clearly testified that the orders came from Estevan Chengfu. How can we justify accusing his boss, the man who is supporting the Rosales families? How about the deed to the property they live in? The kids' education and support? We don't have any evidence of Diego's direct involvement in the murders."

"Perhaps," said Nate. "But a man like Diego Montemayor, who is obsessed with avenging his wife's death, will devise brilliant plans to reach his objectives. Why he wanted the Rosales twins' death, I still don't know. But—and this is the central matter—we need to get to Diego himself. If the legal system cannot pin the murder on Diego—I will accomplish it, even if I do it alone."

"Tell me what you're thinking." In the next breath I added, "For example, what motive would Diego have for ordering the killing of two young kids—who are unrelated to you—if he wants revenge against you and your family? You know that Diego's attorneys will argue that Estevan acted on his own."

"That's my point, Max. If Diego can weasel out of this double murder, he'll continue to haunt me and my entire family—including you." Nate walked to the breakfast area window. He took a deep breath and looked out onto the patio. Hands in his trouser pockets, he admitted, "For the longest time I've deliberately ignored my intuition—maybe it's the Holy Spirit; I don't know. I'm learning to heed those tugs inside me…to listen to my 'inner voice.'"

"The renowned psychiatrist confesses to using non-rational methods! Sorry, Nate, but this is novel, coming from you. I need to celebrate it."

"If you ever repeat this in public, I'll deny it," Nate said with a chuckle.

I smiled briefly. Reaching for a voice of reason, I said, "You must remember, Nate, that Diego Montemayor deeded the property to the Rosales families, and he established a trust for the kids' education. As far as we know, nothing has changed."

"True," said Nate, "but what if he slowly eliminates each one of them? Have we investigated who would inherit the Winnetka property if that happened? Would the estate revert to him?"

"I don't know, but we could find out."

Nate would not be dissuaded. He returned to the kitchen counter and sat next to me. "We could spend a year investigating clues to these murders and reach the same conclusion that is evident to me—Diego killed the twins. And, frankly, after knowing how Diego works, it should be evident to you also."

Nate was frustrated. In his exasperation, he agreed that the two of us should at least approach FBI Special Agent Edmunds. He opened his fridge, took out two bottles of my favorite Mexican ale, and immediately downed half a bottle. He soon realized he didn't like the flavor of beer, set it down, and dialed Ram Edmunds's number.

. . .

Ram was unavailable, but he returned Nate's call within a couple of hours. He informed Nate that he'd been traveling to the DC headquarters often. In fact, Ram was not certain when he'd be able to meet with us. He did assure us that he was investigating the Rosales incident and that he was interested in hearing Nate's take on the case.

"However," Ram added, "at this point, the abduction and murder of the Rosales kids is still centered on the person who admitted committing the crime, Lucas Williams."

"Okay, Ram," said Nate. "I promise to make time for a meeting with you as soon as you're able. I'm counting on you to help me ensure my family's safety."

. . .

CHAPTER TWENTY-THREE

[Chicago; four months after the twins' drowning]
(March 2022)

n the first week of March, Ram Edmunds returned from an extended trip to DC. He personally called Nate to set up an appointment. Fully recovered from his common cold, Nate was eager to "present his plan" to Ram Edmunds. Graciously, Nate included Max in his plans for the meeting with Ram and he promptly accepted.

Upon arrival at Chicago's Field Office of the FBI, Edmunds and Nate greeted each other as if it were a family reunion. The two men had developed a relaxed familiarity. The three sat at the conference table. Laurie, the executive assistant, always in a cheerful mood, pranced in with three settings for coffee and a full carafe. "Please let me know if there's anything else you need."

Allowing Laurie to return to her desk, Ram opened the meeting with an update. "While in DC, I took care of some matters involving Lucas Williams, a person of interest to you. For several weeks I've dealt with an attempt on Lucas Williams's life. While incarcerated, Lucas was attacked twice by inmates. We think someone on the outside ordered a hit on him, so like Dr. Ivo Wu, I placed him under federal protection."

"I think we all know who ordered the hit, Ram," Nate said.

Nodding vigorously, Ram said, "You're probably right, but we do not have proof."

Nate quickly got down to business. "That's partly why we're here, because I think that you can help unravel a final thread to this global blanket of evil—I believe the murder of the Rosales twins will lead us to the capture of the world's number-one fugitive, Diego Montemayor."

Ram was amused. "Nate, although we have an idea where Diego is now, we cannot presume to even come close to capturing him. So far he has stayed two steps ahead of us. The latest intel suggests that he is no longer at his Corsica estate."

"Any clues as to his whereabouts?" Max asked.

A dejected Ram Edmunds said, "None."

"You surprise me, Ram. Have you capitulated?" Nate asked. "It may be that Inspector Sánchez has had undue influence on me, but his *Art of War* wisdom has encouraged me. Diego Montemayor is not invincible."

"What have you learned about Diego Montemayor that makes you such an optimist?" With a rare smirk on his face, Ram Edmunds got up and walked to the buffet behind the conference table. Picking up the carafe, he walked around the table pouring for us the Jamaican Blue Mountain brew. He then filled his own cup and said, "Please forgive me. I'm not normally a cynical man, but Diego has been out-witting us at each step…. Unless you've discovered evidence, I won't buy your Kool-Aid."

Nate walked to the credenza to sweeten his coffee. "I'll provide one quote from Sun Tzu: '*The whole secret lies in confusing the enemy, so that he cannot fathom our real intent.*' You see, Ram," Nate said, holding his cup while stirring the contents, "I believe that with your resources—and, with Interpol's help—we can devise a ruse, a sting operation, that can ensnare Diego Montemayor once and for all." Sipping his cup of joe, Nate winced and walked back to the credenza to add sugar to his cup.

"Sounds rational—ambitious, but rational. Do you have some-thing in mind?" Ram asked as both stood by the credenza.

"I'll need help, but yes, we've developed a rough outline of a plan," said Nate as he looked at Max. Returning to his seat, Nate turned to his brother-in-law to chime in.

Sounding too apologetic, from his seat Max added, "At least a *very* rough outline."

Ram looked at Max and smiled. "Let's hear it."

Max blurted out an initial question. "Okay, Ram—what has been the principal motivating obsession for Diego Montemayor for the last six years?"

"I suppose we've all concluded that the man is full of anger and hatred toward Nate and Miró. He wants to avenge the 2016 death of his wife, Yael. He confessed to that aboard *The Black Pearl*, and he's demonstrated that throughout." Ram walked over to his enormous window that gave him a view of the Chicago skyline in the distance.

"Exactly," Max said. "Diego is obsessed with revenge. But what if he were to discover that his wife Yael is still alive?"

Turning away from his view and looking at Max, Ram said, "Of course, that would be a game-changer. Yael Montemayor, however, died in that hospital fire. It became public record."

Nate interrupted, "What Max is saying is what if we could convince Diego Montemayor that instead of perishing in that fire, Yael survived? What if Yael's godfather—the chief investigator for Las Palmas PD, who investigated the fire and pronounced her dead—secretly rescued her?"

In his excitement Max added, "And since Chief Inspector Sánchez wanted to protect his loved one and keep her from being charged with numerous crimes, he instead pronounced her dead, kept her alive, and provided protection for the past six years."

In tag-team fashion, Nate jumped in. "In effect, Sánchez would be protecting his goddaughter from law enforcement and from returning to a life of crime with her husband Diego Montemayor."

"You guys have seen too many movies," Ram said, chuckling. "Do you realize how difficult it would be to pull that off?" He was now laughing. "No disrespect, but to convince a shrewd and seasoned criminal like Diego Montemayor, such a scheme would require enormous resources, not to mention enormous risks to countless other individuals. And a well-planned sting operation would also require a professional cast of actors…plus *beaucoup* financial resources."

As if he had just stepped into a more imposing persona, Nate stood and walked over to Ram Edmunds. He squared his shoulders and deliberately invaded Ram's personal space. Nate set his cup of coffee on the conference table and after pausing a few seconds, he looked at Ram without a smile on his face. "I don't think you realize, Special Agent Edmunds, what my family has lived through these last six years. Not for a single moment have we forgotten the constant threat that Diego Montemayor poses for us. While Diego's disappearance and elusiveness have become a 'cold case' for the authorities, we have lived with one realization—that while Diego Montemayor is alive, no one in my family can be secure."

Taken aback, Ram placed a hand on Nate's left shoulder. "Nate, I did not mean to downplay the gravity of your situation. Nor can I ignore how the rest of your family must feel. Yet I need to clarify that your plan might be difficult to pull off."

Hoping to defuse the tension in the room, Max added, "Ram, you must remember that we might have significant resources at our disposal."

Ram was thankful for Max's interruption. He sat at the head of the table again and invited Nate to sit next to him. "Fine. Enlighten me."

• • •

For the next two hours, Nate assumed a professorial role by commandeering a pull-down dry erase board on the wall behind Ram Edmunds. He laid out the "Pygmalion Project," as he called it, and presented a compelling strategy. Ram appeared to be impressed. Several times Nate deferred to Max as he provided details regarding interviews that he'd conducted with Commander Rob Rivers from the Chicago PD.

Although on two separate occasions Edmunds had to step out and reschedule his afternoon appointments, he listened attentively. Other than asking for clarifications, he did not interrupt. Nate segmented his presentation by introducing his basic premise first. In a remarkable gamble, he offered Special Agent Edmunds a compromise.

"Listen, Ram—give me—and my family—six months. During this prep time, we will develop our Pygmalion Project. Miró and I will play Professor Henry Higgins and work on Raquel Rosales's elocution, her training in traditional European and Spanish culture and even Yael Montemayor's favorite recipes. We may not even require six months, since Mrs. Rosales is quite well educated, unlike the original Eliza Doolittle."

"Okay, Nate—run by me the whole *Pygmalion* thesis. What is it exactly?"

"My whole project is based on the classic play *Pygmalion*, which became the musical *My Fair Lady*. It's the story of an uneducated flower girl in England who is given lessons by a professor of linguistics to pass her off as a cultured, well-educated woman."

"Sounds familiar," said Edmunds.

"Yeah, Ram," Max said. "You and I probably better know it as the story in *My Fair Lady*. You remember Professor Henry Higgins giving elocution lessons to Eliza Doolittle?"

"Max, do you mean Rex Harrison playing Higgins and Audrey Hepburn playing Eliza?"

Nate jumped in. "Bingo. Although on Broadway, Eliza Doolittle was played by Julie Andrews. Of course, the movie *My Fair Lady* had Audrey Hepburn playing Eliza."

"So," Ram Edmunds asked, "why do you insist on calling it *Pygmalion*?"

"Well," said Nate, "that's the title of the original play, which was written by George Bernard Shaw. It was based on Greek mythology. The Greeks spoke of Pygmalion, who fell in love with one of his sculptures. The sculpture came to life."

"Fine. Refresh my memory, though. Remind me and go over the fine points of the play," said Ram Edmunds.

"Okay, Higgins and another scholar by the name of Pickering, who is also an avid student of languages and dialects, encounter this poor flower girl who has a strong Cockney accent. Higgins insists that poor speech patterns determine lack of social success. He brags to his friend Pickering that he would be able to transform the flower girl into a cultured lady if he had six months to give her elocution lessons. Pickering disagrees, and he is willing to wager that it cannot be done. So the bet is on."

"Ahh, yes, I remember the phrase '*The rain in Spain stays mainly in the plain,*'" said Edmunds.

"After several months of training, that's the one phrase that Eliza masters in order to convince Higgins that she is ready for a test."

"Which brings me to a major point," said Ram, "who would determine in our case if Raquel Rosales would be ready to pull off passing for Yael Montemayor?"

"Good question, Ram," said Nate. "Let me remind you that Miró and I are willing to play Henry Higgins. My wife is a university professor who has studied languages, and she is also well versed in art and European literature. As a psychiatrist, I understand social dynamics and a little about upper-crust manners. We will enlist Yael's godfather, Eduardo Sánchez, who knew Yael from birth. Give us six—max, seven months—to prepare her. I promise you'll be convinced."

"I'm not your problem. It's Diego, the husband," Ram said.

Without batting an eyelash, Nate responded, "We can do it—with your help."

"Nate, you cannot be serious," Unconvinced, Ram Edmunds got up from his conference table to serve himself more coffee. Turning, he asked, "Are you saying that you intend to transform Raquel Rosales into the deceased wife of Diego Montemayor? And you expect Diego Montemayor to be convinced that his wife is alive—and that this woman is actually Yael Montemayor—his wife?"

"I am convinced it can be done," said Nate.

Ram Edmunds shook his head. In apparent exasperation, he loosened his tie, unbuttoned his suit vest, and sat down at the head of the conference table. While he rolled up his shirt sleeves, he said, "In addition to the impossible task of persuading a loving husband of his wife's resurrection, you forget that Diego Montemayor knows Raquel Rosales well. For at least four months they lived steps away from each other. For Pete's sake, Nate—she lived in his Winnetka compound. He probably saw her daily."

"We understand all that," said Nate. "Just listen to me. Between us and Inspector Sánchez, we can determine to the most minute details Yael Montemayor's facial features. We've contacted Sánchez, and he is willing to share as many photographs as necessary. In addition, he will offer his own personal recollection, all his memories, to ensure that we get it right."

Ram's voice rose several octaves, "What are you talking about?" He shook his head. "Granted, I haven't met Raquel Rosales, but you haven't mentioned that she is Yael Montemayor's double. I haven't even heard you mention there's a passing resemblance. Remember it's not only about working on her facial features, but there's also complexion, birthmarks, intimate details regarding her total person."

"There is a better than passing resemblance," said Nate. "The two women shared much in common—the same height, same color of hair and eyes. Even Raquel Rosales' demeanor is like the deceased Yael Montemayor. By that I mean that her posture and the way she carries herself reminds me of Diego's former wife."

Still shaking his head, Ram objected, "That's a far cry from what we'd need to accomplish in order to convince someone like Diego Montemayor."

"This is where we add the second major part of the plan," Max said.

"Yes," said Nate, "Max is addressing the need to enlist the services of Dr. Ivo Wu. During our preparation period, Raquel Rosales will require a skilled plastic surgeon. We need for him to transform Raquel into Yael Montemayor."

"Are you out of your mind? Do you realize what you're asking?"

"I do. I do indeed," said Nate. "Furthermore, I think it can be done."

"Nate, I don't think Dr. Wu even has a license to practice medicine in this country," said Edmunds. Again, he rose from his table to dispose of his coffee mug, mumbling to himself.

"Just listen to me," Nate insisted. "I've spoken to Gabriel Picard, and he assured me that we will have full cooperation from Interpol… and from his good friend Inspector Eduardo Sánchez."

"Tell me again what Picard's role is at Interpol."

"Picard is the deputy secretary general."

"Pretty big shot. I forgot that you worked under him in Europe."

"Ram, I'm certain that transferring Dr. Wu's European license to practice medicine in this country can be handled easily," Nate said. "And we know Wu is extremely capable, being that he performed some astounding work on Diego himself and countless others. If he was able to transform Diego into Rodrigo Díaz, he can accomplish what we demand from him. Just keep an open mind."

Nate Shelley could be extremely persuasive when he put his mind to it. Like a shark coming in for a kill, he circled around the table and approached Ram. In a calm, methodical voice he added, "And, to satisfy your deliberate and cautious approach to all this, I promise you that before putting our plan in motion, we will allow Inspector Eduardo Sánchez—the person who knew Yael Montemayor all of her life—to approve of Raquel Rosales. In other words, if he's not convinced that Raquel Rosales will be able to persuade Diego Montemayor of her identity, I will personally cancel the plan. I give you my word," said Nate.

"So your plan includes three facets." Ram Edmunds seemed to ask a question: "First, you will transform Raquel Rosales into 'my fair lady.' Second, she undergoes plastic surgery. Third, we *all* test her—with Inspector Sánchez being flown here to give the final approval. Is that right?"

"With one minor correction," added Nate. "Because of our short timeline, facets 1 and 2 must be carried out simultaneously. By that I mean that our training will begin immediately; however, we will ask Dr. Wu to also perform the surgery as soon as possible. While Mrs. Rosales undergoes surgery and recuperates, her training will be ongoing."

"Are you certain she is willing to undergo all this?"

Max quickly responded. "She is ready for the challenge."

Nate added, "We will let you be the judge. Max has offered to bring her in for an interview as soon as your schedule allows."

CHAPTER TWENTY-FOUR

[Chicago; four months after the twins' drowning]
(March 2022)

=MAX=

learned to consult with my brother-in-law before conducting interviews. Nate, he's a world-renowned psychotherapist, and it would
be foolish not to tap his expertise. Gaining Ram Edmunds's support was critical for the success of the Pygmalion Plan that we'd
forged, so I wanted to ensure that before introducing Raquel Rosales
to Edmunds, I would present the best case to him. I had one opportunity to present our best "Eliza Doolittle," and I did not want any
missteps on my part being the reason for Ram's rejection of the plan.

Since Nate and Miró knew Ram well, I inquired about his personality—his virtues, his character traits, and temperament. In short,
I wanted to know what "made him tick," as my grandpappy used to
say. Nate provided unbelievable insights that evening. Although during my first meetings with Ram I'd recognized some obvious traits—
his adherence to established rules, his preference for tradition and the
status quo rather than change—Nate gave me some invaluable nug-
gets that helped me understand Agent Edmunds much better. For
example, Nate had learned that Ram was peculiarly nostalgic, remaining loyal to his good friend Angelo Calabrese, who had turned out
to be a rogue federal agent. In addition, despite the disloyalty of his
superiors, he remained strongly bound to his work and to the FBI.

Nate was emphatic: "Ram will resist doing things differently for as long as he can, Max. If I could think of a personal motto for Ram, it would be 'If it ain't broke, don't fix it.' However, you must remember that in addition to being so rigid and unwilling to try the unfamiliar, he is a deeply moral man."

"You make it sound like we're fighting a losing battle with Agent Edmunds," I said.

"You must understand that as a young boy, Ram grew up in a home that lacked stability. He grew up in a very conservative community, and his parents were probably the only ones in his circle of friends who were divorced. Though he was surrounded by good kids and supportive friends, he was still humiliated by the 'untraditional' home environment of his youth."

"So are you saying that, now as an adult, Ram seeks out…no… that he actually needs predictability in his world?"

"That's exactly right, Max. Special Agent Edmunds *needs* predictability."

"Okay, well—I'm taking Raquel Rosales to see Ram in three days. He agreed to see us for a late afternoon meeting."

* * *

(Three Days Later)

"Ram, it's past five. Come on. Rise and shine."

Special Agent Ram Edmunds grunted, looked out the window, and realized it was another gray, wet Chicago morning. Though he was wearing winter pajama bottoms, his top was a short-sleeved T-shirt. He shivered and thought twice about going back to bed. It was his day for his short jog around the small, Oak Park Village community. He would circle the development twice to reach his daily quota. Five miles and back home for a shower and breakfast. The faint streetlights streamed in through the plantation shutters and bathed his bedcovers with a silvery light. He finally stumbled out of bed and picked up his eyeglasses from the cherry nightstand.

"When you get back, I'll have your banana waffles ready." Claire

Edmunds yawned. "Your favorite ones with caramelized bananas. By the way, Ram, it's getting more difficult to wake you each morning. Are you okay?"

Ram did not acknowledge his wife. He didn't speak much the first few minutes after waking. In fact, he hardly spoke before his first cup of java. He grabbed his sweats mechanically and stepped into them. He laced his New Balance 1080 v11's. Almost to himself he said, "Most mornings I'd rather get back in bed."

Stepping out into the dull, overcast morning, Ram noticed a musky, earthy smell emanating from the flower bed in his tiny front yard. It was what the TV meteorologists refer to as "petrichor." His mind wandered as he picked up his pace. *If I get caught in a downpour, it'll give me a perfect excuse to go back home.* He trudged along the rest of the way—with no further signs of rain.

He circled the last cul-de-sac and headed home. Other than the smell of rain, Ram could detect only the exhaust fumes from the IH 290 freeway traffic blocks away. Did he want to remain with the FBI if he got promoted to deputy director? *Will I return to Chicago after retirement? A home down in Florida or Texas would be nice… maybe even Arizona. With my home equity, I could probably afford a nice spread of land…right now. And to be able to golf ten months a year would be a treat.* Ram trotted the last two hundred yards while he continued his daydream.

"I'm back, Claire. I'll shower and then join you for those waffles. Please brew my Jamaican java…. Oh, and pick out my shirt and tie for today." Ram knew exactly which tie Claire would pick. It would be the boring gray and sky blue she preferred, her Christmas gift to him two Christmases ago.

Claire placed the caramelized bananas, already sliced, back in the fridge. She stood in front of Ram's electronic tie rack and took her favorite tie to match his blue button-down medium-starched shirt. "Rambo, would you like your coffee by your toiletries, so you can take a drink or two after your shower?"

"Not necessary. I'll scramble to the table right away," Ram called out from the shower.

Funny, thought Ram. *We always follow the same routine, and Claire still asks the same questions. I wonder if she gets bored by it.* Ram wore his suit pants to the table but skipped the shirt, wearing only his T-shirt.

"It's warm in here, Claire. Did you raise the thermostat?"

"Two degrees only. Want me to adjust more?"

Ram smiled. "If you don't mind."

While Claire rushed to set the table, Ram checked his emails on his phone absentmindedly, considering that it was rather nice having an empty nest and being able to ease into such predictability. It hadn't always been this way.

Little did Ram Edmunds know that his routine would be so unexpectedly upset by the developments of that day. His 3:00 p.m. appointment with Max Kempball and Raquel Rosales would bring his customary routine such upheaval that years later he would realize this day would be pinpointed as the day he embarked on a new phase of his life—the phase when he doubted his mental stability and resolve.

. . .

That same afternoon, Laurie, Ram's executive assistant, announced to him at 2:55 p.m. that his visitors were waiting outside his office. "Give me five minutes, will you? I need to collect my thoughts."

Ram Edmunds had been dreamily contemplating his approaching retirement—or perhaps a potential promotion and a move to DC. In truth, he was also acknowledging how regimented, ordinary, and unexceptional his home life had become. Oh, he appreciated the familiar. He even desired the predictability of his life with Claire. He knew her likes and dislikes. She knew his. He had learned to accept her faults and annoying habits. To Claire's credit, most of the time she kept quiet about his own thoughtlessness and his caustic remarks. However, it was unusual for Ram to be so distracted. That's what contemplating retirement was doing to him.

"Laurie," Ram said over a vintage intercom system he had refused to give up, "please bring me the Shelley files. And be sure to include the transcript of the last meeting."

He was neither eager to meet with Max and the Rosales widow nor was he ready. Garnering all the discipline he could muster, Special Agent Edmunds collected his thoughts and resolved to be as objective as he could be. He would humor Nate Shelley and comply with his promise to at least contemplate the outlandish "Pygmalion Project" that had abject failure written all over it. What Nate and Max had convinced him to consider was a long-shot effort to deceive Diego Montemayor, the European mastermind who for years had managed to evade law enforcement officials throughout the world. Yet here was Ram Edmunds, who was preparing for retirement, about to engage in a risky, improbable, and fanciful scenario that had little chance of success. *Why on earth are you doing this, Ram?*

Laurie walked in with file in hand and asked, "Should I wait five minutes and walk them in, or do you want to come out and greet them?"

"I'll walk out in five."

Ten minutes later, a puzzling enigma began to unravel for Ram Edmunds. It began with the woman who waited for him in the lobby. She wore a gray wool-twill blazer over a black dress that came to one and a half inches above the knee. After the meeting, Ram would learn from the staff photographer that her stunning outfit was "très chic."

• • •

(30 minutes after Ram's meeting with Max and Raquel)

"Saint Laurent, Spencer cropped blazer," Remington said. Moving his golden locks away from his forehead with his pinky, the photographer added, "that piece alone is very, very expensive." He was holding photos he'd taken, using concealed cameras.

Ram had asked for the entire meeting with Max and Raquel to be videotaped, without their knowledge. He asked his staff photographer, Remington Lake, to come in for a de-briefing.

"How expensive?" asked Ram.

"I'd say the jacket alone runs about $2,800...and those heels are... ahem...Manolo Blahnik." Remington gasped audibly.

"I'm sorry, Remington, but that doesn't mean a thing to me. Please explain," said Ram.

"It means," said the flustered photographer blinking repeatedly, "that the shoes would put you back about five grand." He added breathlessly, "And the clutch, or the purse, if you will, was a Lana Marks Cleopatra Clutch." Remington paused for effect. He sat at the edge of Ram's guest chair. Both hands on his knees, Remington repeated, "Lana Marks, Mr. Edmunds."

"Again, Remington, you need to enlighten me," said Special Agent Ram Edmunds.

"Okay, that purse—you might need to sit for this one—probably cost close to $400,000."

"What? How many zeroes are you using?"

"You heard correctly," said the young photographer as he pursed his lips and blinked repeatedly.

"How do you know all these things, Remington?" asked Ram Edmunds. "Are you sure you're not pulling my leg?"

"You must remember that in my previous life in L.A., I used to photograph celebrities who paraded up and down the red carpet. I shot that video—and the pix of Mrs. Rosales—for you and immediately researched every single item she wore. Those items were not fake, and I can assure you she was wearing more big bucks than the combined cost of the furniture on our floor—no, the entire building probably. Most film stars would have salivated seeing her wardrobe."

"You mean that small crocodile purse cost more than her shoes... than her entire outfit?"

"Mr. Edmunds, that tiny flap with glitter was encrusted with pink diamonds and pink gold." It appeared that Remington had to stop to catch his breath. He fanned himself with the splayed fingers of his right hand.

Ram Edmunds walked to his window. The last rays of light coming in through his west window reflected off the Picasso reproduction of the sculpture in Daily Square. Unlike the giant, unnamed, steel original, the small *Orangutan* was made of silver. It reflected the light and shone on his crystal glassware. The reflection danced through the conference room, flitting playfully like an angel's wings, quivering above his computer screen.

Ram's mind reeled at the extravagance of Mrs. Rosales' clothes, but more stunning was her sheer beauty. He thought of Raquel Rosales and remembered being struck by his wife, Claire, in the same fashion the first time he saw her. Claire had almost taken his breath away. No, she *had* taken his breath away. She was that beautiful. When he first met Claire at the age of eighteen, she was a raving beauty. Tall and stately, she had been like an apparition to him. Did Raquel remind him of his wife, Claire?

Max and Raquel Rosales had left after a three-hour meeting. Ram had no idea what had happened, but he was convinced that the svelte Hispanic beauty who had just left his office was right for the role of Eliza Doolittle. What bothered Ram Edmunds was his complete acceptance of a risky and reckless plan to get involved in a sting operation of such magnitude. *Why, at this point in my life, am I willing to risk a career and a placid retirement?*

Ram attempted to summon Laurie, his executive assistant, using his intercom. There was no response. Then he realized it was past seven in the evening. Laurie had left an hour ago. He'd place the call himself. Ram desperately needed to meet with his friend Nate Shelley first thing in the morning. Better still, he needed to meet with Nate Shelley, the psychiatrist, because he needed counseling, therapy—psychoanalysis perhaps.

CHAPTER TWENTY-FIVE

**[Chicago; four months after the twins' drowning]
(March 2022)**

Ram could not erase from his mind the image of a painting he'd viewed at the Museum of Art some time ago. He didn't remember the artist, but it was called *The Tambourine Girl*. In that painting a forlorn, melancholy beauty was leaning against a marbled background, her eyes thousands of miles away, wistfully imagining a better future. Ram couldn't help it. When he'd come out to invite Raquel Rosales into his office's conference room, Raquel was leaning against the marble pillar in the waiting area. Her look—and her beauty—captivated him. It was the look of *The Tambourine Girl* in the painting.

After a brief dinner of leftovers with his wife, Claire, they both retired for the night at 9:00. Ram had been distracted all evening. He told Claire about the meeting with Max and Raquel Rosales, but he left out the part of the young woman's appeal.

That night he had a dream about a younger Ram running after a fugitive kite in an open field. Distracted by the fluttering tail on the kite, he approached a cliff and fell down the precipice to a certain death. He woke in a sweat. Ram got up and drank some warm milk at the kitchen counter. After returning to bed and falling asleep, he had a similar dream where Ram found himself in an impossible situation of persuading Claire, his wife, of his innocence. They sat on the bed, Claire holding several pieces of paper. She had found incriminating evidence of something worthy of divorce, and he pleaded with her not to be unreasonable. She walked out, packed her bags, and left the house. Ram woke up again in a sweat and close to tears. Instinctively, he turned to Claire and asked her to forgive him. Still groggy, Claire woke and asked, "For what, honey?"

"For everything, Claire, everything I've ever done to hurt you." Ram realized he sounded silly, kissed his wife on the cheek, and asked her to go back to sleep. It was 2:30 in the morning.

Following the last dream, just before his alarm rang at 4:30, Ram woke up, thanking the alarm and Providence for interrupting another disturbing nightmare. This time Ram had jumped off a cliff—possibly the first one in the kite dream—and fell into the arms of a hairy minotaur, a powerful-looking creature with the body of a muscular man and the head of a bull or an ox. The creature was grinning as he walked toward a raging fire in a furnace.

Later that morning in Nate's office he related to him the three dreams. "I've never been so happy to be awakened, Nate. I've never had this kind of excruciating mental issue. As you can imagine, in my job I've experienced danger—my life has been threatened hundreds of times—but this kind of psychological trauma, self-doubt, delusional infatuation, or whatever you want to call it...I'm embarrassed to say it, but I'm obsessed with this woman."

"How long has this been going on?" asked Nate.

"What do you mean?" asked Ram Edmunds. "This just started after she left my office yesterday after 6:00. When she left with Max."

"So you're referring to Raquel Rosales?" asked Nate.

Embarrassed, Ram said, "Yes, I thought Max had shared with you. I spoke to him briefly last night."

"Okay, Ram—let's go back to the beginning. What precisely happened?"

"Yesterday, Max and Mrs. Rosales arrived before the time of their appointment. Laurie informed me they were waiting, but I'd been daydreaming. So I wasn't ready to see them. I had been worrying about my retirement, which is coming up in less than a year."

"Umm…hm."

"To be honest, Nate, I was also wondering why I was considering such a crazy and foolish sting operation. I was at the point of cancelling the meeting with Max and Mrs. Rosales. Regrettably, I was ready to call the whole thing off…I was ready to break my word to you. Instead, I had the meeting videotaped so that I could use it as evidence…to justify my rejection of the plan."

"And now?"

"Now, my dear friend, now…I don't know. My heart is telling me to go forth with the plan no matter how slim the chances for success, which is not my rational self that is deciding. If the old Ram Edmunds were to be thinking clearly, I would be telling you right now to forget the whole improbable plan."

"Ram, I know you at various levels. I believe I can consider you a friend. I also know you as a consummate professional. I will trust your final judgment," said Nate. "So to get that matter out of the way," said Nate, "as much as I would hate starting from scratch with an alternate plan, I would understand your decision perfectly."

"I trust you also, Nate."

"Now you can proceed knowing fully that during this discussion I will not attempt to sway your judgment one way or another. Is that clear, and are you comfortable accepting my objectivity?"

"Totally."

"What happened when they both walked in?" asked Nate.

"That's the thing. I asked Max to walk into my office first for a private word. I asked Max to tell Raquel, whom I had not yet seen, to wait outside my office. Then I shared with him what I just admitted to you. I said that as I reconsidered your 'Pygmalion Project,' as you call it, I realized it was too risky and that it was doomed to fail."

"What did Max say?"

"He begged me to at least meet with Mrs. Rosales. He was confident that upon meeting her, I would change my mind." Ram Edmunds chuckled. "Boy, was he right!"

"Then you went out to greet her?"

"No, a strange thing occurred. Laurie walked in and excused herself for interrupting. She took me aside and said, "You need to meet with this lady. Everyone in the office is flabbergasted."

When I asked her why, she merely said, "You'll see when you walk out there."

"Please explain," Nate said. "I've met with Mrs. Rosales previously, and as attractive as she might be, I did not find her to be particularly stunning or ravishing."

"Well, when she walked into that office, she certainly left an impact," said Ram. "As I was speaking with Laurie with the door to my office slightly ajar, a change in the level of my staff's voices told me they were talking about her. Without returning to Max, I walked out to greet Mrs. Rosales…. At that point, Nate, I was still determined to simply apologize and explain to her that I had decided not to involve my office in your plan."

Nate remained silent.

"I walked toward the small waiting area, assuming she'd be seated in a guest chair. She had moved closer to the exit and was standing, leaning against the lobby's marble pillar. She had this forlorn look, as if dejected and sad. Instantly I thought of a painting that I'd seen a month before at the Chicago Museum of Art. There was an exhibition of pre-modern artists. I can't remember the artist's name, but the painting was called *The Tambourine Girl*."

Nate did not want to interrupt Ram's flow, but he merely added, "His name was Godward, John William Godward."

"Yes, that's it. The artist was Godward. I remember the painting, and I could swear that she had posed—that Raquel Rosales had posed—for the painting…. Nate, I can't stop thinking about that painting."

"Can't stop thinking about the painting or Raquel Rosales?"

"Both, I suppose," said an embarrassed Special Agent Ram Edmunds. "Nate, I'm sixty-five years old and I'm about to retire. I'm a grandfather. I love my wife, but…"

"But you can't stop thinking about Raquel Rosales. Is that it?"

"That's exactly right."

"Ram, the dreams you shared. Do you think they were caused by this momentary obsession?" asked Nate.

"Of course. What else *could* it be?"

Nate did not respond.

"Nate, when I approached her, I smelled that fragrance—I have no idea what it was—on her suntanned skin…it could've been the smell of soap, I don't know. But I stood there, stunned, as if I'd seen an angel or heavenly being of some sort. I felt like a stupid teenager."

"Why do you say that?"

"That's exactly how I felt. Like I said, I'm an old geezer, and I've seen female beauty before. I don't normally turn into a blithering idiot."

"Okay."

"I finally introduced myself," said Ram, "and she smiled and didn't shake my hand. I invited her to join Max and me in my office. She slipped past me, and she grazed my arm. No skin—she was wearing a tasteful jacket over a black dress. But when she grazed my arm, it was like a blaze inside of me was incinerated. She looked straight ahead and did not look at me as she sat down next to Max."

"Did she do anything suggestive or inappropriate?" asked Nate. "Did she say anything that could be interpreted as seductive or prurient?"

"On the contrary. Her words were measured and formal. She seemed cultured. When Mrs. Rosales sat down, her posture was the posture of a model or a ballerina. She was somewhat aloof and very reserved—almost austere, I'd say. Something about her said, 'class,' 'elegance.' Not at all what I expected."

"Please explain, Ram."

"Well, Nate, you and Max had told me she was the wife—widow, I should say—to one of the Rosales brothers. Those two were Diego Montemayor's lieutenants, but they were—again sorry for the term—two-bit gangsters from the hood. For such a woman to be married to their kind frankly amazed me."

"Understood."

"I know what you said earlier, Ram, but have you—before this, I mean—been vulnerable to a woman's elegant beauty, as you describe it?" Nate was taking copious notes in his notebook.

"By the way, Nate, should I be lying down on a couch or something?" asked Ram.

Nate smiled. "No, Ram—that's not necessary. Go on."

"You can probably tell better than I can, but this is truly bothering me. No one has had that effect on me...except maybe my wife many years ago. At this point I'm obsessed by a young woman, and I have no business even contemplating anything ever developing. Furthermore, I have no intention of leaving my wife, changing my life, or doing anything irrational. Yet I can't get some things out of my mind. Am I making any sense?" asked Ram Edmunds.

"Yes, you're making sense. And I believe that I can help you. Please, is there anything else you'd like to get off your chest?"

"Much more, Nate. But I cannot remember every detail. Most of what I do remember embarrasses me."

"We are bound by doctor-patient confidentiality."

"Did you just become my doctor?" asked Ram, smiling for the first time.

"Yes, among other things—friend, colleague, and therapist," said Nate.

"Okay, here goes.... I'm spilling my guts here. A little after 5:00, I offered Max and Raquel a drink. I went to my cabinet and took out a couple of bottles...three actually, 'Scotch, vodka, or bourbon'?" I asked. "Max and I went with bourbon, but she took scotch with a splash of water."

"I'm not judging," said Nate. "It was officially after five."

"No, that's not what I meant," said Ram. "When I offered her the drink, her hand was an inch away from mine, and my entire focus—all my senses went on stand-by mode. A sophomoric hope of a single touch rushed down into that hand of hers that was accepting my drink. I felt an electrical charge, a heat inside of me that made me feel ashamed of myself. When I stared into her eyes, she averted my look. There was no touch, of course. However, there was in me a total awareness of her person. I got a whiff of her hair, a glorious floral fragrance different from her perfume. Having her in front of me to enjoy visually was not enough. Enjoying the visual banquet did not quench my need for more sensual satisfaction. I wanted to touch her, even taste those full lips."

"Sounds very intense, Ram," said Nate.

"Nate, in my mind I was thinking, 'Please, let me kiss you'. The thought was so forceful that I thought I'd vocalized it. I stepped away from her and went directly to my seat at the far end of the table to continue our conversation. But all the while I thought, 'She is so beautiful…so unbelievably beautiful.'"

Nate had a smile on his face. He rose from his seat, closed his notebook, and walked behind his desk. Nate remembered that Miró and Max had met with Raquel the previous two nights to coach her before her meeting with Ram Edmunds. *Did Miró and Max launch the training of Raquel Rosales without informing me?*

CHAPTER TWENTY-SIX

**[Chicago; four months after the twins' drowning]
(March 2022)**

For the next five minutes Nate did his best to set his friend Ram Edmunds at ease. He reassured Ram that the level of stress he was experiencing was a "temporary glitch."

"I promise you, Ram, that we will converse tomorrow, and after our conversation, you will feel much better about this situation. For the time being, take the rest of the day off, and take Claire out for a walk, or drive her to the park…. Go shopping, whatever Claire would like to do. Only one caution. Do not—under any circumstances—discuss with Claire your momentary obsession with Raquel Rosales."

"Nate, you seem extremely confident about this. Please understand that I'm not doubting your judgment, but something like this doesn't magically disappear," said Ram. "What I mean is that you appear dismissive, as if this 'condition'"—Ram made quotation marks in the air— "is common. I don't believe that it is."

"Please trust me, Ram," said Nate. "After our conversation tomorrow, if your stress levels don't diminish, I promise that we will take more aggressive measures. At this point, I'll prescribe some benzodiazepines. Take one tonight only if you think you need it. I ask that you tolerate this for only twenty-four more hours."

• • •

Alone in his office, Nate recorded his clinical synopsis in the New Patient files. With a smile, he texted Max and Miró to request a late afternoon meeting. Max responded almost immediately, stating that he had been expecting his communication. "Miró and I will update you on our first coaching sessions with Raquel Rosales," he added.

Miró, on the other hand, responded after an hour. Her brief text to Nate indicated that she had scheduled a faculty meeting for mid-afternoon. She would not return home until 6:30.

"Let's meet Max at *Va Pensiero*, my love. Shall we make it 7:00-ish?"

Miró simply responded with a thumbs up.

Va Pensiero had been Nate and Miró's go-to Evanston restaurant for many years. It had been the venue that Miró had selected for their first date, and it had remained their sentimental favorite.

By the time Nate arrived, Max was already there, drinking a Moretti beer. Nate joined him at the table and quickly ordered a chardonnay. "The usual *Planeta*, Dr. Shelley?" Lorenzo, the friendly waiter, asked. Without waiting for a response, the waiter turned and brought the chilled Italian white. A moment later he showed up with a warm plateful of Ciabatta, focaccia, and some brioches. "On the house." He smiled as he placed the mounds of softened butter between the two men.

By the time that Miró arrived, Max had consumed one brioche, most of the ciabatta, and was in the process of "tasting" the focaccia.

"By the looks of it, you boys have been here quite a while," said Miró.

"Yes, a basketful of bread ago," said Nate, smiling at Max. "Your brother has been here fifteen minutes, and I arrived five minutes later."

Nate and Miró exchanged pecks, and Max hugged his sister. "Good to see you, sis."

Nate wasted no time. "Okay, now you can break it to me. What did you two do to Raquel Rosales? Ram Edmunds asked to see me this morning, because—in his words—"he was tied up in knots because of a serious development".

"Sorry I did not give you a heads-up, Nate," said Max, "but Ram called me late last night, stating that everything in his gut told him to proceed with our plan. Furthermore, he said that Raquel Rosales was perfect for the part, but he was afraid he was eager to proceed with the plan for the wrong reasons. Frankly, Ram was not making sense. I thought he'd had a drink too many."

Without being summoned, the waiter showed up with a Bellini in his hand. "I hope it's to your liking, Dr. Epstein-Shelley." Miró smiled and nodded.

Turning to Nate, Miró said, "We should've mentioned that the last two nights we've spent hours with Raquel in her home. After choosing her wardrobe for the meeting with Ram—which, incidentally, is as tasteful and extravagant a wardrobe as Yael Montemayor would've owned—we dedicated our time to coaching her attitude and behavior."

Nate proceeded cautiously, "Don't know what you guys did, but she managed to conflict Ram sufficiently for him to seek my therapy. For obvious reasons, I took him on as a temporary patient, but I will end that relationship after tomorrow. In the meantime, I cannot share details about our first session."

"Frankly, my main objective was to turn Ram Edmunds into a lovelorn lunatic," said Max. "Last night when Ram called me, he confessed that he couldn't think of anything else—he developed what he thinks is a serious infatuation."

Miró and Max smiled. Miró turned to Nate and asked if he could possibly imagine Ram as a "lovelorn lunatic." Nate did not comment. Instead, he turned to the waiter to request another Moretti for Max.

Before his sister, Miró, had a chance to add a comment, Max said, "Miró invented a persona for Raquel, a role that we wanted her to play. At the end of last night, we thought Raquel was ready for her meeting with Ram. She's a quick learner."

"Nate, remember how Max quizzed you about Ram Edmunds?" asked Miró. "He used all your information to allow us to formulate a plan. The plan may even take on a slightly different twist once you resolve this issue with Ram Edmunds."

"You must elaborate, my love. What specific information did I give Max that proved so helpful?" Nate seemed confused.

For the next fifteen minutes, Miró and Max explained to Nate that they both suspected from the beginning that Ram would not proceed with the Pygmalion Plan.

"Remember, Nate," said Max. "You outlined for me critical characteristics that made Ram what he is. You specifically mentioned how much respect Ram has for established ideas; how he is opposed to change; how he resists new styles, fashions, and trends. Bottom line, Ram is rabidly conservative," said Max.

"But," said Miró, "Ram is staunchly loyal to friends, to his employers, and to family. Like Max says, he prefers the status quo, and he rejects situations that appear to be strange or risky. He fears change."

"Yes, I described to Max the preferences of a conventional personality type," said Nate. "What does that have to do with the coaching of Raquel Rosales?"

Miró said, "Nate, you gave us the key to the preparation of Raquel for her meeting. Your description of Ram's personality type told me that Ram's personal identity depends on sameness."

"Yeah, so—"

"So my hunch...and Max's hunch also...was that Ram was *not* about to agree to our Pygmalion Plan—not in a million years. His comfort level is predictability. And in his mind, a Hispanic woman married to an uneducated drug dealer from the Chicago hoods had no chance of convincing the world's most wanted criminal that she was a poised, well-spoken, well-read, woman of culture. Ram probably assumed that a woman of Raquel's background—although he'd never met her—would need a lifetime to pull off a plan like the one being proposed."

"So, Nate, what was our best...our only...hope?" asked Max.

Before Nate could answer, Miró said, "Shock him with a persona that would shout the extreme opposite of his presuppositions."

"Yeah," Max said. "Present him with a demure, sophisticated, yet alluring woman who is perfectly comfortable in her own skin."

"Whoa!" said Nate. "That's not what I was thinking."

"Think about it, my love," said Miró. "Ram would have dismissed anything predictable."

"Exactly," Max said. "In truth, however, we didn't think she would have a seductive impact on Ram."

"I met with Mrs. Rosales briefly," said Nate, "but she didn't strike me as a seductress. She's attractive, yes, but someone that can send Ram into a frenzy, no…definitely not. What coaching did you give her?"

"*Mi amor,* listen," said Miró. "Raquel Rosales is like many new starlets who are transformed by their handlers, their managers, and marketing gurus. Raquel has always known she's an attractive woman. What I had to do was convince her that she would need to play a character that is more than attractive, that such a character is more than beautiful…a *femme fatale* who is mysterious and desirable."

"Hopefully, a *femme fatale* who is not villainous?" Nate asked.

"Precisely."

"Well, the only thing I'm able to tell you is that she did an outstanding job," said Nate. "You transformed her role into one that inspires reverence. If you can continue to create a virtual apparition, an angelic image…a woman who can pose for a classic painting… the ruse will be a success."

Miró seemed pleased. "We spoke about a sophistication that would set her apart. Now, I think she—or at least this 'new Raquel Rosales,' this new persona—knows she's beautiful. I'm not sure she knows what to do with her beauty, though."

"What I can't understand," said Max, "if Ram is smitten, as he told me, after a single meeting—how's that possible, Nate?"

"Tolstoy once said that 'the biggest surprise in a man's life is old age,' Max. And, I suppose that old age creeps up on you. For some men who are facing retirement, their identities and family stability are called into question."

Miró asked, "Is Ram contemplating retirement?"

"In less than a year," said Max. He's shared that with me. "I think it's very unsettling to consider a disruption of a life that revolves around your work and your home life. His work has given Ram his identity. Now he meets a woman that jars his entire perspective of the world—the predictable paradigm—and he falls down a precipice."

Miró jumped in. "I thought Ram had a strong marriage. When he refers to his wife, Claire, he speaks of her with such fondness, such love."

"That may be the problem. Ram may feel guilty about these

thoughts, thinking he's betraying his marital vows. He's not contemplating leaving Claire, is he?" Max asked.

"Nothing like that," Nate said.

Max shook his head. "Please clarify something, someone. Does Ram regret being married to Claire or not?"

Miró took a sip of her wine. Instinctively, she reached for her pen to write down an explanation but returned the pen to her purse. "Growing up, in Ram's world if you wanted to have sex, you had to beg for it—or get married. Isn't that right, Nate?"

"During his times, that would be accurate," said Nate.

"So Ram got married?" Max asked. "That's as good as saying that Ram regrets his marriage."

"Not at all," Miró objected. "What it means, however, is that the thing that most satisfies Ram—predictability—is what you and I disrupted with the coaching of Raquel Rosales. Ram literally does not know what to do with his reaction to Raquel...doesn't know what to do with his feelings. He is facing a perfect storm in his life that brings everything into question."

CHAPTER TWENTY-SEVEN

[Chicago; four months after the twins' drowning]
(March 2022)

After a satisfying dinner of pan-fried sea bass, accompanied by a Pouilly Fumé, Nate and Miró were ready to retire early. Max, however, opted to have his favorite *Va Pensiero* dessert.

"Tell me, Max—since you opted for the salsa verde on your roasted potatoes, how did you enjoy the Vermentino that Lorenzo recommended?" asked Nate.

"Who?"

"The waiter, Lorenzo."

"Oh, it was good, Nate. Are you sure I won't keep you if I order the cannoli?"

"Go ahead. Miró and I will order the decaf cappuccinos," said Nate. "You and Miró did say earlier, though, that your coaching of Raquel Rosales led you to consider a 'slightly different twist' to the original plan. Which twist?"

"That was me, *corazón,*" said Miró. "I believe—and I think Max agrees—that we should consider a modification of our original Pygmalion Project."

"Please explain."

Smiling, Miró said, "I know that you are not Ram Edmunds. And I also know that you are not always resistant to change; however, you sometimes are reluctant to tweak carefully thought-out plans."

"Okay, okay," said Nate. "I admit to having a tinge of stubbornness. I prefer to refer to it as *tenacity.*"

"Exactly," said Miró. "When we realized that Raquel was doing so well in following our instructions, Max and I discussed the possibility of removing the need to convince Diego Montemayor that Raquel is actually his deceased wife."

"Whoa! That's a significant change. It turns our strategy upside down," said Nate. "Why did you call it merely 'a slightly different twist'?"

"Should I rest my case at this point, my dear husband, or should I continue? Are you not willing to consider any kind of change?" Miró asked.

"Yeah, Nate. Just listen to her reasoning," said Max.

Since Lorenzo was approaching the table with an over-sized cannolo, Miró knew that they would lose Max for the next fifteen minutes. His concentration would be dedicated to the enjoyment of his delectable dessert.

"Listen to me. If you consider this 'tweak'—and I will defend the choice of words—it will allow us some flexibility," said Miró. She primarily addressed her husband. Of course, Max was somewhere in gourmand heaven. "Our training, our process, will remain the same. Raquel will be transformed into Yael Montemayor's double. After the surgery, Raquel will look like Yael. Her preparation, her elocution, her cultural education, her ability to appreciate fine wines and to prepare Spanish cuisine will continue to be part of the plan. Her walk and her demeanor will be exactly like Yael's. With the use of videotape, we will constantly update Yael's godfather, Eduardo Sánchez. We will seek his approval each step of the way."

"Okay, I feel better," said Nate. "So, what changes?"

"What changes, *mi amor*, is the following. Permit me to present my argument just like your favorite Spanish philosopher would. Do you remember that José Ortega y Gasset said that often he would reject a linear approach? He preferred to use reasoning that would resemble the flight of a 'gyrfalcon'?"

"I do remember quite well. Ortega would also compare that style of reasoning to the way the Israelites led by Joshua marched around Jericho for seven days. Each day the Israelite army marched once around Jericho—"

"But the seventh day," Miró finished Nate's thought. "The seventh day, the army marched around Jericho seven times, and after the seventh cycle, Jericho's walls fell."

"In other words, Ortega often used non-linear thinking, which is not the same as 'circular reasoning,'" said Nate.

"Exactly." Pausing to collect her thoughts, she continued.

"In our case, we will use—with your help, of course—Diego Montemayor's personality profile…just like we used Ram Edmunds' profile, to prepare Raquel. Although our understanding of Diego Montemayor—by that I mean mine and Max's—is limited."

At this point, Max figuratively rose for air. He put his fork down and turned to Nate and Miró and nodded in agreement. Although he did not say anything immediately, Max grasped for words to support Miró. He cleared his throat. "Although our understanding of this criminal mind is limited, we know a few things that you have shared with us. For example, we know some obvious things. Diego is self-centered, self-indulgent, and explosive. He has no compassion for others. I personally think that he is actually very dependent on those around him, although he would hate to admit it."

"Agreed," said Nate. "All that is true."

"We also know," said Miró, "that Diego is arrogant, and he thinks he's above the law—therefore, he doesn't see himself as a criminal."

"Accurate so far," said Nate. "While Ram Edmunds' greatest need is for sameness and predictability, Diego Montemayor's greatest need is to be admired. Diego craves admiration. That's why he went to great lengths to develop sophisticated gadgets to incinerate his victims. Those gadgets were his inventions."

"Wow—that's pretty sick," said Max.

"Well, Max, have you decided to rejoin us in our conversation, little brother?" his sister asked.

Before swallowing his last mouthful, Max smiled, but Nate continued. "Those instruments of death—which were meant for us—had to be unique, grandiose, and technologically advanced. He shows off because he *needs* admiration. He could've attempted to incinerate us a hundred different ways, but he needed to put an imprint on his choice of weapons."

"I agree with Max," said Miró. "Diego must have a twisted, psychotic mind."

"I cannot dispute that," said Nate. "Furthermore, in the same way that Diego has extreme views of himself, he also has extreme views of others. If you cross him, regardless of your previous loyalty to him, he will consider you a totally bad person—in all ways. As difficult as it may be for us to understand, Diego considers himself 'all good,' while considering his enemies 'all bad.' There are no gray areas for him."

"So," asked Max with a smile, "would you say Diego has an *epically* inflated self-image?"

Nate cleared his throat, "Let me qualify that thought. Although it may sound contradictory, Diego Montemayor—in reality—has low self-esteem. He is less than meets the eye. He is a classic narcissist."

"So, is it all about Diego in his world?" asked Max. "Me, me, me?"

"Totally."

"Well, my dear husband, although as Raquel's coaches *we* will need more coaching, how do you think we should approach this?"

"That's a laugh. This whole discussion is about you telling me how we should adjust our Pygmalion Project," said Nate. "I know you better, dearest wife, your 'gyrfalcon reasoning' is only halfway complete. And I am waiting for the 'seventh day'—as in the fall of Jericho—the seventh point of yours to see my walls of resistance tumble down."

Miró laughed and took a sip of her cappuccino. With eyes glimmering, she proceeded playfully flirting with her husband. "In the same way that Max and I approached Raquel's preparation for the meeting with Ram Edmunds, we will study how best to prepare Raquel for Diego Montemayor. What I will tell you is that like the plan for the meeting with Ram, we will attack at the heart of Diego's greatest need."

"Explain what you mean," said Nate.

Max jumped in, now fully focused on the discussion. "Nate, focus on how we prepared Raquel Rosales for Ram's meeting."

"Okay."

"The key to Raquel's preparation was acknowledging Ram's greatest need. His greatest need, according to your account, was predictability and sameness."

"Correct," said Nate. "And your solution was to shock Ram with a persona—Raquel's trained persona—that would be the opposite of his presuppositions. You actually chose to go against Ram's greatest need."

"That's exactly right, Nate. So, Miró is proposing the same strategy. Number one, what is the key for Raquel's preparation for Diego Montemayor?" Without waiting for a response from Nate, Max added, "The key is the acknowledgment of Diego Montemayor's greatest need—the need for admiration, the need to feed the grandiose feelings of self."

"Okay, if I follow you and Miró, point number two, the way to approach Diego Montemayor, is to shock him with a persona that will not fulfill his greatest need. Like Yael, his deceased wife, Raquel will challenge his expectations and instead of feeding his illusions of grandeur, will be aloof and deny him the admiration he craves."

"*Exactly*," Max emphatically stated. "His resurrected Yael—this goddess whom he idolizes—will have zero admiration and love for him!"

"Wow…wow…" Nate was speechless. "I'll have to think about this one. That's quite a plan…and a risky one."

Rising from the table, Miró said, "Boys, I have an early meeting tomorrow. Can we fully discuss this entire plan after we get a good night's rest?"

With that, the strategy session was over.

. . .

[Isle of Corsica, France; late March 2022]

"Estevan, please ask Ciccio to get my SUV ready for a drive down to Bonifacio. I'd like to treat you to an afternoon drink at the Hotel Solemare. From their bar, we can scout the various yachts coming in and out of the harbor. It's time we select one for our use." Diego had a need to bring up delicate subjects, but considering his *consigliere's* overreaction to the Lucas Williams matter, Diego was treading carefully. Though Estevan had an explosive temper, he was a good soldier, a loyal friend and associate. In fact, Diego could still trust him with his life.

Within minutes they were on their way to downtown Bonifacio. Isabella, Diego's "chambermaid," as Diego referred to her, joined them, since she also served as interpreter for Estevan. In the short time that she'd been employed by Diego, she had mastered sign language quickly, and it facilitated conversations between Diego and Estevan. "You seem more sullen than usual, Estevan. Is anything wrong?" Diego asked aboard the SUV.

Just tired. Estevan kept his signed response simple for Diego's sake.

"Is that why you skipped our *tai chi* session this morning?" Diego asked. Estevan nodded in agreement.

Isabella, who was sitting in the front with the driver, Ciccio, turned to look at Diego and said, "He's been *depresso*...has the blues, you know, *Signore?*"

"You mean depressed, Isabella—what about?" Diego inquired.

"He doesn't say, *Signore.*"

"Well, after a few drinks, we'll cheer him up," Diego said. "By the way, tell Ciccio to park by the square. I noticed you're wearing heels, so we'll take the train that the hotel provides instead of walking uphill."

The cloudless skies of a spring afternoon greeted the three as they sat at their favorite spot in the bar, which allowed them a full view of the harbor. A smiling waiter approached them and addressed Isabella first: "For the *bella donna?*" Isabella ordered a *limoncello* and Diego ordered two gin martinis for them.

Taking his first sip of his martini, Diego asked Estevan, "Out with it, my friend—why so downcast?"

Estevan took a long look at Diego and finally signed, *Our organization is not doing well.*

Although Isabella started to interpret, Diego interrupted. "It's okay; I'm following."

Estevan continued. *I know you wanted Lucas Williams eliminated...*

"So?"

He suffered stab wounds, but he survived...twice.

"The man is incarcerated. He's defenseless; how could he survive?" Diego asked. "What the devil is happening? Who are these clowns you're contracting, Estevan? Is he still in the same prison?"

All are people we've used before. People the warden recommended. Lucas is now under federal protection and has been moved. That's not all.

"What do you mean, that's not all? What more can possibly go wrong?" Diego asked.

Estevan had not touched his martini yet. Clearly upset, he signed rapidly. *When our man inside the FBI was discovered, he apparently committed suicide. He shot himself and left a horrible vacuum in the federal channels that we've controlled. He may have...*

Turning to Isabella, Diego asked, "Okay, I need your help here."

"He say that he commit suicide...our man with the American federals. A *vuoto*...how do you say...a, a..."

"You mean a void, a *vuoto*, yes?" Diego asked. "But who committed suicide, Isabella?"

Turning to Estevan, Isabella pressed for the name of the contact inside the FBI. She then turned to Diego and said, "It was H-O-M-E-L-Y...the man in FBI."

In disbelief, Diego covered his face for a long while, then asked in a whisper, "Did he leave a suicide note?"

Estevan responded. *We don't think so, but uncertain.*

Isabella started to interpret, but with a wave of his hand, Diego stated, "I understood that." Standing, Diego told Estevan to pay the tab. He then added, "Whose boat is that? The largest one out there?"

Estevan signed to Isabella as he paid the bill. Isabella followed Diego outside and said, "Estevan says it's the *Shenandoah of Sark*. He doesn't know owner."

"Tell him to buy it."

[Chicago; four months after the twins' drowning] (March 2022)

That following afternoon, approximately twenty-four hours after Ram's session with Dr. Nate Shelley, Nate and Ram drove to Winnetka to meet with Raquel Rosales. Although Ram was anxious about meeting with Mrs. Rosales—the object of his obsession— he had been persuaded by Nate that his second meeting would help "in his recovery."

Upon arrival at the Rosales mansion, Raquel greeted both men at the door. Ram, like most visitors, was overwhelmed by the size, beauty, and extravagance of the estate. Raquel smiled and asked both men for their windbreakers to hang in the guest closet. Attractive as she had seemed the previous day, Raquel appeared more relaxed, friendlier, more talkative, and even hospitable. Her long hair was down, and she wore jeans and a long-sleeved work shirt. When she noticed Ram Edmunds admiring her home's architecture, she asked if he would like a tour of the house. Embarrassed, Ram declined.

Raquel Rosales addressed Ram, "I apologize for my behavior yesterday evening, Mr. Edmunds. I'm afraid I may have given you the impression that I was aloof and distracted. I had the impression that you were reluctant to have the meeting. When you asked Mr. Kempball to come into your office without me, I assumed that you were about to dismiss both of us."

Sheepishly, Ram said, "That's perceptive of you, Mrs. Rosales. In truth, I had intended to cancel the meeting. But when I met you, I was…"

Nate interrupted. "What the special agent means, Mrs. Rosales, is that he was very impressed with you. He does believe that we should proceed with the plan, but our visit in your home will clarify certain things to him—and to me also."

"Again, I must apologize for my poor manners. Please do sit down and make yourselves comfortable." Raquel led them into the great room in the center of the downstairs floor. Each guest chose an armchair, and Raquel sat at the sofa.

"Dr. Shelley, since I've come to know your wife quite well and Max Kempball also, I'd like for you to call me 'Raquel.' And, if you're comfortable doing so, Mr. Edmunds, please do the same."

"Ahem, it may take me a while to adjust, but I'll certainly try," said Ram. "Today you seem much more relaxed, more comfortable with your surroundings. I suppose that's a silly comment to make, since you're at home, of course. But what I mean to say is that your behavior yesterday seemed guarded, maybe…"

Raquel Rosales chuckled. "Yes, I was quite nervous…and aloof, like I said. Also, Max and Miró—Mr. Kempball and Dr. Epstein-Shelley—had strict instructions for me. I was supposed to play the role of a different person, a person who is spoiled, rich, and—I'm embarrassed to say it—sexy. I'm sure I didn't do a very good job of acting sexy. I'm not very comfortable playing that kind of role."

Ram quickly interrupted, "Oh, I can assure you that you played your role very well, Mrs. Rosales. You made a huge impression on… my photographer…in fact, everyone in the office. I was very struck with your role, as you call it."

"Thank you for the compliment, Mr. Edmunds. I have much to learn."

"From what I heard," said Nate, "you were fabulous. Everyone, including Laurie, Ram's executive assistant, was extremely impressed."

"Yes," Ram chimed in. "I even mentioned your visit to my wife."

"Well, that makes me feel better. I will need six months to get prepared. Like I said, I have much to learn."

The next half hour was dedicated to breaking the ice. Nate took the lead in raising innocuous matters, such as the well-being of Raquel's sister-in-law and her children.

"Rosa María and I visit daily. She's been very good about keeping me company and checking on me constantly. Even her kids come to drop over a dessert or to share news about their school accomplishments—they're great kids."

Nate went on to raise questions about Raquel's wardrobe and how she had come to acquire such expensive tastes. Raquel responded that most articles were gifts from her deceased husband, who apparently had paid for her shopping trips to New York City and abroad. As the conversation progressed, Ram appeared more comfortable being in the presence of the *femme fatale* whom he'd met the day before. For some reason, the aura around the mystery woman had disappeared, seemingly the result of an actress stepping out of her role. He was getting to know a more casual version of the woman of beauty who had removed several masks of intrigue. Privately, Ram thought that in his many years of law enforcement, he had never encountered such a total transformation.

"So, Mrs. Rosales—or Raquel," asked Nate, "do you feel comfortable sharing the specific instructions you received in preparation for your meeting with Special Agent Edmunds?"

"Oh, no, Dr. Shelley—your wife and Max gave me strict instructions not to divulge any 'trade secrets,' as they called them. They specifically asked me never to share details about the preparation for my new persona."

"Wise counsel," said Ram. "From my perspective, you passed your first test—convincing me you can step into a fictional role."

"Raquel, this may be an appropriate point to change the direction of our chat," said Nate. "Ram and I need to also address some delicate subjects. Are you comfortable discussing those matters?"

"I can only guess what those things might be, Dr. Shelley, but nothing can be more difficult than losing my husband and two sons. And I am convinced that Rodrigo—I apologize, because I knew him only as 'Rodrigo,' but I realize now that his real name is Diego

Montemayor—is responsible for those losses. He killed my husband, and in my heart I know that he is responsible for the death of my boys. If I can do anything to bring him to justice, I will. When I lost my husband, I was left with Matt and Paul—they were all I was living for." Although Raquel was clearly a remarkably strong woman, her eyes welled up. She went on. "Now, with the loss of my twins, I would sacrifice my life if I had to."

"We promise you that we will protect you as much as possible," said Ram Edmunds. "However, we all know that Diego Montemayor is a dangerous killer."

"I am very aware, Mr. Edmunds."

"Would you use the word *hatred* to describe your feelings toward Diego?" Nate asked.

"There are no words to describe the way I feel toward that man. He revolts me; he is the most despicable human being I've ever known," said Raquel.

"Yet in playing the role of a resurrected Yael Montemayor, are you aware that you may need to entertain some of his advances? You may even find yourself in…intimate situations. Would you be able to go to that extent, since you find this man to be so hateful?" Nate asked.

"Gentlemen, I hope you can excuse me for being blunt. But if I have to play the whore in order to see that man hanging from a rope, I am determined to do it."

"I am very impressed, Mrs. Rosales," said Ram Edmunds. "Please forgive us for bringing up such unpleasant topics."

Smiling, Raquel rose from the sofa. "I have behaved so badly. I meant to offer you something to drink or perhaps some assorted cheeses, a charcuterie of sorts." From the kitchen, she added, "I haven't kept any alcohol in the house for a while except for an occasional bottle of wine. Some coffee, perhaps?"

"I would appreciate a glass of water," said Nate.

"I'll have the same," said Ram.

Raquel rolled in a serving cart with two glasses of water and a pitcher of iced tea. In the center was a platter, the charcuterie that she had mentioned. As she took some berries and drank her green tea, she asked, "If you don't mind my question, Agent Edmunds, what does 'Ram' stand for?"

"Not at all," said Ram. "My first name is Raymundo, but everyone knows me as Ram. I've been called Ram since childhood. My dad, Steven Edmunds, married a 'Mexican beauty,' as he called her. My mom's name was Larisa."

"Interesting," said Raquel. "So you're bilingual?"

"Unfortunately, I lost most of my Spanish growing up in the Midwest."

Raquel agreed, "Yes, that is unfortunate."

● ● ●

On the return to Ram's office, the two men discussed their meeting with Raquel Rosales. The meeting had been relatively short compared to Ram's initial meeting with her and Max.

"Yesterday I promised you that your obsession with Raquel Rosales was only a 'temporary glitch,' Ram. I also promised you that after our meeting today, your stress levels would be diminished."

Ram Edmunds readjusted his seatbelt and sighed deeply. "You also promised me that we would take more aggressive action if the stress levels were not diminished."

"What are you saying, Ram?"

"I am saying," said Ram with a poker face, "that you were correct. My stress level has diminished, but I need to add that I still find Raquel Rosales extremely attractive."

"What are you suggesting, Ram?"

Ram smiled. He turned to Nate and said, "You know you're a heck of a therapist. You nailed it. When I was sitting there in front of Mrs. Rosales, I realized that I had been obsessed with a persona, as you called it. She herself said it, she was playing a role—a role, by the way, that she plays very well."

"So do you think she can pull off the role of Eliza Doolittle?"

"Huh? Who's Eliza Doolittle?"

"The woman who was transformed in *My Fair Lady*, Ram."

"Oh, yeah. That's right. Eliza Doolittle. Don't know about *that* role, but she certainly can play Yael Montemayor. If anyone can convince Diego Montemayor, it will be that lady. She will need very little training," said Ram.

[Chicago; four months after the twins' drowning]
(March 2022)

That following morning Ram was up before the alarm rang. In fact, before suiting up for his morning jog, he prepared the only breakfast dish he'd mastered—his spinach frittata with bacon and cheddar—a specialty that Claire refused to prepare. Long ago she had learned to allow her husband the opportunity to surprise her on special occasions, such as Mother's or Valentine's Days. He placed the concoction in the fridge, hoping to return from his run before Claire was up to cook the breakfast in his iron skillet and then place it in the oven to finish cooking.

After his five-mile jog, he rushed back into the house, showered, and snuck into the kitchen to prepare his surprise. There were telltale signs that Claire had awakened but gone back to bed when she realized what Ram was planning. The coffeepot was on, the table was set, and even the butter dish was out. Five minutes into his preparations, Ram called out to her, "Rise and shine, my special blossom. Your breakfast is ready."

Acting appropriately surprised, Claire sat down at the table "without even having a chance to fix her hair." Ram could tell that she had brushed it earlier. She was wearing his favorite night gown, silk instead of flannel.

"And what, my dear, is the special occasion?" asked Claire. She had a smile as she savored her first sip of coffee. "Wow—you even used the perfect amount of cream!"

"No special occasion—just feel like it's a brand-new day, a day that I can look forward to," said Ram.

The bright sun coming in through the plantation shutters announced a cheerful end to the gray and misty days that Chicago had been experiencing. "The weather forecast indicates we'll have sunshine all day," said Ram. "And temperatures may rise to the mid-sixties."

"This is so enjoyable, dear. I wish we had more time, but I just want you to remember that you've got early meetings starting at 8:00 sharp. I spoke to Laurie last night, and she asked me to remind you." Claire rose to serve Ram his second cup of java.

"No, no. You sit. It's my turn to spoil you," said Ram.

Claire smiled, but she had a suspicious grin on her face. "Are you sure you don't have something up your sleeve?"

"Frankly, my dear, that's for me to know and for you to find out."

"Now you're worrying me, Ram. What's up?"

"If you must know, I believe we are due for a romantic weekend somewhere away from home…even if it's somewhere nearby. An Airbnb or something to that effect," said Ram. "I'll take care of it."

"That would be nice, dear."

●　●　●

(Evanston-Skokie, IL)

=MIRÓ=

Nate, Max, and I were discussing the menu for the Sunday family meal. Taking advantage of a brisk, invigorating sunny break in the weather, we sat around the outdoor clay *chimenea* and occasionally huddled around it to warm ourselves. The chilled breeze rustled the pine and fir cones enough for them to fall onto our wooden deck. Occasional gusts of wind caused the smaller blue firs to bend in the direction of the lake. Though we still had a few hours of daylight, we all drank hot Mexican chocolate, like the one Mom used to prepare. I referred to her written recipe because she had specified amounts of cinnamon, nutmeg, and even a tiny pinch of chili powder to create her amazing blend. Also, I carefully used the ancient wooden *molinillo*, or whisk, to achieve the proper froth. "Never give this *molinillo* up, Miró," Mom would tell me. "It's the one that your *abuelo* used when he taught me this recipe."

It was our turn to host the Sunday meal. For many years when Mom was alive, Sunday meals were hosted by my parents. Since Mom's passing, we've alternated between Dad's home and ours. Max, of course, has become Dad's chef. Although my culinary skills do not come close to the world-class cuisine that Mom prepared, I learned a thing or two from her. Max, on the other hand, has probably surpassed my own skills partly because he's had access to all her recipes. At Max's suggestion, we settled on *coq au vin* (modified Julia Child's version) for Sunday's early dinner. Max reminded me that unlike Julia, my mom always used cornstarch rather than the chicken's blood to thicken the sauce. More importantly, she waited until the chicken was done to add the Romanian pastrami, her substitute for salt pork, because she thought that if you cooked it in the sauce, the process would turn it into a soggy mess.

Two years had passed since Mom's death, but it was still fresh for me. The scar on my heart was still raw. I couldn't think of her without shedding tears. Nate said my grieving was incomplete. Only Dad can refer to her in the most natural way, as if she were alive. His casual yet firmly held belief was evident. "Well, she *is* alive, *Mi'jita*...she's very much alive." That is always Dad's response. "We believe that in our hearts," he says. "When your mom and I—and the rest of us—are reunited in the New Jerusalem, we will bask in God's presence for eternity."

Max understood. To Nate's delight, he also could now fully understand. "Where...where is this New Jerusalem?" I asked. "And when will this happen, at the end of times or immediately after our deaths? When will we be reunited with Mom?" Although I was raised by Jewish parents, I had vacillated between Judaism and Christianity. This was possibly the result of a Catholic education. However, now, like Nate had done, I wanted desperately to believe. I have a certain jealousy when Nate seems to share Dad's faith—and even Max's.

So that Saturday afternoon, when I recommended that we bring Dad into our consideration of the Pygmalion Project, Nate didn't object. He gave no outward sign that he opposed it, and he even added, "I thought by now you and Max would have brought Abraham into our discussions. From the beginning we've collaborated as a family," said Nate. "And this should be no different."

"I'm glad you agree, *mi amor*," I said. "I've been concerned about Dad."

"Concerned?" Nate put his chocolate down. Though he was jotting some notes on his electronic daily planner, he stopped. "In what way?"

"Are you aware that since Mom's death, he hasn't returned to the basement?"

"Are you serious? Why hadn't you raised that issue?" Nate asked. Nate furrowed his brow. He blinked repeatedly and bit his lip, "I should have a talk with him. How about we drop in on him this evening?"

Knowing that Dad is not fond of surprises, I called and asked if he would welcome a visit at approximately 8:00. Of course, he agreed.

When we arrived at Dad's home later that evening, Max greeted us, took me aside, and whispered, "Dad already has some ideas about the Pygmalion Project. I know how Nate dislikes adjustments to a plan, but I think the additions will strengthen it."

"I wouldn't worry too much. You'd be surprised how much Nate respects Dad's ideas," I said.

Dad and Nate walked into the kitchen and interrupted our private conversation. "Hmm," said Nate. "Already plotting against me?"

"Honey, stop that." I followed Nate to the den area. "By now you should know that we're all together on this. Max and I have given you full control and veto power over any recommendations we make. And, Dad, you'll be glad to know that Nate wants your input into this new scheme he has in mind."

As he followed us into the den, Dad asked, "Before we begin our conversation—which will take a couple of hours—I must ask about Minerva. And don't tell me that she's on a date with Cal because I know that they're no longer an item."

"You're right, Dad," I said. "They've mutually agreed that neither one is ready for a permanent commitment. My soon-to-be seventeen-year-old is already planning for college, and she is busily studying for her AP classes."

Turning to Nate, Dad said, "I must say that the little I've heard of this new plan sounds brilliant".

"Oh, I see where this is going," Nate said. "Since you plan to gang up on me later, you're buttering me up so that I can let my guard down. Then—pow!" He gestured by punching his left palm with his right fist.

"Nate, please. We're doing no such thing." I turned to Dad and said, "My dear husband fears that his well-thought-out plan will be sabotaged by us. Now he believes that we've brought you into the discussion to outnumber him some more."

"Well," Abraham said, "I can only assess all points of view and offer my honest opinions, so I'm making no promises. And I believe that you respect my integrity. If I'm brought into this discussion, I'll provide my opinion, but I'll also abide by your final judgment."

"Abraham, I like pulling my wife's leg…in truth, I adore my wife's legs," said Nate, smiling.

"Let's keep this conversation from becoming R-rated," Dad said as he chuckled while covering his ears.

"What I started to say," said Nate, "is that I welcome your opinion. Believe it or not, I also welcome Miró's…and Max's input also."

I interrupted. "We have a pressing issue before considering the Pygmalion Project."

"Is that what we're calling it—the 'Pygmalion Project'?" my dad asked.

"Yes, Dad. Originally Nate and Max conceived the whole thing, and they were already using the name when they came to me," I said.

● ● ●

CHAPTER THIRTY

[Skokie, IL; four months after the twins' drowning]
(Late March 2022)

My love, I believe I know the pressing problem you're about to present. Could I ask you to withhold any discussion of 'obstacles' until after your dad hears the plan?" Nate patted the seat next to him and gestured to Miró to join him on the sofa.

"Since you're trying so hard and since you're being so sweet presenting your request, I'll agree," Miró said with a forced smile.

Max walked in from the kitchen and offered everyone something to drink. Abraham, who remained standing in his den, accepted a glass of *tempranillo*. After pouring his dad's favorite wine, Max joined them in the den and sat on the raised hearth around the fireplace.

The four agreed to a full discussion of the Pygmalion Project. As each step of the Pygmalion Project was outlined for Abraham, everyone got another opportunity to review—and even tweak—minor points. Then Abraham summarized the discussion. "So although I'm about to vocally enumerate the major points of the sting operation, I'll ask Max to use his easel to help us see the entire summary." On cue, Max retrieved the easel from his office upstairs. "As I understand it, we need to plant in Diego's mind that his deceased wife has been resurrected. In my estimation, the easiest portion is the physical transformation. With the talents of the infamous Dr. Wu, that should offer no major challenge."

"What would you say, Abraham, is the principal challenge?" asked Nate.

"Transforming Raquel into a cultured European who studied at the Sorbonne and who is wealthy, educated, and very refined. That, my dear ones, is *one* of the major challenges," Abraham said.

Max jumped in. "Dad, that was also Ram Edmunds's worry. Well, not the only one, but the biggest one."

"And I hope that you can appreciate why, son."

"We should add, however, that Raquel carries herself well, is well educated and well read," said Max.

"Nonetheless, we can all agree that Raquel, born an American Hispanic—sheesh, has a mountain to climb, no?" asked Abraham.

Nate did his best to reassure his father-in-law. "We—principally Miró and Max—will play the role of Professor Higgins from *My Fair Lady* and prepare Raquel to take on the persona of Yael Montemayor. True, it's important that Raquel should successfully take on the role of a highly educated woman who got her collegiate training at the most prestigious French university. We acknowledge that she also must learn about European history, geography, and culture. In addition, she must master Spanish cuisine, which we understand was one of Yael's many talents."

Miró removed her reading glasses, which she was beginning to wear more often. Reluctantly she added, "And I've been biting my tongue this far. Here is the major 'pressing issue' to which I referred. We must not forget that Yael Montemayor in her youth was a famous international ballerina, a flamenco sensation in Spain."

"That, my dear daughter, will be an impossibility," said Abraham. "If you believe that Raquel Rosales will master flamenco in six months, you are sadly mistaken."

Nate, who'd been seated, stood next to the sofa. As he bit his lower lip and looked at Abraham, he asked, "Do you consider that liability a deal-breaker? Does that mean you don't believe the Pygmalion Project can work?" Nate complained, "You sound more negative than Ram Edmunds."

"That is far from what I'm saying. I believe the plan can work—with a few minor tweaks." Abraham stepped across the room to Max's easel and took a marker for the dry-erase board. "Let us all consider the following. What if we prepare Raquel Rosales as diligently as possible so that she can pass as Yael Montemayor's double? We continue with the ruse and attempt to persuade Diego Montemayor that his deceased wife is alive." There was an interrogation mark in Abraham's voice. Abraham paused a long time.

"We're all following, Abraham," said Nate, somewhat impatiently.

"So, where is your so-called tweak?" asked Max.

"The first minor tweak will entail one simple contradiction. Instead of Raquel Rosales attempting to persuade Diego Montemayor that she is indeed Yael, she will forcefully deny it. In fact, she will identify herself as a Spaniard who was raised in the US."

"But, Dad," said Miró, "it's critical that Diego *think* that Yael is alive." At this point, Miró was playing 'devil's advocate,' presenting Nate's previous objection. "He needs to be convinced that she is alive and fall in love with her—again."

"Yes, Dad," said Max. "That's the point of the Pygmalion Project. That's why Raquel, like Eliza Doolittle, will be transformed into a wealthy, cultured European. Diego, he needs to fall in love with his wife, who's been resurrected."

"All that is perfectly understood. And the plan is a good one; however, the minor tweak I am proposing," Abraham said, "will allow us some flexibility. If we have Raquel play an alluring woman of mystery, who *denies* that she is Diego's former wife, she can be allowed some imperfections. In fact, it may even help Diego be persuaded that those who kept Yael alive—namely Inspector Sánchez and Interpol—are in fact trying their best to hide the truth—by fabricating inconsistencies."

"Go on, please. Elaborate a bit more." Nate was now intrigued.

For the next five minutes Abraham suggested that Yael's impostor instead fabricate a tale about a skiing accident that in turn forced her to rehabilitate for a year in the US. Although the healing was complete, she would never be able to engage in competitive or even strenuous sports. "Inadvertent slips and contradictions to her story will only convince Diego Montemayor that 'Yael' is hiding her true identity."

"That's brilliant," said Nate. "Abraham, it may even play perfectly in Diego's case. Diego is such a narcissist that he will be convinced that his suspicions are accurate. The more that Raquel denies that she is his deceased wife, the more he will believe it. We can even have Yael's godfather, Eduardo Sánchez, forcefully assert that Yael perished in the hospital fire. Once we have successfully planted those doubts in Diego's mind, he will go with his own convictions—not anyone else's."

"I don't know," said Miró. "It seems risky."

"*Mijita*, no riskier than passing off Raquel as the real Yael. If this new version of Yael Montemayor cannot dance flamenco, if she forgets Yael's favorite wine, or if she reveals a scar unfamiliar to Diego, she simply asserts that she is her own person—and emphatically will state that she is *not* Yael Montemayor. And the minor surgical scars that might be unveiled during their courtship will be attributed to a skiing accident. In fact, the scars from the plastic surgery may explain—in Diego's twisted mind, at least—why her flamenco abilities have disappeared."

Now apparently in Abraham's corner, Nate added, "Remember that we are counting on Diego being self-centered and self-indulgent. With Diego, it is always about himself. A narcissist often gets caught up in his own grandiosity. So he often rejects opinions, and even facts, if these don't align with his own conclusions."

"Once Diego is convinced that his Yael is alive, nothing—or no one—will dissuade him," said Abraham. "Like Nate is saying, Diego possesses this self-inflated power of deduction."

"So what you're saying, Dad," said Max, "is that regardless of Raquel's denials that she is Yael, Diego will still believe it."

"Exactly, son. Once he is convinced in his mind, nothing will persuade him otherwise."

"You've convinced me, Abraham. Well done," said Nate. "However, you said earlier that you'd be proposing *a few* tweaks—plural. What else?"

"Only one more tweak. I propose that we include a genealogical component," said Abraham.

Smiling, Nate asked, "Why am I not surprised?"

"Bravo, Dad. I knew that you would introduce family histories, blood lines, that kind of thing." Max stood up and applauded. Miró and Nate good-naturedly joined in.

Taking a bow, Abraham smiled and added, "Although this should be fairly simple, it may require the cooperation of Ram Edmunds and Interpol. Given sufficient time, it can be done."

"Okay, tell us what you have in mind," said Miró as she walked over to Nate, who was now serving himself a glass of *Bermejo* that had been placed in a chiller next to the sofa.

"Do you remember what a difficult time we had tracing Diego Montemayor's genealogical past? The reason for that was that Angelo Calabrese, his biological father, had destroyed most public records to erase his connections with his son. As a member of the intelligence services, it was easy for Calabrese to destroy his son's birth records, familial ties, even educational history. Interpol was able to discover a trail only after Diego began his university studies."

"Of course. It also enabled Diego to escape the authorities so easily. He was a man with no past," said Max.

"I propose that we do the same with Raquel Rosales. Rest assured that once Diego meets this mystery woman—who could pass as his deceased wife's double—he will investigate her history, her background, her birth records. I propose that Diego should discover that his resurrected Yael—the new Eliza Doolittle— will have no public records anywhere. The only records he will find will be the records of his deceased wife."

"Brilliant," said Nate. "It will further convince Diego that Interpol and Eduardo Sánchez—those whom he will assume rescued Yael from the hospital fire—are also the ones responsible for creating this fictional persona, who, incidentally, has no personal records."

At this point, Abraham sat in his favorite easy chair. "Like I said, these tweaks will give our Pygmalion Project greater flexibility."

CHAPTER THIRTY-ONE

**[Chicago North Shore; four to eleven
months after the twins' drowning]
(Late March–Early October 2022)**

From late March through the spring and the end of summer, Raquel Rosales endured the most stressful and intensive period of her life. Nate and Miró dedicated the collegiate spring break to the design of a curriculum that would ensure a strong preparation for Raquel's transformation. Acknowledging that she would need at least three weeks to recover from the initial facial surgeries, they developed a complete curriculum that would include more "pragmatic" areas like dining etiquette, culinary skills, and general European demeanor and customs. In addition, Nate and Miró compiled a more "academic" set of modules on European history, art, music, and literature, with a concentration on Spanish culture and the French language.

Max himself, on the other hand, received several weeks of intensive preparation on the culinary customs in Europe with a concentration on Spanish and Mediterranean cuisine. He asked to be taught the basic recipes of the Canary Islands also. To take on the role of the culinary expert, Max needed to be formally instructed to pass on to Raquel the cooking skills needed. For this instruction, Nate requested the help of Interpol to contract the best culinary experts available. Four famous chefs—Aitor Zabala, Yottam Ottolenghi, Martín Berasategui, and Alain Ducasse—each dedicated a week to Max's instruction.

In addition, Nate asked Inspector Eduardo Sánchez to accumulate all the photographs and videos of Yael Montemayor that he could obtain. By the third week in April, Nate's training team was ready to begin.

Naturally, Nate had enlisted the help of countless resources, such as a handful of Miró's Northwestern University colleagues, the European chefs recommended and hired by Interpol, and FBI trainers and "consultants" provided by Ram Edmunds. In addition, a team of post-op and aftercare nurses were hired, based on recommendations from Abraham Epstein, to handle all aspects of Raquel Rosales's physical care—such as pain management, emptying drains, changing wound dressings, applying heat or cold packs, and acting as liaison with Dr. Wu to update prescription and care instructions.

After lengthy consultation with Dr. Ivo Wu, it was determined that to "sculpture a Yael Montemayor" who was six years older than the one that Diego knew, only facial procedures with slight bone reconstruction and body contouring would be needed. No limb or skeletal reconstruction was necessary; however, very minor breast reduction would be needed to approximate Yael's bosom shape. Because Yael Montemayor had not borne children, Raquel Rosales would require minor body contouring procedures that would reduce her lower body curvature.

During the first week of the post-operative phase, Raquel's recovery was extensive and painful. She woke during the middle of the night with sharp pains and twice had her prescriptions changed to control the pain. In addition, the wound care was ongoing. With drainage constantly occurring, Raquel was concerned about the scarring. Thanks to the 24/7 aftercare nurses, Raquel was satisfied that everything was being done in accordance with Dr. Wu's orders.

Scarring was negligible and her discomfort was minimized. Because Raquel did not require a facelift or a neck lift, and because there was no need for rhinoplasty, the recovery process was shortened. She underwent some eyelid and brow lifts in addition to cheek and jaw enhancements, but within two weeks, Raquel asked Nate and Miró to begin their training. Though the nurses' care continued, primarily to alleviate the breast reduction and body contouring surgery aftereffects, the pupil proved to be not only a courageous and tough patient but also an extremely fast learner. After the eighth week following the surgery, Raquel Rosales proclaimed that she was fully recovered, although Dr. Wu ordered the nurse care to continue for at least two more weeks just in case any recurring problems arose.

. . .

Raquel Rosales's training had a rigorous daily schedule starting with the "academic" portion during the morning. The more "pragmatic" training took place in the afternoons and evenings. Nate's training team chose dining etiquette to be the first topic of pragmatic instruction, since they had observed Raquel as a hostess in various other situations, including a dinner at the Shelley home. They correctly assumed it would be the easiest part of the training. Raquel Rosales evidently had either received solid training at home or picked up most table manners along the way. Miró decided to concentrate on the differences between Continental and American styles regarding the proper handling of utensils, place settings, and order of seating at a formal dinner.

Raquel was surprisingly open about her own personal doubts regarding table manners. She inquired, "Miró, here in America I've been to rather formal gatherings where even the hostess will use a knife to break her bread roll. Is this ever appropriate?"

"Great question, Raquel. As far as I know, it is not. However, we tend to be more informal in the US, but to stay on the safe side, in Europe use your fingers to break bread, never your knife."

"Thank you," said Raquel. "I have another question regarding the passing of dishes at the table. Is it ever proper to pass to the left?"

"Never. And whenever you pass a gravy boat or any kind of jug, do so with the handle toward the recipient."

Raquel commented, "So glad you anticipated my next question because it does not always happen in our country. In addition," asked

Raquel, "when I do my table settings, I'm not certain what to do with oyster or seafood forks."

"Because I'm a fan of oysters, Raquel, I can help with this one," said Nate. "As you know, forks are always on your left and knives and spoons on your right. However, there is one exception. Oyster and seafood forks will always appear on your right, next to the soup spoon. You as a hostess are also tipping off your guests regarding the order of your serving."

Miró applauded her husband. "Funny, but my dear husband rarely pays attention to place settings, order of seating, or even the order of wine glasses. Which brings to mind, are you comfortable with your knowledge of order of seating at a formal dinner?"

With a smile, Raquel, looking like a proud pupil, said, "Pretty sure that I've got that, although I don't have much experience hosting truly formal dinner parties. If I'm not mistaken, the male guest of honor sits at the hostess's right. And the female guest of honor will sit on the host's right. Am I correct?"

"Yes, you've got it, Raquel. Did you learn all this at home?" asked Miró.

"My mom had high aspirations for me, Miró. She enrolled me in all kinds of Emily Post trainings, and I recall most of those lessons. My husband, Macario, made fun of me because he claimed that all that—expletives blank, blank—was stuff that people didn't do anymore."

"Do you have any other questions, Raquel?" Miró asked.

"I can think of one more. What happens if I spill something on the table...or on myself?" Raquel asked.

"Use your napkin or ask the waiter if there is one for some sparkling water. Do not, and I say this because I've seen so many people do this, dip your napkin in your water glass to clean up the mess."

"Thanks," said Raquel. "I think I've got it."

"Well," said Nate, "I hate to bore you with more of this, but just in case, we'll still review basic manners and dining etiquette. We'll cover dos and don'ts of behavior at the table; passing dishes and food around the table; your posture and customs; formal table settings; knowing how to use your napkin; using your wine glasses correctly and in the right order; pacing yourself; and since Europeans seem to be stricter than we are, avoiding taboo conversation topics."

Miró added, "One thing that Nate forgot was the tricky subject of being left-handed. Since Yael was left-handed, you'll need to handle being a left-handed diner. Also, since most Europeans, and certainly Diego Montemayor and his colleagues, tend to consume prodigious amounts of wine, not only holding the different wine glasses but also using the correct glasses for the various wines will become very important."

For the next seventy-two hours Nate and Miró handled the training related to dining etiquette. The modules that were designed to be presented over an entire week were completed in three days.

Next on the agenda, Max Kempball approached Raquel to serve as primary instructor for the culinary skills portion. Only one of the four chefs who instructed Max remained in the States. Prior to returning to Europe, Berasategui served as the final judge to assess Raquel's learned skills—and to supervise Max's own missteps. Surprisingly, this portion of the training was one that presented a small challenge to the talented pupil.

Although Raquel Rosales was considered a good cook, her culinary skills consisted of primarily Mexican and American dishes. Because the hallmarks of Mediterranean cuisines include the use of robust wines, basil, briny capers, rich olive oils, and various types of citrus and dried fruits, Raquel was forced to adapt to the preparation of dishes with vastly different ingredients. The seafoods, vegetables, and meats combined with these ingredients offered different twists to the regional dishes to which Raquel was accustomed. The consulting chefs recommended to Max that he clearly present to Raquel the various approaches to Mediterranean cooking. The result was a preparation that differentiated among the unique twists of Spanish, Italian, Greek, French, Moroccan, and Israeli cuisines. In the end, Raquel announced to Nate and Miró that Max had enjoyed his teaching more than the pupil had.

"Because Diego favored Mediterranean cuisine over the dishes of the Canary Islands," Max said, "we've dedicated much time to that style. Of course, we need to spend at least four or five days to the preparation of some fundamental Canarian dishes that, as far as Inspector Sánchez remembers, Diego approved of."

"Such as?"

Max referred to his notes. "Sánchez specifically mentioned a few main dishes from the Canary Islands and some desserts. In the first category you'll learn to prepare *Papas Arrugadas*, *Adobo de Cerdo*, *Sancocho Canario*, and *Ropa Vieja*. For dessert, Diego also appeared to enjoy the *Queso de Cabra* prepared with Tenerife's honey, which came from a plant grown on Mt. Taide's volcano."

"Is that it for Canarian cuisine?" Raquel inquired.

"Oops, almost forgot one that Sánchez himself liked. It's a dessert known as *Bien Mesabe*, a puree of almonds, egg yolk, sugar, lemon zest, and cinnamon. It's served with heavy cream or ice cream."

After more than three weeks of intense culinary training, Raquel reached "acceptable-level" quality—according to the consulting chef—with several specialties. Her specialties were Spanish tapas and paella, Israeli vegetarian delights, the tastes of Tuscany, Marrakech Tajine dishes, Spanakopita and Baklava, as well as panna cotta with chocolate ganache. In a moment of inspiration, Raquel inquired of Sánchez, "Can you recall any particular dish that was Yael's own favorite—not particularly favored by Diego but by Yael herself?"

Within minutes the retired inspector responded by instant message: "Great question, Raquel. Yael had learned of a family recipe that had been brought over from the New World from her great-grandmother. It was a recipe for *capirotada*, a Mexican bread pudding that became a family recipe passed on from generation to generation."

"I will master it," Raquel said. "Thank you."

To no one's surprise, Max gained eleven pounds during his teaching assignment. Raquel was told that to achieve "master level," she would simply repeat the recipes four times a week for the next several months. Raquel agreed to accept that kind of rigor only if Sánchez chose eight dishes for her ongoing, master-level training. Within three days Sánchez responded with his eight top choices.

The ongoing "academic" portion of the training went very smoothly.

Raquel devoured most of the education, except for the historical intricacies of pre-nineteenth century European history. She wisely concentrated on Spanish history and at least a passing knowledge of French and Spanish political relations since Yael had lived and studied in Paris at the Sorbonne.

Fortunately, Raquel had a fairly good background in spoken French. Not much time was dedicated to the French language, except for recorded lessons on fluidity and conversational usage. It was not until shortly after the Fourth of July celebration that Raquel encountered her first serious roadblock.

Arriving on a Monday, Inspector Eduardo Sánchez announced that he would stay in Chicago for three days. The assessment, he said, would be thorough but quick. Upon meeting Raquel Rosales, the inspector was astounded.

"*Increíble y asombrante*," said Inspector Sánchez. At a loss for words, the inspector simply exclaimed that the resemblance to his goddaughter, Yael Montemayor, was beyond comparison, without equal—"*sin par*." In private, he did share with Nate and Miró that he'd discovered a "minor physical flaw." "My Yael," he whispered in Spanish, "had a very slight overbite, which gave her a somewhat sexy, aristocratic look—very appealing, actually."

Much more concerning, however, was Inspector Sánchez" assessment of Raquel's Spanish language skills. Although Raquel considered her Spanish to be more than adequate, when Inspector Eduardo Sánchez arrived in early July, he objected immediately. After a ninety-minute "examination session," Inspector Sánchez provided feedback. Before presenting his assessment to Nate and Miró, he spoke briefly to Raquel. He informed Raquel that her general language skills needed much improvement. His recommendation, he said, would be to concentrate on the improvement of Raquel's Spanish accent, enabling Raquel to speak like a native Spaniard.

Raquel Rosales complained to Inspector Sánchez. Since she felt confident in her Spanish dialect, Raquel told her examiner, "Señor Sánchez, I've traveled extensively in Europe, and no European—certainly no Spaniard—has criticized my Spanish."

Always a gentleman, Inspector Sánchez patiently responded, "That's because your Spanish is quite good. However, I can guarantee you that every Spaniard can detect that you are a Latin American speaking Spanish—proper Spanish but not Castilian. Since my goddaughter was a Spaniard, it will be necessary for you to master certain pronunciations."

"Such as?" said a defensive Raquel.

"Although I'm not a linguist, I can give you some specific telltale signs. For instance, the way you pronounce the letter *z* in Spanish sounds exactly like the letter *s* in the English word *sun*. But my Yael, my goddaughter, pronounced the letter *z* like the *th* in English words like *theater* or *thing*. Her husband, Diego Montemayor, also uses the same pronunciation. I believe it's called *distinción* by linguists."

Somewhat annoyed, Raquel complained, "I suppose I've always considered such pronunciations a sign of…affectation or pretentiousness on the part of some Spaniards."

"Not at all, Raquel," said Sánchez, "In southern Spain and the Canary Islands, for example, we pronounce 'gracias' as 'grasyas,' while the rest of Spain will pronounce it 'grathyas.'"

"I thought you'd said that *distinción* applies only to the letter *z*. But *gracias* is spelled with a *c*," Raquel said.

Somewhat embarrassed, Sánchez added, "Your instructors will teach you more efficiently than I can, Raquel, but in addition to the letter *z*, which is always pronounced as a *th*, a letter *c* when it comes before an *i* or an *e* is also pronounced as a *th*."

"Forgive me for my skepticism, but now I do realize that I'll need to brush up on such things," said Raquel. "Any other glaring telltale signs?"

"Now that you bring that up," Sánchez said with a smile, "I noticed you use the word *jugo*, but my *ahijada*, my goddaughter, would use the word *zumo*, as in *zumo de naranja*. Also, you referred to your *carro*, but Spaniards will use the word *coche* to refer to your car. And when you told me that you drove to get here, you used the word *manejar* instead of *conducir*, as a Spaniard would say. Although the word *manejar* is used in Spain, it is limited to 'managing' a business or an enterprise."

"Wow—I definitely agree that my word choice in those instances would be very telling. Can you think of any other glaring ones?" Raquel was now taking notes.

Sánchez replied, "Oh, I will leave that to your instructors, but tell them to concentrate on differences in word usage, specifically the distinctions between Latin Americans and Spaniards…. Oh, yes, another word choice that clearly stood out for me was your referral to your *computadora* to refer to your computer, which in most of Latin America would be fine."

"What would a Spaniard have said?"

"We in Spain would use the word, *ordenador*. And we prefer to say *móvil* rather than *celular* when we speak of our cell phones. My duty is to ensure that you sound exactly like Yael Montemayor, and your pronunciation and word choice will be noticeable," said the inspector. After pausing and taking a deep breath, he said, "Also, and sorry to bombard you in this manner, you must speak a little faster. My countrymen—and women—speak faster and from the diaphragm."

"What do you mean 'from the diaphragm'?" Raquel asked.

"I believe that one of the first things that people notice when they travel to Spain is how Spaniards seem to speak not only fast but forcefully, as if they are forcing air from their lungs. Your language trainers will know when you mention it," said Sánchez.

"Anything else?" asked a frustrated Raquel.

"Please don't take offense, Mrs. Rosales. I am merely doing my best to prepare you before you confront a dangerous criminal who is no fool. If he is to be deceived, it must be a flawless ruse—or 'sting operation,' as *Señor* Kempball calls it."

"I'm sorry if I sound defensive, Inspector."

Eduardo Sánchez smiled. "I've prepared a list of things that I will recommend to your trainers. When I return in six weeks, I will concentrate on those items."

"Can I see the list?" Raquel extended her hand. When she started reading the list, which was lengthy, she exclaimed, "Oh, my…is my Spanish that bad?"

"Not at all, like I said. These items are primarily things that may trip you up, rather than the most obvious concentration on the academic instruction."

"But there must be…what…two hundred items here." Raquel went on to read a few. "You ask, 'How do you pronounce the letter *v* in Spain?' I did not know there was difference."

"The letter *v* is pronounced *uve*," said Sánchez.

"You also list *bolígrafo* versus *pluma*. Isn't *pluma* used in Spain?"

"In Spain we would use *bolígrafo*. Only in Latin America is a pen a *pluma*," Sánchez said.

"And I suppose the same applies to *nevera* versus *refrigerador*?" Raquel asked. Before waiting for an answer, she added, "And the word for *peach* is not *durazno* in Spain—it's *melocotón*, eh?"

"That's correct." Sánchez was smiling.

Raquel continued: "Miró and Nate's academic portion of the training is concentrating on the arts, the history, the music and the politics of Spain, but are you saying these common mistakes are the 'giveaways,' the things that will trip me up?"

"Not exclusively, Mrs. Rosales," said the inspector. "Nate and Miró are correct. They want to give you the learning with which Yael was familiar. Diego also is well read and extremely bright. Yet I believe it's the little things that can tip off someone who is testing your story," said the inspector.

To Raquel's dismay, Nate immediately contacted Gabriel Picard. He informed him that his good friend, Inspector Eduardo Sánchez, was not satisfied with Raquel's preparation. Nate asked Picard to secure the services of the best linguist that he could find who could coach Raquel in the use of Spanish like a native Spaniard.

. . .

Professor Miguel Peñate arrived two days later. A noted scholar from the *Real Academia* in Madrid, he immediately attacked his task with diligence and precision. Not only was he able to address every single item in Inspector Sánchez's list, but he also added his own points of conversational Spanish that "transformed" Raquel Rosales into Yael Montemayor within two weeks. Because the scholar's leave of absence was short, he insisted that his portion of the training take priority and that Nate should postpone the rest of the training while he concentrated on his intense Castilian instruction. He also recommended that Raquel use every spare moment to listen to recordings of Spaniards in real conversations. He also recommended countless Spanish films that would fill Raquel's free time.

When Inspector Sánchez returned six weeks later, Raquel passed her examination with flying colors. Not only was Raquel able to impress the inspector, but she also delicately corrected the inspector in a few Castilian peculiarities, namely the use of the informal pronoun *vosotros*. When Raquel invited the training team as well as Inspector Sánchez to an informal luncheon in her home, she surprised Sánchez by using the irregular conjugation of accompanying verbs: *"¿Qué os gusta comer?"*

"Wow!" responded Max, "That's a form I had not heard. Is that the formal way of addressing us all? Does that mean, 'What would you like to eat?'"

"Yes, that's what it means," Raquel said, "but it's the informal use of a pronoun rarely used outside of Spain."

Miró was impressed. "We'll need to brush up on that one and be tested by you now, Raquel."

"Tenéis que estudiar mucho para el exámen," Raquel replied with a laugh. "For your benefit, Max, that means, 'You all have to study a lot for the exam.'"

"I think I've got it," said Max. "It's the Castilian way of saying 'y'all.'"

Laughing, Inspector Sánchez said, "Indeed it is, Mr. Kempball. Indeed it is."

● ● ●

PART FOUR

THE DECEPTION

*"The supreme art of war is to
subdue the enemy without fighting."*

SUN TZU

CHAPTER THIRTY-TWO

[Jerusalem; six months into the Pygmalion Project]
(October 2022)

That particular Friday was a crisp early-autumn day in Jerusalem and Professor Ari Weiss was looking forward to enjoying the small pleasures in life before sundown, like enjoying a stroll in a blossom-filled, solitary garden, having an ice cream while seated at a park bench, or listening to his favorite music on his iPods. "Time to relax, Professor. Leave all the fretting and combativeness to the Americans," said his Palestinian colleagues at the center, "but let us all enjoy this golden fall afternoon."

Mustafa Yavuz, a Turkish research assistant who greatly admired his mentor and teacher, said, "Yes, let's give thanks that we were not born 'privileged,' Professor Weiss. Go out and enjoy yourself."

Not all his colleagues, however, considered Professor Weiss harmless. Through the years, he'd given enough people reason to both admire and question his writings. It was not clear to critics how one so outspoken could escape the wrath of governmental "fact-checkers." Professor Weiss's strength, however, was his ability to raise questions without accusing any perpetrator of wrongdoing. He remained objective and thorough in his research.

His legion of detractors, of course, were not all scholars. Many journalists, international critics, and political figures spoke against the "dangerous teachings" of the brilliant scholar. Members of the intelligence agencies in the US and Western Europe discredited his viewpoints.

Weiss not only had been educated at Oxford but also had taught at Cambridge. Presently, in addition to running the Center for Middle Eastern Peace Studies, he also taught at The Hebrew University of Jerusalem. Rarely did Professor Weiss engage in didactic or prescriptive dialogue; however, nervous nellies from all walks of life feared his "exposés" because he was willing to publish what compromised journalists diligently avoided. Nonetheless, heads of state often secretly consulted his publications to collect the wealth of historical and authoritative perspectives on global developments. It was rumored that even the Vatican monitored closely what he had to say.

Dr. Weiss employed three scholars in residence at the Center for Middle Eastern Peace Studies. In addition, he was also assisted by five graduate researchers of various political leanings. Simply put, the professor sought out the best minds and the best writers who had an interest in unraveling convoluted political statements made by politicians. He focused on separating propaganda from truth. Each passing day the task became more difficult.

In one of his latest publications, Weiss questioned why a Middle Eastern theocracy, a sworn enemy of the US, could invite so much financial and political support from the current American administration. A sworn political independent, Professor Weiss had simply posed the question, but the retaliation from the left-wing American administration, as well as "woke" supporters throughout the world, had been immediate and vicious. As a result, the professor attracted plenty of disapproval and even censorship.

As the center's director, he had also published numerous authoritative reports and articles criticizing the threats posed by militant jihadists inside Europe's borders. His most recent book documented that Europe was under a systematic assault of jihadist Islam. Not only did he document the rapid increase in Muslim immigration, but he also published interviews of countless immigrants who had been questioned by government authorities. According to Weiss's data, the plan of these immigrants was to make Islamic law, or "sharia," reign supreme in all of Europe. Without commenting on the benefits or dangers of these developments, Professor Weiss simply published the documentation.

The recently elected American administration called his writings "white supremacist nonsense." "Hysterical racism," said others. Most journalists suggested that Dr. Weiss "and all his researchers at the center" were inciting violence and general opposition to non-white people seeking asylum. They argued that the recent influx of minority Muslims required not hateful rhetoric but tolerance and dialogue. The irony, said Professor Weiss, is that it was his publications that were being taken down from the Internet and removed from bookshelves, not the veiled physical threats against him. "By all means we need tolerance and dialogue—but not censorship," he stated.

Soon imams in the US and Europe were calling for dealing with people like the professor very severely. They went on to suggest that loyal Muslim martyrs should step forward and complete the task of "religious obligation." Instead of condemning these statements, members of Spanner's American administration obliquely recommended that the professor go into hiding.

At thirty minutes past ten in the morning, Ari Weiss heard a faint knock and looked up to find one of his scholars-in-residence, Sanura Gamal, leaning against the doorjamb. She placed a pile of files on his desk. She was part secretary, part brilliant researcher and office manager. More often she served as "mother hen," a trait she had learned from her Egyptian mother.

"I hate to disappoint you, but you have a busy Friday, Professor. You will be interviewed by *Al Jazeera* here in your office at 12:30 p.m., so you will need more than coffee in your tummy."

"Is it the same journalist that called me a dangerous right-wing conspiracist last year?"

"Of course not. It's Benjamin Green. The reporter who called you names would not have made it through my gatekeeping," Sanura said with reassuring emphasis.

His efficient colleague stood over him and started straightening his desk. "Remember that after the interview you will go straight to the local TV station to appear in their 'Celebrities Today' show. They will dispatch a limo to collect you."

"You mean the 'Celebrities Unmasked' show, don't you? That host believes that his only job is to 'unmask,' embarrass, and humiliate his guests." The professor scratched his head, muttering to himself, "Why I agreed to the skewering, I don't know."

After the unpleasant mid-day interview with the young reporter from *Al Jazeera*, the professor wolfed down a bagel toast sandwich with feta cheese, green olives, and a side of hummus that Sanura had prepared for him. At a quarter before two, the professor walked out of his office and headed toward the black Jaguar limo that was sent by WXBS to deliver him to its studio.

As he approached the TV station, a gaggle of reporters was there to document the arrival of the celebrity about to be maligned. With his shock of gray hair and customary gray tweed jacket over khaki slacks, he was one of the most recognizable celebrity-scholars in the country. Behind the photographers, leaning against the white brick wall, were two young Middle Eastern males dressed in oversized denim jackets. A third member of the trio was resting his feet and smoking his Turkish cigarette in a crouched position. As Professor Weiss approached, the youngster tossed his foul-smelling cigarette to the curb and, staring at the professor, assumed the position of an American major league baseball catcher ready to receive a pitch from his pitcher.

Thinking the young man was asking for his attention, Professor Weiss stopped and asked, "Excuse me—are you addressing me?"

Smiling, the crouched young man said in a loud voice, "A swing and a miss." His other two companions leaning against the wall broke out in laughter. The professor turned around and entered the building.

At the end of the first twenty minutes of the TV interview, Weiss realized the TV host was behaving in a restrained and civil manner. Despite some condescending remarks related to the sordid history of the Western world's hatred of non-white civilizations, the show ended with some good-natured banter regarding political hypocrisy.

Exiting the TV studio, the professor realized that the limo that had transported him to the studio was unceremoniously dismissed. It meant the professor would need to find his own way home.

Just as well, he thought. *I still have a few hours of daylight left. On this day I will sit at my favorited café across the park and read.*

Walking across the lush gardens of the park situated across from the TV station, he was reminded of his grandmother's fondness of hibiscus. Vibrant bushes bordered the central elevated platform, which often attracted political speeches and declarations. The bright orange cornet blossoms of the hibiscus took him back fifty-five years when he watched "Bubbe," his amazing grandmother, planting and transplanting her blooms in the greenhouse. She had an amazing green thumb, one that produced an impressive array of thriving vegetation in a semi-arid and inhospitable climate. The crisscrossing paths of the park were lined with a double rank of jasmine and taller lavender. The professor stooped merely to inhale the crisp scent of the Mediterranean plants. *I would have been denied this treat if the station's limo had delivered me back home,* he thought. Inhaling deeply one more time, he pinched some rosemary leaves and brought them to his nostrils to continue enjoying this olfactory feast.

As he crossed the cobblestone street, he caught the familiar whiff of Turkish tobacco that he had smelled two hours prior. Professor Weiss stepped onto the curb of the Café Alkalay. The tobacco stench dissipated. He approached the maître d' station of the sidewalk portion of the café. Although he had not frequented the establishment located in the Armenian Quarter in years, the maître d' recognized him.

"Professor Weiss! How nice to see you again!"

He was promptly situated at his favorite spot of the café. From that perspective he had a magnificent view of his favorite park, the one he called "Bubbe's Garden." The crosswalks of the park, crushed red granite walkways that approached the center of the park from each of the four corners, were lined with a mixture of annuals and perennials—hostas, pomegranate blossoms, and desert roses. Front and center of the park, situated on a five-foot concrete pedestal, was a massive replica of the Knesset Menorah Monument. At the base of the pedestal was a bronze plaque that described the rich history of the state of Israel and how it was influenced by the formation of the Knesset. Surrounding the monument was the most awe-inspiring, multi-colored rose garden this side of paradise.

To the left of the park, the steeple of the Greek Catholic Cathedral peered above the large cypress trees that spread a canopy over the gardens. The central steeple soared a couple of hundred feet into the air, and beneath its supporting arch hung a large bell at the center of the façade. Although the central elevation spread the full breadth of the church, Professor Weiss only had a partial view of the entire limestone front. The two-hundred-year-old cypresses blocked part of his view and provided a welcome shade for even part of the café. At either end of the cathedral also hung smaller bells that would toll in consonance with the central one. Thrice daily the bells would announce to parishioners the arrival of each midday as well as at six o'clock, morning and afternoon. Only for funerals would the bells be rung half-muffled.

Directly opposite the church, and to the right of the professor's perspective, sat the magnificent structure of the Chinese embassy, which had just moved from Tel Aviv. It dominated the view on that right side of the park since the tinted glass structure seemed to reflect the image of the cathedral on its soaring mirror-like exterior twin towers. It was the structure that most resembled a skyscraper in the city of Jerusalem. Unfortunately, it lent a garish blue hue to a cityscape that was dominated by a more subdued architecture, which in Professor Weiss's estimation, provided a "visual eloquence" much better suited to the region's culture.

After ninety minutes the professor finally acknowledged his accommodating server, who had inquired more than once if he needed more than coffee. He decided to order a glass of *albariño* accompanied by a cheese board. Rarely did he drink alone, but he'd decided he would summon Sanura, his assistant, after one glass. He would then offer to treat her to a relaxing dinner near the center's headquarters.

Before the *cheese board* arrived at his table, the Greek Cathedral's bells began tolling. *That's funny*, thought Professor Weiss. *It is not six o'clock yet—and the bells have been partially muffled.*

Just then, two red Ducati motorcycles stopped at the café's curb-side. Three individuals wearing oversized denim jackets and black helmets walked up to his table. The middle one took off his helmet and grinned. In his best imitation of a star baseball pitcher, he reared back, and one of his partners handed him a Molotov cocktail. Before tossing the homemade weapon, he exclaimed in perfect English, "You're out!"

Professor Weiss saw the long-necked projectile coming in his direction. He tried to evade the incendiary device, but the detonation was instantaneous. According to newspaper publications the next morning, the death toll amounted to six, including the professor, the maître d', and one of the assailants.

CHAPTER THIRTY-THREE

[Jerusalem; six months into the Pygmalion Project]
(October 2022)

Upon hearing of Professor Ari Weiss's murder, Nate and Miró decided to travel to Jerusalem the following day. Nate wanted to be present for any funeral or memorial services that would be organized for the professor. Not only did he recognize Ari Weiss as his spiritual mentor, but Nate considered him a friend. Miró had joined Nate in various Zoom conversations with the professor, but she had never met him or the rest of the center staff.

Yosef Peretz had telephoned Nate the same evening when he received the terrible news. When Yosef learned that Nate wanted to be present at the professor's memorial services, Peretz insisted that he and his wife would host Nate and Miró while they stayed in Jerusalem. Nate protested that he did not want to impose on Yosef's family, but Yosef declared that he and Mrs. Peretz would consider it a serious affront if they chose other lodging. Nate accepted, not realizing that his encounter with the rest of Yosef's family would unlock the portals to a deep and dark enigma that extended to Diego Montemayor's cartel.

Nate and Miró landed in Tel Aviv late in the evening. Yosef was waiting at the exit leading to the parking lot, and after loading the luggage and his passengers, he transported them immediately to his Jerusalem home. Loni Peretz was waiting for them when they arrived and offered them refreshments and some light evening fare. She was a young, pleasantly plump lady who seemed to enjoy baking, given the assorted offerings and the aroma of cinnamon in her kitchen. She obviously also took pride in growing orchids, which were present in every room of their cozy and serene two-story house. Sitting on the Peretz balcony, they briefly chatted about their flight and Professor Weiss's memorial events for the next few days. Within two hours after their arrival in Jerusalem, Nate and Miró were in the guest bedroom sound asleep.

Nate woke early the following morning despite the jet lag. For some reason, he had a nagging sense that he had met Mrs. Peretz previously. It was a feeling of familiarity, of déjà vu, that puzzled him. When Miró woke, she found Nate sitting on the bench at the foot of the bed. His crunched-up brows, the narrowing of his eyes, and the slight tilt of his head told her that her husband was struggling to make a connection. Yawning and sitting up, she asked, "What is it, honey?…Couldn't sleep?"

"It's not that…I just have this impression that I've met Mrs. Peretz before. Of course, that's unlikely, unless…"

Putting her robe on, Miró asked, "Unless what, honey?" Not getting a response, Miró asked, "Would you like me to go downstairs and bring you back a cup of coffee…you think they drink coffee?"

"No, no—wait for me and we'll both go down after we clean up." Chuckling, he shuffled to the small bathroom, joining Miró at the double sink. "You know, I've presented a couple of papers on this phenomenon, but none of my conclusions fit what I'm experiencing."

Miró rinsed her mouthful of toothpaste, and she asked, "What phenomenon—what are you talking about, honey?"

"This déjà vu I'm experiencing. It's as if I've talked to Loni Peretz before," said Nate.

After twenty minutes the Shelleys met their hosts downstairs for breakfast. The aromas of freshly baked bread and pastries beckoned them to the breakfast table. The couple's two daughters, ages four and three, were seated at the table, but they immediately rose to greet their guests. Loni Peretz told both girls, "These are good friends from America. Please welcome them to our home."

In unison they smiled and sang, "Good morning, Dr. Nate and Dr. Miró. Welcome to our residence." Then the older child said, "I am Sarah." "Me, I am Tamar," said the three-year-old.

Walking into the breakfast area, Yosef said, "You may sit back down, girls." Turning to Miró, he asked, "Were you able to rest well?"

"Indeed, we did," said Miró, "But I must say how impressed we both are with your children. I can see you are educating them well."

Loni Peretz was already at the table serving coffee for the adults. "I hope you enjoy strong coffee," she said. "Yosef and I prefer very dark roasts, so let me know if we need to adapt to your tastes."

"From experience I can tell you, my dear, that Nate likes his coffee strong, just like I do," said Yosef. "However, I cannot speak for you, Miró. Please let us know."

"This is a delicious brew—thank you," said Miró.

For the next forty minutes the two families enjoyed an assortment of *bourekas*—cheese and fruit-filled—which Loni had been told was Nate's favorite pastry. In addition, she had prepared a platterful of chocolate *rugelach*, which was Yosef's preference. Both types of pastries were a hit. While Nate and Yosef dominated the conversation for the first ten minutes, Loni then inquired about Miró's familiarity with Israel and about her background. Yosef had informed her that although Miró's parents had Sephardic Jewish heritage, Miró had converted to Catholicism. Somewhat embarrassed, Miró admitted that because of the Catholic schooling she had growing up, she had become skeptical of her Jewish background. Later she had become skeptical of all faiths. Although not agnostic, Miró said she could not identify as one or the other. As a family, they worshiped in the Catholic church for the sake of providing stability for Minerva, their daughter. She added that Nate's recent spiritual conversion was fascinating to her because she saw the radical transformation that Nate had undergone.

While Loni cleared the table, Yosef asked her to leave the dishes in the sink. He offered to do the dishes and then dismissed Sarah and Tamar. They politely excused themselves and ran outside for some play time in their small backyard.

"Yes, we are a unique family, Loni," said Nate. "My father-in-law grew up as an orthodox Jew, but he has recently become Messianic. My brother-in-law is a devout Christian, and I recently underwent a salvation experience, thanks to Professor Ari Weiss."

"And I," said Miró, "well, I'm sort of stuck in the middle."

"Don't feel bad," said Loni. "I resisted God's call for many years. Thanks to my husband, my life has been transformed. He was patient with me."

"Forgive me if I'm out of line," said Nate, "but I woke up with a distinct impression that I had met you before. I know it's virtually impossible, but I didn't meet you in my previous two visits to Israel, did I, Mrs. Peretz?"

Yosef and Loni exchanged amused looks. Loni answered with a huge smile, "Yes and no. I am not the same person you met some years ago. I go by 'Loni,' but my real name is Álana…" Loni Peretz paused, not knowing if the name would jar Nate Shelley's memory.

Still perplexed, Nate shook his head. Obviously Nate did not recall the name Álana. Nate bit his lower lip; he tapped his fingertips on the olive wood breakfast table and rested his forehead on his free hand. "No, I simply can't remember the occasion, Mrs. Peretz."

Leaving Loni alone so that she could respond to Nate's confusion, Yosef walked to the kitchen sink to wash the dishes. Loni began her explanation: "I was sixteen or seventeen at the time. I had taken on the surname of my common-law spouse, Rollo." When Loni pronounced the consonant of the *ll* as a Spanish *y* sound, Nate's mouth fell wide open.

"I'm sorry that I had not brought this up before," said Yosef Peretz from the kitchen, "but I think you'll understand that the information—if you'd found out before—would have complicated our relationship tremendously."

Six years before, when Nate and Miró had first visited the Canary Islands, their lives had been inexorably and drastically changed. Not only had Nate and Miró been falsely accused of a murder they did not commit, but they had been imprisoned and had suffered great personal distress. Additionally, their eleven-year-old daughter, Minerva, had been kidnapped by Diego Montemayor's crew. The individuals who kidnapped and held Minnie for several days were a teenage couple by the name of Sonny and Álana Rollo.

"Our paths crossed in the Canary Islands, Dr. Shelley. I assure you I am a different person now," said Loni Peretz.

"After being mentored by Professor Ari Weiss—both professionally and spiritually," Yosef said, "I received a job offer at the University of Las Palmas—in the Canary Islands. I moved there to teach and conduct research. Since my Spanish skills were quite good, I also volunteered as a counselor in a prison ministry where Álana was imprisoned for the kidnapping of your daughter."

"When Sonny, my common-law husband, and I were arrested by Inspector Eduardo Sánchez, we were both convicted and sent to prison," Loni said. "After being imprisoned, I never heard from Sonny again, but I was blessed to have met a prison counselor, a wonderful man, who led me to a true repentance and a wonderful spiritual conversion. Although Yosef was willing to wait for me to complete serving my sentence, I was released early, and we got married here in Israel. I am now a different woman."

Nate and Miró were so numbed by the revelation that they remained seated at the breakfast table in complete silence. Nate finally opened his mouth to ask for details, but Miró interrupted him.

"We're obviously speechless. As I recall, my daughter described how Nate rescued her from Diego Montemayor's home. She had been held in the wine cellar for several days…in the dark…with no bathroom privileges or anything," said Miró. "A very young girl held her hostage…and that was you, Loni?"

With tears in her eyes, Loni Peretz had trouble responding. "I'm afraid that's true, Miró…. I was a terrible human being…. I was lost…to drugs, crime, all kinds of things. I'm very sorry, and I'm truly ashamed of what I did. I hope you can find it in your heart to forgive me."

While Miró looked away, Nate responded for both, "Of course, we forgive you, Loni. In fact, if I recall correctly, I didn't behave well either. And I used some pretty harsh language."

Loni Peretz chuckled and said, "I've described the encounter to Yosef, word for word…. Don't worry—you were justified under the circumstances."

Miró, in amazement, could only say, "What are the chances that we would be sitting in front of the kidnapper who traumatized my eleven-year-old daughter? I've also heard accounts of the heroic rescue from my husband. Since he's fond of embellishing stories, can I hear from you how he snatched my daughter from Diego Montemayor's wine cellar?"

"Please listen to me, Miró—although this may sound repetitious, I'm not proud of anything I did in the past. I do not glamorize any of it, nor can I claim that my unhappy childhood justified my actions. Your husband, however, was quite bold, and I remember that somehow he entered Diego's mini-mansion. I was alone in the house, holding your daughter Minerva hostage."

"How about Diego and his wife, Yael? Where were they?" Miró asked.

"They were already on the run because the authorities, including Inspector Sánchez, suspected that they were involved in the kidnapping. Since Diego's house was a multi-level structure on the side of a mountain, I was downstairs where Minerva was locked up inside the wine cellar. Your husband came up behind me and grabbed me by the hair. He held a letter opener to my throat and using the whisper of Clint Eastwood told me that he would kill me if I didn't cooperate. I was terrified. I opened the heavy metal door to Minerva's cell and let her out."

Miró then asked, "Then what happened?"

Loni Peretz sheepishly said, "He locked me in the cell where I'd held Minerva, your daughter. He also took my cell phone away from me. My boyfriend didn't find me until the next day."

Clearly embarrassed, Nate apologized. "I'm sorry for the names I called you, Mrs. Peretz."

"No, I deserved it." She chuckled, and turning to Miró, Loni said, "He called me a 'skinny bitch'—which I was."

Nate asked, "Do you know what happened to Sonny Rollo?"

Yosef walked back into the small breakfast area and said, "We believe he is still serving time in a Spanish prison."

CHAPTER THIRTY-FOUR

[Jerusalem; six months into the Pygmalion Project]
(October 2022)

After a brief walk around the neighborhood, Yosef and Loni Peretz described to their guests the elaborate preparations being made for Professor Ari Weiss's memorial services. The Shelleys were astounded by how massive and elaborate the operation would be. Yosef stated, "The border police, the Israeli defense forces, the Shin Bet security service, and various government ministries have been asked to ensure security and deal with traffic arrangements to maintain public order. While Professor Weiss lies in repose at the Knesset, many dignitaries and even heads of state will visit. In addition, Israeli flags in all government offices and military bases will be lowered to half-mast. They will remain that way until after the funeral."

"Forgive my ignorance," Miró said, "but when you say the professor's casket will 'lie in repose,' is that the same as 'lying in state'?"

"Before this memorial service, I don't believe the Knesset had allowed this practice. Only state officials can officially 'lie in state.' Since the professor did not hold public office, he cannot be offered such an honor with official government guard," Yosef said. "However, the tribute being bestowed on him—'lying in repose'—is making history. The Knesset Plaza will remain open for a few hours to world dignitaries and will then be open to the public for the remainder of the day tomorrow."

Loni Peretz added, "The following morning his coffin will leave for Mount Herzl, where the memorial service will be held."

Raising her eyebrows in surprise, Miró said, "I had no idea that Professor Weiss was so widely recognized."

"Although humble, he was a great man, Miró." Yosef's eyes teared. "I'm honored to have rubbed shoulders with greatness."

If Nate and Miró had been surprised to hear the description of the following two days of commemoration, the actual events exceeded their expectations. As Yosef and Loni drove up as close as they could to the Knesset Plaza, they parked in a spot reserved for dignitaries. Yosef explained that as special guests from the Center for Middle Eastern Peace Studies, he had received certain privileges. Despite the light mist, throngs of people were being held behind cordoned-off areas to allow the government officials and heads of state to pay their respects.

The international media was present with aggressive photojournalists pushing themselves into strategic locations to catch the various celebrities as they approached. The Shelleys and the Peretzes were granted entrance along with the government dignitaries. "I had no idea this would be so well attended," said Miró. What she privately meant was that she had no idea that Dr. Ari Weiss was such a well-respected man throughout the world. In truth, after spotting so many dignitaries, Miró felt underdressed.

In addition to the US Secretary of State, numerous heads of state from the EU attended the funeral, including those from France, Germany, and the Netherlands. Charles, the Prince of Wales, was present as well as the prime minister of Canada, the president of Mexico, and the European Union president. Two former British prime ministers were escorted through the Plaza, as well as the Australian governor general.

Nate turned to ask Yosef a question when he witnessed two Middle Eastern security groups separately escorting obvious dignitaries. "Do you know who they represent?"

"Yes," said Yosef. "That first couple—they're members of the royal family from Jordan."

"And the second group behind them?" asked Nate.

"Those individuals are representatives from the Egyptian government," said Yosef. "The professor did much to improve Israeli relations with both countries."

The following morning was an early one. To arrive on time for the 8:30 funeral, the two couples left the house at 6:30 a.m. Although the center staff and their guests occupied specially reserved seats, the grounds around Mount Herzl were wet and soggy, which made their walk to their seating difficult. Nate noticed that the grave for Professor Ari Weiss was adjacent to the tombs for a section labeled "Great Leaders of the Nation."

Nate whispered to Yosef, "How common is this to be granted such an honor—to be adjacent to the national leaders of Israel?"

"Not common at all, Nate. The Knesset approved such a thing for the first time," said Yosef with a smile.

• • •

For the following two days Nate and Yosef determined that they would dedicate their time to cataloging much of Professor Weiss's research files. What they discovered was extraordinary. Although a decent effort had been made by the center's research assistants and the professor himself, thirty-one boxes of files had remained untouched and certainly not archived nor catalogued.

Meanwhile, Loni Peretz and Miró decided that their own time would be better spent touring and shopping. They would tour Israel and allow Miró to make stops at various locations that Nate had gotten to visit with Professor Weiss. So Loni and Miró set out to visit Haifa, Capernaum, Caesarea, Nazareth, and the Sea of Galilee. On their way back, they would tour a kibbutz or two. At Miró's request, Loni also promised to stop at the Dead Sea and perhaps Masada.

During the next two days Nate got to reacquaint himself with the center staff, probably better than his first visit. They researched together, ate together, and debated various issues sometimes in vigorous manner but not in any way disrespectful. Nate, who primarily disagreed with his Middle Eastern colleagues on their view of

America as a hopeless imperialist country, admitted to various serious blemishes in US history. However, he was quick to defend American support for Israel, at least, for much of its history. His colleagues pointed to recent American "betrayals," which they considered "egregious" and "distressing."

Working for twelve and fourteen hours, each day the team discovered unpublished research notes and essays written by Ari Weiss. The findings included original documents, photographs, newspaper articles, and lecture material—which informed the entire staff on future research challenges. Nate and the research staff agreed to collaborate regardless of the time it would take.

The most interesting finding, however, was voluminous material that Professor Weiss accumulated to describe a little-known political relationship. In fact, the professor had collected original communications between the Chinese Communist Party (CCP) and the Palestinian Authority to suggest that long-standing ties existed between the two parties. The communication between the two entities had begun since Mao Zedong's rule in Communist China.

"What possible motive could Mao and his bunch have for befriending our Palestinian brothers?" asked the Center's research team.

"That's what we will uncover," said Nate. "I predict that it will illuminate us all."

According to Professor Weiss's early findings, Chairman Mao himself sent personal letters to Palestinian officials indicating his strong support for all Third World liberation movements. The professor had several letters in his collection. In the post-Mao era, the CCP evidently continued to support the Palestinian Liberation Organization (PLO) and consistently endorsed Hamas as the rightful rulers of the Gaza Strip. Also, they refused to label Hamas as a terrorist organization.

In several recent public lectures Professor Ari Weiss also made mention of personal correspondence between the current leadership of the CCP and the PLO. In those lectures he referred to the center's "files" on the fabrication of a false narrative, one that would implicate conservative organizations in the US—including Christian conservative groups—in order to deflect attention from Palestinian terrorism in the US. The professor's personal journal entries suggested that enormous amounts of money were being channeled to specific media in the US by the CCP to propagate this myth. Unfortunately, those "files" were not in any of the boxes being reviewed by Nate and the research team.

"Wouldn't this contradict your Interpol bosses' convictions that a right-wing conspiracy is underway to overthrow the present American administration?" asked Yosef.

"I would be contradicting my boss if I were to bring this forth, yes," said Nate. "But I cannot do so without the files themselves."

Yosef agreed. He repeated, "If found, these files would serve as evidence that would contradict Interpol's suspicions of a right-wing Christian group seeking to foment political unrest in the US."

"And," Nate said, "it seems that since Mao Zedong's regime, the Chinese Communist Party has cultivated a relationship with Palestinian leaders to bring liberation for them at the expense of everyone else. I wonder if these files had anything to do with Professor Weiss's assassination."

Yosef lamented, "I doubt the professor's assailants will ever be captured. Their terrorists usually retreat to the Gaza Strip, and there they enjoy the protection of Hamas. Not even with an act of the Knesset can we extradite people, regardless of the evidence. And in our case, we don't have any."

"We have the photographs of the media outside the TV station," said Nate.

Yosef chuckled. "Ha—the photographers are usually complicit. They've refused to hand over any of their files."

The following evening while in their guest bedroom, Miró was eager to share information. Nate and Yosef had worked on the professor's files until late in the evening, and they had devoured falafels on their drive home. Nate was exhausted and sleepy. As he put on his favorite Wolverine gym shorts, which substituted for pajamas, Nate searched for his blue and maize University of Michigan T-shirt.

"I promise you that it will only take a minute. You need to hear this nonetheless," said Miró. She took Nate by the elbow and sat him down at the bedside bench. She reached into Nate's luggage and handed him his T-shirt. "Loni had much to share."

"My love, if you consider it urgent, I'll listen, but forgive me if I fall asleep," said Nate. "The professor's old files have been fascinating but frankly very difficult to categorize. I'm drained."

"Okay, try this on for size," said Miró. "If this does not grab your attention, nothing will…. What if I told you that your boss is a child molester, Mr. Big Shot Psychiatrist?"

As he removed his glasses to pull on his shirt, Nate stopped. "What on earth are you saying?"

"I'm saying that Loni claims that from the age of ten until the age of fourteen—for four years—" Miró paused for emphasis. Then almost in a whisper she added, "she was sexually molested by her stepfather, Gabriel Picard. That's the reason she ran away from home."

Nate dropped his shirt on the bench. He put on his glasses and rose. He walked around the room shirtless and barefoot. Finding his flip-flops under the bed, he returned to the bench and sat once more. "Miró, that's a serious accusation…. Do you…what I mean is…does Loni sound credible?"

"In my estimation, yes." Miró came to sit beside Nate at the foot of the bed.

"Did Loni ever complain to her mom?"

Nodding, Miró responded, "We had long discussions while we drove across this wonderful place. She was sweet…still hurt from the childhood trauma…and she is still in mourning for losing contact with her mom. She stated that from the very first signs of her stepdad's inappropriate behavior, she confided to her mother. Instead of coming to her aid, her mother dismissed her claim as a vengeful accusation."

"So Picard didn't stop?" asked Nate.

"Since Álana disapproved of her parents' divorce and since she missed her biological dad tremendously, her mom ignored her complaints. Álana pleaded to her mom several times to no avail…. Her mom always sided with her stepdad."

"So what happened?" Nate asked.

"At the age of thirteen," Miró said with admiration in her voice, "Álana took matters into her own hands and complained to the local police. She even took the bus downtown and filed a report at the Brussels police headquarters. Since her dad was already a big shot at Interpol, her accusations fell on deaf ears."

Nate was motionless, speechless. He listened dumbfounded.

Miró continued. "Feeling helpless…without support from her mom or the authorities, the poor girl left home. She was homeless for a year until a small-time drug dealer came to her rescue. That was Sonny Rollo, the one who took her to the Canary Islands and later worked for Yael Montemayor and her husband, Diego."

"How did she survive…living on the streets, I mean?" asked Nate.

"She implied that she used and sold drugs, pawned stolen goods, and got money for sexual favors," Miró said. "I can only imagine."

Nate cautioned: "Honey, you do realize, don't you, that every prison inmate claims innocence. Ninety-eight percent of all criminals say they weren't guilty."

"My dear husband, please give me a little credit for being able to discern dishonesty. I am not a human lie-detector, but this girl… this woman…sounds sincere. I cannot guarantee it, but I believe she's credible."

"She does admit to kidnapping Minnie—Minerva—doesn't she?" asked Nate. "And she admits to drug use, drug dealing, and theft…yes?"

"Absolutely," Miró said. "Furthermore, she states that she deserved her prison sentence. However, she remains steadfast in her claims about being molested by her stepfather."

"Do you think it's possible that she's seeking revenge for Picard providing most of the testimony that convicted her and Sonny Rollo?" asked Nate.

"What are you saying?" Miró asked.

"Well," explained Nate, "I learned from Inspector Sánchez that Gabriel Picard provided most of the incriminating evidence that helped convict Sonny and Álana."

"I did not know that, but it seems to me that you're looking for reasons to absolve your friend…and your boss, Picard."

Nate objected, "Miró, I'm simply asking us to consider all relevant matters."

"Nate, which evidence did Picard have that Inspector Sánchez did not have?"

"According to Sánchez, Picard offered written statements of Diego Montemayor and Tío Dante, employers of Sonny Rollo and Álana, and submitted the evidence to the presiding judge," Nate said. "Remember that at the time, Diego and his associates were not under suspicion."

With a wry smile on her face, Miró asked, "So now are we willing to side with the testimony of two dangerous criminals to discredit Loni Peretz?"

"My love," Nate pleaded, "can we sleep on this new information? Perhaps after getting some rest we'll be able to consider and digest more clearly."

Within three minutes Nate was sound asleep.

• • •

It became clear during the next twenty-four hours that Nate had not received Miró's revelation about Álana well. Although he did not always agree with his former boss, Interpol's second-in-command Gabriel Picard, he respected him greatly. From the first day that Nate had approached Picard, he had been cooperative and keen on assisting Nate in his quest to remove Diego Montemayor's threats. Picard had even offered to combine resources with his American FBI colleague Ram Edmunds to capture Diego.

So the following morning Nate promised Miró that he would consider Álana Peretz's claims, but he asked Miró what she thought about his return to Europe—this time with the entire family. He suggested that a move to Lyon, France, might be exciting for Minerva and wondered if Miró could perhaps join a European university as a visiting scholar. He explained to Miró how being in Europe, closer to their nemesis, would enhance their chances of success. Armed now with much more information and a solid plan to capture Diego

Montemayor, Nate, as part of Interpol, could then launch the Pygmalion Project from a European locale.

To Nate's surprise, Miró did not reject his proposal outright. She seemed willing to consider the move. "I do have one condition, however," said Miró.

Nate bit his lip, stopped in his tracks, and braced himself, "What condition is that, my love?"

"Well," said Miró as she took a sip of the coffee that she'd retrieved from Álana's kitchen, "in exchange for my agreement to move to Europe, will you allow me to ask Dad to do a bit of research into Picard's past?"

"Do you mean a tracing of his genealogy? How would that help us?" asked Nate.

"As you know, Dad can come up with all kinds of interesting data other than birth certificates, educational records, and such. Who knows? He may even trace some nefarious connections," said Miró, only half-joking.

"Just tell Abraham to be delicate. Researching the background of a master spy—behind his back—can be difficult…and dangerous."

"Don't worry. I'll tell Dad we don't want you getting in trouble with your future boss."

The following day, Nate approached Picard to present his plan to rejoin Interpol. He suggested that the Pygmalion Project could be executed from Europe much more efficiently. Picard listened attentively and asked several questions. Then he promptly agreed to a collaboration.

Before agreeing to anything, Miró wanted to discuss her own doubts. "If Loni Peretz's claims are true," asked Miró, "could you ever trust Picard? What if he's complicit with Diego himself, Nate? Wouldn't that endanger us even more?"

"If Picard is complicit with Diego Montemayor, then isn't it better to keep him closer rather than at a distance?" Nate could see that Miró agreed, although she might not be ready to admit it.

"Okay, okay," said Miró. "You're overselling the case. I may not be convinced you're right. However, I think I can request a leave of absence at Northwestern. Although I've been dean for less than a year, my former boss would not mind holding up the fort for another year…if necessary. But to be honest, our main challenge may be our daughter, Minerva. She will not be thrilled about moving."

"I thought of that," said Nate. "Will you consider leaving her behind while she finishes high school? She could then join us and study at one of the finest European universities."

"That would be tough on me. I'm willing to consider it, though," Miró said. "I do have two questions. Would it be out of line if you asked Picard to assign you to Israel?"

"I don't even know if Interpol has an Israeli NCB, a National Center Bureau. When I was here before, Picard never asked me to check in on them, if they exist at all," said Nate.

"My second question is…" Miró hesitated. "Do you think I could become a part of the Center for Middle Eastern Peace Studies?"

"I'm willing to look into both matters immediately if you're serious," said Nate.

Nate felt he maintained maximum objectivity when it came to Álana Peretz. Of course, he could not forget how the younger Loni had subjected Minerva to days of fear and trauma. Against his better judgment, he did hold it against his daughter's kidnapper—any parent would. But he thought he could deal with the kidnapping with objectivity going forward.

It turned out that Interpol did have a National Center Bureau in Jerusalem. Picard, however, was reluctant to assign him to that location. He preferred to reassign Nate to the Lyon office. As for the appointment of Miró to the Center for Middle Eastern Peace Studies, Yosef Peretz was confident that the appointment could be accomplished, especially if Northwestern University approved an exchange of sorts. One of the center's scholars-in-residence would certainly advance his or her academic career if that could be arranged.

CHAPTER THIRTY-FIVE

[Chicago; last two months of Pygmalion training]
(October 2022)

After a week's delay, Nate and Miró returned and immediately set the stage for their move to Europe. As Miró predicted, Minerva was the principal challenge. Minerva informed them that she could complete her high school requirements by the end of the year because of her accumulated credits. However, she refused to finish her remaining coursework via online instruction. That option was out of the question.

After numerous family discussions, it was decided that upon Nate and Miró's departure, Minerva would move in with her grandfather Abraham Epstein. Her Uncle Max gladly agreed to be chauffer, chaperone, family chef, and enforcer of all digital communication and social media restrictions imposed by Nate and Miró. Abraham, who was already in semi-retirement from hospital duties, agreed to limit his teaching duties at Northwestern's Feinberg School of Medicine. He joyfully accepted all "grandfathering duties" that would be developed during the few months left before Minerva's high school graduation.

"In addition to all my grandfathering tasks, I took seriously your request to investigate the deputy secretary general of Interpol, Gabriel Picard. I've only been at it eight or nine days, but I've uncovered some fascinating information," Abraham said.

"Thank you, Dad," Miró said. "I knew you could come up with something."

"And spare us all the family lineage, his ancestors, and other juicy facts about his royal heritage," joked Nate. "What did you discover?"

"For one thing," Abraham said, "Picard has been a frequent traveler to China, more specifically to the Port of Shenzhen. Over the last six years he has been there two dozen times."

Nate objected: "Abraham, Picard flies all over the world. He is with Interpol, after all. I don't find his travel to China to be unusual at all."

Abraham added, "Allow me to point out that the former chief of Interpol, a Chinese national, vanished from the face of the earth in 2018 after returning to China from his office in Lyon. Yet Picard, his underling, can travel freely to and from China. Now that I find peculiar."

Miró interrupted: "Dad, were you able to determine the purpose for his travel to China? Why must he go there so often?"

"I can't tell for sure because Interpol's China headquarters is in Beijing—not Shenzhen. However, what I found fascinating was the discovery of newspaper clippings that show Picard shaking hands with board members of a certain Pan Asian Shipping Enterprises."

Looking at his watch, Nate said, "It's not that I don't appreciate what you're doing, Abraham. I know you have good intentions, and I also know the request came from us, but we've got a lot on our plate. Our imminent move to Europe has us involved in dozens of chores. Do you really think we need to discuss Picard's travels and connections around the world?"

"You're absolutely right," said Abraham. "My background search on Picard can be ongoing and I'll continue to keep you informed. However, let me add one small detail that I left out."

"Shoot, Dad. What is it?" asked Miró.

"The surname of one of the board members of that shipping company—it's Chengfu. And if I'm not mistaken, that's the same last name attached to Diego Montemayor's *consigliere*."

Nate laughed, "Now, that, my dear father-in-law, is what journalists call 'burying the headline.' That could be a coincidence, or it could be significant. It's not as if Estevan has sole claim of his name, and 'Chengfu' is probably a common surname in China. Please keep us informed if you uncover any further connections."

. . .

In addition to the need for countless family meetings, Nate and Miró summoned the training team for the Pygmalion Project to their Evanston home. They announced that Raquel Rosales's training needed to be accelerated and brought to its conclusion. The other principal players—including Raquel, Max, Abraham, and FBI Special Agent Ram Edmunds—regrouped to ensure that Raquel was sufficiently prepared, although she had already declared herself to be ready.

As the Pygmalion team was getting ready to endorse Raquel's "graduation," Miró admonished, "Not so fast. Although Inspector Sánchez gave Raquel passing marks, don't you remember the final observation that he made in private?"

"I do," said Nate. "To be honest with you, I'm not sure how to proceed with that one."

"Wait a minute—I don't remember any objection from Inspector Sánchez. What are you talking about?" Abraham asked.

"Sorry, Abraham," said Nate. "We must've failed to mention that before leaving the last time he was here, Inspector Sánchez stated that Dr. Wu got everything right—except for Yael Montemayor's slight overbite. According to the inspector, it was very minor, but a very sexy and appealing feature that added to Yael's charm."

Miró added, "But when we spoke to Dr. Wu, he indicated that attempting to replicate that facial or dental feature would be virtually impossible to do. Eliminating bad bites is common, but 'fabricating' something like that requires the collaboration of orthodontists and maxillofacial surgeons. If something like that were to be attempted, the 'facial harmony' of the patient could be severely compromised. And the recovery period could be extensive."

"So are you saying that Wu is against attempting something like that?" asked Abraham.

"Yes." Max added, "Not only that, but to be honest with you, that physical flaw—if you want to call it that—is making Ram Edmunds very nervous."

"In that case, grasshoppers," Abraham said with a smile, "we will treat it like we've been planning all along. We will blame it on the alleged surgeries following the skiing accident."

"What skiing accident, Dad?"

"Well, we've already decided to attribute any scars, even Raquel's inability to do flamenco, to a fictitious skiing accident. If questioned, Raquel will say that those surgeons went ahead and fixed her bad bite, her overbite."

"Hmm," said Nate. "And Diego will again assume that it was all part of the scheme concocted by Yael's godfather, Inspector Sánchez. Brilliant, Abraham. Simply brilliant."

Abraham took a brief bow. He continued, "As I recall, we've decided that the name of Raquel Rosales's fictitious persona will be 'Eliza Durazo'—in honor of the character in *My Fair Lady*, Eliza Doolittle. If that's the case, have you asked Picard to remove public records regarding any connection between Raquel Rosales and the fictitious 'Eliza Durazo'? Remember that before removing those public records, we must first create them to be convincing to Diego's goons who will be conducting searches throughout the Internet."

"I confess that I have not followed up on that matter. I'll ask him to address it immediately," said Nate.

When Nate and Ram Edmunds explained how necessary it was to wipe clean any birth, marriage, employment, or educational records of Eliza Durazo, Picard not only agreed but also went a step further. He first created false birth and educational records for Eliza Durazo, then left a trace of the destruction of those records—sufficient evidence for Estevan and Diego to uncover that "someone" had tampered with the public records of this mystery woman. In fact, Picard proved to be more creative than any of them in fabricating false records and leaving crumbs of evidence for Estevan and Diego to uncover.

Inspector Sánchez and Picard even created a series of communications in which they discussed the "unfortunate fire" that destroyed vital health records of a Sánchez relative who had received medical attention in various hospitals and clinics in Europe. These phony records that were presumably destroyed all occurred a week after Yael Montemayor's death—further planted evidence to convince Diego that his wife was still alive. An officially redacted email communication, which had inadvertently referred to a "Ms. Durazo, from the Canary Islands," was "carelessly" filed in the official records that included Yael Montemayor's death certificate. All these false leads were planted by Interpol at the request of Gabriel Picard.

Picard, of course, ensured that Yael's records before her death were intact. He ensured that every detail of her life be available for anyone searching for her life's details prior to the hospital fire that killed her.

· · ·

(Early November 2022)

After leaving his Chicago practice in the capable hands of his mentor and friend Dr. Michael Stein, Nate and Miró traveled to Lyon, France, the first week of November to assume his new duties with Interpol. Officially, Nate's new title included being the head of Operation Millennium, a worldwide effort to combat Eurasian organized crime. Although the operation had been an ongoing project since early 2021, Nate took on the duties of "administrator in charge" while the operation across France arrested twenty-five suspects, including a high-valued target thought to be a major world player in international crime. According to information released to the press, a new Interpol Director of Operations, whose name was withheld for his protection, destroyed the top of the criminal hierarchy responsible for drug trafficking, extortion, contract murder, and money laundering. According to published reports, the crime leaders arrested were responsible for "polluting economies throughout the world by investing the proceeds of their criminal activities into legitimate funds and businesses." In his first formal interview, the new administrator in charge (Nate) stated, "Interpol stands ready to offer expertise and support to any member country in their efforts to dismantle the criminal web of Eurasian organized crime."

In truth, Gabriel Picard offered to Nate a one-year appointment in Lyon to launch the Pygmalion Project, which, of course, was kept secret and was shielded from the press. Within a year or less, Picard's plan was to move Nate to the National Center Bureau in Madrid. Because Diego Montemayor was presumed to be in either Spain or France, Nate would need to familiarize himself with both criminal environments. Following the information provided by the former deputy director of the FBI—Jacoby Homely—and the convicted Lucas Williams, credible information had been discovered that indeed Diego Montemayor and his *consigliere,* Estevan Chengfu, were in seclusion in Diego's compound on the French island of Corsica— Bonifacio to be precise.

* * *

Interpol insisted that Raquel Rosales travel to Europe with Nate and Miró in a private aircraft. During the trip to Europe, Raquel Rosales officially assumed the identity of Eliza Durazo. Because of the whirlwind transfer to Europe, multiple challenges presented themselves. Although Nate began his assignment immediately, Raquel/ Eliza and Miró had an opportunity to furnish and prepare Nate's and Miró's new apartment in Lyon. In addition, Miró and Eliza reviewed the final preparations for execution of the Pygmalion Plan. As they multi-tasked, the two women also did extensive shopping to bring Eliza's wardrobe up to date with French and Continental fashions. On day ten, after their arrival in Lyon, Nate and Miró prepared Eliza for the first encounter with Diego Montemayor. They met in Nate's new Interpol office, where Nate addressed the cultural and linguistic peculiarities of Corsica. "If you've never been there, you will be in for a treat, Raquel…uh, Eliza…. I must get used to your new identity…. Not only is it a beautiful place, but the culture and the people are truly unique."

Eliza was curious. "I've been in France numerous times. What makes Corsica so unique?"

"Don't be surprised if you hear the locals speaking Italian," said Miró.

"Or French," added Nate. "In fact, locals have developed a curious mixture of Italian, French, and the Sardinian dialect. They actually call their language 'Corsican' or 'Course.'"

Eliza hesitated. "Oh, dear—we've been concentrating on my French and Castilian, but now you're telling me I must learn Italian—or a version of it?"

"No, no," Miró reassured her. "When you order from a menu, you—like everyone else—will have three choices, Italian, French, or Corsican. In your case, you'll be safe with French. Besides, remember that you're not passing as a local Corsican."

"Exactly," said Nate. "Like Italy itself, the island of Corsica has had a varied history, with a succession of different cultures and governments. Although it is officially a French island, local people are proud of their heritage, and it's reflected in their language, customs, and food."

"Somewhat like the Basque area in Spain," said Raquel. "Or like your native South Texas, Miró. I remember my husband telling me that when he traveled to the South Texas border, in some places, Spanish—or, as he called it, "Tex-Mex"—was more common than English."

Miró continued. "That's true. So no need to worry about the language while in Corsica. You will be escorted by one of Gabriel Picard's best Interpol agents, an agent whose real name has been withheld from us. He will be known as your fiancé, Ruel Levant. His passport is French, and he's supposed to be a wealthy businessman from France with British and French family roots. His public records, as well as yours, have been carefully filed to create credible histories and backgrounds. His English and French language skills are quite good, and his martial arts skills are superb."

"We hope you will not be uncomfortable, but you will be traveling as an engaged couple, sharing bedrooms, et cetera," explained Nate. "Will that be a problem?"

"Thank you for asking, but I believe I am capable of maintaining boundaries," said Eliza.

* * *

Gabriel Picard also summoned his friend, retired Inspector Eduardo Sánchez, to Lyon. In his counter-surveillance of Diego Montemayor, Picard had discovered a mysterious message that Diego Montemayor had received in April 2020. When Diego first arrived at his safe house in Corsica after the murders aboard *The Black Pearl,* a message had arrived from an unknown source. It was addressed to Diego and simply read, "*Gachupín*, I got you home safely. Now, let's part ways."

Picard remembered that Nate had informed him that Tío Dante—Diego's former right-hand man—had left a note that would be delivered to Nate in the event of Tío's death. That note, according to Nate, indicated the identity of Diego Montemayor's "handler." Although Nate had never revealed to Picard that he'd learned the identity of such a handler, Picard made a "conceptual leap" and formulated the hypothesis that Nate had learned from Tío who Diego's handler was. Picard wondered how much Nate knew.

In an ambitious gamble, the Pygmalion Team created a trap to lure Diego Montemayor into a meeting with Inspector Eduardo Sánchez. Since they knew that Diego and his assistant, Estevan, monitored their online and telephone communications, they fabricated a series of false communications between Picard and the inspector. The various emails and phone calls suggested that Interpol was more interested in going after a "bigger fish" than Diego. In the fabricated communications, Interpol was less interested in apprehending Diego than his "handler."

The final puzzle piece came from Inspector Sánchez. "Where shall we meet?" the inspector asked in an online communication. Picard's planted response—which was, of course, intercepted by Estevan Chengfu—stated, "Since I'll be in the vicinity of Marseille, let's meet there." As soon as Estevan opened Picard's bogus attachment, a doctored photo of the Sofitel Marseilles, he unleashed a sophisticated counter-intelligence attack on his own entire communication center that instantly seized control of not only his phone's operating system but also his boss's data. Within seconds, Estevan had unknowingly exported all his emails to Interpol, his contacts, as well as private messages to Diego Montemayor. His metadata, as well as his entire browsing history, was exposed. In addition, Interpol now had a live feed of Diego's and Estevan's every move.

Picard and Inspector Sánchez waited for forty-eight hours. Then, early on November 13, a message from an encrypted address arrived in the inspector's inbox. "*Padrino*, this is Diego. since I know you will be close to me in Marseilles, I would like to host you for a late breakfast at the Hotel Solemare in Corsica. Will you come?"

CHAPTER THIRTY-SIX

[Corsica, France; Pygmalion
training project completed]
(November 2022)

D on't move," Diego whispered. He froze in place, turned pale, spellbound by the vision. The two men trudged uphill through the narrow cobblestone alleys of Bonifacio, and Estevan knew that after unusual physical exertion, Diego reacted with short-lived flushing of the face. Instead, Diego's face turned pasty. Arrested by Diego's firm open palm on his chest, Estevan peered at the open window, then at his boss. Immobilized, a whitewashed Diego stood there dumbfounded. Mouth hanging open, Diego tried unsuccessfully to articulate his unbelief. He mouthed inaudible questions.

Though the cloudless November skies shone brightly with a late morning sunshine, a crisp Mediterranean breeze blew in between two-story, pink stuccoed structures. The tiny centuries-old homes leaned toward each other almost touching across the narrow cobblestone alleys in Bonifacio. Neighbors reached out of their second-story windows to hang their morning wash to dry and greet each other with melodious *Ciao's* and *Buongiorno's*. Neighboring house-wives often shared a common clothesline spanning the six-foot space across the alleys.

Since traffic was not allowed through the narrow walkways, Diego and Estevan had hiked the stone alleys after parking their vehicle at the town square. Their one-half-mile walk to the Hotel Solemare took them through the small-town center, a charming mixture of sidewalk cafés, private residences, and open-market vegetable and fruit stands. They could smell the rich Italian roasted coffee as they passed the sidewalk cafés, all adorned by pink and purple bougainvillea. The fragrance of lavender that permeated the air throughout the island of Corsica was subtly enhanced by various herbs in hanging planters. The soothing smell of spearmint and rosemary emanated from every café in Bonifacio.

Diego and Estevan stood outside *La Loggia,* where most customers seated inside at the small tables consumed pastries—assortments of *bocconotto, cannoli,* and *sfogliatelle*—with espresso. The elegant woman at the window, who was deep in conversation with the man seated across the table, appeared to drink hot tea with a side of half a *cannolo.* She did not notice the two men standing on the other side of the opened window. Her raven black hair, which was sternly pulled back, and her animated smile transfixed Diego.

"That's my wife," said Diego. "That's my wife," he repeated, clearly confounded.

Your wife has been dead for years. Estevan was signing, but Diego's attention was exclusively on the woman sitting inside the café.

Diego's trusted *consigliere* tried again to communicate with his boss, using simplified sign language, *She's dead—it's not her.*

Although both men were behind schedule for their meeting, Diego was frozen in place outside the café, bewildered by the ghostlike image of his deceased wife. Suddenly, on the other side of the window a waiter approached the table and noticed the two men standing outside the restaurant. He stood between the window and the table, giving the two ogling passersby his back to block their vision. The waiter appeared to fill the customers' glasses with fresh water and slowly fussed with the tablecloth, trying valiantly to provide his patrons' privacy.

"Estevan, I must speak to her," said Diego. "I'm certain it's Yael, my wife."

Holding Diego by the elbow, Estevan insisted with agitated signing, *You'll be late for your meeting.*

Ignoring his mute *consigliere*, Diego stormed into the small restaurant. Estevan followed. The stunning beauty, dressed entirely in black, noticed the intruders approaching the table. In a ballerina's posture, noticeable even while seated, the woman pursed her lips in the middle of a sentence and gave Diego a patented look of annoyance. Speechless, Diego stood for a moment at the table. After his awkward pause, he managed to say, "Yael, what are you doing here?"

The woman's engaging smile vanished. "*Je suis désolé, mais est-ce que je te connais?*" She used the flawless inflection of a native French speaker.

"I'm your husband, Yael—of course you know me," said Diego in Spanish. "*Claro que me conoces, Yael. Soy tu esposo.*"

The woman turned to her friend and said, "*Allons-y.*" Her companion quickly left money on the table and escorted her out. Although Diego attempted to stop them, Estevan intervened by gripping Diego's elbow and slowly shaking his head. As Estevan led Diego out the café, the loud honk of a bicycle ridden by an old man kept them from a collision. "*Guardi dove va!*" complained the unsteady octogenarian. Estevan guided Diego in the opposite direction, toward the Hotel Solemare, where the meeting with Eduardo Sánchez was scheduled.

"Estevan, I know it's insane, but that woman is my wife. We need to follow them."

In their trek to the meeting, Estevan signed very slowly, deliberating between phrases. *It's impossible…. Your wife died in the hospital fire…. Her DNA was found…and confirmed.*

CHAPTER THIRTY-SEVEN

[Corsica, France; November 2022]

A s Estevan Chengfu led him to his appointment at the Hotel Solemare, Diego Montemayor stewed. *If that woman in the café was Yael, how could she have willingly betrayed me? Estevan is right—how can she be Yael? Am I going mad? Was that merely a vision back there? Is she Yael's double?*

Diego had lost his wife in a gut-wrenching fire that occurred in a Canary Islands hospital in 2016. Or had he? For six years Diego had assumed that his wife, Yael Vidaurri Montemayor, was dead. He had been forced to go into hiding from the authorities and moved his business to the Americas, partly because his most trusted friend and business partner had repaid him with treachery. Now Diego lived for one thing, and one thing only—his *raison d'être* had become revenge—not fame, nor riches, nor power, but plain revenge against the ones responsible for his wife's death—Nate Shelley's family.

Could that woman in the café truly be my wife? If so, how did she survive that catastrophic fire six years ago? Was she saved by her godfather? And was Interpol complicit in allowing her to live under legal protection to save her from me—and my organization's reach?

Diego Montemayor's safe house in Corsica was more of a *palazzo*, an enormous villa at the southern tip of Corsica. His new home overlooked the Mediterranean in all its splendor. But laughter, merriment, and joy eluded Diego.

Diego had married in his late thirties. He fell in love with his best friend's wife and convinced her to forsake her marriage vows, a serious matter for a devoted Catholic. The marriage had been tumultuous in the early years, but it settled into a stable and respected union. The couple had become esteemed community leaders and generous philanthropists of numerous causes, especially those promoted by the Catholic diocese in the Canary Islands.

Eventually Diego's wife had become his soulmate, his friend, and the love of his life. She became his sounding board. Because of the great respect for her husband, the strong-willed Yael had submitted to him in most instances. Then suddenly she died in a tragic fire, and an acrid, somber cloud darkened Diego's tormented soul. He lived embittered, convinced that his only relief would arrive through a justified revenge that would calibrate the scales of divine justice.

Estevan led Diego toward the Hotel Solemare. The trek uphill was brisk, but the two men walked in silence. Diego's mind was still back at the café, where he was convinced that he had either witnessed an apparition or a resurrected spouse, the love of his life, his Yael.

Retired Inspector Eduardo Sánchez sat alone at the Hotel Solemare's main dining area. A distracted waiter refilled his cup with a touch of coffee and plenty of froth. As the foamy concoction overfilled Sánchez's cup, the taciturn waiter mumbled an apology: "*Mi dispiace.*" He quickly disappeared to the kitchen and returned with a fresh saucer. "*Spero che mi perdoni.*"

When the waiter departed, two men approached him. The lanky one with the pallid complexion spoke directly to Sánchez.

"I never thought I would see you again," said the lanky stranger.

Sánchez recognized the voice, but the man's appearance confused him. "I beg your pardon. Have we met?" Both men were using Spanish, their native language. The man with Diego, with Asian features, did not say a word.

"*Padrino*, it's me—Diego."

Still confused, Sánchez rose to his feet and extended a hand in greeting. "You're taller and your face, well, it's different. *Una nariz aguileña.* You look—younger."

"Yes, well, *Padrino*, the Roman nose, the whole facial reconstruction was necessary. Also, I underwent limb-lengthening surgery. Thanks to you and your friends at Interpol, I was a wanted man here in Europe, so I had to disappear for a few years."

"I was doing my job," said the retired inspector.

Still standing, the three men paused without breaking the silence. "Tell me one thing, Inspector—is Yael still alive?"

"What?" The former inspector stared at the stranger and shook his head. "If you truly were Diego Montemayor, you would not be asking such a question. I don't know what you want from me, but please have a seat. You can join me for coffee," said Sánchez. Turning to the silent man next to Diego, he said, "I'm Eduardo Sánchez. Diego's wife was my goddaughter." Estevan smiled and accepted the invitation to sit at the table.

"At great risk, I asked to meet with you, *Padrino.*" Diego appeared to be a man with a heavy burden. "I have a proposition for you, but first…answer my question. Is Yael still alive?"

"With your enormous resources, I doubt you consider me a threat. Furthermore, why are you asking such a preposterous question?"

"I just saw her—here in Bonifacio," said Diego.

"She was like a daughter to me. I loved her dearly, but she perished in a tragic fire," said Sánchez. "If you are who you say you are, you would know that."

"We talked to her at a café nearby," said Diego. "I know it was her."

"That's impossible. She's been dead several years."

Estevan placed his hand on Diego's forearm to remind him of the business at hand. He tapped his watch. He then hailed the waiter.

"Estevan reminds me we have important business to discuss. I'm ready to offer your friend Gabriel Picard of Interpol a compromise of sorts," said Diego.

"Why come to me? I'm retired," said Sánchez. "Listen, Diego—if that's who you truly are—go to Picard. He and I haven't communicated in years."

Diego laughed, and Sánchez remembered the cynicism in Diego's mirth. Even Diego's lightheartedness was always tinged with a sneering disbelief. "My dear, dear inspector, certainly you must know that

I'm aware of your comings and goings. I know to whom you speak and your entire circle of contacts. My associate here, Estevan, keeps me fully informed."

"Then you must know that I cannot speak for Picard or Interpol."

"No such request is being made. I simply want for you…and Picard…to hear my proposition," said Diego.

"Go on. Just realize that I can offer no guarantees," said Sánchez. His words were interrupted by the listless waiter wearing a white dinner jacket. He was delivering a large carafe of Italian roast. On a platter he also offered a choice of pastries to the three men.

"Leave the entire platter and do not return until I summon you," said Diego. Turning to Sánchez, he said, "I can deliver to Interpol the man who has orchestrated the most widespread web of corruption in the Western hemisphere."

It was Sánchez's turn to mock Diego. "I thought the man responsible for that corruption might be *you*, Diego."

"I cannot complain about my enterprise, *Padrino*, but I am offering you—and your friend—a bigger fish."

"Hmm. And in return I suppose you'd like a détente with Interpol, perhaps complete immunity…and protection?" As the inspector waited for Diego's response, he detected a deep melancholy in his eyes. He remembered that sorrowful expression.

"Ha!" said Diego. "I've accomplished all that on my own. I cover my own tracks. I'm insulated. But I know my handler's M.O. He intends to frame me for every one of *his* crimes, and he will leave me fully exposed for the vultures to consume."

"So you do want protection?" Sánchez asked.

"Like I said, I can protect myself. I only want Picard to get to him, my handler, first."

"I always thought Diego Montemayor was 'independent,' shall we say?" I'm surprised that he—or you—would confess to having a 'handler.'"

"Such puppeteers exist," Diego said.

"Is that the compromise?" asked Sánchez.

"Yes, and, of course, one more thing. I want the truth about my wife, Yael," said Diego. "I know that you and Picard investigated the hospital fire that supposedly killed her. I also know that you blamed me for her involvement in the Nate Shelley case. You could've easily faked her death to provide her legal immunity and an escape from my crime syndicate, as you called it."

"Hmm. You seem convinced that she's alive," said Sánchez.

"Are you protecting her? I want to know the truth. Is my wife, Yael, alive?"

CHAPTER THIRTY-EIGHT

[Corsica, France; November 2022]

Eduardo Sánchez took a croissant, buttered it, and smiled, "It appears, Diego, that nothing that I say will convince you. So go on thinking that my goddaughter Yael is still alive. Believe me: I *wish* she were still with us."

Encouraging Diego to bring closure to the meeting, Diego's mute assistant signaled to his boss the lateness of the hour. He tapped his watch one more time.

"Estevan reminds me that we should be leaving. Can we count on you to convey my offer to Interpol?" Diego asked.

Still with a smile on his face, Sánchez responded, "I must admit that your persistence is reminiscent of the man I knew as Diego Montemayor. Tell me one thing. What was the favorite recipe that your wife would prepare for me?"

Without hesitation, Diego said, "*Paella Valenciana*, and the last time you joined us was in our home in Las Palmas. It was a Sunday afternoon, and Archbishop José Gómez blessed us with his presence."

"Very impressive. Either you're an accomplished researcher, or..."

"Say it, *Padrino*. I believe you're convinced that I'm Diego Montemayor."

"I suppose that I'm willing to accept the facial reconstruction, but the 'limb lengthening' is difficult to swallow. I'm not even certain medical science can accomplish that kind of thing," said Sánchez.

"You'd be surprised."

"When you were in the Canary Islands—in Las Palmas, in fact—you hired an assistant from the Middle East. What was his name?" Sánchez asked.

"If you're referring to Aamir Farooq, he's the person who supposedly perished with my wife in the hospital fire," said Diego. "Unless, of course, you and your Interpol friends also helped *him* survive the disaster."

The retired police inspector showed surprise in his placid glare. He admitted, "Like I said before, very impressive. Of course, most of that information was splashed across various news sources." After pausing, Sánchez continued: "One thing that I noticed when you raised your arm is that you have a nasty burn scar on your forearm. The Diego that I knew did not have such a scar. And please don't tell me it's the result of your so-called 'limb lengthening.'"

"Inspector, before leaving the United States, I had an unfortunate accident that scorched my arm rather badly. It took more than a year to heal," said Diego.

"Unfortunate."

"Why don't you simply share my proposition with your friend Picard from Interpol—and let him decide?" asked Diego.

"If I decide to go along, how do I communicate with you...Diego?"

"As I said, *Padrino*, we are constantly monitoring your communications. Estevan will let me know when you and Picard have spoken."

● ● ●

After the meeting with Diego, Eduardo Sánchez met Interpol's assigned contact, Guy Blanchet, who played the role of ferry steward on the boat back to Marseilles. Executing perfectly a "dead drop," Sánchez passed on to Guy his iPhone and switched on his secure satellite phone provided by Nate and Picard. Upon arrival at the French mainland, Guy Blanchet now wore the inspector's customary three-piece suit and traveled to Las Palmas via Iberia Airlines. He had traded costumes with Inspector Sánchez. From Marseilles, Sánchez—wearing the steward's ferry uniform—traveled directly to Interpol headquarters in Lyon.

Nate and Picard's counter-monitoring of Estevan and Diego Montemayor indicated that Estevan had digitally tracked Sánchez's impostor, Guy Blanchet, back to the Canary Islands, where the retired inspector's iPhone was being used to transmit false information back to Estevan. With the assistance of the American NSA, Nate and Picard scrambled the iPhone's video imaging to transmit pre-recorded videos of Sánchez's activities in his home in Las Palmas, Gran Canarias. Furthermore, Estevan's and Diego's own communications were now being monitored.

Upon arrival in Marseilles, Eduardo Sánchez had partially undressed to remove his wired audio recording equipment. The retired chief inspector from Las Palmas had used his vintage instrument many times before, and he was proud of its lasting usefulness. Now safe in Picard's office in Lyon, the three men—Picard, Nate, and Sánchez—listened to the entire recorded conversation with Diego Montemayor that had taken place at the Hotel Solemare. After the fourth replay of the conversation, Nate congratulated Eduardo Sánchez.

"You played your role in masterful fashion, Inspector. We think you convinced Diego that you doubted his identity, and on numerous occasions you forced Diego to persuade you. You put him on the defensive. Well done." Nate was genuinely impressed.

Inspector Sánchez smiled. "You must remember that in warfare, Nathaniel, one must adopt the opponent's own weapons. 'To know your enemy, you must *become* your enemy.'"

"Is that one of Sun Tzu's quotes?" asked Nate.

"Indeed it is."

"What also went incredibly well was Raquel Rosales's—or Eliza Durazo's, I should say—impersonation of your deceased goddaughter in that café in Bonifacio," said Picard. "I think Diego is convinced that Yael is alive or is close to being convinced."

"You know, Raquel could've convinced me, and I remember Yael well," said Nate. "What about you, Inspector Sánchez? You knew Yael all her life. Could she convince even you? Is Eliza good enough to fool someone that knew Yael that well?"

Sanchez cleared his throat. He picked up the vintage recording equipment as if to re-evaluate its usefulness. He paced the room and after a long silence, he finally said, "Nate, as far as her physical resemblance is concerned—despite the absence of her slight overbite that was so charming in my goddaughter—I am amazed not only at the ability of the surgeon to match Yael's facial features, but also her total physique. The rest, however—her ability to refer to life in Spain, to describe her childhood experiences, to even prepare Yael's favorite recipes—remains to be seen."

Picard addressed Sánchez's concerns. "I realize that Dr. Ivo Wu is an artist with his surgical skills. I do believe that Eliza Durazo could convince even Yael Montemayor's parents of her physical identity. However, Eduardo, are you saying it's impossible for her to speak with familiarity about the Spanish—and European—culture? Do you still have serious doubts?"

Eduardo Sánchez admitted that he was worried about an American Hispanic impersonating a Spaniard. "To be honest, I'd still like to quiz Eliza on some highly personal details, family history, her appreciation of art, Spanish cuisine, wines, et cetera. The fact that Raquel—or Eliza—already had a familiarity with the French language is helpful. But you must remember that my Yael studied at the Sorbonne, and the French language was second nature to her."

"We'll see how our Pygmalion Project worked," said Nate. "We trained her intensively for seven months. She was tutored by the best. Just remember that for all practical purposes, her training is over. We may fine-tune some details, but the execution of our plan must begin soon."

"Allow me to correct you," said Picard. "Our execution *has* begun. And the first test at the sidewalk café in Bonifacio was good enough for Diego to swallow the bait."

· · ·

CHAPTER THIRTY-NINE

[Corsica, France; November 2022]

Estevan drove Diego back to his "*palazzo* on the cliff," as Diego now called it. Diego was silent and could not understand Estevan's skepticism. He considered Estevan's abject refusal to accept that Yael was alive a sign of stubbornness, or worse, as a tinge of disloyalty. As they rode in Diego's Range Rover, "Westminster," Diego realized that whatever Estevan's motivation, his *consigliere* was questioning his judgment. "Okay, Estevan," Diego finally said. "I want you to investigate everything there is to know about this mysterious woman we met at the Café *La Loggia*. If you can confirm that she is not Yael, I will accept the evidence. Until then, I'd prefer that you respect my judgment."

Signing while he drove, in rapid sign language, Estevan said, *Also I will monitor closely Inspector Sánchez's communications.*

Diego turned to Estevan, "What are you implying?"

Now agitated, Estevan signed, *It is too much of a coincidence that you met this mysterious woman on the same day that you met with Inspector Sánchez.*

"So now you're suggesting that the person who probably kept my wife alive—and has kept her away from me—is handing her over? That does not make sense, Estevan."

I am pointing out that something is not right. You must be careful, Estevan warned.

Upon arrival, Estevan parked the SUV at the front entrance.

Estevan left the keys in the ignition for Ciccio, the compound's driver, who immediately came out to park it in the motor shed.

"Welcome back, Signore." Alessandro, Diego's Corsican valet, opened the door to the *palazzo* and bowed to Diego. He also nodded to Estevan, who had become his respected advisor because of Estevan's experience attending to Diego's needs back in the US. Often Alessandro would consult with Estevan to learn about Diego's moods, his preferences, his likes and dislikes. As a result, although Diego still turned to Estevan for assistance, he was learning to trust Alessandro's ability to fully assume the valet and bodyguard duties.

Surprisingly, Diego was also beginning to depend on Isabella, the "chambermaid," or *cameriera*, whom Estevan had hired upon Diego's arrival. Although she had not mastered English, her progress was notable. She appeared to be loyal, discreet, and pleasant. She was also attractive and bright.

More than once, Estevan had calmly reminded Diego, *You pay Alessandro and the rest of your staff healthy salaries. Show them that you trust them. One day you might need to trust them completely.*

"Are you planning to leave me, my friend?" Diego asked.

No, signed Estevan. *However, Alessandro is a very talented young man, and he knows this culture better than I do.*

For several years after his move to the Americas, Diego had learned to depend on Estevan's help. Though mute, Estevan was a valuable resource. He was astute, deeply loyal, and had a good understanding of organizational dynamics. Through sign language and written notes, Estevan was remarkably articulate and clear headed. Now back in Europe, Diego Montemayor had elevated Estevan to a different role. Estevan had become more of a full-time confidante, a colleague, and almost a partner. In fact, Estevan had assumed full control of most of Diego's finances. Plus, Estevan supervised Diego's *tai chi* training regimen. Although Estevan kept his sign language simple, Diego was improving his skills and becoming more proficient at understanding lengthy conversations with his favorite *consigliere*.

However, the latest incident in Bonifacio unsettled Diego. *Was Estevan's loyalty wavering?* "Let me ask you, Estevan—did you ever send my condolences to the widow, Raquel Rosales, for the loss of her twins?"

After thinking about it, Estevan, placing his right palm on his forehead, signed apologetically, *I must have forgotten. I don't believe I did.*

"Well, send her flowers even if we're a year late," said Diego. "Also, when I read the proposal for the 'gain of function' grant, I was shocked. I'm a businessman, not a misanthrope. Why didn't you remove the funding for the Wuhan vaccine? I hear it's ongoing."

With a blank stare, Estevan responded in simplified sign language, *I don't remember you giving me those instructions. We're still involved.*

Diego grabbed Estevan by the arm and said, "We thoroughly discussed it, and I clearly said I was not in favor of creating a lethal vaccine. The virus was fine; it was never intended to be worse than a bad cold, but this—this is a vicious attack on humanity. I will not be involved in it. End it now!" With insolence and fury in his eyes, Estevan nodded his head but pulled his arm away from Diego's grasp and walked away.

● ● ●

The following morning after a mid-morning espresso and a crostino with ricotta, figs, and honey, Diego announced to Estevan, "Let's go outside." Estevan followed. Stopping at the French doors to the gardens, Diego admired his property. He opened the doors and stepped out onto the *palazzo's* magnificent expansive manicured gardens. Above them, the rooftop terrace cast a late-morning shadow over the turf. Beyond the well-mown grass, a waft of wild lavender and rosemary filled the air. The red-granite cliff descended in a precipice to pink sandy beaches a mile below. There, away from the zenith upon which his estate was located, the aquamarine-blue waters of the Mediterranean Sea completed the *palazzo's* imposing canvas.

Numerous gas heaters burned the chill from the sea breeze. Diego stood there soaking in the Mediterranean sun, mesmerized by its beauty. Estevan deliberately moved in front of Diego to block his view. Turning to face Diego, he admonished. *Listen to me,* he signed. *The woman we met at the café is not your wife.*

"How can you be so certain, Estevan?"

Estevan used his notepad to scribble his question. *Have you heard of Occam's Razor?*

Diego smiled. "Are you saying that the most obvious and simple solution to my quandary is the correct one? That the woman simply has a remarkable likeness to my wife?"

Exactly.

"Unless you discovered something last night during your Internet searches, stop telling me what to think. Show me some evidence." Walking away, Diego was upset. Looking at his impeccably cut grass, he said, "Estevan, I'm telling you that the woman at the café was Yael. I should know. For the love of God, I was married to her." All Diego could think of was, *If Yael is alive, I can again enjoy life.*

Estevan followed his boss. He took his forearm from behind, stopped him, and signed, *You* want *it to be your wife.*

Diego walked away and left Estevan brooding. Estevan stood there and wondered, *Is Diego that blind?* He pondered, thinking that Diego was out of control.

CHAPTER FORTY

[Lyon, mainland France; November 2022]

nterpol's special team, the Pygmalion Team—composed of Gabriel Picard, Nate Shelley, and Inspector Eduardo Sánchez—had prepared the undercover agent who was now occupying Inspector Sánchez's home in Las Palmas, Gran Canaria. The team warned Guy Blanchet, a trusted agent and analyst, regarding the specifics of Diego Montemayor and his cabal. Fully aware that the inspector's iPhone, his computer, and all his communications were being monitored, Blanchet fabricated a series of communications sent to Interpol.

Writing under the inspector's identity, Blanchet wrote an urgent message to Picard, "Need to meet you immediately to discuss my meeting with Diego Montemayor." He signed it "Eduardo." In addition, Blanchet sent multiple sham follow-up emails to Picard. The emails falsely confirmed that the meeting with Picard could be conducted online; however, he was concerned about the sensitive nature of a troubling "discovery" that Diego Montemayor had made.

Curious about Interpol's counter-monitoring of Estevan's snooping, Nate wanted to know if the team had learned anything new about Diego's operation. Nate asked Picard, "I know it may be premature, but are there any interesting findings at this point?"

"Funny you should ask that," said Picard. "Diego appears to not only be upset about Estevan's refusal to accept his resurrected wife, but he's also questioning why Estevan made 'business decisions' without consulting Diego."

"Any decisions that concern us?" asked Nate.

"It's certainly of concern to Interpol, but it may not be relevant for the Pygmalion Project. It appears that without Diego's approval, Estevan funneled billions of dollars to the American NIH and CDC to get the experimental drugs they've labeled as 'vaccines' approved for distribution worldwide. In addition, Estevan compensated some 'expert physicians' and immunologists to endorse the vaccines."

"Are you speaking of the vaccines used worldwide to combat the effects of the deadly virus created by Diego in the first place?" asked a confused Inspector Sánchez.

Picard corrected Sánchez, "Technically, Diego funded the Wuhan laboratories to develop the virus; he did not 'create' the virus himself. But yes, my friend, Diego oddly claims that the virus was intended to have lethal effects on fewer than one percent of the infected population. He is incensed because the series of vaccines and boosters that were disseminated to the population are intended to claim vastly more innocent lives."

"So the monster may have a conscience after all," Inspector Sánchez quipped. "Just for clarification, I'm assuming 'CDC' and 'NIH' are American acronyms for…"

"Yes, I apologize, Eduardo. NIH stands for 'National Institutes of Health' and CDC means 'Centers for Disease Control and Prevention' in the US."

"*Gracias*," said Sánchez.

"It also appears that we're not the only ones who have hacked into Diego's digital fortress, one that was impenetrable up to six months ago."

"Did the Americans finally catch up with him?" asked Sánchez.

"Not at all, my friend. The Mossad is also collecting all his information. It appears that the Israelites had ties to Diego before he started collaborating with the CCP, but somehow those ties with Israel were cut after the new partnership with the CCP began."

"I'm sorry, but who is the CCP?" asked Sánchez.

"It's the Chinese Communist Party, Eduardo," said Picard. "I'm using the English designation for Nate's benefit. For you, it's the *Partido Comunista Chino*, or *PCC*."

Inspector Sánchez chuckled. "The plot thickens, my friends."

. . .

[Bonifacio, Corsica; November 2022]

"Since you're not convinced, Estevan, I will leave this in your hands. I want that woman followed and tracked down, if she's still on the island, that is. Although I'm certain she is Yael, I want you to confirm it for both our sakes. I want to learn everything about her. What name is she using? Who is her escort? Above all, I want her history, her birthplace, her education, et cetera. I'm certain that you will find out she is indeed Yael, my wife."

Estevan smiled. He started to jot in his notepad, but instead, he decided to sign his message. It was a simple one. *It will tell us nothing that we don't already know.*

"And that is?" asked Diego.

Diego, she is not alive. Your wife, Yael, perished in a hospital fire in the Canary Islands. Who knows who this woman is?

"Use our staff to follow her. On this small island it should not be difficult," said Diego.

Estevan signed, *If you like, I will involve myself.*

"Perhaps initially you can get involved. Find her. Identify her; then leave someone else in charge of following her, especially if she leaves for the mainland."

Shaking his head in obvious disagreement, Estevan signed, *I will do my best.*

That same evening, Estevan—accompanied by the driver Ciccio and one of the armed guards of the villa grounds, Nicolo—scoured the bars, restaurants, and various venues in Corsica. Estevan personally inquired at *La Loggia,* where he and Diego had spotted Yael's look-alike, but no information was available. All the waiters and staff present during the late-morning visit from the mystery woman remembered her well. Yet no one could inform Estevan of her whereabouts or her identity. Estevan's posse visited every hotel, every beach, and every tourist attraction, but without success.

Slightly past midnight, Ciccio turned onto the unlit two-mile gravel road leading to Diego's villa. As they approached the first building, the one that Diego had initially mistaken as his own home, all the interior lights were on. Music and laughter suggested that a celebration was ongoing, something that Estevan had not witnessed since their arrival in Corsica. In the past, the building had been owned by Diego Montemayor's holdings, but through his attorneys, he had sold the impressive but "charmless" home to a British couple who visited only during the summer. Out of the ordinary, the Brits appeared to be visiting their second home and entertaining guests.

Estevan signaled to Ciccio to stop. Signing to Nicolo, he asked him to follow him inside. Climbing the granite steps, they approached the door, and an officious-looking butler-type opened the door and asked for their invitation.

Tell him we're the neighbors who live up the road, signed Estevan to Nicolo. *We just want to welcome them to the neighborhood.*

The unsmiling Brit said to Nicolo, "Don't bother, sir. I mastered sign language long ago." Unceremoniously, he shut the door, a serious affront to the men. A moment later the butler opened the door and a stunning beauty in a black evening gown approached the door.

"*En quoi puis-je vous être utile?*" Recognizing Estevan, she turned to the butler and said, "Oh, dear—please get Monsieur Levant." Leaving the door ajar, the woman addressed Estevan, "Didn't we see you at the café?"

As the tuxedoed Mr. Levant approached the entrance, Nicolo in broken English said, "The owners of the palazzo…welcome you. We not intend…we don't want…intrusion from us."

Noticing the rifle slung on Nicolo's shoulder, Levant stated, "We would invite you in, but I'm afraid we're having a rather intimate family gathering. I hope you understand."

Tell him that if he needs anything—security, transportation, or assistance—to please contact us. We're just a mile up the road, Estevan signed to Nicolo.

Malcolm, the butler, intervened. "I will translate for Mr. Levant and his fiancée."

• • •

Upon arrival at the *palazzo*, Estevan informed his boss that their efforts to find the mystery woman in Bonifacio had been a total failure. However, Estevan and his team were able to locate her within the grounds of the compound. *Evidently, the property down the road, the one you sold to the Brits, is being leased by your friend and her fiancé.* "Did you get her name?" Diego asked.

"Well, she will soon be 'Mrs. Levant' because that is her fiancé's name. Knowing that Diego would not be able to interpret the signed surname, Estevan spelled the name, *"L-E-V-A-N-T,"* on his notepad.

After Diego inquired about the specifics of the encounter, Estevan explained that the couple was entertaining family and were not receptive to any outside contact. He further explained that Levant was obviously French and the mysterious woman spoke English in addition to French.

Encouraged by the successful search, Diego turned in but asked Estevan to dedicate time to investigating the name "Levant" and the identity of the man by her side, the "temporary obstacle."

Unable to sleep soundly, Diego woke up before dawn and created a fancy invitation done entirely in calligraphy. It was an invitation for his new neighbors in the Bonifacio compound. He informed them that in five days he would be hosting a soiree for a small group of friends and that he would request Mr. Levant and his fiancée to be his guests of honor.

Upon receiving the invitation, the former Raquel Rosales—who had fully assumed the persona of "Eliza Durazo"—commented to her fiancé, Ruel Levant, that she had never seen such an elegant and beautiful invitation. To Diego's dismay, however, the couple sent back the invitation via a courier.

The following morning Diego received the invitation without an RSVP. The courier simply indicated that "The recipients regret to inform you that their schedules will not permit their attendance." Diego immediately asked Estevan to drive him to the leased property so that he could speak to Levant and his fiancée. When Malcolm, the officious butler, received him, Diego discovered that Levant and his lady friend had moved to another location.

I told you that they did not welcome any outside contacts, Estevan signed. *Let's return home.*

Driving back to his *palazzo*, Diego said, "Unless you give me evidence that she is not Yael, my wife, I want you to do what I say. Find that couple. They can't be far."

For the next twenty-four hours Estevan and his team scoured the island of Corsica. After checking every boutique hotel and villa in Bonifacio, they proceeded to inquire about nearby establishments. At noon the following day Estevan found that the couple had checked into *Le Grand Hotel de Cala Rossa*, which was approximately twenty-five kilometers, or fifteen miles, from Bonifacio.

Diego was having a salad in his garden when Estevan arrived with the good news. A delighted Diego left his lunch, threw his napkin on the wrought iron table, and rushed to shower and shave. "Estevan, you and I will visit them this afternoon."

When Diego and Estevan arrived at the Grand Hotel lobby, they asked the concierge to ring the couple. The concierge discreetly covered the mouthpiece to conceal his own embarrassment, but it was obvious the couple did not wish to be disturbed. Since Diego had slipped a generous tip for him, the accommodating concierge was able to convince Monsieur Levant to at least speak to the "refined gentleman" who was seeking an audience with Levant and his companion. Instead of inviting Diego and Estevan up to their suite, Levant suggested they meet at the bar by the pier. After twenty-five minutes, Levant and "Eliza Durazo" showed up at the outside bar overlooking the Mediterranean, appearing relaxed and refreshed. However, they were clearly distant, suspicious, and reticent.

In the most charming manner that Estevan had ever seen in Diego, his boss gushed, "Thank you for allowing me to extend again the invitation which you...understandably...rejected." For the next twenty minutes Diego apologized for his rude behavior at the street café in Bonifacio. More than once he insisted that he would "make it up to them" by introducing them to the charming community of Corsica, even if they had judged him to be an "absolutely boorish" neighbor.

After Diego delivered a lengthy and embarrassing diatribe—at least in Estevan's estimation—Ruel Levant shared a little about his own background. He even curtly accepted Diego's apology. And to Diego's delight, the couple agreed to attend Diego's end-of-the-week soiree. Appearing to encourage his fiancée to be courteous to Diego and his associate, Levant added, "My fiancée Eliza may have much more in common with you, Monsieur Montemayor."

Playing her role perfectly, Eliza looked first at her fiancé, then back at Diego, and exclaimed, "I truly doubt such a thing, my love."

"Where are you from, if I may ask?" Diego asked.

"I'm a Spaniard. However, I was raised in the US, so I doubt that our paths ever crossed, Mr. Montemayor. In fact, I've forgotten most of my Spanish." Acting totally bored, Eliza turned to look at the beautiful scenery from the bar that overlooked the water.

Turning to the waiter, Diego summoned him and asked the couple, "Would you allow me to order some beverages for us?"

After the waiter took the wine orders, he promptly left. Diego continued, "As for forgetting a language, I find that learning a language is like riding a bicycle, Ms., Ms.…."

"Durazo…Eliza Durazo."

"Well, I can see that you have not forgotten your *distinción*, Ms. Durazo. If you had forgotten your native language, you would have lost it and pronounced your surname as 'Duraso,' with an *s* sound." Diego smiled. After the wine was delivered, he added, "And 'Eliza' would not have been pronounced with a *th* sound."

"Oh, my—I thought I'd lost my annoying lisp," said Eliza. As she took her first sip of her bubbly, she observed Diego making his mental notes. The rest of the afternoon was uneventful. Although Diego insisted on buying them dinner, Levant and Eliza claimed to have a previous engagement.

"Well, at least I will get to entertain you at my soirée this week-end," said Diego.

Somewhat disappointed, Diego returned to his *palazzo on the cliff* to plan his next steps. Before dismissing Estevan, Diego sat at his office desk and asked, "Well, my friend, what do you think now? Isn't it curious she claims to have forgotten Spanish, yet she slips constantly by using her native pronunciation? They may have brain-washed her, but I can tell she cannot resist my obvious interest in her. I don't care how many years have gone by, but my wife, Yael—or whoever she claims to be—still loves me."

Standing above him, Estevan shook his head, *It can be a trap. Maybe Sánchez and Interpol want you to believe it is Yael. Who knows?* Estevan wanted to object some more, but Diego stopped him. "I have repeatedly asked you to provide me with evidence. If you had found any proof, you would already have thrown it at me. By tomorrow noon I want Eliza Durazo's history—her birth records, her work history, her educational history, and her marriage certif-icate, if any."

The next day Estevan joined Diego for lunch in his own dining room. Diego challenged his *consigliere*: "Let's have it. Where is your evidence?"

She does not exist. Eliza Durazo does not exist; there are no public records for such a person, Estevan signed. *She is fictitious.*

Smiling in triumph, Diego stated, "By any chance, did you attempt to review my wife's public records? Are they there?"

Of course, Estevan said. *Yael's records are intact. But I could not find anything for her following her death.*

"Listen, my friend," said Diego, "We are looking at the same evi-dence, but we arrive at different conclusions. The fact that you cannot find records for Eliza Durazo means that she is indeed fictitious—because she's my wife, Yael Montemayor."

What I did not mention, Diego, signed Estevan in exasperation, *is that I found evidence of Eliza Durazo's birth certificate, educational records, even an employment record that had been destroyed. Whoever did this wants you to think Eliza Durazo is your wife.*

"No, Estevan. What it proves…is that my theory…that this alleged 'Ms. Durazo'"—at this point Diego used air quotation marks— "is Yael," said a smiling and smug Diego.

. . .

CHAPTER FORTY-ONE

[Lyon—Corsica, France; November 2022]

Since Estevan and Diego were closely monitoring Eliza Durazo's and Ruel Levant's every move, Nate arranged for Eliza to schedule a two-hour massage session at the Hotel Solemare in Bonifacio. Nate and Miró donned white clinical uniforms normally worn by masseuses and entered the hotel's large "spa and well-being" area thirty minutes before Eliza's arrival. A makeshift meeting area was set up for Eliza's final training inside the spa. Eliza wore loose gym attire and was given large white towels to change into before her "Swedish massage session."

It was now time for Nate to complete the final tweak of preparation for Eliza Durazo. It was perhaps the most sensitive piece of the coaching. Nate and Miró traveled to Bonifacio from Lyon, France, to coach Eliza. The final session would entail training that could transform a psychologically sound individual into a manipulative and dangerous operative who would be capable of psychopathic actions.

Nate's opening statement was "Like the former chief inspector says, 'In order to vanquish the enemy, you will need to become the enemy,' Raquel."

Eliza Durazo was in character. In fact, she was rarely *out* of character because she believed that to appear believable to Diego Montemayor, she would play her role 24/7. "Forgive me, Dr. Shelley, but you should call me by my new identity, 'Eliza Durazo.' I've been playing a role, the role of 'Eliza Durazo,' full-time. Am I to under-stand that you're asking me to become a psychopath?"

"I like what you've done, Raq…er, 'Eliza'. I like how you're using the *th* sound for the letter *z*," said Nate.

"Yes, Dr. Abe, and the inspector says linguists call it *distinción*. It's intended to throw Diego off. Since Eliza is claiming to be a Spaniard brought up in the US, I've chosen to use distinctly Spanish pronunci-ations to further confuse Diego into believing his own self-deception."

"Very nice move," said Nate.

"Okay, as far as turning you into a so-called psychopath, let me explain," said Nate. "Miró and I will guide you each step of the way. You will simply use techniques that Diego himself uses to manipu-late other people. We're not brainwashing you."

"But if Diego uses those techniques, won't he recognize them immediately?" asked Eliza.

"True, we must acknowledge that Diego is a brilliant man. He is a deranged criminal, but still brilliant."

"What Nate is saying is that a narcissist like Diego Montemayor has a need to be in control," said Miró. "Whether you are a friend or an enemy, his need is to be in total command. Friends become willing participants of his plans; enemies are put in positions where their lives depend on conforming to his wishes. In both instances, he is the manipulator."

"That is so true," said Eliza. "When I was around him in Win-netka, under my real identity, I disliked the man from the beginning. Now that you explain it in such a way, it becomes clear." Eliza sat at the conference table and drank her tea. "Do you mind if I take off my shoes?"

"Yes, during our coaching you can become yourself," said Miró.

"For now only," said Nate. "At all other times you are the new per-sona, Eliza Durazo."

Nate went to the dry-eraser board and assumed a professorial role. "When it's necessary, Diego is a master at controlling the behavior—and the minds—of others. He can use subtle strategies of mind control, or when necessary, he will use what we normally call 'brainwashing.'

The difference is that with his enemies Diego uses brainwashing but with people to whom he is close, he becomes a manipulator who merely uses strategies common to 'mind control.'"

"We want you to use the same techniques that Diego uses on other people. In this case, you will be manipulating Diego," said Miró.

"In my case," said Eliza, "you will want me to use 'mind control' since you do not want me to become Diego's enemy."

"That's correct," said Miró. "As you turn the tables on Diego, you will become his manipulator. At the beginning you will be aloof, distant, and completely disinterested in Diego. After all, we must remember that we've given you Ruel, a Frenchman who is your supposed fiancé. But gradually you will allow Diego to woo you 'back' into his clutches."

Walking barefoot to the tea and coffee station, Eliza asked, "So, what am I supposed to learn about mind control?"

Standing at the head of the table, Nate said, "Without getting into the weeds, I'll keep it simple. Like most psychopaths, Diego Montemayor uses four techniques that I'm convinced are ingrained in him. The steps he takes may even come naturally. You must those four techniques that Diego himself uses on other people."

"He is an expert at this, and you expect me to manipulate *him*?" asked Eliza in disbelief. "He'll read through me. Even you admit, he's a master at it."

"Remember, however," said Miró, "that in your case, Diego is already at a disadvantage. He's convinced that you are his deceased wife come to life. He believes that Yael Montemayor never perished in a fire—that Chief Inspector Sánchez and Interpol created this fictional person by the name of Eliza Durazo. To keep Yael alive, to save her from prosecution, and to shield her from a life of crime, the authorities invented Eliza. So for Diego you are not the mark. He is convinced that he has uncovered a plan by the authorities to deceive him."

Nate jumped in: "Being a narcissist, Diego has a deeply embedded need to be right. In his mind he is superior—smarter and more analytical than anyone else. Diego will not accept any evidence, any opinions, or any information that contradicts his own conclusion.

In this case, he is consumed by his own self-deception. In a way, he's already on your side."

"Okay, let's go through those four steps or four techniques," Eliza said. She appeared to be unconvinced.

Without hesitation, Nate moved to his dry-erase board mounted on an easel. "First thing, Diego pours upon his victims nothing but approval, affirmation, affection, and even love. Step two is a disabling, even self-effacing, effort to convince the victim that he is just like him or her—that he is also an imperfect person."

"You must be careful, though," said Miró, "that you do not gloss over the steps. Although the steps may sound unimportant and informal, each one is important."

"Yes, and each step must be accomplished before proceeding to the next one," said Nate.

Scratching the side of her nose, Eliza asked, "But you're not telling me that Diego walks around with notes in his pocket in order to know the steps to take, are you?"

Nate chuckled. "That's what is so remarkable about psychopaths and sociopaths. They seem to have an instinct about how to proceed. That's why I said earlier that with people like Diego Montemayor, such behavior is almost instinctive. He knows when he's ready to move on to the next step. With us—those of us who have healthier psychological makeups—we must work at it."

"Okay," said Eliza. "I believe I need to ask Miró something in private, Dr. Shelley."

"I will allow that only if you remove titles from our conversation," Nate smiled. "You have dropped titles when you address Miró and Max. Even with my father-in-law, instead of calling him Dr. Abraham Epstein, you call him Dr. Abe. In my case, you still call me Dr. Shelley."

Eliza covered her mouth. "I'm embarrassed. I suppose that's because I started my training with them. I feel like I've gotten to know them a little better, but I didn't mean to…"

"No apologies are necessary. Just call me Nate, okay?"

Eliza nodded her head, and said, "I'll try…. So if I can ask Miró a few questions in private—is that acceptable?"

"Yes, of course it's acceptable," said Miró. She and Eliza rose and walked to the other end of the small conference table.

While they were chatting, Nate jotted down on his dry-erase board the two points discussed:

TECHNIQUES OF MIND CONTROL

1. I approve of who you are; *I like you*, admire you, and respect you. *[Reinforce the other person's persona.]*

2. *I'm just like you*; there are many similarities between you and me. *[Strengthen the bond.]*

He underlined some key points, stepped back, and put his marker down. Glancing at the other end of the table, he realized Eliza and Miró were privately discussing lengthy questions. Nate left the room for a restroom break.

● ● ●

Returning to the meeting room, Nate discovered that Raquel and Miró were back at the table with smiles on their faces. "Should we order additional tea or coffee?" asked Nate.

"No, Raquel—rather, Eliza—and I thought it would be safer to keep going, continue with the coaching," said Miró. "We're certain that Estevan and Diego are monitoring every move that she and Ruel are making. And we dedicated only two hours to this brief session."

After reviewing the first two "mind control" techniques used by Diego Montemayor, Nate scribbled number three on his dry-erase board.

3. *I understand you*; you can trust me; *your secrets are safe with me.* [*Offer safety and security.*]

"Remember, Eliza, that Diego is a master manipulator. He knows when to begin to confide 'intimate details'—even flaws and insecurities—with his prey. He is willing to trust others with personal details about his own life to suck them into his 'inner circle.'"

"And that, my dear," said Miró, "is what you will do to Diego. You will gradually share intimate details with Diego to allow him to completely let his guard down. He will be eager to share his own intimate details with you because he will trust you implicitly."

"Those are only three techniques. What about technique number four?" asked Eliza.

Nate paused. He approached Eliza and almost pleaded. "This probably will be the most difficult request we will make." He locked eyes with her. "We would not make this request if we thought it were unnecessary."

Miró added, "If you refuse to go along with step number four, we'll understand. If you're unwilling, Nate and I will think of an alternative."

"I believe I know what's coming," said Eliza. "So…if I'm unwilling, what alternative did you have in mind?"

"We don't have one…at the moment," said Nate.

Still in her bare feet, Eliza rose from the table and poured the last few drops of tea in her cup. "Let's hear step number four."

Unable to muster the courage to verbalize it, Nate walked back to the easel and jotted on his board,

> 4. *I am the perfect friend, partner, companion…lover…for you;* now that you know all my deepest secrets, hopes, and desires—even the same weaknesses that you have— realize that I am the perfect match for you. *[This bond is special.]*

Nothing but the rattling sound of the ceiling vents caused by the hotel's A/C kicking in could be heard for the next ninety seconds. Eliza turned to the wall, put her shoes on, then removed them. She said nothing. Nate sat back down and studied his notes. Miró started to utter encouragement but changed her mind.

When Eliza turned back to look at Nate then Miró, she had tears in her eyes. "Back in Winnetka I told you that I'd be willing to become the whore to see Diego pay for his crimes. I suppose you took me up on it?"

"Mrs. Rosales, I promise you that we will come up with an alternative plan if you refuse to go through with this," Nate said.

"Would you like to think about it?" Miró asked.

"We've worked for almost a year to get here. I will not jeopardize our plan," said Eliza. "I've got nothing else to live for."

For the next fifteen minutes the three summarized the four points on the board. As Eliza asked pointed questions, she also took notes from the material on the board. Nate and Miró clarified the possible scenarios that could arise. Miró ensured that the entire session had been duly recorded. She put away her own notes in her satchel for future reference and dissemination to the rest of the Interpol team. Before erasing the items on the board, they reviewed the four steps one last time.

TECHNIQUES OF MIND CONTROL

1 I approve of who you are; *I like you,* admire you, and respect you. *[Reinforce the other person's persona.]*

2 *I'm just like you;* there are many similarities between you and me. *[Strengthen the bond.]*

3 *I understand you;* you can trust me; *your secrets are safe with me. [Offer safety and security.]*

4 *I am the perfect friend, partner, companion...lover...for you;* now that you know all my deepest secrets, hopes, and desires—even the same weaknesses that you have—realize that I am the perfect match for you. *[This bond is special.]*

While Eliza returned from her supposed spa massage to meet Ruel at the bar, Nate and Miró took the Hotel Solemare's service elevator wearing white masseuse uniforms. They carried with them the various towels and oils that had presumably been used for the massage that Monsieur Levant's fiancée had ordered.

CHAPTER FORTY-TWO

[Lyon–Corsica, France; late November 2022]

The special aircraft that Interpol provided for Nate and Miró for their return to Lyon was modern, if not luxurious. The captain, Juliette Martin, accompanied by her first officer, Ethan Durand, greeted them at the *Figari sud Corse* Airfield, which served as the most convenient private jet airport in the island. They provided Nate and Miró sandwiches, fresh vegetables, and an adequate bottle of wine. On their trip back to Lyon, Nate was curious.

"What girl-to-girl talk did you have with Raquel—uh, Eliza?"

Miró could only smile. "The questions became moot after you introduced point number four, Nate. Poor Eliza. After you introduced the first two steps of mind control, she wanted to know just how much affirmation to give Diego, to whom she referred as a 'monster.' She was concerned about her own ability to pull off any kind of intimacy with Diego—how much admiration, respect, and approval could she offer a man who repulses her? During our brief conversation, she was ready to establish some boundaries, but I convinced her to listen to your entire presentation first."

"What is your impression? Do you still believe she can pull it off?" Nate asked.

"I have grown to respect Eliza. She is a strong-willed, resourceful woman. And she is committed. I believe she will work on herself; she will take on the role that will give her the only satisfaction she needs now. When she takes on the role of a *femme fatale*, she can be very effective—remember what she pulled off with Ram Edmunds, of all people!"

. . .

Diego Montemayor had anticipated securing a crewed yacht for his extravagant end-of-the-week soirée. Diego's original plan had the floating party sail along the French Riviera to witness a spectacular sunset and the breathtaking beauty of the coastline. However, Estevan persuaded Diego to have a more proper starting time for celebrities who began their festivities at midnight or later. And Estevan also prevailed upon Diego by convincing him to invite his celebrity guests to his magnificent mansion. Diego heeded Estevan's advice.

The dress code was strictly enforced—formal wear and masks. The champagne was unlimited and the entertainment superb. Tasteful, unobtrusive stringed lighting was installed along the gardens and swimming pools. Various bars were situated throughout the premises. The finest Beluga caviar was offered at each bar in addition to the champagne. At 3:30 in the morning, an assortment of *pintxos*, *montaditos*, and tapas were offered for any guests who cared about some other form of sustenance.

Of course, the numerous Spaniards so well known to American moviegoers were present without their entourages. Bardem and Penélope were there. So was Antonio, who was unaccompanied. The hip-hop-turned-politicians rubbed elbows with Wall Street tycoons who had flown in just to attend the event. Of course, several members of the CCP were present to encourage the grooming of the young newcomers to the American Congress. Seasoned US senators were also present, but they discreetly remained masked throughout the event. The director of the Health Organization of the World (HOW) sat with the CEO of CNBS and a tall gangly and awkward American who dominated the conversation. They, along with some Google magnates, chose a dimly lit table close to Diego's private gardens. Removing his mask, the image of the person commandeering the conversation was captured by the property cameras. Billy G., who had appointed himself the healthcare spokesperson of the globe, spoke endlessly and indiscriminately. "All I know," he said, "is that we must limit the world's population—one way or the other."

Yo-Yo Ma attended but did not perform. The beautiful voice of Andrea Bocelli serenaded the guests with "*Con te Partiro*." He went on for a scant fifteen minutes. Even Ringo Starr briefly accompanied Julian Lennon and Elton John, but he refused to stay when various movie celebrities began to partake of the suspicious powders that were circulating the grounds. Brad, sans Angelina, was there smiling his million-dollar smile. Numerous other international stars of the cinema and the world of entertainment were present. At least three best-selling authors were present, including the one who had collaborated with a former US president to publish a book. The string quartet who started the festivities at 11:00 p.m. took leave thirty minutes after midnight, and the less-inhibited guests—viz. Elton and Tina T. without their spouses—started dancing well after midnight on the decked dance floor set up by Estevan and his crew.

A special table reserved for Diego and some "close friends" offered the "*Almas*" version of Beluga. Ruel Levant and his fiancée Eliza Durazo arrived past midnight at 12:15. Estevan met them at the door and led them to Diego's table. He had Isabella Rossi by his side for the purpose of translation. In addition to learning English, Isabella, Diego's *cameriera*, had also mastered sign language in an inordinately short amount of time. Isabella wore a revealing beige *La Femme* lace column gown and she looked ravishing. However, when Eliza Durazo arrived, the men's stares shifted from Isabella to Eliza. She wore a stunning blue Bergdorf Goodman plunging-neck, sleeveless gown that perfectly accentuated her tall, slender figure and her perfectly shaped legs.

Without fail, every Hollywood and international celebrity took note of her entry. The women could not help but stare. Men—it could be said—drooled unabashedly. In fact, the star of the movie classic that depicted the tragic sinking of a celebrity ship taking its maiden sailing was so distracted by Eliza's entry that he spilled his date's champagne glass on her flat, anemic bust. Apologizing profusely, the embarrassed actor, instead of looking at his date, could not keep his eyes away from Eliza, and he proceeded to grin stupidly at her while pat-drying his date's drenched breasts. Finally the livid actress, herself well-known and well-respected, took the famous actor's champagne glass, tossed its contents onto his face, and walked away. Laughing hysterically, other men at the table of starlets applauded as the emaciated actress trudged away.

. . .

Timing his arrival perfectly, Diego joined Eliza and her fiancé at his table, which was squarely in the middle of his private garden. Immediately Diego opened the conversation by openly criticizing his own behavior during the past two meetings.

"I would have responded in the exact manner you did. I congratulate you, Monsieur Levant, for your actions and the way that you've protected your fiancée from the insolence of an intruder. I beg your forgiveness," said Diego. "As for you, Ms. Durazo, I doubt if I can convince you that I meant no offense—I was captivated by your charm, your glamour, and—forgive my forthrightness—by your loveliness."

Casting an apologetic look at Levant, Diego added, "My admiration to you, my friend. You are a fortunate, a very fortunate man to win the favor of such an enchanting beauty."

Eliza Durazo made mental notes of Diego's skillful use of the first strategy of "mind control" that Nate and Miró had identified. He will, they said, initially "approve of who you are." Be aware of it, they had warned, and master it yourself.

"We hardly know you, Mr. Montemayor," said Levant, "but we are flattered by your attention. In truth, we still question why you douse us with such compliments."

"I will be very direct, Mr. Levant. I lost my wife, Yael, six years ago in a tragic fire. And your fiancé is my wife's double. She could be her twin."

Turning to Eliza Durazo, Diego looked into Eliza's eyes and, leaning toward her, said, "You look exactly like Yael. My wife possessed such alluring beauty, and I believe—"

"Monsieur Montemayor," said Eliza, "*tu me mets mal à l'aise.*"

"I do not intend to make you uncomfortable. But you could be Yael's clone, her duplicate," said Diego. Fidgeting with his bow tie, Diego straightened up in his chair, took a sip of the champagne—his first one—and allowed Ms. Durazo to seek reassurance from her fiancé.

Addressing Eliza, Levant asked, "*Souhaitez-vous partir?*"

"That won't be necessary," said Diego. Although he was not confident speaking the language, Diego understood French perfectly. "If anyone should leave the table, it is I. After all, I do want my guests to enjoy themselves."

While Eliza looked away, Levant asked, "I understand my future wife is your wife's look-alike, but I assure you she was raised in America, and she attended American schools."

"May I be so bold as to ask when you two met?" Diego asked.

Eliza turned to Diego and spoke directly to him. In flawless English she said, "We met nine months ago in Paris, Mr. Montemayor. Is there anything else you need to know?"

As I assumed, Diego thought. *She just came into his life.* "¿Yael, cuándo vos me admites quién eres?" Diego insisted. (When will you admit who you are?)

"¡Basta! Me llamo Eliza Durazo y no Yael." In responding, Eliza had used *distinción*, the use of the "th" sound for the letter "z".

Diego noted the pronunciation. *Though my Yael was raised in the Canaries, she picked up the pronunciation, the distinción, from the greater part of the mainland—exactly as Eliza is doing.* "Please do not be upset," said Diego. "I will allow you and Monsieur Levant to enjoy the rest of the party. I will welcome my other guests."

Before walking away, Diego caught Estevan's eye. With a look, he summoned him, then turned to Eliza. "I have great respect and admiration for you, Miss Durazo." As he left the table, Diego signaled to Estevan, and immediately two tuxedoed caterers offered Eliza and Ruel Levant fresh flutes of champagne and small servings of caviar. Diego pondered and made mental notes: *Yael is not covering up her identity very well.*

Instead of mingling with his guests, Diego chose to view the rest of the soirée from his magnificent terrace, which gave him a view of the two hundred guests in attendance. The full moon was reflected on the intensely blue waters of the Mediterranean, foreboding things to come.

CHAPTER FORTY-THREE

[Lyon–Corsica, France; December 2022]

As Abraham Epstein had predicted, the changes made to the Pygmalion Project offered Nate and his team enormous flexibilities. Now the Pygmalion Project could be accelerated. Rather than pretending to be Yael Montemayor, Eliza Durazo vehemently affirmed a separate identity. Every time that Diego Montemayor suggested that Eliza could pass for Yael's twin sister, Eliza Durazo discounted it as nonsense. The more that Eliza denied any familiarity with Diego's deceased wife, the more Diego became convinced that Eliza was indeed his lost love.

Initially Nate and Picard depended primarily on Eliza's and Ruel's information to keep abreast of Diego's reactions to the ruse. Although Estevan's digital communication was already compromised and the Interpol team was able to listen to most conversations via cellular microphones, not all of Diego Montemayor's interactions were completely monitored. Yet Nate and Miró, along with Eduardo Sánchez and Gabriel Picard, recognized that Diego Montemayor seemed to be convinced, beyond a doubt, that Eliza Durazo was "in reality" Yael Montemayor.

The Pygmalion Team, made up of the three men, quickly added Miró to their crew. They were headquartered in Picard's office in Lyon, France. However, they also assigned three additional Interpol operatives to spy on their quarry in Corsica. Their principal objective was to inform the Pygmalion Team of Diego's interactions with Eliza Durazo and her "fiancé," Ruel Levant.

Upon arrival at a neighboring villa in Bonifacio, the Interpol spies got settled in. The visitors' luggage was unlike other ordinary tourists' belongings. The sophisticated electronic equipment included voice-activated receivers and transmitters, satellite phones, radios, a late-model Flir infrared camera, plus an assortment of Sony, Canon, and Nikon cameras. In their luggage they also had three sets of binoculars and four handguns, all 9mm semi-automatic Beretta pistols.

Although Nate had requested that Diego's villa be bugged by the operatives in Corsica, Picard considered the effort too dangerous. With Estevan's level of communications expertise, Picard was certain any attempt at bugging Diego's villa would be detected. He knew from the surveillance already in place that Estevan regularly swept the premises for any foreign and unwanted intrusion. So far, however, Estevan had not discovered the malware that allowed Interpol to trace Estevan's digital communications.

What the newly appointed Interpol spies were able to accomplish on their second day in Bonifacio was to attach GPS tracking devices to Diego's two vehicles. While Ciccio, Diego's driver, ran an errand to the local market in Bonifacio, the talented "Bluto" from Interpol had attached the device to the Range Rover's undercarriage. As Ciccio picked the best produce at the outdoor market, Nicolo drove Diego and Estevan to the marina in Bonifacio. The other two Interpol spies—"Olive" and "Popeye"—followed them. Nicolo drove the Mercedes-Benz G-Class and parked in front of the Harbor Master's office. While Diego and Estevan conducted business with the harbor master, Nicolo strolled toward the nature reserve. Popeye planted the device successfully on the Mercedes-Benz and Olive drove them back to their own villa safe house.

From cumulative information, Interpol's Pygmalion Team concluded that Diego was convinced that "they" –Sánchez and Interpol—had brought Yael back to health after the hospital fire and kept her from having any contact with her husband and her former life. The Pygmalion Project was progressing smoothly. The fortuitous turn of events, given Diego's self-deception, pleased Nate. Even the sole member of the team who still expressed doubts regarding Eliza's performance, Eduardo Sánchez, was beginning to feel more confident. Impressed by Eliza on her first encounters with Diego, the inspector's buy-in would solidify their chances for success.

. . .

On their return from the marina, Diego smiled broadly and asked Estevan, "Aren't you enjoying this beautiful day…the fresh air and sumptuous fragrance of the flora? What on earth is wrong, man?"

I believe you are falling into a trap, Estevan signed.

"What are you talking about? Estevan, are you still doubting that my Yael is alive?" Diego was using English to keep the discussion from their driver, Nicolo.

You run across this strange woman at a local café on the same day that you meet with Inspector Sánchez. Don't you find that "coincidence" to be improbable?' asked Estevan in his signed efforts to persuade Diego. Estevan was signing rapidly, frustrated and fearful that his boss was falling into someone's web of deception.

"What are you calling an improbable coincidence?" Diego asked.

You meet with Inspector Sánchez, whom you haven't seen in years, and on that same day you also coincidentally *run into Yael. What are the odds?*

Diego could not keep up with Estevan's sign language. "Estevan, please write me a note. I can't follow your argument."

After reading the scribbled note, Diego challenged Estevan. "So now you're saying that Inspector Sánchez brought his goddaughter, whom he's concealed from me for six years, so that I could accidentally meet her at a café in Bonifacio. Estevan, that is preposterous".

Nicolo arrived at the villa, and Estevan climbed out of the Mercedes G-Class and walked away totally exasperated. He dropped his notepad on the entrance pedestal and stormed into his office.

Diego remained inside the vehicle and considered Estevan's objections. He had directed Estevan to investigate Eliza Durazo's past, but no records could be found. Obviously someone had eliminated "Eliza's" entire history by deleting birth, educational, marriage, and work records. Yael's life records, on the other hand, were intact, up to her death, of course. In Diego's mind, this had been done to keep him off the trail.

Diego Montemayor reminded himself that he had outwitted his enemies for decades. Yet Diego could not discount Estevan's intuition and his powers of analysis. In this case, however, Estevan appeared to be close-minded, unwilling to consider the evidence. Yes, perhaps Sánchez and Interpol had fabricated a ruse to deceive him, but he—Diego Montemayor—had caught them red-handed. For years Sánchez might have successfully deceived Diego, but it was now time to unveil the masterfully prepared cover-up. Couldn't Estevan see that it was Diego who had uncovered the plot to keep Yael alive and away from him?

It was clear to Diego. In his delusion he assumed that Yael had been brought back to health after the hospital conflagration. She had probably undergone plastic surgery, which restored her beautiful skin and removed all scars from the disastrous fire. Her beauty was intact. Yes, certain telltale surgical scars may have been evident—tiny ones along the jaw line and above her brow—but Yael was still Yael. After all, Diego Montemayor, her husband, should know! No ploy by the law enforcement agencies—not even Estevan's suspicions—was going to convince him otherwise.

Meanwhile, Estevan grew more suspicious. He was unconvinced. He had met Yael only twice before the hospital fire, primarily in business settings, but there was something about Eliza Durazo that made Estevan skeptical. True, the resemblance was astonishing. As he reviewed countless photographs, he had to admit to Diego that the uncanny likeness was difficult to ignore. However, Eliza Durazo—as alluring and mysterious as she might be—was simply "too perfect." He could not identify a single piece of evidence to disprove Diego's theory, but he remained doubtful.

The following day, shortly after Diego had completed his early morning *tai chi* session, Estevan walked onto the manicured lawn of the private garden and approached Diego at his customary wrought iron patio table, where he enjoyed his first cup of espresso. Eyes shut, Diego smiled at the sun's rays that bathed his face in warmth. Without any preliminary signing or other form of communication, Estevan simply dropped the local morning newspaper, which splashed the front-page photograph of Ruel Levant and Mademoiselle Eliza Durazo, along with news of their wedding scheduled for the following week. Diego opened his eyes and glanced at the front page. If he was dismayed by the news, he did not show it. He simply stated to Estevan, who was walking back to the *palazzo,* "We'll need to accelerate our efforts, Estevan." Estevan kept on walking and simply shook his lowered head.

Diego waited until the following day to approach Ruel Levant and Eliza Durazo. He and Estevan traveled forty minutes to reach Lecci, which was forty kilometers northeast of Bonifacio on the island of Corsica. Upon arrival, he rang the couple from the lobby of *Le Grand Hotel de Calla Rossa.* "First of all, my congratulations for the upcoming wedding. I come bearing gifts," Diego said.

As was his custom, Ruel did not invite them to their suite. Instead, he curtly stated, "Give us ten minutes, and we'll join you for some cocktails, Monsieur Montemayor." Diego and Estevan waited downstairs at the decked and shaded area overlooking the marina.

Countless yachts were docked in one of Europe's chicest ports. Key berths in this coveted harbor were hard to come by, with waiting lists being full for months. During this gloriously sunny day, it appeared that a megayacht had arrived overnight. Several curious onlookers had left their tables at the bar to admire the recent arrival. Without a cloud in the sky, only the high-flying marsh terns dotted the sky. Diego Montemayor smiled as he enjoyed the view.

As Diego instructed Estevan to order their favorite sipping wine, his guests arrived. Visibly despondent, Eliza showed up arm in arm with Ruel. She was wearing a knee-length sleeveless beige eyelet linen Bottega Veneta cover-up with matching beach hat. Her glowing bronze skin contrasted alluringly with her fitted shift. Not bothering to mask his obvious approval, Diego noticed the teal one-piece swimsuit underneath. In unison with most of the male patrons, he lecherously admired the view, which surpassed the marina's view of the Mediterranean.

Making a show of the fact that their entertainment had been interrupted, Eliza held her jeweled teal Bottega Veneta flat sandals. Her other hand propped up her matching teal sunglasses on top of her head. Her expression made it clear she preferred to return to her sunbathing.

Diego took his Panama hat and rose from his seat. Estevan remained seated. "Please have a seat," Diego said. "And forgive my friend's rude behavior."

Noting Eliza's facial expression and her nonverbal communication, Diego said in apology, "How thoughtless of me to simply barge in, interrupting two lovebirds on their romantic vacation." We drove here merely to be the ones to offer the first wedding gift to the soon-to-be newlyweds. Diego leaned over and handed Ruel Levant the title and paperwork of the *Shenandoah of Sark*, the three-masted schooner megayacht moored within sight. "Are you fond of sailing, my friend?" he beamed.

Scanning the papers quickly, Ruel was genuinely stunned and speechless. "Uhm…yes, Monsieur Montemayor. I do sail…but we can hardly…I don't know what to say."

Eliza interrupted: "Say no, darling." She took the folded documents from Ruel and, turning to Diego, forced a smile and affirmed, "Although we appreciate your generosity, Señor Montemayor, we cannot accept it. You must understand—we hardly know each other."

Diego shook his head and refused to take the papers that Eliza was attempting to return to him. Ignoring her, Diego with a smile said, "Do you see that one-hundred-eighty-foot classic yacht in the distance?" He was partly shielding the sun from his face. Estevan pointed to the magnificent yacht in the marina. "I had bought it for my retirement, but I'm afraid I've used it only once since I bought it. My business does not allow such frivolity."

"The answer is no, Mister Montemayor. Thank you, but no…" Eliza said in a slightly flawed English. She had practiced with Miró to inject an "ee" sound into the word "Mister."

"Miss Durazo, I must admit I am deeply saddened—and more than slightly hurt," said Diego, genuinely contrite in voice and actions.

His gaze was lowered, and he seemed to struggle for his next statement. "I assure you," he said humbly, "there are no conditions and no strings attached."

Ruel Levant quickly said, "Monsieur Montemayor—and Monsieur Chengfu—please take your seats. I've already ordered our drinks. We can at least toast to a beautiful afternoon and our upcoming marriage."

Eliza Durazo got up and took her sandals. As she walked away, she put on her hat and sunglasses without saying a word.

"Gentlemen, please understand that Eliza does not mean to offend you. She merely…" Levant started to explain but stopped. In well-practiced regret, he continued: "We cannot accept your generosity, as well-intentioned as it might be. I beg you to understand."

● ● ●

Gabriel Picard's office in Lyon was not as well-appointed as Ram Edmunds' FBI regional office in Chicago. However, Interpol's technological equipment was unparalleled. Picard's furnishings were comfortable but practical. It could be said that his office was industrial in its appearance, with huge open areas and exposed brick walls. The exposed A/C vents and exposed wiring made for several digital cable "rats' nests" at every desk in the open area.

The few windows in the large office/conference room had been covered, which prevented any natural light to penetrate Picard's *sanctum sanctorum*. Sitting gloomily at his desk, Picard listened carefully to the conversation between Levant and Diego. He approved of Eliza's performance. She was playing her part extremely well. His own agent, Ruel Levant, on the other hand, was taking extreme risks. Levant was alone with Diego and Estevan. Since Levant had refused to wear ear buds for sound reception, Picard was unable to advise him. Picard wanted to remind his agent that he was dealing with dangerous criminals.

Although Ruel Levant was wearing a voice-activated transmitter, the wind noise made the voice quality less than ideal. As Gabriel Picard and two of his communication specialists monitored the conversation between Ruel and Diego Montemayor, he wanted desperately to impress upon Levant, an experienced Interpol agent, that he needed to exercise caution. Levant was not armed. Picard thought to himself, *Diego will not hesitate to eliminate you to claim Eliza for himself.*

In his next transmission to headquarters in Lyon, Levant appeared to accept Diego's invitation to walk up to the marina. Picard could not believe it. Two minutes later, he heard Diego barking orders for the disembarkation of his professionally trained men from the yacht to allow Estevan and Ruel Levant to take a quick look at his wedding gift for the couple.

In a subsequent garbled transmission, Picard heard the voice of a certain Isabella Ricci, who was introduced as Estevan's translator, greeting Monsieur Levant. She appeared to be aboard the *Shenandoah of Sark*. However, Picard again heard Levant inexplicably accepting an invitation to "look around" the magnificent vessel.

From the thunderous sound of static interference, a moment later it was obvious that the sailboat's diesel engine had been started and they were seaborne. The wind noise prevented any further transmission to Interpol's Lyon headquarters. Picard wondered if Diego had boarded the yacht. He turned to his communication specialists and asked, "Did either one of you hear Diego Montemayor's voice as they boarded the yacht?" The two men shrugged, indicating they could not verify whether he was aboard. Picard sat morosely as he visualized the *Shenandoah of Sark* heading into the Gulf of St. Cyprien.

● ● ●

Rescue for Ruel Levant was not an option. Picard knew that the entire operation would be sacrificed if any attempt on saving Levant was made. He immediately contacted the two Interpol operatives who were near the marina. "Is the yacht within your range of vision?" Confirming what he already knew, Picard acknowledged Popeye and Olive's response. They could no longer see the schooner. Their next words, however, clarified to Picard what Diego's next move would be. "What we can confirm is that Diego is walking back by himself to the decked bar overlooking the pier." Picard ended the communication and waited…. *Estevan is going to kill our agent.*

PART FIVE

THE EXECUTION

"...earthly riches can never... pacify divine wrath."

<small>SOREN KIERKEGAARD</small>

CHAPTER FORTY-FOUR

[Lyon and Corsica, France; Palma
de Mallorca, Spain; December 2022]

Word of the unfortunate drowning of Ruel Levant in the Gulf
of St. Cyprien near Lecci, France, reached the Lyon Interpol headquarters the following day at exactly noon. Gabriel
Picard was in his office on the third floor when he was informed by
the agent on duty. Picard immediately called Nate Shelley and the
rest of his team to advise them that necessary adjustments to the plan
would need to be made immediately. The call was made on a secure
line to avoid the compromised lines tapped by Diego and Estevan.

"Ruel Levant was an integral part of the Pygmalion Project, and
his absence will require Ms. Durazo to 'fly solo,'" Picard said calmly.
As usual, Picard was taking the news as he did most things, with little emotion and supreme composure.

Miró immediately asked Picard if he had heard from Eliza. Picard
responded, "My people in Lecci tell me that she is secure in her suite
at the Grand Hotel. She ordered a late breakfast, but she has not left
her room since last night."

"Has Diego attempted to communicate with her?" Miró asked.

Picard quickly responded, "No efforts have been attempted from
Diego nor Estevan."

"How did the press report the news?" Nate asked Picard.

"Very predictably. A distraught couple—perhaps Isabella Ricci and
her companion—reported that their guest, who had perhaps had too

much to drink, was hit by the boom as they were heeling. Estevan was at the helm and the guest, Ruel Levant, drunkenly walked leeward at the precise moment that the mainsail was in motion."

Nate apologized: "I'm afraid you'll need to translate for Miró and me, Gabriel. Neither one of us sails."

"Of course," said Picard. "Estevan was steering the boat. Evidently the vessel was leaning over in the water, pushed by the wind and picking up speed."

Miró interrupted, "Is that what 'heeling' means?"

"Indeed it does," said Picard. "The boom is the thick pole that runs along the bottom edge of the mainsail. So, according to the couple, their guest, Levant, foolishly moved to the side of the boat, the low side, where the yacht was leaning. As the boom, or the thick pole, was moved by the force of the wind, it hit Levant on the head and knocked him overboard."

Miró asked, "Was there any attempt to save him?"

Picard slowly said, "According to Isabella Ricci's interview, she took over at the helm while Estevan jumped into the water to rescue their guest. Estevan later claimed that he went under several times to help his friend…but to no avail."

"Mm, hmm. How convenient!" said Miró.

With resignation in his voice, Picard added, "Sounds perfectly plausible to the public."

Breaking with his usual demeanor and finally showing remorse, Picard added, "We could not risk exposure to stop Diego's cold-blooded attack…. He was my…our…best agent."

● ● ●

Perhaps Gabriel Picard's greatest regret was not being able to honor a valiant fallen agent at his funeral. Since Levant's body was not recovered, a simple memorial service was held at an undisclosed location. According to a false account published in the *Tribune de Genève*, a Swiss newspaper published in French, Ruel Levant's family and fiancée attended an "intimate memorial service." The article did not disclose individual names or locales. Although Estevan was unable to track down Eliza's whereabouts for two weeks, he copied the newspaper article for Diego Montemayor to read.

Using several private jets provided by Interpol and combined resources from France and Spain, Eliza Durazo flew incognito to a series of locales to scramble flight manifests. Two days after Levant's murder, she arrived safely at the Lyon Interpol headquarters to help tweak the Pygmalion Project. The unanticipated elimination of Ruel Levant would require changes in the original plan.

Joined by Eliza, the Pygmalion team determined that Ruel Levant had intended to settle in the western Mediterranean isle of Mallorca with his bride, Eliza Durazo. In fact, the property in Palma de Mallorca had already been furnished and prepared for the newlyweds to occupy after their wedding. With Interpol's resources, not only had Ruel carefully attended to their future home, but also he had created a will that included Eliza as co-owner of his estate.

Within two weeks, Eliza Durazo moved into her new home. An online and telephone trail was left for Estevan to discover. First, Eliza telephoned the concierge at *Le Grand Hotel de Calla Rossa*. She explained to the hotel administration that following the tragic accident that claimed the life of her fiancé, she had left the hotel without packing her belongings and without leaving a forwarding address. She apologized for the inconvenience but requested that her luggage be forwarded to her new home in Palma de Mallorca.

Second, Eliza Durazo sent a series of messages to a fictitious relative who lived in Toledo, Spain. In the messages she shared her grief of losing her future husband and requested her company if it could be arranged. She apologized for having lost contact with her family in Spain after having lived in "the States" for so many years. Traditionally, she closed her last message by expressing affection from a cousin who never forgot her, "*Con mucho cariño, tu prima que no te olvida, E.D.*"

To raise the curiosity of Estevan and Diego, Picard and the Pygmalion team created the false identity for Consuelo Cervantes, Eliza's alleged cousin. The female Interpol agent who would play the role of Consuelo M. Cervantes was, like Ruel Levant, a martial arts and weapons expert and an accomplished information systems analyst who had mastered the blockchain. Her name was also withheld from Eliza and the Shelleys. Within three days, Consuelo joined her "cousin" Eliza Durazo in her new Palma de Mallorca home.

A third series of communications—this time from Cousin Consuelo to Eliza Durazo—offered her condolences for Eliza's loss. According to Consuelo's false identity, she was a "government employee who administered a pharmaceutical supply company." Since her supervisor had granted her a leave of absence, she promised to accompany her relative for as long as necessary. All of Cousin Consuelo's emails were traceable, of course, for the benefit of Estevan's espionage efforts.

Upon arrival at Eliza's home, Consuelo unpacked her luggage. From it she unloaded a Canon EOSM R5 digital single-lens reflex camera and satellite communicator. After touring Eliza's villa, she identified the room that best afforded an unobstructed view of the sky. After Consuelo powered up the satellite communicator, she loosened a small, magnetized antenna and opened the casement windows. Leaning backward, in the direction of the southern sky, she sat on the sill and secured the antenna to an external frame. Next, she plugged the antenna into the communicator and synced it to her phone. The encryptions software ensured that her phone messages could be read only by her intended recipient. Once she locked into Interpol's satellite system, she communicated directly with Gabriel Picard, and only with Gabriel Picard. Through redundant encryption, she prevented her own communications to be traced, even by Picard.

. . .

Reluctantly following Diego's orders, Estevan shared his findings with his boss. He informed Diego that Eliza had moved into her new home in Palma de Mallorca, the home that Ruel Levant had already bought and furnished for his bride-to-be. Understandably, Eliza was in mourning for the loss of her fiancé, and a distant cousin by the name of Consuelo Cervantes had moved in with her to help her grieve the loss of her future husband. Estevan shared printed copies of the email exchanges between both women.

The following day Diego sent multiple messages to Eliza expressing his deepest condolences and sympathizing with her loss. He described how he had felt after losing his wife, Yael, in a hospital fire and how much he had loved her. He poetically described his grief and how he had refused to eat or drink for days, going on minimal nourishment for weeks. He waxed philosophically about his depression, his loneliness, and his suicidal thoughts. Reading his messages, Eliza could not help reminiscing about the loss of her own husband, and even now, the loss of her children. As cynical as she wanted to be, Eliza compared Diego's frailties with her own and admitted to herself that Diego indeed sounded sincere.

. . .

Although a resident of Spain for years, Consuelo had never visited the Balearic Islands, nor the principal destination spot for countless vacationers throughout the world. She walked into Eliza's den and was immediately hypnotized by the view of the Bay of Palma. The beauty of the island did not escape her. Scotch in hand, Eliza approached Consuelo to read some emails from Diego. Eliza wondered if Diego might be undergoing changes.

"Snap out of it, girl," said Consuelo. "You are dealing with a master manipulator. Of course he sounds sincere. If you recall Nate's last training, Diego is merely launching step number two your way. And recite for me what Nate and Miró forced you to memorize. The second step is…"

"I'm just like you: strengthen the bond," Eliza responded, robot-like.

"Exactly," Consuelo said. "And what will come next?"

"Okay, okay. I get it. I can't fall for his manipulation," Eliza said.

"Look, *prima*." Consuelo accentuated the word *cousin*. "I'm not kidding. Review for me the steps that Diego will take. I'm here to help you, not to become your best friend."

"Step one," said Eliza, "is 'I approve of who you are; I like you, admire you, and respect you.' Step two we just reviewed, which is 'I'm just like you; there are many similarities between you and me. Step three will be coming soon, I suppose," said Eliza.

"And that step is…?"

"Step three is 'I understand you; you can trust me; your secrets are safe with me.' And before you prompt me, Step four is 'I am the perfect friend, partner, companion, even lover, for you. I am the perfect match for you.'"

"You better believe it, girl. Those four steps will save you in this process. Engrave them in your heart because you must master those steps yourself. You're going to turn the tables on that monster," said Consuelo. "Remember: not only did this animal murder your alleged fiancé, but he also murdered your own husband and probably your twin sons. As far as he's concerned, he'd rather kill you than lose you. He has methodically completed the first step, which is meant to reinforce his target's persona. What he's doing now is the second step of his deliberate plan to strengthen whatever bond there is between the two of you."

Eliza interrupted. "I know. I know. After that is accomplished, during the third step of his process, he will seek to offer me safety and security. After that's done, he'll move in for the kill. He will seek to convince me that our bond is special."

"I know it's scary," said Consuelo. "But you've got support. I'll be here each step of the way."

. . .

CHAPTER FORTY-FIVE

[Corsica, France; Palma de Mallorca, Spain; January 2023]

During the next three weeks, Diego Montemayor was a respectful, sensitive, and understanding friend to Eliza Durazo. Each day he emailed morning greetings simply to let her know that Eliza had a loyal friend who was a stone's throw away. Although he had gifted her and Ruel his own yacht, Diego offered to gladly rent "a boat" to sail across the Mediterranean to her Mallorcan shore— only if she was willing to receive company. Not once did he show up unannounced. Not only was Diego understanding, but he often apologized for his inability to offer additional comfort.

Occasionally he sent her potted plants, which he had again begun to grow. He shared with her that after his own wife's death, he had neglected his botanical interests and left behind a greenhouse, which he adored. He lamented his lack of enthusiasm and interest in hobbies.

Several exotic flowers arrived by post, and framed photographs of the plants were delivered at odd intervals. His small, thoughtful gifts were infrequent but tasteful. After the second week of communications, Eliza responded with one message, expressing polite appreciation. She thanked him for his gifts but assured him that gifts were not necessary.

For three weeks Diego Montemayor refrained from sounding too optimistic or of good cheer, but on the first day of the fourth week, he announced that he had a resurrected interest in his primary hobby— "gardening." In truth, Diego was a renowned botanist and expert toxicologist.

He shared with Eliza various architectural drawings of his newly built greenhouse, a glass-walled structure built on the side of his personal garden, which appeared to be more of a conservatory. A magnificent array of exotic plants lined the walls of the "greenhouse," some which Eliza had never seen. Various kinds of foxgloves, philodendrons, and calatheas filled each nook and cranny. It appeared to Eliza that Diego was serious about his hobby. Dozens of red, orange, and purple flowering plants adorned the glass dome with hanging baskets. Sizeable Valencia orange plants stood at the entrance, beside which Diego stood proudly showing off his prized fruit blossoms.

Not an easy thing to accomplish this time of year, read the message at the bottom of the picture. Not familiar with growing seasons, Eliza assumed that teasing orange blossoms out of a small tree was indeed difficult in the beginning of the year.

Eliza noticed that in the photograph Diego appeared with a strange magnifier hanging from his neck and in his left hand he held a tiny potted plant. In his right hand he held tiny tweezers, as if he were ready to pluck his own eyebrows. Curious, Eliza asked via electronic mail, "What is it you're holding?"

Within seconds Diego responded, "I'm holding a rare variety of my favorite plant, the foxglove, *Isoplexis canariensis.* In my right hand I hold forceps with which I genetically modify my tubular plants."

"Around your neck—is that a jeweler's magnifier?" asked Eliza.

Curiously, and out of character, Diego responded with a *double entendre*: "Ha, yes, very perceptive. When I do my work with my beauties, I use what is called a 'triple loupe'—which has three antireflective lenses to magnify the body parts…of the plants, of course."

Eliza did not bite. She simply responded, "I see."

• • •

Although Diego continued his daily communications, Eliza waited until the following week to thank Diego for his friendship. In that brief electronic communication, Eliza not only expressed appreciation for Diego's understanding and his genuine concern for her but also went on to note that, in life, her intended husband, Ruel, was also a very sensitive man. In fact, just like Diego, her fiancé had been genuinely concerned for her own safety, happiness, and emotional well-being.

Although Eliza knew that her "cousin" Consuelo M. Cervantes—in addition to the entire Pygmalion Team—was monitoring all her communications, as soon as she clicked "send," she regretted her action. She approached Consuelo, who was upstairs in her "communications office" to ask if she had gone too far.

"On the contrary, Cousin Eliza, that was a master stroke. For the first time, you've expressed approval of your new friend, Diego Montemayor. Your own counterattack, your own manipulation, is underway."

Within minutes Eliza received an endorsement from Lyon. It was Nate: "Well done. For the next couple of weeks, suggest to Diego what he wants to hear: 'I approve of you; I like you and respect you.'"

While Diego dedicated the next three weeks convincing Eliza of his trustworthiness, Eliza responded—infrequently—with gratitude and subtle indications that she indeed took note of Diego's devoted sense of friendship. At one point she apologized for her previous behavior and her own skepticism regarding his sincerity.

Of course, Diego responded by stating how she had been completely entitled to her doubts, given the age differences, and his inappropriate approach to welcoming Ruel and his fiancée to the isle of Corsica. He repeated how he would not dream of betraying her trust, nor would he ever hurt or offend her.

Though a torrential rain had assaulted the paradise of Mallorca all weekend, on Sunday Consuelo asked Eliza to take a walk with her along the Sea Front Walk. "We'll wait until the storm passes, and we can walk to the *Ola del Mar Café*, said Consuelo. "It's only a few kilometers from here."

"I'll walk with you," Eliza said, "but let's stick to the Historic and Architectural Route, and don't meander into Old Town because I'll get lost. We'll stop at one of our favorite cafés if I get tired."

"You mean one of *your* favorite cafés, don't you?" asked Consuelo.

Eliza simply chuckled. It was true. After moving to Europe, she had become more sedentary. In Mallorca, however, there were plenty of pedestrianized streets that allowed the average tourist to discover so many of the historic sights.

After going through the king's palace next to the cathedral and admiring the Gothic architecture, Eliza was ready for a cappuccino. They arrived at her favorite spot, the *Can Joan de S'Aigua*, presumably the oldest café in the city. Eliza suggested a table with a better view than the one usually selected by her "visiting cousin." Consuelo asked for two *cortados*, but Eliza insisted she would have the Mallorcan hot chocolate, almond ice cream, and a couple of Mallorcan pastries.

Although the weather was humid and cold, Consuelo wore her jean shorts and hiking boots. She announced, "Nate and the rest of the Pygmalion Team think we should accelerate our plan."

Biting into her first pastry, Eliza asked, "How?"

"Suggest to Diego that although you appreciate my presence here, you do not find me to be as understanding and helpful as you'd hoped. Share with him how frustrated you get with me and how we often disagree on things. Suggest even that our conversations often get disagreeable."

"In other words," asked Eliza, "you want me to transition to the second phase of manipulation. Are you asking me to reinforce Diego's persona and further suggest that he and I—rather than you and I—have many similarities?"

"Exactly. You are a quick learner, aren't you?" Consuelo asked without an interrogation in her voice.

"There's nothing I would like more than to nail that murderer," said Eliza.

"Just remember to keep your emotions in check," said Consuelo. "You do not want to even hint at any animosity against your prey. Slow and steady."

"How slow? How steady?" asked Eliza.

"Cousin Eliza," admonished Consuelo as she pulled her stray blonde locks of hair into place, "do not get impatient. This is a process. When you're ready, we will spring the trap. Until then—one step at a time."

That Wednesday, Eliza sent several emails to Diego, admitting she had several disagreements with her visiting cousin. Eliza alluded to Consuelo's bad hygiene, her insensitivity, and her crass sense of humor. She described Consuelo's lack of social graces and her general disregard for her looks. In truth, she even wondered if it had been a mistake to invite her cousin into her life.

Like a perfect gentleman, in an email Diego refused to comment on Consuelo's shortcomings. Instead, he focused on his admiration for a relative who cared enough to dedicate weeks to helping his "favorite human being" grieve the death of her fiancé. He went on to state the remarkable similarities between his personality and Eliza's.

For an entire week Diego refrained from criticizing Consuelo. "All I know," said Diego, "is that I thank God that Consuelo has done for you what I could not do. I wanted to be there for you, by your side, to help you grieve for your loved one. Each day my heart broke for you, knowing that you were in pain. Please forgive me if I lack prudence, but I believe a friendship like ours can grow. Perhaps your cousin feels a need to return to her obligations. Perhaps it is time. I believe that you can now trust me to help you the rest of the way."

Like clockwork—just to confirm Nate's predictions—on exactly the eighth week of Diego's communications with Eliza, Diego began his effort to win Eliza romantically. That same evening a courier arrived at her home bearing a long, gilded box with a note in flamboyant calligraphy that said, "Thank you for our sacred bond." In the box appeared one long-stemmed red rose.

Following the advice of the entire Pygmalion Team, Eliza did not respond. Consuelo advised, "Keep Diego off balance. Let that manipulator know that he's crossing a line—but don't close any doors."

Not having received a response for forty-eight hours, Diego wrote a desperate electronic communication, "Have I managed to offend you? I have trouble expressing my feelings when I am in this state of mind. Will you please tell me how I can regain your trust?"

Eliza waited another twenty-four hours to answer. She responded with questions of her own. "My friend, Mr. Montemayor, if I have misled you in any way, please explain. Your concern and understanding are appreciated. I admire you and respect you. We have much in common, yes, but why the red rose? At any time did I inappropriately signal to you that I wanted a romantic relationship?"

Diego was at a loss. How in the world had he misinterpreted Eliza's responses? He stewed for a day. The following day, since the *Shenandoah of Sark's* ownership had been transferred to Ruel and Eliza, Diego instructed Estevan to rent a yacht and sail toward Mallorca for an unannounced visit.

• • •

CHAPTER FORTY-SIX

[Skokie, IL; January 2023]

=MAX=

truly don't know how much Minerva struggled while being away from her parents. Despite the upheaval to her life, not once did she complain or express any kind of emotional difficulties. By the middle of December, my niece had graduated from high school. She had celebrated Christmas and New Year's Day with Dad and me, but it had marked the first year to spend the holidays away from her parents. At the present time she was enrolled in online college courses while she considered her top offers from several Ivy League schools.

I only know that Minerva communicated with her parents daily and I also know that Dad and I were thrilled to have her smart, vibrant, and emotional energy that she brought into our lives. In truth, she rejuvenated us. Before high school graduation, Minerva joined the Ursuline Academy's cross-country team and convinced me to take up jogging again. Her training required early-morning running, so I joined her for five days a week. For my sake, she cut her morning runs to two miles. After three weeks, we extended our shared early-morning training to five miles daily. In Dad's case, Minerva discovered that in his earlier life, Abraham Epstein had been a Krav Maga master. In fact, he had been an instructor for police academies in Texas to help pay for his medical studies. So Minerva requested basic training from her grandfather, which enabled him to spend long hours at the neighborhood gym with his only granddaughter. I believe they grew closer than they had ever been.

Dad and I did our best not to disrupt Minerva's normal schedules, her social life, and her online class regimen. Although early on we attempted to move into Nate and Miró's home in Evanston, it became impractical and costly. With her approval, we moved her to Skokie to live in her grandfather's larger home, and Minerva welcomed every change with anticipation and without complaint. Like I noted earlier, Minerva has always been a model young lady, a well-adjusted and mature human being.

On the last Saturday of the month of January, the three of us decided to take advantage of the first sunny morning in weeks and ventured out to our favorite coffee shop in Skokie. Taking off her woolen French beret and mittens, Minerva admitted that although she was sticking to her favorite chai tea, she also intended to order an almond croissant. Although she normally avoided fattening sweets, Kneads & Wants Cafe's almond croissants were her weakness. She fought off a modicum of guilt, nodded in self-approval, and asserted that she had earned a treat.

Removing his winter gloves, Abraham announced to Minerva, "I've discovered some things that your mom and dad may be anxious to know. Much of what I'll share with you I'd hoped to bring with me to Lyon on your spring break, but my latest findings cannot wait."

"Dad, before you get started," I said, "what should I order for you?"

"I'll get whatever you're getting," said Abraham.

After waiting in line, I returned with a platter of pastries, Minerva's chai tea, and two coffees.

"My goodness, son—are you feeding a private army?"

"Sorry. Everything looked good, so I got one of each."

Minerva just shook her head and laughed as I handed her the almond croissant.

"Dad, is it more information on Picard's connections to the Chinese shipping magnates? If it is, remember that we need to be careful with any communications that may incriminate Nate's boss—"

"Whoa—hold on!" said Minerva. "I don't think I've heard anything like that."

I explained to my niece that Nate had given Abraham a green light to examine genealogical connections and public records of the people involved in the Pygmalion Project. "In fact, before your parents left for Europe, your gramps informed Nate that recent newspaper clippings and photographs suspiciously placed Gabriel Picard in Beijing numerous times. Apparently, Picard was conducting business transactions throughout the South China Sea. In several photographs he even appeared with the board of directors of Pan Asian Shipping Enterprises."

Embarrassed because her mouth was full, Minerva put her hand over her mouth and took a sip of her tea. "Would that be unusual for a person who works for Interpol, Uncle Max?"

"That's exactly what your dad said, *Mi'jita*. However," said Abraham, "one of those members has the last name of Chengfu…and that's Estevan's—Diego's assistant's—last name."

"Umm—that does make it interesting!" my niece exclaimed. "I remember that sinister character quite well from that horrible day aboard *The Black Pearl.*"

"Although we don't know if there's a connection with Diego's assistant," I said, "we thought it was worth investigating some more."

"Well, just to bring us back to your question, Max," Abraham said, "my most recent findings do not relate to Picard's frequent contacts with the Pan Asian Shipping company. My new findings do concern Picard, though."

"Ooh," Minerva said as she rubbed her hands together in anticipation. "The plot thickens."

Turning to his granddaughter, Abraham asked, "Do you remember how Diego's wife, Yael, was so convinced that our family had cheated her great-grandmother out of the deed of ownership to a huge land grant in Texas?"

"Yes, Gramps. How could I forget? It drove that poor woman crazy to the point that she wanted to kill Mom."

Abraham nodded. "Exactly. In the end, if she could not have that original title, she preferred to die—along with your mom and dad— in that hospital fire."

"Thank God that Dad was able to rescue Mom."

I added, "Your dad has been quite the hero—several times."

"Well," Abraham continued, "I went back and reviewed some of our old files. Nate shared additional material since joining Interpol—new files that were collected by Picard's staff contain some fascinating information, and I'll need your help, Max, with the interpretation of some terminology favored by law enforcement types. I may be wrong, but it appears that Picard passed on these files to Nate without reviewing them."

"Thank you all for including me in this conversation," Minerva said. "Maybe I'm wrong, but although I'm merely seventeen—soon to be eighteen—I think I can help...even in small ways."

It was such a treat for me to see my niece maturing before my eyes. "You, my dear one, are a very bright and perceptive young lady. I know your opinions and insights will help us a great deal."

Minerva smiled and turned to her grandfather. "Sorry for the interruption, Gramps. Please go ahead."

"I discovered a brief exchange between Yael Montemayor and Picard while she was employed by Chief Inspector Sánchez...back in 2016. It appears that while Yael was helping her husband, Diego, in the family business, she employed Sonny Rollo to pry into Miró's history," Abraham said. "Although she had arrested him for minor crimes, Yael was impressed with Sonny's vast hacking and cybercrime know-how. She began using him for her own illicit purposes."

"Again, sorry for the interruption, Gramps, but isn't Sonny Rollo the one who kidnapped me when we traveled to the Canary Islands?"

"Yep, the same one, *Mi'jita*. When your dad rescued you from Diego's home, it was Sonny and his girlfriend, Álana, who had kidnapped you. But they were holding you in Diego's home."

"Go on," I said. "I'm sure that's not the fascinating information that you discovered in the files."

"Exactly right, Max. The fascinating part is this. When Yael Montemayor hired Sonny, she found out from Sonny's girlfriend that as a child she had been sexually abused by her stepfather."

Surprisingly, Minerva forgot about her croissant. As she put it aside, she peered intently at her grandfather and appeared totally engrossed in the conversation. "That's horrible."

"Here's the clincher," said Abraham. "Her stepfather is Gabriel Picard."

"My goodness—talk about a small world!" I said. "No wonder you said this was fascinating, new evidence."

"Keep up with me here. Back in 2016, when Álana informed Yael about being sexually abused by her stepfather, in her official capacity as deputy inspector of the Las Palmas PD, Yael Montemayor telephoned Gabriel Picard. At the time, Picard was assisting Inspector Sánchez solve the murder of an American citizen."

"I have to ask," I said, interrupting. "Why would Interpol get involved in solving a murder that occurred in the Canaries?"

"Because at the time, Interpol suspected that the murderers were part of an international sex trafficking ring."

I asked, "Did Yael Montemayor blackmail Gabriel Picard?"

"All I know is that the recovered files indicate that Yael confronted Picard with Álana's allegations. The next day, Yael was offered a handsome sum to serve as liaison to Interpol in the investigation of an American woman's murder."

"In other words, Picard wanted to keep the allegations from becoming public," I said.

"And," said Minerva, chiming in, "Yael Montemayor was able to conceal her guilt in the murder of the American woman, Penny Rhodes."

"Precisely," said Abraham. "The unholy alliance between Gabriel Picard and Yael Montemayor was formed to conceal two crimes. Picard agreed to look the other way when Yael eliminated evidence that implicated her in the murder. And Yael agreed to keep quiet about Álana's accusations against Picard regarding his sexual molestation."

"I need to remind you, Dad, that we must be careful in communicating this information to Nate and Miró. After all, Nate is now working for Gabriel Picard."

* * *

CHAPTER FORTY-SEVEN

[Palma de Mallorca, Spain; February 2023]

Although an accomplished sailor, Estevan hired a small crew to help steer the yacht that Diego rented. Estevan disapproved of Diego making an unannounced visit at Eliza Durazo's villa; so instead of assuming the helm, he skippered the vessel so that he and Isabella Rossi could speak sensibly to Diego. Given to reckless and impetuous decision-making, Diego often needed counsel to prevent disastrous business and personal mistakes. This time, Estevan feared that Diego was falling into a dangerous web of deceit concocted by an invisible enemy.

If anything, Diego was usually in control of his senses. He was the one who manipulated circumstances in his favor. With Estevan's help, he had outwitted international law enforcement and had manipulated global politics to amass a fortune. From funding the development of a mysterious virus to controlling numerous political elections throughout the world, Diego had stayed one step ahead of his enemies. Now—an alluring and mysterious woman was making a fool of him. But why?

Standing at the yacht's port side of the bow, Diego looked out onto the horizon and contemplated the Mediterranean's sapphire blue spectacle. Using sign language, Estevan beckoned Diego to the stools by the bar. Behind the bar, Isabella prepared gin martinis, which had become Diego's favorite cocktail.

"Let me stand here five more minutes to soak in the sun, my friend," said Diego. "I'll join you in a while." Estevan knew that following the facial reconstruction and limb-lengthening surgeries, Diego's skin was not able to tan normally. He required the use of lotions and oils to attain a pigmentation on his pasty complexion that looked natural. Unfortunately, the lotions had the regrettable effect of aging Diego's skin. Before leaving for Mallorca, Diego had asked Isabella to select for him a white, or beige, cotton crew-neck sweater "that would be most becoming." Standing before his full-length mirror for thirty minutes, Diego had changed his off-white slacks four times until he settled on his favorite pair.

Amused, Isabella mentioned to Estevan that Diego was behaving "like a lovelorn teenager on his first date," *un adolescente inamorato*. Estevan just shook his head.

Finally Diego joined Estevan and Isabella at the bar. Although Estevan stuck to his customary all-black attire, Isabella wore a chic winter white blazer with gold buttons sans any kind of blouse. Her slacks matched Diego's. After using the silver shaker, the full-breasted Isabella leaned over the bar and proceeded to pour Diego's martini. "I hope you're enjoying the view, *padrone*," said Isabella.

Avoiding her stare, Diego responded, "Very much so. *Bellissimo*."

Estevan did not waste any time. Knowing that he would be signing too rapidly for Diego's skills, he asked Isabella to interpret. *I think you are making a big mistake. We need to vet this woman and even her cousin to find out what their motives are. And don't tell me that you still think that Eliza Durazo is your deceased wife.*

Diego waited for Isabella's interpretation. Then Diego smiled. Looking straight at Isabella, he said, "Estevan is acting like a betrayed lover. I think he's jealous."

Estevan smacked his head with his left palm, walked around the bar, and poured the rest of his cocktail down the drain. *If you are asking me if I think this woman is a threat to our relationship, then, yes, I believe that she is dangerous. Someone planted her in your life. For what reason, I don't know.*

As Isabella vocally interpreted Estevan's hurried signing, Estevan interrupted to correct her. *No, no. What I'm saying is that she is a threat to Diego's entire enterprise!* The labored dialog lasted for several minutes with an impasse at every juncture. It ended when Estevan stormed below deck to the bow's cabin.

. . .

When they docked at the assigned berth, Diego told Estevan and Isabella not to wait up. Ignoring the incoming rain clouds, Diego looked up at the sky and smiled. He refused to acknowledge the incoming storm and inhaled the piscine smells mixed with petrichor. *Amazing,* he thought. *Just being close to her invigorates me.* Still smiling and thinking of his beloved, he took a cab to the St. Regis *Mardovall,* where Estevan had arranged for his rental car to await him.

Before driving to Eliza's villa, Diego consulted the GPS in his BMW to stop at a flower stand to purchase a white, long-stemmed rose. He realized he needed a truce for Eliza and a clarification for any misunderstanding. As Diego traversed the various narrow, winding roads up the scenic hills in the island, he practiced his greeting. He desperately needed to undo his foolish miscalculation. *How could he have misunderstood Yael—or Eliza—so badly? What a blunder.*

Perhaps distracted by his thoughts, Diego twice retraced his route to make sense of the maze-like map on the screen of his rental. Signage for the various roads radiating from the main road was not always prominent and most of those roads were narrow and barely double-laned. And with the change in elevation, the foliage, although verdant and colorful, was consistently patterned—bougainvillea, queen palms, as well as tall hedging lining the roads on either side. The star jasmine groundcover seemed to be ever present, replacing the odors of the bay below. All roads leading up the hilltops resembled each other.

Driving the steep hills that dotted the residential area, Diego stopped twice to admire the view of the Bay of Palma. Amazing how this view of the Mediterranean could be so different from the one he enjoyed from his Bonifacio estate. After three false attempts, Diego finally arrived at Eliza's entrance. He admired the privacy offered by the topography. Each hill on the island could accommodate only

two or three modest villas ascending toward the crest of each elevation. Rather than sharing a single view of the bay below, each villa
enjoyed a unique perspective ranging from the lowermost dwelling
at the base of a hill to the mid and top levels.

Like Eliza's dwelling, the neighboring villas, of relatively modern
construction, were all tri-storied. The first story consisted of a two- or
three-stall garage, plus presumably an ample basement. The second
story included the various living areas, each with multiple floor-to-
ceiling windows facing the sea. Third stories consisted of three or four
bedrooms. The second and third stories boasted of multiple balconies
and windows overlooking the marvels of the Mediterranean. Most
of the villas were white or beige stucco with steep-walled driveway
entrances to the first-story garage. The dark rock used for the driveway entrances contrasted with the pastels of the stucco constructions.

Parking his vehicle at a steep incline, Diego climbed out and
quickly determined the area surrounding Yael's—or Eliza's—home
was not pedestrian friendly. No real sidewalks were present. Homes
in this community were meant for one thing only—to admire the
glorious view of the most beautiful body of water on earth. Eliza's
tiered garden in the front included various dwarf palms in addition to taller queen palms, bougainvillea, and what Diego's expertise told him was "hypericum balearicum" shrubs. Diego did not
have the flowering plant in his Bonifacio estate because it is native
to Spain's Balearic Islands. The pretty yellow flowers of the shrubs
lined the walkway to the second story, which led to the front door.
Stepping up the brick-on-sand walkway, Diego, somewhat winded,
noticed the arched wooden double doors. They were massive and
worn. When he pulled on the hanging rope that announced his visit
at the front door, it chimed with an unexpected aria from Puccini,
"*O mio babbino caro.*"

The door opened and the unexpected greeter threw Diego off
his scripted dialog. When he saw the tall and muscular perspiring
female wearing a biking outfit and a white fabric headband, he forgot his memorized greeting. She held her well-worn shoes and asked
the stranger who just stood there, "Well, what is it?"

Diego stammered, "Is this…?" He stepped back to look for the address at the front entrance but did not find one. He again looked at the greeter and said, "I may have the wrong address."

"Well, that would depend, wouldn't it?" The tall blonde, who was wearing a sleeveless top, dropped her shoes onto the floor and took off her headband. Diego noticed the pronounced and well-defined biceps on the bicyclist and the unshaven underarms. She spoke Spanish with a German accent.

"Does Eliza Durazo live here?"

"Are you Diego—Diego Montemayor? Because if you are, I don't think I should let you in…. She was afraid you'd show up." Just then Eliza appeared behind the rude greeter and tapped her on the shoulder. She murmured, "Let him in, *prima*."

Diego squeezed by the perspiring blonde and took one step into the foyer. *Prima* hardly moved to allow him in. She stood there looking at Diego from head to foot. She was taller than him by two inches.

Eliza had stepped behind the greeter, and as she visually acknowledged Diego, she turned slowly to walk the length of the white marbled foyer. She stepped down to the living area and called out, "Please come in, Mr. Montemayor."

Diego noticed that the entire southern wall of the living area was encased in floor-to-ceiling glass doors. Outside an infinity pool graced a large patio, and beyond the pool, which seemed to disappear in the horizon, was the *Bahía de Palma* with its magnificent beaches. The patio appeared to extend the back side of the villa and it was walled with volcanic rock that contrasted with the pink flagstone of the floor. The extent of the western wall of the volcanic rock wall was lined with white and radiant red rose bushes. The eastern wall was partially covered with the aromatic star jasmine.

"I regret that you appear forced to use titles, Eliza. Among friends—"

"It became clear to me," said Eliza, "that you misinterpreted our friendly exchanges. Now you show up unannounced…. Frankly I'm unclear about the purpose of your visit."

Diego realized he was still holding the long-stemmed white rose and awkwardly extended his arm. As he did, he said, "Perhaps this will convince you that I'm offering a small token to make amends for my stupid assumptions...my thoughtlessness."

Eliza looked at the rose, but she did not make a move toward Diego. Without a word, she turned and sat at a white leather *capitonné* easy chair. Diego noticed that the dark wooden walls contrasted with the white marbled floors, which were dotted with thick, contemporary, hand-tufted wool rugs that invited a person to go barefoot. Also, the coffered ceiling of the living area was done in intersecting white acacia squares. Subtle LED lighting was recessed into the periphery of the entire room's ceiling. The raised abstract design on the rugs was repeated in blacks, whites, beiges, and oranges, which reflected the outside colors in the patio. As she sat, Eliza used a remote control to light the room with three large chrome, arched floor lamps—a very tastefully done living area but much too contemporary for Diego's taste.

From behind Diego, the blonde, whom he now assumed was Eliza's visiting cousin, walked up to him, took the rose, and moved toward a black-marble sideboard to grab a crystal vase. In her first conciliatory act, she said, "Sit...wherever you like." Diego looked around and saw a *pouf rond*, or round ottoman, and a massive sofa opposite Yael—or Eliza. Both pieces were done in matching white leather *capitonné*. He chose to sit on the sofa.

Before walking away, the Amazonian cousin asked Eliza, "Would you like me to stick around?"

"It won't be necessary, Consuelo."

Attempting to make a recovery, Diego stated, "Eliza, I somehow managed to destroy whatever trust I may have built as a friend. I have no intention of offending you. Nor do I want to make you think that I will ever be disrespectful of your wishes. I came to reassure you that I am a friend...a friend who considers our friendship—what I foolishly described as a 'sacred bond'—to be special. By no means did I intend to be disrespectful."

"The red rose, Mr. Montemayor, to me the red rose indicated that I had opened the door to a romance...between the two of us." Eliza stood up and walked to her sliding doors. She looked in the direction

of the magnificent rose wall. "Each one of those rose bushes outside...
I planted each one to symbolize the love between Ruel and me." Eliza,
as if holding back tears, swallowed hard as she walked back to her
seat. "I cannot forget him. Can't you understand?"

Diego seemed genuinely moved. With a smile he nodded. "Who
better than I can understand, my friend? Remember how I described
to you my agony after losing my wife? Because you allowed me to
share my pain, I believe that much of my heartache was healed. In
my renewed interest in life, I became so excited that I thought I could
do the same for you."

Eliza paused. She made a show of looking out into the distance.
Nodding, she said, "Maybe now, after your explanation, I begin to
understand your mistake...a little better."

Diego continued, "However, in my enthusiasm I stupidly imagined
more of a 'bond' than what was there." Bringing his right hand to his
chest in a show of humility, he added, "For that I deeply apologize."

Eliza smiled and rose to her feet. She extended her hand in a gesture of peace and said, "You are forgiven, my friend." As she started
walking toward the front door, Diego rose from his seat and quickly
said, "I was hoping to take you out to dinner to solidify our friendship."

Garnering all the grace she could, Eliza said, "Perhaps another
time, friend."

Walking out the door, Diego said good-naturedly, "I will come
calling soon to treat you to a fabulous Spanish dinner."

"And, if you could, please include my cousin, Consuelo, in your
invitation."

"Of course," said Diego as he put on his fedora.

. . .

CHAPTER FORTY-EIGHT

[Corsica, France; Palma de Mallorca, Spain; February 2023]

Using Consuelo's satellite phone, Nate and Miró communicated with Eliza to congratulate her on her meeting with Diego. "That was a stroke of genius," said Nate. "You were in total control of that conversation, Eliza, and the entire team is very proud and impressed," said Miró.

"When you mention the entire team, does that even include Inspector Sánchez?" Eliza quipped. Acknowledging that the primary skepticism from the team came from the inspector, the three participants in the call laughed. To Eliza's surprise, the inspector's voice intercepted the exchange: "You can count me in as an admirer, Eliza," said the inspector. "I believe my goddaughter, Yael, would have handled that situation exactly as you did. *Enhorabuena*."

Using perfect *distinción*, as Inspector Sánchez had advised, Eliza responded, "Gracias." She then switched to English: "I confess, however, that I was extremely rattled by his visit."

Miró said, "No one here detected any sign of anxiety. On the contrary, you were firm, assertive, and—"

"Manipulative?" asked Eliza.

"Yes, exactly," said Nate. "As the inspector stated, you did spectacularly well. You managed to put him on the defensive, but you left the door open to allow him to fall into *your* trap. You have reversed roles."

Eliza expressed caution. "But I am merely at step two. I have a long way to go."

Miró reassured Eliza, "You are being deliberate, and you are pacing each of your steps, which is confusing Diego. Remember, he is accustomed to being in control and you have removed that advantage."

Since Consuelo had been standing by listening to the call, she commented, "And that extra touch that you added about planting rose bushes to remind you of Ruel—wow! That was special. I don't think you've ever planted anything in your life."

Eliza chuckled, "That's probably true."

"Forcing Diego to invite Consuelo to your upcoming dinner date," Nate said, "was also a stroke of genius."

"I do have one question," said Eliza. "If Diego invites us to dinner at his estate, should I decline?"

"Absolutely. Let him come to you in Mallorca. Preferably, you recommend a place, possibly a restaurant that you and Consuelo know well," Nate said. "Also, it may be advisable to reject his first invitation. Use a scheduling conflict as an excuse."

. . .

Exactly a week after his visit, on a Sunday afternoon, Diego extended an invitation for dinner. A courier appeared at Eliza's front door with another boxed long-stemmed white rose and an invitation—done in Diego's customary calligraphy—inviting Eliza and Consuelo to dinner the following weekend aboard the *Maltese Falcon*, a megayacht that Diego intended to lease. Dinner would be served at 10:00 p.m., but cocktails would be served at 7:00 p.m.

Consuelo did not allow the courier to leave. She asked the courier to deliver a response to Diego indicating that Eliza Durazo and Consuelo M. Cervantes had a prior engagement. They regretted not being able to attend.

For the next five days Diego proposed several alternative dates for their mini soirée. Each date was rejected by Consuelo since her intensive training for a "road-bicycle racing competition" would allow for only limited windows in her calendar. On the fifth day Eliza intercepted the exchange of emails between her cousin and Diego.

Apologetically, she confided with Diego that the absence of social graces in her cousin did not reflect her own reluctance to "share a meal with a good friend." In her own email she clarified that she still had great respect for him and even appreciated the "many similarities" between the two. In closing, she went on to say that Consuelo failed to recognize the special friendship "between us."

Encouraged, Diego proposed two alternative weekend dates for the threesome to have dinner. He requested that Eliza speak to her cousin and allow them to select a venue of their choice. By the following day, Eliza responded with a cheerful acceptance, indicating that a Saturday dinner at 9:00 p.m. at Fera Restaurant in Palma would be ideal. Diego promptly responded with a request of his own—*would Eliza consider having cocktails at 7:30 prior to dinner?*

Following Nate and Miró's suggestion, Eliza responded, "I will definitely join you for cocktails. Regretfully, Consuelo will decline the offer of cocktails, but she will join us at 9:00."

On the evening of the "mini-soirée," as Diego had named it, Diego arranged for Eliza to be transported to the restaurant. An Audi limousine arrived promptly at her home at exactly 7:20, but Eliza kept the chauffer waiting until 7:35. Arriving at the restaurant, Eliza realized that a tuxedoed Diego had rented an entire section of the restaurant to celebrate their "reconciliation" as friends.

Eliza commandeered her entrance like a cinema celebrity in a fishtail dress of aqua lamé fabric by Dolce & Gabbana. Noting her arrival, a small crowd of individuals formed at the front entrance. When she walked in, the crowd parted with murmurings of an international celebrity who was arriving. The maître d' immediately notified members of the press and several photographers captured every move Eliza made during dinner.

Upon entering, Eliza noted that Fera Restaurant had not only deliberately fused a Spanish-Japanese confluence into its menu but had also incorporated the Asian influence into its architecture, décor, and ambiance. A sensation of warmth and aesthetic design welcomed clients. The dark parquet wooden floors and beige walls of the "library" section of the restaurant were accented by black charcoal wooden bookcases and cornerpieces. The lamp shades adorned with blossoming cherry trees created an atmosphere for more intimate diners in this section. The longer terracotta and soft earth tones of the gray dining room were dedicated for larger parties. Aided by a gallery of fine art, the establishment added a sense of accord and harmony with nature.

Diego received Eliza with great fanfare. He had arranged for a photographer to capture every move that Eliza made. Photographs were taken of Diego greeting Eliza, Diego presenting Eliza with a bouquet of white roses, Diego pouring the first glass of champagne, Diego posing with his "friend" for an endless series of pictures in the niches of the restaurant. The owner and chef, of course, was included in various photos.

With each photograph taken, Eliza found it more difficult to smile. She looked away from the camera and found it easier to look into Diego's eyes. Diego, of course, was delighted since he interpreted her interest in him as a sign of a growing affection and attraction.

As her anxiety intensified, Eliza's behavior became more demure. Diego interpreted this reservation to be the disintegration of her brainwashing administered by Yael's godfather, Interpol, or whoever had designed his wife's indoctrination. It was clear to Diego that he was breaking down Yael's—or Eliza's—resistance.

Eliza, on the other hand, was tempted to consume more wine than advisable to tolerate an evening with the man she despised the most. Communicating electronically was one thing. Being in his presence was another. Going against the Pygmalion Team's suggestion, Eliza accepted a second glass of 1996 Louis Roederer Cristal Vinotheque. From the first wafting of raspberries mixed with honey, she was captivated by the champagne. Although she could not taste the "blanched almonds" that Diego described, Eliza took a healthy sip of her second glass. Studying closely the surveillance cameras that had been installed by Interpol at the restaurant, Picard remotely noted Eliza's indiscretion. Immediately he instructed Consuelo to arrive twenty minutes earlier.

Surprisingly sporting a tasteful one-shoulder black cocktail dress by Just Cavalli that the Pygmalion Team had selected for her, the blonde Amazonian who had looked so unattractive three weeks before looked radiant when she arrived. Although she did not command the attention of the photographers in the same fashion as her supposed cousin, Consuelo did receive plenty of stares from patrons and staff. The angle of the one-shouldered neckline was somewhat acute, revealing her ample breasts, but the choice remained a tasteful one that was flattering to her figure. The hem hit two inches above the knee and the center back slit was modest. Her light blue eyes matched her perfectly chosen sequined clutch. A recent haircut unveiled a short, choppy feminine appearance that reminded Diego of a younger version of the American actress Jamie Lee Curtis. Wearing heels, Consuelo passed for a charming, even alluring, diva. To Diego's horror, however, she still sported unshaven armpits.

Cousin Consuelo joined them at the table and asked, "What are you drinking, *prima*?" Without asking, she took Eliza's champagne and downed it. "Hmm—not bad."

"Yes, Ms. Cervantes, it's French. I'm glad you approve," said Diego. "Could I order you one?"

"I will accept. Thank you." Turning to Eliza, she said, "But you, dear cousin of mine, have had your fill. You look as if you've had enough."

Eliza laughed and turned to Diego. "I'm afraid that Consuelo has taken her duties very seriously. When she said she would travel to Mallorca to take care of me, she meant it."

Since Consuelo was fully wired, the Pygmalion Team had auditory as well as visual surveillance. The team was thrilled that Consuelo was removing the edge from Eliza's stressful encounter with Diego. With her rude and tactless behavior, she was diminishing the tension and hopefully also preventing Eliza from nervously drinking too much wine.

Consuelo asked, "So what do you do, Mr. Montemayor—or can I call you Diego?"

"Yes, of course." Diego cleared his throat. "I import and export primarily, but I'm not very active right now," Diego said.

Impatiently glancing at the bartender, Consuelo, without looking at Diego, asked by forming air quotations marks, "What exactly do you 'import' and 'export'?" Still awaiting her drink, she sighed loudly. Acting totally bored, she looked around the restaurant. Without waiting for a response from Diego, she turned to Eliza and asked, "This place is dead. Where did everyone go?"

"Diego has rented this entire wing—the 'library'—for greater privacy," explained Eliza. Just then the tuxedoed waiter, rushing from the bar, served Consuelo's wine.

Consuelo took her first sip and on second thought decided to down her glass. "Nice. Very nice. I'll have another."

Estevan had vetted both women repeatedly. Diego had been informed of Consuelo's fake heritage. Although her father was a Spaniard, her mother's maiden name was Müller. Born in Heidelberg, Consuelo moved to Spain after she completed her secondary education. She attended the university at Salamanca. Diego suspected a dubious sexual orientation since Consuelo's public records and communications did not include any heterosexual interests. Of course, Interpol had hurriedly fabricated Consuelo's digital trail of false information for Estevan to uncover.

"Tell me, Consuelo, why you speak Spanish with a German accent. I find it charming," said Diego.

"My mother is Teutonic in all ways, and I lived in Germany throughout my childhood," Consuelo answered. "Have you ordered dinner yet, Diego? I'm famished."

"If Eliza is ready, I suppose we can move to the main dining room." Turning to Eliza, he asked, "Eliza…?"

Before Diego could escort both of his guests to the dining room, two members of the staff who were wearing business suits rushed directly to the table, pulled the ladies' seats, and directed all three to the dining room. Three tuxedoed individuals were waiting for them. Candles were lit at the table and dark guest linen napkins were placed on their laps. Speaking Spanish, the taller of the suits who had directed them to the dining room approached Diego with the chilled bottle of the Montrachet Grand Cru that Diego had obviously ordered.

He wore the *tastevin* around his neck. "This is the 2016 vintage that you prefer, Señor Montemayor."

"*Humos sagrados*," exclaimed Consuelo. "What's with the huge medallion hanging on a silver chain?" The wine steward, of course, was wearing around his neck a shallow, faceted silver cup called the *tastevin*.

Embarrassed for her, Diego explained, "Sommeliers often wear it to identify themselves and also to ensure the bottle contents are not flawed." He turned to the steward and said, "Yes, go ahead and serve it."

"Wait, wait, Diego. Can I taste it first?" asked Consuelo.

Pausing, the sommelier turned to Diego, then explained to both ladies, "Since you're having the appetizers the gentleman ordered, *escargot à la Bordelaise*, we believe this bottle will be exquisite."

Consuelo insisted, "I'd still like to taste it."

Diego nodded in the sommelier's direction.

After taking a small sip, Consuelo stated, "I'll have a dry German Riesling instead."

Good naturedly, Diego told the sommelier, "A bottle of German Riesling for the lady, and we'll have the Montrachet." In his mind, Diego assumed that Consuelo had no idea what a treat she was missing when she selected the pedestrian fruity offering over the world's best chardonnay.

In gratitude, Eliza leaned over and placed her hand on Diego's forearm. She mouthed the words, "*Thank you.*"

Meanwhile, the entire Pygmalion Team in Lyon was in stitches. Consuelo's performance was hilarious, and the way she had eliminated Eliza's jitters by injecting comic relief was a thing of beauty. "She ought to win an Oscar for her performance," Miró said.

"If we were filming the scene, we could submit it to the Cannes Film Festival," said Inspector Sánchez. "I've never seen Diego so flustered."

Throughout the two-hour dinner, every time Diego attempted to have a meaningful conversation with Eliza, Consuelo was there to deflect his attention. Although Diego had carefully selected the various dishes, Consuelo criticized his choices for dinner and declared the dishes tasteless. For appetizers Diego had selected the *foie gras* and *duck dim sum*. He had selected two main entrees for them—the sea bass (done in coconut, carrot, and lemongrass) as well as the filet of lamb. From the dessert menu he selected the Apfelstrudel with walnuts, vanilla, and cinnamon. Although neither Spanish nor Japanese, the chef used a delicious Austrian recipe stretching the dough by hand until it was wafer thin and adding the local ingredients to provide a perfect ending to a feast of a meal.

Expecting gracious compliments, Diego asked "his ladies" what they thought of the dinner. However, instead of responding directly to his question, Consuelo suggested an exercise and dietary routine for Diego that could enhance his "pallid and unhealthy" appearance. "If I were to stay here longer, I would wager a small fortune that I could get you back in shape," Consuelo said as she reached over to feel his flaccid arm muscles.

With a valiant attempt at a smile, Diego was momentarily speechless. "When you say that you might not stay longer, are you suggesting you might leave Mallorca soon?" Diego asked.

"I plan to leave next week, or the next. I believe my cousin is ready to fly solo," said Consuelo.

Although Diego did not notice, Eliza gulped her last sip of wine. She went still and again swallowed hard.

. . .

CHAPTER FORTY-NINE

[Palma de Mallorca, Spain; February 2023]

To his credit, Diego Montemayor behaved as a consummate *caballero*. Not only did he tolerate Consuelo's ill manners and uncultivated etiquette, but he was also gallant toward Eliza and courteous toward Consuelo. After the delicious dessert, he ordered Fera Restaurant's specialty coffee, "wild *kopi luwak*." Rather than explaining the process by which the *kopi luwak* coffee is made, Diego decided to withhold the civet cats' involvement prior to the packaging of the beans. Instead, he begged his two guests if he could escort them home in the limousine that he had secured for them.

Eliza accepted. To her dismay, Consuelo chose to ride with the chauffer in the front, since she discovered that the driver hailed from Toledo. The driver immediately mentioned several favorite restaurants that Consuelo also frequented, and the two engaged in conversation all the way home.

Stuck with Diego in the ample soft-leather back seat, Eliza thanked Diego for the "fabulous" dinner. Diego chuckled and suggested that he "would do better" next time. Since Eliza had initiated physical contact in the restaurant when she'd thanked him for being patient with her cousin, Diego casually touched Eliza's hand twice and even "accidentally" brushed her upper arm with the back of his hand while in the back seat. Although Eliza was prepared to brush away his next attempt at physical touch, Diego resisted any efforts until he bade good-bye at the entrance. Surprisingly, Consuelo left the two at the front door as she hurried upstairs to "get ready for her training" the following morning.

In a gallant gesture, Diego merely took Eliza's hand, looked into her eyes, and said, "My good friend and stroke of good fortune, I will say good night. And should your cousin leave for the mainland, I promise to be here for you whenever you need me."

Eliza was relieved when she walked inside. Standing with her back against the door, Eliza exhaled deeply and thought, *Thank you, God—the night is over.* Consuelo was waiting in the kitchen, but she signaled to Eliza to follow her to her upstairs office, where a communications tent had been set up to prevent any intrusion from Estevan's listening devices.

Once there, Consuelo asked Eliza to sit beside her for a debriefing meeting with Lyon's entire Pygmalion Team. Consuelo started the meeting, "We just returned from our dinner, but I have significant concerns."

"Explain," said Picard.

"I'll address Eliza, but I want for the team to be part of this." With a stern and intense look, Consuelo turned to Eliza and said, "Eliza, if you seriously intend to take the next step, you'll need to do better than tonight—much, much better. I will not be a part of this if you continue to behave in the half-baked, wimpy fashion you did tonight. And I certainly will not be rescuing you every time you meet with Diego. Either we *all* pull out now, or you make up your mind that you will comply with the plan. Do not waste our time."

Eliza remained silent. For a long while no member of the team intervened. Miró finally asked, "Eliza, do you have anything to say?"

"I suppose I need to thank Consuelo. Before Consuelo arrived at the restaurant, I froze when I realized I was having drinks alone with Diego. To eliminate the disdain for the man, I was determined to use alcohol to dull my senses. That was a mistake."

"You *bet* that was a mistake, girlfriend," said Consuelo. "Tonight you had an excellent opportunity to advance your manipulation, your plan, your ruse. Instead, you were paralyzed. When you're with that man, you cannot let your guard down. You—not Diego—must be in total control."

"I'm afraid that Consuelo is right," Nate said. "Tell us what we can do to help."

Eliza paused. "I don't know what to say. I thought it would get easier, but I was wrong. And tonight you hit me with a bombshell, Consuelo. Will you truly be leaving next week?"

"I'll need to leave sometime, *prima*." Consuelo accentuated the word *prima* (*cousin*) to remind Eliza that her stay was only temporary. "You'll need to take the next steps on your own. I won't be there when he makes his final intimate advances, and—make no mistake—that is the goal. We want him making those advances."

Picard interjected, "Eliza, there have been some developments that may help you as we move forward."

"If help can be offered, this is the time," said Consuelo.

Picard continued, "We have intercepted communications that suggest that a serious rift is occurring between Diego and Estevan. It appears that Diego is extremely unhappy that Estevan has not carried out Lucas Williams's murder while he's in federal protection."

Nate added, "Regarding Jacoby Homely's conviction, there is even a worse rift. Diego found out that news sources indicated that Homely had provided information that was 'incriminating.' When Diego wanted to know, 'incriminating to whom?' Estevan had no answers."

"That's useful information," said Consuelo. "We can use the growing tension between Diego and his *consigliere* to our advantage."

"What about Estevan's suspicions?" asked Eliza. "Has he convinced Diego that I'm trying to deceive him?"

Picard responded for the team. "It appears that Diego's infatuation with you is the main reason for the tension. The more Diego commits to you, the more that Estevan becomes convinced that he must assume control of some—if not all—of Diego's empire."

"What does that mean for me?" Eliza asked.

"For one," said Picard, "it means that you have an opportunity to take advantage of the wedge between Estevan and Diego. You can even widen the chasm between the two by becoming the one Diego turns to. You may even become Diego's confidante, the person he can trust."

Nate added, "The more Diego doubts Estevan, the greater the chance that he can trust *you* with his most intimate secrets."

Miró intervened to offer some encouragement. "Listen to me, Eliza. Trust your training. Trust your instincts. Yes, tonight's dinner may have been a small setback, but you can use it to your advantage. I want you to concentrate on your resolve to avenge your husband's and your children's deaths. Use that to remind you why you are in the middle of this battle of wits."

Nate said, "When you decided to join us, Eliza, you counted the cost. You knew what it would entail. You agreed."

Eliza interrupted: "to become the whore if I had to."

To Eliza's surprise, her principal critic—Inspector Sánchez—chimed in: "Remember that the whole secret lies in confusing the enemy so that he cannot fathom our real intent. Use this temporary setback for your benefit. We all trust you. Now let's move on to our next step."

• • •

[Lyon, France; February 2023]

Nate and Miró left Picard's cavernous office past midnight. When they arrived at their leased apartment in Lyon, it was nearly 2:00 a.m. Four hours later, Nate's phone chimed. "I hope it's not too early," said Abraham, "but Max convinced me this could not wait." For the next thirty-five minutes Abraham outlined his latest findings regarding the "unholy alliance of 2016," the alliance formed between Picard and Yael Montemayor. He explained that the Interpol files that Nate sent included damaging information that Picard had obviously overlooked.

"These files may finally explain why the authorities so swiftly convicted Sonny Rollo and his girlfriend for kidnapping, yet they were incapable of apprehending Diego Montemayor," Abraham said.

"I've had only three or four hours of sleep," Nate said. "Connect some dots, please. You called it damaging information—damaging to whom?"

"I'm sorry, Nate, but what Max and I discovered is that back in 2016, when we were in the Canary Islands, the primary written testimony of Diego Montemayor quickly enabled the courts to convict the young couple for Minerva's kidnapping."

Nate ambled to the small kitchen and started his espresso maker. "I'll need caffeine to digest this information. While I wait for my coffee, correct me if I'm wrong. Wasn't there an Interpol Red Notice for Diego's arrest at the time?"

"Dad has you on speakerphone mode," Max said. "So I'm also on the call. That's just it, Nate. Diego was not under suspicion at the time. But the significant point is that when Picard shared the Interpol files with you and the Pygmalion Team just a few weeks ago, he failed to redact some incriminating evidence that clearly states that back in 2016 he hired Yael Montemayor as 'liaison' to Interpol to keep her quiet about Álana's—his stepdaughter's—child molestation charges."

No longer mumbling his words, Nate said, "I get it now, Max. I had to clear some cobwebs with espresso. I know it's not even midnight in Chicago, but I had not started my morning. So what you're saying is there was a *quid pro quo* between Picard and Yael Montemayor…. Are you certain of that?"

"Positive."

"Do you think Gabriel Picard has been compromised by Diego? Is Picard working for him?" Nate asked.

"At this point we cannot say for certain," said Abraham. "What I do know is that Picard has connections with the Pan Asian Shipping board of directors."

"Forgive me, Abraham, but just because Diego's assistant's surname is Chengfu doesn't mean that Estevan—much less Diego—is related to board members of a shipping company."

"Hold on, Nate," said Abraham. "I promised you that I would continue researching, and I've done that. Although I'd hit a roadblock a few weeks back, I discovered that by the seventeenth century, Chinese genealogy was started by people recording their histories in manuscripts called *Jiapu*. Although much of that information is available, the surviving *Jiapu* are scattered throughout libraries in Asia and the

US. Unfortunately, many of these documents were destroyed by Mao during the Cultural Revolution."

Nate also had his iPhone on speakerphone mode. Laughing as he served another cup of espresso, he said, "Be kind to me. It will take twenty of these cups to wait for the punch line. Max, can you help your dad come to the point?"

"What Dad is trying to tell you," Max said, "is that because Estevan's clan was close to Mao, not only did they have the resources to preserve and print their *Jiapu*, but those documents also survived the Cultural Revolution of the 1960s. Estevan's family has been involved in shipping for many decades, even preceding Mao's rise to power. It appears that the Pan Asian Shipping company is not only suspected of being involved in the shipping of weapons and cyberweapons, but they are also suspected of child trafficking."

"Then your hunch is that Picard at least has connections to Estevan's relatives. Is that right?" asked Nate.

"That is exactly right," said Abraham. "No more. No less."

• • •

CHAPTER FIFTY

[Lyon, France; Chicago; February 2023]

By noon, Nate and Miró had received multiple attachments that Max had encrypted to prevent snoopers from intercepting his communications. Armed with circumstantial evidence, Nate and Miró began to plan their meeting to confront Gabriel Picard. With much forethought, they decided to return to Abraham and Max to seek their advice. On their second telephone conference of the day, Max recommended that they include Minerva in their conversation. "Dad," Max suggested, "Minerva has proved herself to be mature, insightful, and obviously very interested. I believe we should include her." Abraham concurred.

"I'll wake her," said Abraham. "With her online coursework all week long, Sunday is her only day to sleep in. I'll give her an opportunity to join us." To no one's surprise, Minerva jumped at the chance. She thanked them both for "thinking of her."

After a thirty-minute telephone discussion regarding the pros and cons of confronting Picard, the entire family decided that before any confrontation with Picard, they should provide copies of the evidence to two entities—the Department of Justice in the US and the International Court of Justice at The Hague. Abraham convinced the family that the move would prevent Picard from sabotaging their efforts.

"If it's okay with you all," said Minerva, "why don't we also include your friend Ram Edmunds since he was recently appointed deputy director of the FBI? I know the FBI may be limited to preventing domestic terrorism, but Ram is familiar with Diego's vendetta against our family—he might be helpful."

Miró jumped into the conversation, "*Mi'jita*, I know you're around Uncle Max all the time. Just remember that as an aspiring writer, when you address more than one person, *you* may be used as the plural form without a need for *you all* or *y'all*." To ensure that Minerva understood her lightheartedness, she chuckled.

"Of course, Mom. As soon as I said it, I knew you'd correct me."

Max stated, "You know, my niece is right. Ram is also one of the few straight arrows that has remained clean as a whistle. He helped us develop the Pygmalion Plan, and he offered to continue his support. Would you mind if I shared this information with him?"

"I thought he was already in DC," said Nate. "Did he remain behind?"

"Ram will make his move at the end of the summer. Presently he's still involved in working out the plan of succession at the regional office here in Chicago," Max said.

"How much time do you need, little brother?" Miró asked.

"Give me until tomorrow or Tuesday. If he's in town, I'm certain he'll see me." Max asked if anyone had anything to add.

With the family's blessings, Nate ended the conference call.

• • •

The following Tuesday Max met with Ram Edmunds. And as usual, Laurie, Ram's executive assistant, made time for Max late in the day. Arriving at 5:45, Max was invited to Ram's conference room. After several pleasantries, Ram asked for the documents that Abraham had collected. He reviewed the documents and quickly agreed that Picard appeared compromised. Ram could not help showing his disappointment—and a certain embarrassment—about another fallen colleague.

"You know, Max, I began my career in law enforcement when this profession was honorable…and trustworthy. Yes, there were some bad apples, but those were the exceptions. A few abused their power, but they rarely survived on the job."

"Do you agree that Nate and Miró should confront Picard?" Max asked.

Ram unbuttoned his vest and said, "Why don't you let my men investigate this a bit more, Max? I've had various conversations with Picard, and he and I have collaborated at a distance, more recently after you trained Raquel to become Eliza Durazo."

"Fine," Max said. "See if you can come up with anything related to the child molestation charges brought up by his stepdaughter, Álana Peretz."

"We will definitely start there and dig further into Picard's relationship with Estevan Chengfu's family. If Picard is working with Diego or his assistant, Nate and Miró need to tread carefully."

That evening Max used the secure line to call Nate and Miró. Nate reluctantly agreed to avoid confronting Picard until Ram Edmunds got back to Max.

* * *

Forty-eight hours after their Tuesday conversation, Ram Edmunds requested a meeting with Max. His "boys" had discovered a back channel to tap into vast communications that required a full investigation. Showing up at 7:30, Max arrived at the Chicago Field Office before Ram entered the building. Seated at Ram's conference table, Max was having his first cup of coffee when Ram walked in.

As soon as they were both seated, Ram received his java from Laurie and opened the meeting. "Max, I'll get right to the point. As you know, I'm not that tech savvy, but my communication specialists are second to none. Evidently, immediately after I assembled my team, they discovered a cache of information that will dumbfound you."

"Explain, Ram. Are we still concentrating on the two major concerns we discovered related to Picard, or something else?"

"Yes, regarding Abraham's research, we came up with incriminating information about Picard. But in addition, we unearthed a payload. I'll explain. When we dug into Interpol and their own back channels to listen in on Diego's and Estevan's digital communications, our team came up with another layer of counter-espionage."

Max interrupted: "Uh, oh. What you're saying is that Estevan or Diego discovered that Interpol had them bugged, and so they returned the favor. Using Interpol's malware, they gained access to Interpol's internal data."

Ram stood up, and as he stirred his coffee, he emphatically shook his head. "That's what we initially thought. We assumed Diego had discovered the malware. However, someone else installed very advanced equipment at a safe house in Palma de Mallorca that has compromised not only Diego's internal communications but also Picard's systems—including Picard's personal and, up to this point, 'secured' lines of communication."

Max was now taking notes. "Did you pinpoint the location of that equipment? Who in Palma is collecting all this data? Who infiltrated both systems?"

"I can have the precise coordinates within minutes." Ram texted the communications supervisor as he filled his second cup of java. "What will blow your mind is the information we've uncovered."

Max laughed. "Will you keep me in suspense, or will you share?"

Ram returned to the conference table and sat by Max. "To tell you the truth, I don't know where to start.... Okay, as Nate would say—at the beginning."

Just then Laurie walked in with the information Ram had requested. "Sorry for the interruption, but Mr. Roy from the Intelligence Division asked me to give you this. He preferred not to answer in a text message."

Ram read the scribbling, "I can barely read my head techie's writing. He's providing the precise coordinates and a physical address in Palma...#7 Andratx, Palma, Mallorca. I'm sure I massacred the pronunciation."

Max immediately responded: "You're right in saying it's an Interpol safe house, but the strange thing is that it's the temporary home of Eliza Durazo. I'm certain that Eliza is not capable of pulling that off, and for the life of me, I can't figure out why the Interpol plant who is playing the role of Cousin Consuelo would be hijacking Picard's communications...unless she infected Picard's computers inadvertently."

"No, Max, the data we uncovered came from deliberate spyware," Ram said.

"Okay, Ram—you've kept me in the dark long enough. What else have you uncovered?"

"First of all, Picard definitely is connected to Estevan's family and to Estevan himself. Second, Picard has been hiding child molestation allegations for many years, and he paid off Yael Montemayor handsomely for keeping it quiet. However, he is uncertain whether Diego Montemayor ever found out what his wife knew. It appears that he wants to eliminate Diego as much as Nate does—but for a different reason."

"In other words," said Max, "Picard believes that if he can help Nate and the Pygmalion Team apprehend Diego Montemayor, he can have Diego eliminated before his own reputation is exposed."

"Exactly, but there is more," Ram said. "There is a serious conflict between Diego and Estevan."

Max nodded, "Yeah, we're already aware of that. We, the Pygmalion Team, also listen in on communications between Diego and Isabella, who does most of Estevan's interpretation. Estevan not only finds Diego's infatuation with Eliza unacceptable, but also he is actively opposing it. He's made that clear to Diego."

Ram went on: "It's more serious than that, Max. The info that we uncovered suggests that Diego is not aware how deep his conflict with Estevan may be. There are indications that Estevan is plotting to appropriate Diego's fortune."

Max asked, "How can he possibly do that?"

"Somehow Estevan was either given power of attorney to manipulate Diego's finances, or he assumed that power on his own. Estevan has begun to transfer ownership of Diego's holdings throughout the world. The Mazatlán compound now belongs to the entity called Pan Asian Shipping Enterprises. Even properties buried in blind trusts have been seized."

"Have you confirmed all this?" Max asked. "How could Diego be so careless about his holdings?"

"What we know," said Ram, "is that Estevan has…or had…gained

Diego's trust. Although Diego began to question some of Estevan's decisions, he gave Estevan enormous control."

"What about the property in Winnetka?"

"My sources indicate that the Bonifacio estate is still under the sole control of a complicated series of shell companies that Diego controls. And the Winnetka estate is in a trust owned by the Rosales widows. The ownership of a megayacht by the name of the *Shenandoah of Sark* was recently passed on to Ruel Levant and Eliza Durazo.

• • •

CHAPTER FIFTY-ONE

[Chicago; Palma de Mallorca; February 2023]

As the newly appointed deputy director of the FBI, Ram Edmunds assumed oversight of the operational division at the Washington, DC, headquarters. Although the FBI was originally created to protect the US from its internal enemies, during the last seven decades the agency had established more than sixty offices staffed by special personnel overseas. The intent of these international offices was to help protect Americans by building relationships with law enforcement, intelligence, and security services throughout the globe. These legal attaché offices—also known as "legats"—were established through mutual agreements with each host country.

While the American legal attachés work with law enforcement of each country to coordinate investigations of mutual interest, they coordinate with the head of the operational division of the FBI. Within five days after meeting with Max, Ram Edmunds directed the legat offices in Madrid, Paris, and Rome to join his *Galatea* force, Ram's FBI team who would ensure the success of the Pygmalion Project.

Before traveling to Palma de Mallorca to meet with the legat from Madrid, Ram communicated with the secretary general of Interpol, Jurgen Wagner, to ensure that he would have "Cousin Consuelo's" cooperation in the joint effort. In his conversation with Wagner, Ram Edmunds discovered that when Gabriel Picard was being considered by the General Assembly as the obvious candidate to assume the office of secretary general, rumors of Picard's indiscretions had come to the surface. Although Picard was able to bury the accusations, his promotion was not granted. He did, however, retain his post of deputy secretary.

The same day that the General Assembly appointed Wagner as the new secretary general, he received orders to surveil Picard, his second-in-command, for possible misconduct. Immediately Wagner created an undercover team who would report directly to him. While being allowed to operate without obstruction, Picard's subordinates, in addition to being supervised by Picard, also reported directly to Secretary General Jurgen Wagner.

Unbeknownst to Picard, while Ruel Levant played the role of Eliza's fiancé, he was also reporting to Picard's boss. As part of the secretary general's undercover team, Levant uncovered information damaging to Picard, including Picard's stepdaughter's accusations and Picard's connections to the trafficking of minors. More specifically, Levant had uncovered Picard's connections to Pan Asian Shipping. All this information had been submitted to Secretary General Wagner and had been passed on to Consuelo Cervantes, Interpol's replacement, who took over Levant's post after Levant's death.

• • •

After multiple conversations with Max, Nate learned of Ram Edmunds's willingness to lend his resources to resolve the present dilemma. It appeared that the Pygmalion Project was evolving into a multi-layered plot not only to capture Diego Montemayor but also to probe a rogue executive of Interpol, the world's largest police organization. Little had Nate Shelley—a practicing psychiatrist and forty-nine-year-old member of his daughter's high school PTA—expected to end up in the center of criminal and global law enforcement intrigue.

In a conversation with Miró, Nate shared the new information that he had received from Max and the new collaboration established with Ram Edmunds. Although relieved, Miró expressed concerns: "Nate, just remember that we need Gabriel Picard's cooperation. We cannot afford to jeopardize the trust that has been established with him."

Nate acknowledged Miró's concern, and he assured his wife that Ram would exercise necessary precautions. Privately he enumerated the various risks involved. *What if Picard, Diego, and Estevan are preparing a trap for us? What if Diego—or Estevan—has been Picard's plant all along? Is the rift between Diego Montemayor and Estevan Chengfu real, or is it a trap for us? Has the Pygmalion Project truly been successful, or is Diego playing us?*

Although it was 5:00 a.m. in Chicago, Nate decided to dial Ram Edmunds's home number. Ram answered after the second ring. As he prepared to leave for his early-morning jog, he donned his ear warmers and mumbled, "I thought you might be calling soon, Nate. What's up?"

"I've spoken to Max, and I'm relieved that you're involved. Frankly, I'm feeling overwhelmed."

"I'm out the door for my jog, and I hope you're not distracted by a sexagenerian runner's huffing and puffing. If it bothers you, I'll gladly give up the run."

"Ha—it sounds like you're begging for an excuse, Ram. No such luck. Okay, first let me apologize for the early call, but it couldn't wait." Nate cleared his throat. "Although we're getting very close to springing our final trap for Diego, I'm worried. Frankly, I've got several doubts…. It appears I'm dealing with too many unknowns. I'm trying to shield Miró from those concerns, but I know she can figure it out on her own."

"Spell…it…out…for me," Ram said between labored breaths.

"Well, what if Diego is playing us? What if he's discovered the ruse and he springs a trap on us? What if he and Estevan are Picard's plants? I'd like to confront Picard with the evidence we've discovered, but…I can't afford to jeopardize the trust that I've established with him…do you understand all my concerns?"

Ram was exhaling sharply. After a moment he chuckled. "Nate, I don't know…if you acquired a cape…when you joined Interpol, but—listen, let me take a breather…. I just made it to a bus shelter." Ram, who was contemplating retirement, was winded. He sat down at the bus shelter bench. His labored breathing and the wind noise had made it difficult for Nate to make out the conversation. Ram continued: "I need to remind you that all superhero positions are taken…. Why is it that you feel it's your sole responsibility to bring down Diego Montemayor…*and* Gabriel Picard?"

"What do you mean, Ram?" Nate paused, then continued: "I suppose you're saying that you can lend a hand." Again Nate paused, indicating that he was asking a question.

"Of course…. Or have you forgotten that I signed on to collaborate in the Pygmalion Project?" Nate noticed that the traffic noise in the background had increased. Still sitting on the bench, Ram said in between deep breaths, "I've reached the half-way mark— I'll walk the rest of the way." Ram sounded exhausted, but he continued. "Nate, you have a variety of resources now. It's not solely up to you…. And the reason I want to meet with you and your entire family in Palma de Mallorca is that we've uncovered valuable information…. There are significant dangers that I do not want you facing without help."

"When you put it that way, I realize that we're no longer alone— Wow. I feel an enormous weight being lifted," Nate said. "We can surely use your help, and since our situation is getting more delicate—"

Ram reassured his friend. "I've put together a team—I've called it the *Galatea* Force. I've enlisted the help of our resources through our legal attachés in Paris, Madrid, and Rome. In addition, I'm in communication with Interpol's secretary general, who, by the way, has been surveilling Picard for a long time. So we have the good guys from Interpol also involved."

"You've called the team what?"

"The *Galatea* Force," said Ram, "in honor of—"

Nate interrupted, "Yes, in honor of Pygmalion's statue. I'm impressed, Ram. You've been doing your research."

"I thought you'd like it," said Ram. "Plus, I want my new subordinates to know that I'm at least literate."

Nate laughed. "On another note, you mentioned you wanted to meet with the entire family in Palma de Mallorca. Who are you talking about?"

"I'd like to have Abraham and Max join us there. Although I cannot pay for Minerva's travel expenses, I will hire Abraham and Max as consultants, since they've provided the bureau valuable information."

"For your information, Ram, Minerva has graduated from high school. About the information that you've uncovered, can you elaborate?" Nate asked.

"Let's wait until we get together in Palma. As for Minerva, Max thinks she can help us. We'll have plenty of time to discuss. First let's coordinate our travels."

• • •

Using "spring break" as a pretext, Nate and Miró arranged with Picard for a leave of absence from Interpol. Picard agreed they should have a "family European vacation." Max, Abraham, and Minerva traveled to Palma de Mallorca ahead of Ram Edmunds. Because Ram was concerned about Estevan's ability to hack their personal credit cards and personal travel information, he provided travel documents, including passports, with fictitious identities for the three family members.

When Max and Abraham informed Minerva about their false identities and travel documents provided by the FBI, she thought it was the most exciting thing she had ever experienced. "I can't wait to write a short story for my online coursework about this young female working undercover for the government," she told her Uncle Max.

With an apology in his voice, Max stated, "The downside to this arrangement is that any writing that you publish in the future will be scrutinized by the feds for the rest of your life. I'm sorry."

"That's the price that we intelligence operatives have to pay," a smiling Minerva said.

For the next three days, Max and Minerva allowed Abraham—the family patriarch—to take on the dominant role of supervising their packing, their travel itinerary, and their preparation. To his credit, Abraham delegated the collection of digital and journaling to Max and Minerva. All the genealogical data—including collected photographs and copies of birth certificates and other public records—he asked Max to digitize. In addition, he spoke to Ram Edmunds and firmly declined the bureau's offer to pay for his travel.

Of the three, Max was the only one who had never traveled abroad, so he tried to keep his excitement to a minimum. However, it was obvious to Abraham and Minerva that Max looked forward to the new experience with the most childlike anticipation.

Abraham picked up the family's travel documents and passports at Ram Edmunds's Chicago Field Office. Laurie, Ram's executive assistant, informed him that her boss had laughed hysterically when reviewing their chosen identities. "That Dr. Epstein has a special sense of humor," he had said. "Abraham chose the name 'Dr. Hugo Hackenbush', a Groucho Marx character in one of his movies."

"One has to have a little fun," Abraham said with a grin. He went on to explain to Laurie that *A Day at the Races* was one of his favorite movies.

Laurie asked, "And Minerva's assumed name—did you also pick that one?"

"No," said Abraham. "She picked 'Kinsey Millhone' because that's the name of a detective in Grafton's murder mysteries. She intends to be a writer, you know."

Following Ram Edmunds's explicit instructions, the family took different routes to arrive at the Spanish island of Mallorca. Traveling under the name of "Dexter Haven," Max offered to drive from Chicago to Dallas. He took an American Airlines flight from DFW to Miami, then connected to another American Airlines flight to Barcelona. From Barcelona he took a ferry to the island of Mallorca. Abraham and Minerva, on the other hand, drove from Chicago to St. Louis. From St. Louis they took an American Airlines flight to Miami. In Miami they boarded an Iberia flight to Madrid and from there flew to the Palma de Mallorca Airport.

Upon arrival at the Palma Airport, Abraham and Minerva were greeted by "Cousin Consuelo" with cursory kisses on both cheeks. She immediately took Minerva's suitcase and told Abraham, "I hope you can handle your own, *Abrám*."

Dressed in light gray sweats, Consuelo addressed them as if they were old friends. Her gait was swift and self-assured. She led them out of the airport without hesitating to check if both were keeping up. As she walked toward her Peugeot 3008 SUV, she asked, "You must be famished. What's your pleasure?"

"We'd like to settle in first," said Abraham. "Then we think of dinner."

Consuelo shrugged her shoulders. "That suits me fine. Just remember—we have dinner at 9:30."

"I keep forgetting," said Minerva. "It'll take me a few days to adjust to the Spanish schedule. I'll need something in me before that time."

Consuelo smiled. "I thought so." On the drive to the unimposing townhouse that Ram Edmunds had secured for them, Consuelo stopped at an "*hamburguería*" that served American-style burgers. She bought a burger and fries to hold Minerva over until dinner. Consuelo explained that she had swept their townhouse for any electronic bugs or unintended wiring that would compromise their discussions. She and "the team" had everything under control, as far as they could ensure. "Of course, we know we're dealing with master hackers on both sides of the fence," Consuelo added.

As Consuelo handed Minerva her bagged snack, Minerva thanked her. Minerva then discreetly turned back to Abraham, who was sitting comfortably in the backseat, and smiled. He simply acknowledged his granddaughter, and he also thanked Consuelo for her thoughtfulness. The unspoken message from Minerva was *Consuelo has no way of knowing that I rarely eat hamburgers.*

Upon entering the townhouse, Minerva exclaimed, "Oh, it's got a swimming pool…and a barbecue grill, Gramps! I'll return to Chicago with a tan, just like most of my friends who were traveling to Florida. I know it's chilly, but if the sun's out, I'll get a tan."

"Well," advised Consuelo, "take advantage of every free moment because we'll be busy. When your Uncle Max—sorry, when 'Dexter'—gets here, we'll review the timeline, and you'll see what I mean. Which brings me to the question, what's his time of arrival?"

Abraham responded, "He's scheduled to arrive tomorrow by ferry."

"He'll need to get his own transportation because I'm scheduled to bike for three hours tomorrow," said Consuelo. "He's a big boy; I'm certain he can find his way."

. . .

Unbeknownst to Max, Ram Edmunds had arranged for the Madrid legal attaché to meet him at the ferry port in Palma. When the trim and well-dressed man approached Max, he addressed him in Spanish: "*Hola, Dexter. Me llamo Marc…Marc Hugot. Me envió mi jefe, Ram Edmunds.*"

Max noted that Marc was not wearing the typical dark suit, white shirt, dark tie that American FBI agents normally wore. Marc had chosen a light ecru cotton sweater under his light blue blazer. His trousers, just a notch darker hue than his sweater, were pressed perfectly. Smart Italian loafers completed the sartorial masterpiece. The affable but disheveled Max responded, "The only thing I understood was 'Ram Edmunds.' Sorry—I'm not fluent in Spanish."

"My apologies. I should not have assumed you were bilingual," Marc said. "I was introducing myself. My name is Marc Hugot, and my boss, Ram Edmunds, sent me. Allow me to help with your bags. And you won't need the heavy jacket you're wearing."

"Thanks. Ram had mentioned we'd be working with legats in Europe. I'm assuming you're stationed in Madrid."

Although Max measured six-foot-three, Marc was perhaps less than an inch shorter. His hair was as blond as Max's but cut shorter. Max estimated Marc was about thirty-three years old. "Yes, I joined right after university, and I have not regretted it. I enjoy what I do. From what Ram tells me, you're also in law enforcement."

Max clarified, "I'm a private investigator, but Ram keeps telling me that I should consider the bureau. I'm flattered, but my focus is elsewhere right now."

"I understand. You've been instrumental in keeping your family safe," said Marc. "Listen, Max—or do you want to be called 'Dexter'?"

"By no means—I believe that our identities were changed for travel purposes only. Call me Max. Ram wanted to ensure that our nemesis did not track us as we traveled to Europe."

"Fine," Marc said. "I started to ask whether you'd like to go directly to your leased townhouse, or would you like to stop elsewhere?"

"After an overnight ferry ride, I need a quick shower, Marc. Could you please drive me directly to our temporary home?"

"Sure. It's a short drive from downtown Palma," Marc said. "Your dad and niece are there…Not sure they're awake, though. It's barely 8:00."

Marc drove a Maserati *Grancabrio*. Almost embarrassed, he explained to Max that Ram wanted to ensure his role of a wealthy bachelor visiting Palma de Mallorca was believable. He was a member of the "rich and famous" on extended holiday. Max now understood why Marc was not wearing the customary bland dark suits worn by agents in the US.

Upon Max's arrival, Abraham greeted them at the door. *"¡Bienvenidos!"* he exclaimed. He shook hands with Marc and gave his son a warm embrace. "Glad you're finally here." Abraham proceeded to give them a tour of the two-story townhouse and offered them coffee. Although Marc gladly accepted the offer, Max opted to take the shower he desperately needed.

By the time Max had rejoined his dad at the *piscina*, Marc had left. "I had no idea we'd have access to a pool," he said. "It's such a beautiful morning, Dad. I expected it to be cooler."

"I understand that it can warm up most days," said Abraham, "but so far the weather's been ideal. Minerva came down earlier this morning, found out we had an empty pantry, except for coffee, and decided to go back up to change into her tanning suit, as she called it. She said she'd enjoy the sun while you and I go shopping for groceries."

Max asked, "And what are we using for transportation?"

"The rental car agency is delivering our SUV. I opted for a sensible Toyota," Abraham said. "With a GPS."

That evening the *Galatea* Force, assembled by the recently appointed deputy director of the FBI, met at the townhouse that would become their base of operations. Abraham, Max, and Minerva hosted the meeting. Master Chef Eliza Durazo arrived with her "cousin" Consuelo, who was laden with so many Spanish delicacies that it seemed as if a catering agency were making its delivery. Consuelo and Eliza even unloaded from the SUV chafing dishes, stoneware, dinnerware, and silverware. Various teas, soft beverages, and eight bottles of wine quickly filled the kitchen counters. Marc—whose full name was "Marceline Hugot"—arrived with additional bottles of wine and plastic goblets for use by the pool. At exactly 7:30 that evening, Ram Edmunds and retired Inspector Eduardo Sánchez, who had picked up Nate and Miró at the Palma Airport, arrived to complete the gathering. After the crowd extended greetings to each other—embraces and European double-cheek kisses, of course—the ten individuals finally sat by the pool for a delicious meal of tapas, paella, and charcuteries that included meats, cheeses, and dried fruits.

Max in particular experienced "porcine euphoria," as he called it. When asked by Consuelo what he meant by the term, he simply responded that where he came from the comment would be "I'm in 'hog heaven,' which means, "I can't imagine being happier." He added, "Since I want to prove to y'all Europeans that I'm cultured, I chose the term 'porcine euphoria.'"

Consuelo and Marc laughed hysterically, and they both bowed elegantly to suggest deference to such a distinguished and eloquent guest. To accentuate her respect, Consuelo belched loudly, which inspired more laughter. In a private comment to her mother, Minerva proclaimed she could not believe that she, a seventeen-year-old, was behaving more maturely than the rest.

Miró whispered, "Don't worry, *Mi'jita*. This group will get down to business, and when they do, you'll realize that this team is bright, talented, and very, very professional."

* * *

CHAPTER FIFTY-TWO

[Palma de Mallorca, Spain; February 2023]

At exactly 10:30 that evening, Ram Edmunds rang the cowbell that Max had gifted him. It was the cowbell that Max's grandmother had used at the family ranch in Three Rivers, Texas, to summon the family to their meals. In this case, Ram used it to gather his *Galatea* Force and to formally initiate the meeting. He thanked everyone and outlined the major plan of operation. He provided the history and the origin of the Pygmalion Plan, the effort to capture Diego Montemayor, who had eluded international authorities since 2016. He explained how Nate had been recruited by the deputy secretary general of Interpol, Gabriel Picard, to serve as a profiler and investigator in this effort.

"At this juncture," Ram Edmunds stated, "it has become necessary to form an undercover operation, which I am directing. The operation, for our purposes, will be called the '*Galatea* Force.' The primary objective, with which the Pygmalion Project started, remains the same—capture and bring to justice Diego Montemayor. However, we have added certain dimensions to the original plan since new information has been uncovered."

After Ram's introduction, Consuelo Cervantes took the floor. She efficiently described how she had assumed the role originally filled by Ruel Levant. "After he was assassinated by Diego's crew—consisting of a male and female—the role of Eliza's fiancé disappeared, and I took on the role of Eliza's cousin from Toledo, Spain. Fortunately,

I benefited from the masterful accumulation of data that had been prepared by Ruel. In his investigation, he discovered evidence which, unfortunately, implicates the deputy secretary general of Interpol. We now have incontrovertible evidence that Picard has had ongoing conversations with the Pan Asian Shipping company owned by a Chinese family. That company has been implicated in various crimes against humanity. I have provided all the evidence to this team, but we need to ask all relevant questions now before we proceed."

Marc Hugot asked a question: "Have we continued to monitor Gabriel Picard's private communications with Diego's assistant?"

"We certainly have; however," said Consuelo, "very little communication occurs between the two. As far as we can tell, they have not communicated in weeks."

Minerva raised her hand, and after being acknowledged by Consuelo, asked, "First of all, thank you for including me and not treating me as a kid. Do you mind if I ask whether Mr. Picard has ever communicated directly with Diego Montemayor?"

Somewhat brusquely, which was her manner, Consuelo responded, "Because none of us sees you as a child…you don't have to raise your hand to join in. What you're asking is a very good question. The last known communication between Picard and Diego Montemayor was when Picard's office summoned Diego to testify against his employees Sonny Rollo and Álana Aguirre-Rollo…in the kidnapping trial that sent the couple to prison. Although the summons was signed by Picard, we don't have any evidence that he ever communicated directly with Diego at any other time."

"Wow—that's interesting!" Minerva said.

"I've been instructed by Interpol's secretary general, Picard's boss, to provide the *Galatea* Force access to all the information that I gather through my back channels," Consuelo said. "Max, I understand from Ram that you are a talented computer nerd and techie. So I look forward to collaborating with you."

"As do I," said Max. "Which leads me to my question: How is your relationship with Diego progressing, Eliza?"

Eliza smiled. "Despite a few setbacks, I've taken control of the situation. I believe I'm ready to accelerate our friendship and move it to the next step."

"What she means," Consuelo jumped in, "is that my *prima* is ready to communicate to Diego that she has 'the hots' for him." As she did, she looked in Miró's direction, non-verbally asking her if she could speak frankly in her daughter's presence. Miró nodded and smiled.

Marc Hugot asked Eliza, "In Consuelo's files she refers to a curious fascination that Diego appears to have in botany. Is this a new development?"

"No, on the contrary," said Inspector Sánchez. "Diego had abandoned his love of botany since he lost Yael, his wife. Now, with the ongoing...romance, if you will...he has resurrected his avocation in botany. Maybe *avocation* is the wrong term because his publications in botany and other subject matters—biochemistry, for example—have been recognized by respected scholars."

"I recommend you study Diego's background more thoroughly, Agent Hugot," said Consuelo.

Not hearing any additional questions, Consuelo addressed the group: "Diego regales Eliza with stories of his plants—primarily foxgloves—and sends her flower bouquets, plants, and such."

"I must say," Abraham said, "that I read your notes with much delight. You injected some of your humor into various descriptions of your findings. What do you make of Estevan's and Isabella's plan to drive Diego mad? Has this been going on for some time?"

"Yes, apparently so," Consuelo said. "Before I came into the picture, Ruel Levant had discovered that when the first disagreements between Estevan and Diego occurred, Estevan began to devise a plan to drive Diego crazy. He enlisted the help of Isabella Rossi to start adding small doses of rohypnol—the common date-rape drug—to Diego's late-night brandy. Later, he concocted a cocktail of drugs that included statins, which in Diego caused leg cramps and muscle soreness. He also included olanzapine, which he knew caused hallucinations."

"Absolutely true," said Abraham. "We're usually careful about prescribing those drugs precisely for those reasons."

In deference to Abraham, Consuelo stated, "That's right, Dr. Epstein. As a cardiologist, you know those drugs much better than I would."

Abraham added, "When you explained how Estevan bought Isabella expensive lingerie and exotic makeup, I realized what they were doing. Diego must have had horrible nightmares, and then Isabella would lie down beside him looking like a zombie or demonic being. No wonder Diego gave Estevan temporary power of attorney."

As Consuelo acknowledged Abraham's comment, she signaled to Ram Edmunds to take the floor. Ram made a few comments regarding Diego's auditory hallucinations and how these were completely fabricated by Estevan and Isabella. Estevan had even gone to the extent of creating computer-generated voices played at the subconscious level in Diego's bedroom. Soon Diego began to doubt his mental state.

Meanwhile, Consuelo took Miró aside and walked behind the brick BBQ grill. She quickly consulted with her regarding the next critical disclosure. Although she was eager to engage Minerva as a full member of the team, Consuelo needed Miró's approval to share the remaining piece of information in Minerva's presence.

What Consuelo had withheld from the *Galatea* Team was the sensitive—but now confirmed—issue regarding Diego's dealings with Russia. Before Diego discovered the possibility that Yael, his wife, was alive, his principal goal in life was to assassinate Nate and his family in the most painful and gruesome way possible. In his many studies, Diego selected a radiation poisoning developed by Russia's nuclear research facilities, which if carried in a vial in water, could be transported internationally aboard an aircraft without setting off alarms that would alert airport screening devices. Additionally, Diego required that his weapon be hard to detect in a person who ingested it. He wanted to ensure that after poisoning Nate Shelley and his family, the poison would not be detectable. As Consuelo described Diego's plan to use this sadistically chosen poison that would trigger a slow and agonizing death, Miró asked, "Was he planning to use polonium?"

"Yes, how do you know about this type of poisoning?" asked Consuelo.

Miró responded, "I recall that the Russians had murdered some of their own diplomats who had collaborated with the UK and limited information leaked out to the public."

Consuelo said, "What makes this such a horrible instrument of death is that, unlike other poisons such as arsenic or mercury, which kill by using the metal to interact with the body, polonium-210 actually kills by slowly emitting radiation, which shreds all the organs one molecule, one cell at a time. Miró, if you want, I'll withhold this information until later to spare your daughter this monstrous plan that Diego had…or still may have…against your entire family."

"Let's get back to the group," said Miró. "My seventeen-year-old wants to be part of this. She does not want it any other way."

As soon as Consuelo and Miró returned to the gathering, Ram Edmunds turned to Consuelo. "Proceed, Agent Cervantes. You have one last piece of information that will be crucial for the team."

After Consuelo repeated much of the gruesome information that she had shared with Miró, she fielded numerous questions from the team regarding Diego's choice of poison. Ram Edmunds listed each question on his dry-erase board:

- How is polonium produced?

- If polonium emits radiation, can't it be detected by Geiger counters or other mechanisms?

- How much polonium can be ingested by a human being for it to be lethal?

- How long does a victim last after being poisoned by polonium?

- To cause damage, must the polonium be ingested or can a person be poisoned in some other ways?

- Does the polonium have a distinctive taste?

Consuelo waited until all the questions were listed on Ram's board. As Consuelo, with the help of Ram Edmunds, answered the team's questions, the group became sullen. Her staccato delivery listed the properties of Diego's chosen weapon of targeted destruction. "The substance can be produced only by nuclear reactors. Geiger counters and other instrumentation cannot detect the poison once it has been ingested. This is the reason that, when taken, health officials cannot treat the patients. Quantities less than a billionth of a gram are sufficient for polonium to be toxic. The time taken for half the substance ingested to decay is about a month. That is why death is slow and incrementally painful." She stopped, looked around for effect, and asked if she needed to address any of those characteristics with more detail.

"No," said Max thoughtfully, "I believe you've brought a proper amount of cheer and inspiration to all of us."

Consuelo dropped her no-nonsense attitude and broke out in laughter. No one else in the group even smiled. "Sorry to disappoint you, big boy, but I tell it like it is."

"And that's much appreciated, Agent Cervantes," said Ram. "We need straightforward facts…as depressing as they may be."

"In closing," said Consuelo, "as far as we know, polonium does not have any distinctive tastes; therefore it can be hidden in any beverage."

"Since I'm taking notes," said Minerva, "I missed your response to the question 'Must the poison be swallowed…ingested…or can it be administered in any other way'?"

"Wow!" said Ram. "Very insightful, young lady. I believe you are correct. Consuelo failed to answer that question. The answer that we presently have is that for significant damage to occur in humans, it must be ingested or inhaled. Any other questions?"

Max jumped in. "Without getting into the weeds much, can you describe the symptoms experienced by victims who've ingested the poison?"

"The normal progression," said Consuelo, "is severe vomiting and diarrhea, with a rapid degeneration of major organs that will lead to a weakening of all systems. For several weeks up to about a month, the victim's condition will worsen, and if fortunate, the victim will fall unconscious. It's an excruciating and very painful death."

"Finally," asked Nate, "do we know if Diego still has the poison in his possession?"

Ram Edmunds interrupted. "What we know is that Diego had prepared three vials—containing the substance mixed with water—and he stored them in his office safe. From our investigations, we believe those three vials are still there."

"Why *three* vials?" Marc Hugot asked.

Predictably, all the *older* adults turned to look at Minerva. Acknowledging them, she stood up and told Marc, "Because, Mr. Hugot, Diego has had three targets in mind from the beginning—my dad, my mom, and me."

CHAPTER FIFTY-THREE

[Palma de Mallorca–Corsica; March 2023]

For the next few weeks Eliza and Diego communicated daily. However, each time Diego offered an invitation to meet, Eliza deflected his attention to their improved relationship and how she enjoyed their daily conversations. On the advice of Nate and Miró, she reinforced their budding friendship and how she would like to become a trustworthy friend just as Diego had been to her. At one point, Eliza acknowledged that Diego probably missed his wife and wanted the void in his heart to be filled. She understood, said Eliza, what it was like to lose a loved one. She was tempted to describe how she had lost her own husband and children, but she wisely refrained from saying more.

Meanwhile, Diego was encouraged every time he communicated with Eliza. He became convinced that his relationship with Eliza, or whatever Yael called herself, would be cemented. Instead of becoming despondent, Diego sensed that his relationship with the woman who refused to acknowledge her identity was developing exactly as he planned. Whatever scheme her godfather and others forced upon her was failing. The reason it was failing was that he simply followed what his friend, Archbishop Gómez from the Canaries, used to say: "Love conquers all." And Diego believed it with all his heart. He would continue to love his wife, Yael, as he always had. In his mind he and Yael would renew their vows in short order.

Early on a Saturday morning in late March, Diego received an instant digital message from Eliza. It was the first time that Eliza had initiated a digital communication. Enthusiastically, Diego responded with surprise and gratitude for the godsend that had arrived "in the nick of time."

For weeks Diego had been experiencing suspicious symptoms, frequent nightmares that caused him to wake up sweating and terrified. A frequent visitor to his dreams—the vicious, rabid black dog—hounded Diego more and more. And although he had not shared with anyone, he was beginning to experience visual and auditory hallucinations—or what he assumed were hallucinations. In both instances, Isabella, or her likeness, who wore a veiled face and a provocative negligee, approached his bed and lay next to Diego. As Diego lifted her veil, the grotesque, toothless face of death smiled at him. Although greatly concerned, Diego had remained silent, refusing to share his terrible nightmares with anyone.

Diego gushed enthusiastically, "You know, my dear Eliza, that you've never before initiated a single communication. Thank you. Thank you. I needed to hear from you."

To Diego's surprise, Eliza responded, "I felt a need to reach out to you. You were on my mind this morning. Forget this texting back and forth; let me call you."

Perhaps because of his state of mind, perhaps because of the strange nightmares, Diego teared up. He had always treated all maudlin behavior in men as weak and spineless, yet here was Diego in tears because a woman was initiating a conversation. After his phone chimed, Diego answered. "My dearest Ya—my dear friend—I need to share with you my problems," he responded.

For the next ninety minutes Diego confided in Eliza and shared the details of his dreams. "This rabid dog appears in my dreams and chases me...and the next thing I know I'm in my bed accompanied by a woman."

Eliza froze because she was afraid that the next statement from Diego would describe *her* (Eliza) in his bed. She was not prepared for a response.

Instead, almost in tears, Diego continued: "The woman in my bed is always wearing a provocative negligee and when I remove her veil, the toothless face of death smiles at me. I wake up terrified...I feel small...childish...no, in all honesty I feel ashamed that I'm behaving like a helpless old woman. Please don't think less of me...as a man."

For the first time in their many interactions, Eliza experienced genuine compassion for the troubled man. As instructed by Nate and Miró, she counted to ten and reminded herself that she was dealing with a master manipulator.

"Diego...may I call you Diego?" asked Eliza.

"I wish you would."

"Diego, I do not think less of you. On the contrary, for men like you, it must be difficult to admit adversities in their lives. It takes courage to do so." Eliza bit her lip as she heard herself uttering the words.

Diego continued: "Thank you. There's much more. My relationship with Estevan is deteriorating. Each time I mention you, he becomes moody...he sulks. Instead of rejoicing with me that my... friendship...with you is flourishing, Estevan ridicules me and casts suspicion on your motives."

Eliza laughed. "What on earth does he think? Is he afraid of losing you as a friend?"

"No, no. He believes that you have a devious plan to somehow entrap me...that you and the authorities are attempting to incriminate me in various crimes—some such nonsense," said Diego.

Eliza chuckled. "Quite the imagination."

Diego cleared his throat. Eliza could tell that he was reluctant to share more, but Diego continued, stammering as he said almost in a whisper. "Like I said, there's more.... This morning—it was before dawn—I thought I was having a nervous breakdown."

Not knowing how to respond, Eliza remained quiet. Then she said, "It sounds like you've been under much stress. Are you experiencing problems with your business, your health?"

"It's my emotional state," said Diego. "I've always been stable, sure of myself, resolute in all things. Now, I don't know.... I'm beginning to doubt my state of mind."

"Diego, although you seem to be stressed, you appear fine to me," said Eliza.

"I woke up this morning—before dawn, like I said—and my first words were 'Estevan! Come here at once. Estevan! Isabella! What the devil is going on?'" Diego then paused for a long while. "I was half-sitting on my bed while I called out to them. Also, I was perspiring from head to foot, disoriented and confused. Isabella appeared at my door before Estevan. She looked at me with horror in her eyes. She just stood there, paralyzed."

Diego stopped, fearing he had said too much. Eliza prompted him: "What happened then, Diego?"

"In an instant Estevan burst in and shoved Isabella aside...He also came to a stop when he saw me," said Diego. "From his expression, I could tell he was as clueless as Isabella.... He regained his composure and motioned to Isabella to fetch some towels and alcohol. Within seconds they were both attending to numerous scratches on my bare torso and with damp towels cleaning the soles of my feet. Most of the scratches were superficial wounds, although I did have a couple of deep gashes on my upper arms. Only my arm scratches were bleeding slightly. The rest of the scratches on my upper body had signs of dried blood."

"Oh, dear," Eliza said with genuine concern. "How in the world did you get those cuts? Are you still hurting?"

"That's just it! I do not know. 'What the devil happened?' I asked them. After my wounds were cleaned, I realized there was more to the absurdity. Wet leaves and dirt covered my entire bed. The small bedside rug on the floor was muddy and stained. The caked mud on the soles of my feet matched the soiled rug."

Eliza, who had been sitting at the small desk in her bedroom, rose to her feet. "How in the world did you get all that dirt and mud on your bed and rug? Did they have an explanation?"

"Estevan signed a lengthy question, which I could not understand. So Isabella stepped in to interpret. 'Estevan wants to know if you've been outside...walking in the garden...or *oltre il giardino*...beyond.'"

"Of course not," I complained. "I just woke up."

By now Eliza was walking up and down the length of the sliding doors to her private patio. Consuelo, who was upstairs listening and recording the conversation, was laughing hysterically. Genuinely worried, Eliza did not know what to say.

Diego continued: "However, and this is even more baffling…my legs were sore, as if I'd been walking, or running, a great distance. Isabella went to get me some coffee and hurriedly walked out of the room. Estevan sat at the foot of the bed, and he took out his writing tablet. He scribbled, *Do you think that you might have been sleepwalking?*"

"I was about to ask you that," Eliza said.

"Well, I'm afraid I reacted badly," said Diego. I told Estevan, 'How would I bloody know if I've been sleepwalking? If so, it would be the first time…. I don't know.'"

Since Diego did not get a comment from Eliza, he went on: "It worries me, Yael. I'm afraid I need help."

"Calm down, my friend," said Eliza. "Just a friendly reminder—my name is Eliza; but I'm certain this is not serious. As Estevan says, you might have been out in your garden, sleepwalking. It's not uncommon. You might have had nightmares—who knows?"

"During the last ten days I've been hearing voices—mysterious voices that I do not recognize," Diego said. "Each time, two or three voices in unison ask me to remove my clothes, walk out to my garden, and climb over the granite wall to jump off the cliff. I've wanted to tell Isabella and Estevan about the vocal hallucinations, but I changed my mind."

"Why? I'm certain they're willing to help, Diego."

"I'm ashamed," Diego almost whispered. "As I drank the coffee that Isabella brought me this morning, I wondered if I heeded the voices in my head…. Did I maybe jump off the cliff?"

CHAPTER FIFTY-FOUR

[Palma de Mallorca–Corsica; March 2023]

As Eliza attempted to console Diego by phone, Consuelo appeared at her bedroom door. With arms crossed, Consuelo assumed the mother hen role, wagged her finger at her protégé, and instructed her not to fall into a state of submission. Without saying a word, Consuelo communicated to Eliza what needed to be said: *Caution: you are dealing with a master manipulator.*

Eliza nodded, acknowledging the warning but wondering if Diego was, perhaps for the first time in his life, feeling vulnerable. She continued listening to Diego but exercised greater caution. Consuelo was right; she could not fall victim to Diego's manipulation. Finally, Eliza suggested, "Diego, why don't we plan for another visit, or perhaps for drinks sometime soon?"

Diego could not believe the remarkable turn of events. The woman who had scorned him repeatedly was now ready to move to the next step. She, not him, was proposing a date! Like an eager teenager, Diego suggested he could get a flight immediately. Eliza chuckled and stated, "Well, I was actually thinking that perhaps this coming weekend would be better."

"By all means. This is cause for celebration. If I can suggest that you and I return to our favorite…Fera Restaurant," said Diego.

"Don't forget my cousin," added Eliza. "You know how much she enjoyed your company last time."

With her wireless earbuds on, Consuelo, still standing at the door, rolled her eyes. She smiled and walked back upstairs to her communication center.

"Yes, yes—of course," said Diego. "Your cousin also…. I thought by now she would have returned to Toledo."

"Her plans have changed twice. She's truly concerned about me," said Eliza.

Encouraged and animated, Diego promised to call back the following morning. He proclaimed his devoted "friendship" several times and hinted at his desire for their relationship to grow in favorable directions. In a bold show of affection, Eliza commented, "I would like that very much."

To Eliza's surprise, Diego remained silent. Speechless, Diego simply muttered, "I…I must either be delusional…or I'm still hearing things…. Tell me, my friend—was that an auditory hallucination, or did I hear you say that you would also like that?"

"No," said Eliza chuckling. "You heard right, Diego." She then ended the call.

Diego rose from his bed. With a spring in his step, he stepped outside onto his private garden and breathed in the invigorating morning air. After going through his *tai chi* routine, he summoned Isabella to bring his second cup of morning coffee.

I knew she could not resist…. My wife never stopped loving me. If they brainwashed her, it does not matter. Diego walked around his private garden admiring his estate and dreaming of having Yael at his side. *Yael will return to her senses. During our last conversations, she has begun to sound more like the Yael I know.*

. . .

Everything appeared to be falling into place. During the next days, Nate and Miró, aided by the rest of the *Galatea* Team, coached Eliza. They scheduled daily meetings at Abraham's townhouse near Palma to discuss each of the next steps. At each of the meetings, the atmosphere became increasingly charged with an intensity that reflected the team's unspoken realization that they were approaching the last stages of the Pygmalion Project.

In her brief telephone conversations Eliza had with Diego the rest of the week, she successfully reinforced their growing relationship and the deep respect she had developed for him. With focused coaching, she even repeated how she "*loved* his interest in botany," how she "*loved* his thoughtfulness," and how she "*loved* his notes of encouragement." In a written instant chat, she pointedly mentioned that she "*hated* not being able to replace his wife, Yael." After each conversation with Diego, however, Eliza reminded herself that the monster who had murdered her husband and at least indirectly killed her sons was not worthy of compassion. She vowed to herself and the team that she wanted to see the man suffer a death more cruel than her husband's.

Sitting around Abraham's townhouse pool, the team coached Eliza. "What is coming up may prove to be the most difficult phase," Nate warned. "I say that because so far you have not had a need to fight off Diego's romantic advances. He, in fact, has behaved like a perfect gentleman. But once you proclaim a willingness to accept his advances, be assured that you will be in the most dangerous of situations. You cannot risk showing your repugnance."

"And, dear *prima,*" said Consuelo, "you cannot afford to use alcohol to dull your senses. You must be in full control throughout the process, and you must convince this monster—as you call him—that he turns you on."

Max, who was standing next to his niece Minerva, leaned over to cover her ears. "Uncle Max, please, you certainly must know that one hears much worse on the average TV show or movie," she said.

"Still, I'd like to play the protector...whenever I can," said the smiling uncle.

Ram Edmunds chimed in: "Miró, do you have anything to add?"

"Thank you, Ram. I certainly do." Turning to Eliza, Miró said, "We've reached that point." She paused dramatically. "The next step is to communicate to Diego that you believe your bond with him is 'special.' Furthermore, you must suggest your desire to be his partner."

Eliza agonized over Miró's instructions for forty-eight hours. She knew she was not yet ready to convincingly face Diego and declare her affection. Finally, knowing that she could not vocalize a profession of love, she wrote him a note elaborating what the team had dictated. To her envelope she attached a red rose. With the team's approval, it was delivered by courier the following day.

• • •

Upon receipt of Eliza's love note, Diego immediately packed a bag and arranged for a private plane to fly him to Palma from Bonifacio. He summoned Ciccio, his driver, to transport him to *Figari Sud-Corse* Airport, a twenty-minute distance from his estate. Although Diego failed to ask Estevan to join him, Estevan jumped into the SUV at the last moment to "inform Diego of some recent developments."

On the way to the airport, Estevan informed him that he believed Inspector Eduardo Sánchez was in Palma de Mallorca. Using simplified sign language, Estevan said, *A certain J. Eduardo Sánchez flew into the Palma Airport several days ago. He was traveling "for pleasure," according to records.*

Clearly distracted, Diego asked, "Estevan, do you know how common the surname 'Sánchez' is in Spanish-speaking countries? What makes you think it's Yael's *padrino?*"

Take it as a word of caution. Wouldn't it be a far-fetched coincidence if he and your Eliza were in the same location at the same time…again? Estevan raised his eyebrows. He reached over to shake Diego's shoulder, as if to wake him from a deep sleep.

Diego smiled. He turned to face Estevan and said, "I know you're concerned. For now, let me enjoy my visit with Yael…or whatever she calls herself. So please—you and Isabella keep me informed…if you discover any convincing proof. *Ciao.*" Diego stepped out of the SUV and jaunted youthfully toward his chartered jet.

As soon as he arrived in Palma, Diego telephoned Eliza. He left a voice mail since she did not pick up. While renting a vehicle, he called again. Consuelo answered the call. "Yes, articulate," she demanded.

Now familiar with Consuelo's voice and her terse manner, Diego simply chuckled. "This is Diego, sweet Consuelo. Could I speak to your cousin Eliza?"

"Who did you say this was?"

"Diego Montemayor, Consuelo. Your friend."

"Oh, yes. Let me see if she's here." Although sitting in her communications center upstairs, Consuelo had intercepted the call deliberately. Eliza was downstairs in their villa, speaking with Miró on a secured line, and she was receiving instructions regarding the next steps. Consuelo made a show of loudly calling out to her cousin, then came back to the line to inform Diego that Eliza was unavailable.

"What do you mean, 'unavailable'?" asked Diego. "I'm certain she would like to speak to me."

"What about the word is difficult to understand, Diego? The word *indisponible* is clearly understood by Spanish speakers," said the irascible Consuelo.

"Will you please tell her that I'm here…in Palma, and that I'd like to see her?" asked Diego with uncharacteristic meekness.

After a brief pause, Consuelo stated, "I can do that." Then she ended the call.

Since Diego had not been invited to drive to Eliza's villa, he deliberated, then decided to kill time by shopping for a small present. Two hours later he received a return call from Eliza. "My dear Diego, I just learned from Consuelo that you called two hours ago. I've been doing laps in my pool."

"I could not wait to see you…after the courier delivered your message…and the red rose—" Diego stopped, as if at a loss for words. "I was overcome…with tears." Before Eliza could respond, Diego— sardonically laughing at himself—said, "Five years ago I would have called anyone using those words a *maricón*. How time changes a person."

Whether Diego was truly a master manipulator or not, Eliza was convinced that the version of Diego that she was getting to know was different from the one she had met as "Rodrigo" back in Winnetka. This hardened murderer now spoke as a human being with weaknesses, vulnerabilities, and tenderness. Although she wanted him to die for his previous actions, she wondered if someone like Diego could ever be redeemed. Ahh, but that was not for her to decide. Her mission was clear, and she wanted to maintain the control she now had.

"Why don't you visit with us now? Can you spare some time?" she heard herself addressing the lovelorn Diego.

"I am here for that one reason, my dear," said Diego.

Several minutes later, pulling on the doorbell rope, the same Puccini aria greeted the visitor with the fedora. With a huge smile, in preparation before the door opened, Diego extended the bunch of flowers he had bought at the local florist. The smile disappeared when he saw Consuelo at the door. Wearing her black bicycling jersey and bib shorts with neon lemon-yellow lettering, Consuelo took the flowers from Diego's hand and stepped aside to let him in. Diego noticed that since the last time he'd seen Consuelo, she had added a streak of lemon-yellow to her short blonde hair. The ample amount of perspiration on her forearms dripped on Diego's wrist, and he discreetly took out his kerchief to wipe it off. Consuelo, however, noticed and rather than apologizing, merely said, "Oops." Diego noticed that she raised her armpit up to her nose and sniffed. Making a face, she exclaimed, "Whew! I need a shower." She turned around, carelessly dropped the bunch of flowers on the credenza by the wall, and rushed upstairs.

To Diego's delight, Eliza appeared behind him. Unlike the average person, Diego, an expert botanist, caught the whiff of the most intoxicating fragrance he had ever enjoyed, a whiff of lotus flower and the Asian pear called "nashi" mixed with balsa. Speechless, Diego noticed that Eliza wore a short white smock of eyelet lace, which revealed the lemon-yellow one-piece bathing suit underneath. The ensemble contrasted with Yael's—or Eliza's—deep tan and silk-like skin. Her wet hair was pulled back and tied at the top with a bright yellow tie, which accentuated the raven-like curls that cascaded down to her shoulders. The image transported Diego to the most beautiful waterfall that he had never seen—until now. Her ballerina-like feet shaped by a pronounced arch were shod with burnt orange Italian leather sandals that were strapped halfway up her calves above the ankles. If Diego had been smitten by his wife, Yael, before, he was shamefully many times more stricken now.

Eliza stood there, smiling broadly. She asked, "Diego, didn't you hear my question?"

Diego was still at a loss for words. He stood there, hat still on, ogling without saying a word. Eliza placed his flowers in a crystal vase. "What question?" Diego finally said.

"I was asking you if Consuelo had asked you in," said Eliza. "Since I did not hear the doorbell, I wondered…"

"Yes, yes," said Diego. "She rushed upstairs to take a shower."

Eliza thanked him for such a lovely and thoughtful bouquet of roses. "This makes my day," she said.

"I thought I would bring you another small present," Diego finally said. He took out a small platinum box from his *guayabera* shirt and, with a slight tremor of his hand, showed her a Tahitian black pearl ring on a thick gold band. The ring tapered at the pearl's setting. The 10 mm blue-black pearl was guarded by five diamonds on each side. "It is a token of my undying love and affection, my friend."

"Diego, this is lovely. May I try it on?"

Diego took it and put it on her right ring finger. It fit perfectly.

"How did you know the correct size?" Eliza asked.

"Sheer instinct," said Diego with a suggestive nod.

Diego and Eliza spent that afternoon on her patio drinking gin martinis. In reality, since Eliza prepared the drinks, she had virgin martinis herself. They spoke of their earlier meetings, with Diego avoiding the mention of Ruel Levant. Although Eliza mentioned her deceased fiancé once, she politely stuck to describing her earlier impressions of Diego, acknowledging—falsely—that she had always found Diego to be a distinguished, charming, and very handsome man. At dusk, Consuelo joined them, gin-and-tonic in hand. She cheerfully announced that Diego should treat them to an evening out. "It may be one of the last opportunities you get to see me, Diego. I do plan to leave soon, you know."

After showering, Consuelo had decided to wear a somewhat reveal-ing and seductive outfit that featured her prominent breasts and long bicyclist legs. The plunging neckline almost caused Diego to ignore her unsightly armpit hair. As she leaned close to Diego to set her empty glass on the bistro table, Diego saw that high on her left breast, Consuelo sported a blue-and-red tattoo of a tiny hummingbird.

When Consuelo noticed Diego studying her tattoo, she asked, "Like?" This caused Diego some embarrassment, but Consuelo added, "I keep insisting that Eliza get one, but she refuses."

Without hesitating one beat, Diego said, "Oh, but she does have one on her—" Then, Diego turned red, looked away, and apologized to Eliza. "Forgive me—I still keep thinking of you as Yael…. I meant no…"

"No need to apologize," said Eliza as she smiled, got up, and offered everyone another drink. As she walked inside to the bar area, Consuelo followed her. Inside she hurriedly told Eliza, "You go back out there. Not only will I prepare drinks, but I must alert the team that we may have missed an important detail on Yael's anatomy. Did you hear Diego suggesting that Yael had a tattoo somewhere in a very private area?"

"I certainly did. No one, not even her godfather, had any way of knowing…"

"Back out there, *prima*," said Consuelo. "I've got to communicate to the team that we may have missed something. And we won't be able to depend on Dr. Wu to fix it."

CHAPTER FIFTY-FIVE

[Palma de Mallorca–Corsica; March 2023]

Although Diego, Eliza, and Consuelo had a festive evening, the rest of the *Galatea* Team scrambled to discover what kind of tattoo the deceased Yael may have privately sported for her husband. Of course, Inspector Sánchez had no awareness of any private body art on his goddaughter. Nate and Miró had no clue. Noting the team's bewilderment, Minerva asked, "Wouldn't the medical examiner or a coroner have that information?"

"Young lady, you keep impressing me more and more," said Ram Edmunds. "More than forty years in this business, and it is not I, but you, a seventeen-year-old with abundant common sense, who comes up with the obvious solution." Ram Edmunds rolled up his sleeves. "Let's get to work. We need the report of those medical examiners. We'll work around the clock if we need to."

"Of course, we can only hope that Yael's remains weren't too badly burned to leave any evidence of the hidden tattoo," said Miró.

With the help of Inspector Sánchez, Ram Edmunds attempted to communicate with relevant personnel at the non-existent hospital where the 2016 fire had taken place. In a suicidal effort, and with the intent of taking Nate and Miró with her, Yael Montemayor had incinerated the hospital, which went up in flames. The question was, would a report of the medical examiner be available for the team to replicate the tattoo on Eliza's body?

Meanwhile, Diego Montemayor escorted Eliza and her cousin to various nightclubs in Palma de Mallorca. While the amorous couple occasionally held hands, exchanged occasional suggestive glances and touches to the face or upper arms, Eliza did not allow any physical intimacy other than passing kisses. Consuelo, on the other hand, danced with various partners, both men and women. She did not appear to discourage any of the advanced petting, but she laughed off any invitation to abscond for the night.

Before eleven at night, Consuelo announced that she was famished. "Diego, what about that restaurant you like so much? I suggest you take us there."

"Fera Restaurant it is," said Diego, "if my beloved is willing." He turned to Eliza for approval. Getting it, he summoned a cab, since he had imbibed more than his limit for safe driving. For the next two hours they enjoyed a delectable dinner. Starting with oysters and Nori steak tartare and lobster bisque, the chef recommended the black rice with octopus and mussels. They shared the plate and ordered sea bass as well as Simmental beef filet. This time Consuelo allowed Diego to select the wines, and he ordered several bottles of Pommard and additionally two bottles of the 2016 Montrachet Grand Cru.

It was past three in the morning when they returned to Eliza's home. On the cab ride back to the villa, Consuelo made it clear to Diego that, given the situation of two single females living alone, it would be inappropriate for Diego to spend the night. Of course, Diego agreed but begged to be allowed to return the following morning before departing for Bonifacio.

More than a little tipsy and with her neckline plunging even more dramatically than before, Consuelo declared that as official chaperone to her cousin, she would allow it under one condition.

"And what is that condition, dear Consuelo?" asked Diego.

"I must be allowed to cook a late breakfast for the three of us," said Consuelo.

Eliza discreetly turned to Diego and cringed, knowing that Consuelo was not the most talented cook. "Of course," said Diego in mock elation. "With great anticipation I await a gourmet breakfast tomorrow morning. Until then, ladies, good night." He leaned over to kiss Eliza. From Consuelo he even received the customary double kiss on both cheeks.

. . .

Diego spent a short respite at the Hotel *Can Cera* in the historic center of Palma. To his surprise, he received an instant message on his mobile phone from "Cousin Consuelo" at exactly 8:00 a.m. It was an invitation for breakfast at their villa to be served "at exactly 9:00." A groggy response came back: "I'll do my best to arrive on time—and fully awake."

Although Eliza greeted Diego at the door, Consuelo called out from the kitchen. "Save the romance for later, you lovebirds. Breakfast is almost ready." To Diego's surprise—and to Eliza's amazement— Consuelo momentarily left the kitchen to receive Diego in the dining room with a fresh cup of an aromatic Italian roast. Before Diego had an opportunity to finish his cup of coffee, Consuelo walked in with a perfectly prepared frittata. To the browned Italian sausage Consuelo had added cooked broccoli rabe, parmesan, and fresh basil leaves. Respecting the couple's possible aversion to onions, she served sliced scallions on the side. Although Diego might have been tempted to make a comment about Consuelo's transformation, Eliza signaled to him to refrain from any snide remarks.

Perhaps the rich coffee enabled Diego to rouse his appetite. He consumed his portion and without embarrassment asked for seconds. Consuelo seemed pleased. "You know, Diego, you might not be my perfect choice for my favorite cousin, but if you can make her happy...well, you're not too bad an egg." She took a sip of her coffee, then took the butter knife and playfully threatened, "But if you ever cross my *prima*..."

"I would cut my own throat," Diego responded.

"Hopefully before I would," Consuelo said without even a trace of a smile.

. . .

At Consuelo's insistence, Eliza and Diego took an extended walk along the panoramic harbor walking trail. The morning was chilly, and the brisk breeze invigorated Diego. The aromas of a Mediterranean port that was world famous for the exporting of almonds, fruits, and olive oil also impressed Eliza with its beauty. The rich aromas of an abundance of vegetation and harbor activity gave the island a savory aroma of marine saltiness mixed with woody notes. The two walked in silence for miles. Diego smiled, breathed in the air, and several times stopped to extend his arms toward the sun as if to embrace life itself. He behaved as a man in love who was perfectly content.

As they walked, Eliza wondered if Diego, a man capable of so much evil, could be worthy of divinity's redemption. In his treatment of Eliza, Diego appeared to be not the master manipulator and murderer whom she knew him to be. In her previous life as Raquel Rosales, she had seen the evil version of Diego, a completely different human being devoid of any redeeming qualities. He had sequestered the Rosales families, kept them from each other, and murdered both of his "cartel lieutenants," as the newspapers had labeled her husband and brother-in-law. Moreover, Diego had probably ordered the drowning of her twin sons.

So then, who was this man beside her? Who was this medieval knight who held the door open not only for her but other women also, including her uncouth cousin? Diego even drew out Consuelo's chair in a restaurant. True, Eliza realized these were outdated conventions. But unlike other women, Eliza—and even the former Raquel—had never considered a gentleman's courtesies toward a woman demeaning signals of oppression and male chauvinism.

Although her husband and his brother were considered thugs from the hood, they had always remained "gentlemen" to their wives. She had always regarded those manners as welcome acts of chivalry, despite the mantra dictated by the radical feminists. To her, those manners suggested a man's interest in maintaining standards of courage, honor, courtesy, and a readiness to help the weak. Furthermore, as a father her husband had taught his sons to aspire to those standards. Whether her husband had lived up to those standards all his life was irrelevant. His mere interest in maintaining those conventions told her that he had aspired to live an honorable life. Could this also be Diego's innermost desire?

A small voice told her, *Beware—know that you are dealing with a ruthless killer. You do not have the luxury of examining Diego's heart.*

. . .

Late in the afternoon, Ram Edmunds and retired Inspector Eduardo Sánchez received an urgent message from a Dr. T. Coronado, the director of the *Servicio Canario de Salud*, the Public Health Department in Las Palmas. The director of the department asked for an immediate Zoom teleconference for clarification of some findings regarding the death of Yael Montemayor. Although the entire *Galatea* Team was invited to participate, only Ram, Sánchez, and Miró were able to join the meeting, which was scheduled ten minutes after the initial notice.

From the director's explanation, the original report was filed by a coroner who had decided on the cause of death in addition to other details regarding the circumstances. The coroner himself, according to the director, had since moved to a remote part of Portugal and could not be located. However, in his notes he had mentioned that Yael's body was evidently dragged to a hallway by an unknown individual for momentary safety, where another secondary explosion took her life. Although the body had sustained third-degree burns, the cause of death was declared to be smoke inhalation. In addition to other details mentioned in the report, a tattoo of an unidentified flower on the upper portion of the left buttock was described. It consisted of a reddish copper plant, with trumpet clusters of long, narrow leaves and tubular flowers.

"Does the report mention the size of the tattoo?" Miró asked.

"Yes, the precise dimensions are in the report, which is forthcoming," said the medical director. "The tattoo was exactly 7.62 centimeters. In addition, the exact location of the tattoo is also in the report."

"Thank you, Dr. Coronado, your help has been invaluable," said Ram Edmunds.

After ending the Zoom meeting, Ram turned to Miró and the inspector. "Without a photograph or a clear identification of the flower of the tat, we're still only guessing. We can't replicate that tattoo on Eliza's body, regardless of the description. We can't afford to get it wrong."

"Don't sweat it, Ram," said Miró. "I know exactly the flower that appeared on her buttock. It was the Canary Islands foxglove, the *Isoplexis canariensis*. It's Diego's favorite plant."

Inspector Sánchez smiled, "I believe that Miró is absolutely correct."

• • •

After a four-mile walk, Diego and his beloved stopped at Eliza's favorite café, *Can Joan de s'Aigo*. Diego announced, "My flower, I have a favor to ask. First, let me order your special delight from this cafe."

"Diego, we have never been here. How can you possibly know what my preferences are?" Eliza asked.

"It was last month, and you told me about your stop here with Cousin Consuelo. You also told me during our mobile conversation that you had ordered Mallorcan hot chocolate, almond ice cream, and a couple of Mallorcan pastries, especially the *ensaïmadas with crema quemada*."

Eliza was amazed. "How can you remember those details? Even I had forgotten that particular visit with Consuelo."

"My sole interest in life is to make you happy," Diego said. "Nothing else matters."

Eliza could not finish her ice cream. However, she did order a second cup of chocolate. Smiling at Diego, she reminded him, "You mentioned earlier that you have a favor to ask."

"I do indeed. I need to borrow your yacht, the *Shenandoah of Sark*, for a very private dinner…a special dinner."

"Diego, of course. In fact, I do not even consider it my yacht," Eliza said.

"You must know that the ownership was transferred to you and your former—to you and Ruel Levant," said Diego. "Since the last time I checked, the yacht is still moored at Porto-Vecchio."

"I do not know what to say," Eliza said. "Such extravagance must be reserved for…other special occasions. Our dinners at Fera have been superb, and if you prefer, we can explore other venues."

"My flower," said Diego tearfully, "I am not getting any younger. To be honest with you, if we already have proclaimed our love to each other, I can only think of a single step to make our joy complete. If I propose an eternal commitment, I would like it to be special. I have thought about it, and I want to formally propose in a special manner."

Remembering all the recent coaching sessions, Eliza countered, "From my perspective, my dearest, it is not so simple."

Diego chuckled. "How simple must it get? I love you. You love me. What is there to resolve?"

"Estevan." Eliza got up from their table and walked out of the bistro. As Diego followed, she stated, "Estevan is a significant part of your business…your life. It is clear he disapproves of me. We cannot enter marriage blindly thinking that his objections to our relationship will be insignificant…. You must know that."

Dismissing her comment with a wave of his arm, Diego said, "He will come around. Estevan is merely jealous…. He…"

"Exactly," said Eliza. She stopped and faced him. "He is jealous of how close we are. He is afraid of losing his influence, his status in your life. Perhaps he's afraid of losing you."

"But you are the most important person in my life. I cannot be without you," said Diego. "I will tell Estevan."

Eliza stopped at a gated entrance to the botanical gardens. The sounds of waves lapping on a distant beach broke the intimate moment. "Don't you see that you're afraid of offending Estevan? Otherwise, you would have already clarified everything. Estevan does not accept me. I cannot enter into your life—in the way you want me to—with Estevan in the picture."

"What are you saying? Do you mean that I must choose between you and Estevan?" Diego asked.

Eliza paused for a long time. Then she turned to walk away without answering his question.

"My love, please don't walk away from me. What are you telling me?"

"No, Diego. Obviously, it is all about what you're telling *me*. Don't you see? You don't want to choose between Estevan and me…. You're afraid that Estevan is more important to you than I am." With body language indicating a show of finality, Eliza, glaring at Diego, held up her hands, palms facing him, and without saying a word screamed, *Do not follow me!*

At the gate, Diego stopped in his tracks. He stood there, wavering, facing a dilemma he had not anticipated. Eliza—his Yael—was rejecting him.

CHAPTER FIFTY-SIX

[Palma de Mallorca–Corsica; March 2023]

A braham's townhouse outside of Palma had become the working headquarters for the *Galatea* Force. While part of the *Galatea* team sat around the dining area busily attempting to identify Yael Montemayor's mysterious body art, others—namely Nate, Abraham, and Marc Hugot—used the communication center upstairs to listen to the transmitted conversation between Eliza and Diego Montemayor. Eliza had just left Diego at the gated entrance to the botanical gardens, and their trace on Diego had disappeared. Using Eliza's cellular microphone as the primary transmitter, Eliza had allowed the team to record every word shared with Diego while they were together. Now, the spat had suspended their recording. Though unexpected, the team welcomed the development. Eliza had given them the time to address the issue of the mysterious tattoo.

Of course, the timeline for the team remained complicated. Since the team considered it important to provide Eliza with an exact replica of Yael's private tattoo before any intimacy between Diego and Eliza occurred, the clock was ticking. Thankfully, Diego had not made any sexual advances, but they suspected that Eliza might find herself in intimate situations in a very short period, especially after the spat was resolved.

During this phase of the operation, Ram Edmunds had suggested to Minerva that she enjoy the day sunning by the pool. As for Consuelo and Max, he asked them to track communications between

Gabriel Picard and his connections with the Pan Asian Shipping company.

Immediately after Nate and Abraham left the communication center upstairs, Consuelo joined Max. Since Consuelo had already tapped into Picard's private communications channels, the previous night she had shared with Max a set of files that had been collected by Ruel Levant. "If I'm forced to work with you, I want you to be informed, cowboy. I expect you to do your homework.... Don't come to me with questions unless you've first prepared. Understand?" asked the overbearing Consuelo. She used a distilled water jug to water and fertilize the tall *ficus benjamina* that stood by her northeast corner. Two glass windows gave the thriving tree necessary lighting. Consuelo then rolled her chair back to her desk, where she faced the three large monitors.

Sitting at his own desk, Max said, "Understood.... Are you always this friendly, or is it my charm that brings it on?" He docked his laptop onto the station and signed on to his account.

"It's all tall, blond, sexy men like you who cause me to melt like butter," Consuelo said with a snarl and gave Max a middle-finger salute. She then fixed her hair and briefly smiled.

"Consuelo, I do have a question. Ruel Levant included recordings between Picard and a member of the Pan Asian Shipping company's board of directors. These recordings go back some time. It appears the same board member sustained those communications with Picard until recently. However, the latest communications have all been by encrypted text."

"What's your question?" Consuelo prompted.

"Have you been able to identify that board member...or board members?"

"No, since Ruel first discovered the most recent encrypted texts between Picard and the board member, he suspected that someone within Diego's close circle—possibly even Estevan—was involved because of his familiarity with the operation, but he discounted that hypothesis."

Max asked, "Why?"

"Because…Einstein," Consuelo snapped, "like you, Ruel heard recorded conversations between Picard and that Pan Asian board member…and, as you know, Estevan is mute."

"Could they be two different individuals? By that I mean, could the recordings between Picard and that board member be of a person different from the one writing the encrypted texts?" Max asked.

"It's possible but unlikely," said Consuelo. "When I read the texts, there is a clear indication that he is the same one whose recordings we heard. In his texts he makes references to previous voice conversations that we recorded." Just then Consuelo walked over to the double windows and opened them. "Do you mind if I turn on this box fan? It's stifling hot in here." Without waiting for an answer, Consuelo turned on the fan full blast and stood in front of it. She unbuttoned the third button on her tight blouse and sat at her desk. For the first time, Max noticed the small blue-and-red tat of a hummingbird in flight.

As he stood up to get some coffee, he told Consuelo, "I'll get you a cup." He returned with a full mug, and standing over her, he added, "One more thing. You and Ruel obviously cracked the encrypted messages; however, for some reason, the Pan Asian board member always signs his messages. Why didn't you decipher the signature?"

"The signature was tough," Consuelo said. "In his text messages, the sender uses an extremely sophisticated system of encryption, but his signature is in a different system altogether. Perhaps it's just a closing or some other kind of code. Neither Ruel nor I could crack that one… so we left the signature alone: 'BPQBSXK.' We could not crack it."

Max smiled as he asked, "You memorized the signature?"

"Not by choice," Consuelo said. "I've tried so many times to decrypt the signature that it's stuck in my memory bank. Nothing we have, no program, has been able to crack it."

． ． ．

Dejected and at a loss regarding his next steps, Diego returned to Bonifacio from Palma via private jet. The demands of his beloved did not make sense. Immediately after deplaning, he boarded his waiting SUV. Driving Diego back from the airport, Ciccio attempted a broken conversation but gave up when he noticed his boss was in a distracted state.

To amuse himself after greeting Alessandro at the door, Diego walked directly to his greenhouse to tend to his foxgloves. His foxgloves always had a soothing effect on him. His prized plants were waiting, front and center, the varieties displaying their vibrant yellows, blues, salmon oranges, and deep reds. Putting on his leather apron, he opened the glassed cabinet and strapped on his goggles to begin a mindless nurturing session. Loupe and tweezers in hand, he reached for his vials that he had prepared for Isabella to nourish his foxgloves but noticed that today's portions were missing. He assumed she had already fed his plants. "One vial per plant," he had said. "*Una fiala per pianta.*" He'd prepared the perfect daily amounts, carefully measured tiny amounts, in labeled vials stored in the greenhouse's glass-encased shelving.

As he moved toward the center of his greenhouse, he noticed a rustling of plants ahead of him. As he approached the row of plants on the raised platform, Isabella screeched with horror. She raised her arms in fright and dropped the vials of organic solution on the cement floor.

The goggled Diego just stood there with magnified terror in his eyes. He recuperated and dropped the tweezers and moved toward Isabella to assist her since she appeared faint. That only provoked another unearthly shriek from Isabella, so Diego stood back. At that point Estevan ran in to inspect the commotion. Isabella just ran toward him and fell into his arms.

Turning back to Diego, she said, "*O, signore, scusami…io…*"

"No, no, Isabella. I understand…. I crept up on you and…" Embarrassed, Diego just walked away and let Estevan console the *cameriera*. He called out to Estevan as he walked away, "Please tell her I apologize! I must've looked monstruous wearing my leather apron and goggles!"

Instead of seeking solace in his office, Diego walked to his private garden and fell onto his favorite wrought-iron swivel chair with a plop. Looking out toward the magnificent view of the Mediterranean down below, Diego reflected.

The crystalline waters of the sea below and the rich granite red of the cliffs that descended for more than a mile to the sandy beaches from his terrace no longer took his breath away. Diego acknowledged that the years hadn't been kind to him. He had hoped that the plastic surgery from Dr. Ivo Wu would have shaved a few years off his hardened appearance. He even became a taller, more slender man. But the surgery had not made him a handsome man. And the creases on his face, the lines at the corners of his eyes—these were engraved episodes of grief, hatred, and vengeance in the book of his life. Even the surgical scars that peppered his body were testimonials not of his manhood but rather of his deception and evasion of the truth—a truth that bespoke a profound despair.

Diego pondered if the many years he had dedicated to an obsessive compulsion to destroy the Shelley family had embittered him—if it had twisted and marred his heart, maimed his emotions, disfigured his features. Does hatred leave its mark and mutilate one's being? *Has hatred transformed me into a monstrous human being?* Diego wondered if the hatred for the Shelleys had disappeared since discovering that his Yael was alive. *Could I ever let go of my hatred for them?*

Instinctively, Diego realized that reconciling with his Yael—not letting go of the love that was rekindling was his only salvation. How could he let it slip through his fingers? *Oh, what a wretched man I am!* Diego cried openly. *And yet…perhaps it's not too late. I can have a blissful, placid, reunion with the woman I love…if only I can sacrifice the closest approximation to friendship that I have. Yes, regardless of the cost, Estevan must go. While I still can, I need to recapture the life I had with Yael.*

CHAPTER FIFTY-SEVEN

[Palma de Mallorca; March 2023]

That night at ten o'clock, Consuelo intercepted a call from Diego Montemayor. A contrite and miserable Diego asked to speak to Eliza. In her usual curt manner, Consuelo said to the caller, "If this is you, Diego, you are obviously a clueless and heartless creature. How is it you think my cousin would wish to speak to you after choosing the companionship of a servant to her?"

"You clearly misunderstand...." Then Diego heard static. Consuelo had disconnected. Immediately Diego called again, and Consuelo let it ring. After twelve rings, Eliza answered the call.

"Please do not hang up on me.... Forgive me, please. Forgive me for my callous...my stupid judgment, my flower. To think that I could have ever given you the impression that I would choose Estevan.... In truth, I cannot forgive myself. Please, Yael.... What I mean is...please, Eliza...speak to me." To his own unbelief, Diego sobbed.

Although Eliza said nothing, she did not end the call. Still on the line, she heard Diego say, "I will speak to Estevan first thing in the morning. I have written him a letter, and I have saved you a copy. In my letter I've explained not only the conditions for termination but also my explicit wishes to cease any further personal communications in the future. I will scan and send you the letter. My attorneys will also receive copies tonight."

Several moments passed, but Eliza did not respond.

"Please say something,...my...everything." The pathetic brokenness in his voice suggested to Eliza that Diego was still weeping. After what seemed to Diego to be an interminable silence, Eliza responded.

"Call me back when you've spoken to Estevan." She then ended the call.

After a sleepless night, Diego woke up Estevan at 5:00. He gave him the letter and explained his decision.

In the meantime, Consuelo shared with the *Galatea* Force the transcript of Diego's phone call to Eliza and the emailed copy of his letter to Estevan.

• • •

Gabriel Picard, the Deputy Secretary General of Interpol, had granted Nate and Miró a leave of absence to have an extended spring holiday with family. Their mutual friend, Inspector Eduardo Sánchez, had also asked for the opportunity to handle personal matters during the interim. During their absence, the communications between Picard and his Pan Asian contact greatly increased. Unbeknownst to Picard, Consuelo Cervantes monitored those communications closely. She provided daily reports to Wagner, Interpol's secretary general, and to the *Galatea* Force under the direction of Ram Edmunds, the deputy director of the American FBI.

The increased chatter between Picard and his Chinese associate suggested that a significant event was ready to happen. In his repeated communications, Picard alluded to "mutual benefits," but no further clues were discerned from the encrypted messages. Few would realize that the digital traffic served to bring about monumental, but unidentified, changes that Picard and Pan Asian Shipping did not anticipate.

Since Consuelo had been instructed by Ram Edmunds to collaborate with Max Kempball in the surveillance of Picard's private communications, she outlined multiple tasks for Max to complete. Sitting alone for hours with Max in the communications center of Abraham's townhouse, Consuelo got to know the private investigator from Texas well enough to appreciate his skills. Although Consuelo was not prone to offer compliments, she reluctantly admitted to Edmunds that Max brought many skills to the team and that he was "a quick learner." Privately she admired Max's sense of humor and his ability to ignore her prickly personality. Perhaps she even acknowledged his rugged good looks.

Although Consuelo enjoyed the corner with a view—having two windows that offered a glorious view of the Bay of Palma—Max's desk also offered him a pleasant view of Abraham's pool and landscaped patio. Since the window was across from Consuelo's desk, they sat back-to-back. On his desk also sat three large monitors with access to everything on Consuelo's screens. The only decoration on Max's desk was a potted Crown of Thorns cactus that his maternal grandmother had personally transplanted from her ranch garden in Three Rivers, Texas.

On the early morning of the third day of collaboration, Consuelo and Max discovered several urgent encrypted communications from Picard's Pan Asian Shipping contact: "Need caterers and orchestra." In a curious response, Picard had replied, "I've secured the Vienna Philharmonic and the catering."

Rolling his office chair on the wooden floors toward Consuelo's desk, Max asked, "What do you make of this?"

"Not sure, cowboy, but I must share with the secretary general. I don't like all this chatter," said a concerned Consuelo.

Within minutes, Wagner, Interpol's secretary general, instructed Consuelo, "If Pan Asian Shipping Enterprises is handling a major shipment, Picard is definitely involved. Be prepared to be mobilized at a moment's notice." What this meant for Consuelo was that at any moment she might be deployed elsewhere by Interpol's general secretariat. It would necessarily postpone or delay the *Galatea* Force's operation.

After Consuelo read the secretary general's message, she went downstairs to advise Ram Edmunds that she might be reassigned, depending on her superior's orders. She stood above Edmunds, who was seated at his makeshift desk on the dining table, and reassured Ram that upon her return to Lyon, Max Kempball would be able to assume the digital monitoring of Diego and Estevan. In an uncharacteristic fashion, she said, "I have full confidence in him."

After being summoned downstairs, Max joined Ram Edmunds and Consuelo. Together, Consuelo and Max informed Ram of the encrypted communications and the "climactic" event being planned by Picard and his Pan Asian Shipping contact. They also explained that the execution of this event was imminent. Still sitting at the center of his dining room makeshift office, Ram pointedly asked Consuelo, "Would you advise Eliza to keep on delaying her reencounter with Diego? Remember that the FBI cannot act independently in Europe without European collaboration. I would prefer to have the full involvement of Interpol."

As she and Max stood across from Ram Edmunds, Consuelo said, "Sir, in my opinion, the *Galatea* Force is dealing with a drug dealer's potential engagement party. Although important, the event will not have international implications. The more recent communications that Max and I uncovered suggest that an event with global ramifications may be in the making. So yes, I believe 'my cousin,' Eliza Durazo, should postpone her communications with Diego. It certainly seems less impactful than this shipment that might have huge consequences."

"May I remind you, Agent Consuelo, that Diego Montemayor is no insignificant drug dealer. This international criminal who has eluded the world's law enforcement agencies for several years controls 80 percent of the world's illegal trafficking—human trafficking, drug trafficking, illegal trafficking of weapons and cyber data—"

"I get it, sir, but with all due respect, you asked for my opinion," said Consuelo. "I've given my opinion. It is your call."

"What if," asked Max, "what if we ask the secretary general to assign other Interpol personnel?"

"We don't have time for that," snapped Consuelo. "It would take weeks to train them and bring them up to speed."

"Okay—let me mull that over, Agent Cervantes. You're dismissed," Ram said.

While Consuelo and Max returned upstairs, Edmunds made phone calls and contemplated different scenarios. Most of those considerations entailed significant risks. Within two hours, Ram brought together the entire *Galatea* team and presented the dilemma. He informed them that he would make the ultimate decision whether to instruct Eliza to postpone communications with Diego, but he wanted the team's recommendations.

Ram outlined his expectations from the group and explained that he wanted each team member's input. He even apologized to Minerva for interrupting the break he had promised. Appearing before the team sporting an impressive tan, Minerva had walked in wearing a two-piece turquoise swimsuit. She covered her body with a beach towel and dried her wet hair. "Mr. Edmunds, thanks for allowing me some free time. I do love the breaks, and I know you're trying to shield me from the ugliness of all the spy stuff. But remember that I appreciate being included."

At Ram's request, Consuelo informed the team of their latest findings. It appeared the increased chatter between Picard and his Pan Asian Shipping contact had some urgent implications. And after sharing those findings with the secretary general, Consuelo said, a postponement of the *Galatea* Force's operation might be necessary. Max added some additional details, but it was clear that a significant development was in the making.

Looking at Ram, Minerva asked, "Sir, can you explain what you think about this important event that Picard and his crooked friends are planning? What do you think it is?"

"More than likely, they're referring to a special shipment of contraband. What the contraband is—your guess is as good as mine," said Ram Edmunds.

Looking confused, Minerva asked, "I don't get it. Why would the shipping company ask Picard for catering and an orchestra?"

Ram responded thoughtfully, "Possibly, Minerva, 'orchestra' and 'catering' might be codes for something else…. Think about it: 'catering' could suggest the delivery of provisions or weaponry or even some bio-weapons. As for the 'orchestra,' the code could stand for a band of personnel, or sophisticated listening or scrambling devices involved in espionage. Who knows? If they're expressing such urgency, this operation will be big. This could be enough for Secretary Wagner to nail Picard."

Several questions ensued from the various members of the team, and after much deliberation, most of the members of the team offered their recommendations. Ram thanked each member for their input. His last question was directed at Eliza: "Your opinion—delay or proceed?"

With a placid smile, Eliza said, "Proceed."

It was past three in the afternoon when Ram brought the discussion to an end. "I will have my decision first thing in the morning," said Ram. "In the meantime, keep digging."

That evening before dinner, Max and Consuelo intercepted another communication between Picard and his Pan Asian Shipping contact. The message simply said, "URGENT—Need caterers. Need orchestra." It was signed BPQBSXK.

Ram, who had developed the habit of using the cowbell to make all announcements, called out in a loud voice, "Team, it's time to wind up our day. Get ready for dinner in ninety minutes."

Ten minutes later, Max, still seated at his desk, called out to Consuelo, who was hurrying downstairs to have her evening jog. "Hold on Artemis. We have another urgent message."

Without returning upstairs, Consuelo said, "Read it back to me."

"It's from the mystery contact at Pan Asian Shipping, and it simply reads, 'May need them two days from now,'"

"Oh, lovely," moaned Consuelo as she climbed back up the stairs. "Now we have a specific timeline." She rejoined Max at the communications center and put on her earphones. "What is this 'climactic' event being planned by Pan Asian Shipping, and how is Picard collaborating? Or is Pan Asian Shipping actually planning a celebration?"

Wearing shorts over her swimsuit, Minerva came up the stairs. A few ruby-red spots on her bare shoulders indicated that she might be reaching her sunbathing limit. "Sorry to interrupt, Uncle Max, but do you know where I can find your sunscreen? I've used up all of mine."

Max had his back to Minerva. "It should be in the closet behind you, honey. Hey, Minerva—I need your input. Cousin Consuelo, the bundle of sweetness seated behind me, and I cannot crack this coded word. Do you have a clue as to what this might mean?" Max showed Minerva the word "BPQBSXK."

"Why do you say it's in code? Is it encrypted?" Minerva asked.

Without turning, Max said, "Yeah, we've cracked the entire messaging, except for this word."

"What's this 'we' claim, *Kemo sabe*?" said Consuelo. "I don't remember you decoding a thing."

"Ha! That's hilarious," said Minerva. "Most kids my age don't know the old TV shows, but Gramps shared all those cowboy episodes with me. Consuelo, I had no idea you'd heard of *The Lone Ranger* in this country—or Tonto, for that matter."

"It was my favorite TV show as a child, but it was dubbed in German," Consuelo said with a laugh.

Hesitating, Minerva said, "Well, if you ask me, I'd say it's the simplest code you can think of. As kids we would use what you professionals call 'Caesar's Cipher'—you know, when you just use a left shift of one or two or three letters in the alphabet."

Consuelo rose from her roller desk chair and pushed it back against the *ficus benjamina*. With both palms on her temples, she exclaimed, "I can't believe it. You solved it, kid—sorry, I didn't mean 'kid.' Minerva, you're a genius. That's it!"

Max was still at a loss. He stared at Consuelo, who was now embracing Minerva. "What? What do you mean 'left shift of one or two letters'? Where do you shift?"

"It's a left shift of three," said Consuelo.

As Max looked at his keyboard, he seemed even more confused.

"No, no, not on your keyboard," said Consuelo. "You know, if you lay out the alphabet and you want to encode your name, shift three letters to the left. Instead of writing the letter *M* you will use a *J*. For the letter *A* you will substitute the letter *X*. Instead of an *X* you will substitute the letter *U*...and so on."

"What you're saying is that the first letter *B* in the encrypted signature is actually supposed to be an *E*. The second letter *P* is supposed to be *S*. That's it! E-S-T-E-V-A-N!" Max shouted.

Consuelo said, "So if that's the case, Estevan and Picard are colluding to…"

"They're talking about the planned soirée aboard the *Shenandoah of*

Sark. If Eliza agrees to go on with it, that is, what Estevan is pulling off—that's the big event—without Diego or Eliza knowing it," said Max. "If Estevan is enlisting Picard's help, it means that he's planning to get rid of Diego—and most assuredly Eliza too."

"It doesn't take much imagination, Sherlock, to figure out what the big event will be," said an unsmiling Consuelo. "Remember that whatever Estevan's plan might be, we need to keep in mind that three polonium vials are still in Diego's possession. Our plans must account for an unthinkable possibility. I'll call the secretary general immediately."

· · ·

CHAPTER FIFTY-EIGHT

[Bonifacio, Corsica–Palma de Mallorca; March 2023]

After his early-morning talk with Estevan, Diego immediately called Eliza. Since she failed to answer the 6:00 a.m. call, Diego left a message. In his detailed message he begged Yael, or Eliza, to reconsider. He again promised his undying love and devotion. He even scanned and e-mailed her copies of his attorney's responses to his communication. In an extreme step, he even asked Estevan to sign the letter addressed to him, to prove to Eliza that he had acknowledged receipt and been informed of Diego's decision and commitment to Eliza.

"Please, can we proceed with our *Shenandoah of Sark* soirée?" Diego asked.

At exactly 9:00 in the morning, Diego received a text from Eliza that simply said, "I'll now agree to our soirée."

Diego spent that entire day instructing Estevan on the many details that he had previously specified. He, Estevan, and Isabella worked until late in the evening planning for the event. The following two days, Diego's entire staff was deployed to ensure all was perfectly arranged.

The night before the event, Diego tossed and turned. After three hours sleep, he rose at 3:00 and wanted some coffee. Using the sophisticated digital intercom system that he'd devised, he apologized to Isabella, then said, "*Portami il caffè, Isabella.*"

A woozy Isabella asked, "In your room, *signore?*"

"No, in the garden, please," said Diego. Putting on a cardigan over his T-shirt, Diego, not wanting to disturb the darkness, used a flashlight to walk out wearing his slippers. He agonized over his plans for the evening soirée aboard the *Shenandoah of Sark*. When Isabella delivered his steaming carafe accompanied by the previous day's croissants, she apologized to Diego. "*Scusami*, but bread is not fresh, *signore*. This…however…your favorite fig and date…*marmellata*."

"Don't leave, Isabella. I must ask. Did Estevan order dinner from my favorite caterers? And the orchestra, what about the orchestra… are they contracted? Did you order all the decorations and the lighting…. Is the special lighting for the boat installed?"

"Please not worry, *signore*. Your caterers were not available, but Estevan…how do you say…hired…better caterers recommended by a good friend."

"What friend? Which caterers? I didn't authorize—"

"*Signore*, Diego said caterers have served heads of state…here in Europe. Your caterers not available," Isabella explained. "The orchestra also recommended by same friend. The members of orchestra play for Vienna Philharmonic."

Although Diego did not seem convinced, he finally muttered, "Hmm. I wish Estevan would tell me these things."

"All decorations ready and lights working. Estevan and I…*ispezionare*," said Isabella as she wrapped her flimsy robe around her slim waist. "You rest."

Estevan had fabricated the story about Diego's favorite caterers not being available. He had contacted Gabriel Picard via encrypted text and asked Picard to recommend the members of the orchestra and the caterers. Picard hand-picked the six members of the small orchestra and the special team used by Interpol to serve special functions for dignitaries. In addition to the caterers being legitimate and truly gifted in their work, they also were skilled Interpol agents. The members of the orchestra led a double life by performing with the Vienna Philharmonic as well as serving in undercover operations for Interpol. Estevan knew each of the hand-picked agents to be highly trained assassins.

When Diego confronted Estevan with Eliza's demands for him to break ties with Estevan, to Diego's surprise, Estevan appeared unmoved. He simply asked if Diego was contemplating marriage. When Diego explained that he intended to propose marriage during the soirée aboard the *Shenandoah of Sark*, not only did Estevan congratulate his boss, but he also announced that he would take care of all arrangements as the last official act as Diego's *consigliere*. Playing the role of a gracious loser, Estevan offered to make it the most memorable engagement evening ever. Isabella, who was at Estevan's side translating his rapid signing, leaned over to give *el signore* a congratulatory kiss on the cheek. Not an affectionate man, Estevan merely smiled at his boss, a facial expression he rarely used.

In his communications with Picard, however, Estevan did allow himself to express his full displeasure with Diego's decision. He told Picard that he was ready to turn in to Interpol all necessary evidence to convict Diego Montemayor in multiple murders, racketeering, and crimes against humanity. What he did not mention to Picard was that, accompanied by Isabella, he planned to flee the West and return to China. Since he realized that his dream of expanding Diego's enterprise to complete global control of all human trafficking, cyber and biological warfare, and global contraband was not going to happen, he was prepared to sever bonds. Of course, he had already appropriated most of Diego's holdings and transferred ownership to Pan Asian Shipping Enterprises.

Picard also had hidden motives. Unbeknown to Estevan, although Picard was ready to assist him, Picard was more interested in eliminating Diego before bringing him to trial. The Interpol agents masquerading as caterers and musicians had been instructed by Picard not only to apprehend Diego but also to assassinate him on the spot. Because Picard suspected that back in 2016, Yael Montemayor had shared with Diego the information regarding the molestation of his stepdaughter, he was not willing to risk his career. He wanted to ensure that Diego Montemayor would be silenced completely.

· · ·

The *Shenandoah of Sark* had arrived and moored in the *Bahía de Palma* two days before. Although the enormous yacht could have accommodated Diego's entire staff, they all remained in Bonifacio. The impressive vessel had two well-appointed aft master cabins with their own WC and shower compartments. In addition, three smaller cabins were situated in the fore part of the yacht. The deck from bow to aft was made of fine teak, but an impressive deck saloon was done entirely in mahogany. As in a former boat owned by Diego, the bar had dual fronts that allowed those inside and outside the covered compartment to access beverages. The serving area consisted of two half-moon bar tops—one dedicated to the inner covered saloon and the other, which served the open-air side of the bar. In the center of the two half-moons a battery of low cabinets well stocked with wines and liquors, plus small refrigerators and stainless-steel appliances, provided an ample workstation for bartenders. The enormous foredeck, which took up almost a third of the entire vessel, had an open area that often served as a dance floor.

Diego delegated most of the preparatory chores to Estevan and Isabella. They in turn worked long-distance with a crew that handled the preliminary arrangements. Diego had insisted on remaining behind in his Bonifacio estate, preferring to fly the same day of the soirée to await the special moment. Of course, Estevan and Isabella also remained behind to help Diego choose his outfit and pack for any unanticipated extension of his stay.

"Is my tuxedo ready, Isabella?" asked Diego. "And how about the four-strand necklace that will complement the black pearl earrings that I gave Ya—uh—Eliza? I want the boxed necklace close to me, perhaps beneath the bar where you will be, Isabella."

Isabella nodded and walked over to the next room, Diego's office, and extracted from the safe the four-strand Tahitian black pearl necklace that Diego had personally selected for the occasion. As she took the necklace, she also took the vials that Diego had in his safe. From his bedroom Diego heard the familiar tone of crystal containers tapping. "Careful with those vials, Isabella...very careful. Place them toward the back of the safe." Isabella momentarily cringed. She froze in place without making another move. Not hearing anything else, Isabella took out the vials. She then responded, "*Sì…sì, signore*. Everything okay."

Isabella returned to Diego's bedroom to ensure that his tuxedo's bowtie was prepared to be packed. She then folded his suspenders and packed them. Although she considered cummerbunds to be outdated, she packed them anyway to allow Diego a choice upon arrival. "Alessandro shined your shoes," Isabella added before inserting them in his shoe protectors and packing them.

Before Ciccio walked to Diego's bedroom to pick up the luggage, he also heard the musical ring of crystal being tapped. Looking at Isabella in Diego's office, Ciccio wondered why she was frozen in place. Seeing that Isabella followed him to Diego's bedroom, Ciccio proceeded to retrieve the luggage. As the two walked in, Diego asked Isabella, "Has Ciccio already loaded the two foxglove centerpieces that I've selected for the soirée?"

"Estevan is bringing plants. He will carry plants in SUV," said Isabella.

"Please tell Estevan not to forget the fertilizer containers, one for each foxglove," Diego said. "We need to feed my plants once daily while we're away."

"*Rilassare*…how do you say…relax, *signore*. Estevan has fertilizer. All is ready," Isabella said.

CHAPTER FIFTY-NINE

[Palma de Mallorca; March 2023]

A double-stretch black Mercedes limousine arrived at exactly 7:30 in the evening outside Eliza's door. The slender man wearing a navy-blue tuxedo pulled on the doorbell cord and Puccini's aria played the full rendition of *O Mio Babbino Caro* before anyone opened the door. Wearing her favorite black bicycling bibs and short-sleeve polyester jersey, Consuelo appeared and stared at the tuxedoed stranger at the entry. She looked at him up and down and leaned to see him sideways. The man, wearing white gloves, stood perfectly erect and said nothing. Instead, he handed Consuelo a small card in calligraphy stating he was there to "collect Ms. Eliza Durazo." Imitating two mimes, in complete silence for the first three minutes, Estevan, the tuxedoed stranger, and Consuelo, the cyclist, maintained expressionless facial expressions. Estevan merely extended his arm to offer the card. Consuelo kept her arms close to her body to accept the card. Estevan bowed slightly. Consuelo placed her right hand on her hip while she held and read the card. Estevan returned to his original stand and held his hands by his side, looking straight ahead and ignoring the greeter. In doing so, he indicated he was finished communicating with Consuelo. Cousin Consuelo, standing perfectly straight and expressionless, broke the silence and said, "Wait there." She then slammed the door shut.

Within a minute, Consuelo again opened the door. Eliza appeared at the foyer behind Consuelo and seemed to glide toward the entrance.

She wore a simple black cocktail sheath, a Roland Mouret Garten dress in viscose crepe with a square neckline and a split "V" detail to subtly reveal Eliza's alluringly tanned cleavage. The ruffle cuffs on her long sleeves accentuated the hourglass silhouette of her perfectly shaped body. A deep center back vented hem exposed three inches of Eliza's legs. The statuesque brunette made two broad and fluid motions to take the elegant dark cashmere wrap that Consuelo handed her and partially encased herself in it. She did not waste a single movement.

Although he attempted to maintain the mime's expressionless face, Estevan abandoned his far-off look and stared. Privately he admitted to himself that Eliza's visage was a stunning one. Diego's object of desire, as Estevan referred to her, looked bewitching. Estevan took a deep, slow bow.

"Good evening, Estevan. Thank you for your courtesy," said Eliza.

Left thumb on the top of his cummerbund, Estevan extended his left elbow and led her to the limo. Ensuring that Eliza was situated in the plush leather back seat, he joined Ciccio, the uniformed driver, in the front. Minutes later, spotting the enormous and brightly lit megayacht from the pier, Eliza asked Estevan if it was the *Sark*. Estevan turned to reassure her and nodded. They drove straight to the pier where a motorboat was waiting to transport them to the impressive yacht. Dutifully, Estevan escorted Eliza and helped her aboard the small boat. He joined her aboard the motorboat to transport her to the megayacht.

As Diego's *consigliere* took Eliza up the *Sark's* gangway, Diego appeared at the deck of the *Sark*. Champagne flute in hand, a jubilant Diego, wearing an Ermenegildo Zegna tuxedo, waited for Eliza. As if spotlights were focused on his gold buttons and cufflinks, his jewelry lit up the oncoming darkness. Uncharacteristically, Diego wore his white starched tuxedo shirt without his bowtie, unbuttoned at the neck. His sophomoric expression resembled an awestruck teenager experiencing his first love. He fumbled his greeting, which suggested he had forgotten the memorized wording. He simply said, "You look…so beautiful…. I don't know what to say." As he toasted their first sip and tapped glasses, a bit of champagne spilled and stained the right cuff of his starched shirt. They both laughed.

Still smiling, Eliza took her first sip and said, "You have decorated so beautifully, Diego…planned it so well." Eliza and Diego walked slowly side by side toward the bow. They walked past the long, raised deck saloon on their left, and Eliza could not help caressing the shiny mahogany wall that seemed to sparkle with the decorative lighting. The stringed lighting gave the enormous vessel a festive spirit. As they walked toward the grandiose bow, they came upon the open-air bar, which was decorated with tropical blooms in small crystal vases, presumably from Diego's nursery. Only three leather barstools appeared on the external side of the bar. From their vantage point, Eliza peeked into the raised deck saloon, where she assumed they would enjoy an elaborate dinner. The subdued lighting and candles on a linen-covered table told her she was probably right.

Two impressive centerpieces were still behind their side of the bar, waiting to be placed in the most prominent location of the dining area. Taking a few more steps, Eliza and Diego then approached the open bow, which had a large dance floor. A small orchestra was playing romantic music, and to Eliza's surprise, there was Andrea Bocelli, microphone in hand, facing in her direction and prepared to dedicate her favorite piece, *Con te Partiro*.

Looking into Eliza's eyes, Diego waited until Bocelli finished his rendition and stated, "This time we celebrate this song, praying for an end to the present loneliness. It is time to say goodbye to regret and grief and to start a new life together, my flower."

As Bocelli ended, he raised a glass in the direction of the couple. "Diego, I believe Andrea Bocelli is toasting us—please acknowledge him," said Eliza.

"Yes, of course." Placing his right hand at the tip of his forehead, palm inward, Diego acknowledged the celebrity's well wishes. An attractive blonde at Bocelli's side whispered to the Italian tenor. Undoubtedly, she informed him that Diego was thanking him. Diego even bowed slightly in his direction. "I believe Andrea will be leaving after a few short songs, my dear. I asked him to remain for the evening, but he has to attend to other commitments."

"What have you planned for the evening, Diego?" Eliza asked.

"I've arranged for a fabulous dinner, with romantic music and a slow sailing along the coast of the French Riviera. After we have a few drinks, we will set sail. Later in the evening, I have planned something special, but allow me some elements of surprise...yes?"

Eliza merely smiled. She noticed that Isabella, also formally dressed but in an almost masculine tuxedo, minus the coat, was tending the bar. Eliza caught her eye, and Isabella nodded. Isabella raised a flute in a questioning gesture, wondering if Eliza was ready for her second glass of champagne. Eliza shook her head and pointed to her half-full glass.

Although Ram Edmunds and his *Galatea* Force had planned for contingencies, Eliza worried that the team might not have planned for the additional individuals on board—the members of the small orchestra, Andrea Bocelli and his entourage, the professional caterers Diego had hired, and other potential "surprises." Eliza did not even know if other members of Diego's staff were on board. If so, was the *Galatea* Force aware? *Are members of Ram's team already aboard the* Sark? *Did Diego invite other celebrities to our intimate soirée?* And why had Estevan disappeared? *Was he still aboard?*

"My flower, I believe this is the most important night of my life. I feel as if I've been given a second chance to love again...to restore our...my life. But you seem distracted. What could be wrong? I've planned the perfect evening for us...." Diego furrowed his forehead.

"Oh, no, no, Diego. Nothing is wrong. I just feel like this is all magical. I suppose I'm just overwhelmed by your...well-thought-out plan. Please simply give me an opportunity to relax.... Why don't we have another glass of champagne?"

In an instant, Estevan slithered behind Eliza. With his back to Diego and Eliza, he awkwardly held three glass containers and motioned with a tilt of his head for Isabella to serve another two glasses of champagne for the couple. As Estevan hurriedly moved toward the bar, Diego noticed that his *consigliere* was also handing Isabella the organic fertilizer vials across the bar top. Estevan held on to one vial. Behind the bar, Isabella had momentarily turned away to fill two additional flutes of champagne, but as she faced

Estevan, she set the glasses on top of the bar. Estevan moved to block Diego's view.

Annoyed, Diego thought, *Why the devil is Estevan giving Isabella three fertilizer vials for my foxgloves.... I certainly hope they don't over-fertilize my plants—it will kill my prized beauties!*

As he turned away to set his flute down on a bistro table, Diego in a moment of complete clarity realized, *Estevan is not handing Isabella fertilizer vials.... He is intending to use the polonium I stored in my office safe. Those vials are intended for Yael and me.*

The next few moments froze in time for Diego. He realized that he was weeping. Diego could not believe that his friend, his confidante, could do such a thing. Just like Tío Dante—his former right hand, his friend, his brother, his entrusted partner—Estevan also was betraying him. The tapping of crystal inside his safe—Isabella had removed the polonium containers! *Why?* Diego looked starboard into the distance, where the sun had almost set, and he begged for mercy. *Help me*, he found himself imploring. When he glimpsed at the plants behind the bar next to Isabella, which were probably the most prized foxgloves he had ever grown, the evening shadows dulled their brilliance. As if the bright reds, blues, and oranges had suddenly faded, the vertical blooms became a blur. Even the rich mahogany of the bar turned gray. *Why?* He could not allow the indescribable agony his Yael would endure if she even inhaled that wretched radioactive poison.

As he noticed the gloved Estevan opening the first vial to pour into the champagne, Isabella backed away. Diego noted an acute apprehension in Isabella's eyes. Moving swiftly, Diego took two steps toward Estevan from behind and leapt toward him. Estevan did not see him coming. Diego reached toward him, arms outstretched. As Estevan began to pour, Diego was airborne. Diego's body flew in front of Estevan and knocked the single vial to the floor. Horrified, both Diego and Estevan looked at each other as they heard the ring of the crystal vial breaking. In one quick, graceful motion, Estevan swiveled right, and with his left arm catching Diego behind the neck, he forced him face downward. Swanlike, his right arm extended out and upward as he gained his balance and jumped over a fallen bar-stool. The lethal radiation was released, and Diego inhaled it.

As Estevan leapt over the stool, he turned and hurried around the bar to retrieve Isabella, who had instantly scurried a safe distance away from the broken vial. Pulling Isabella behind him, Estevan ran full speed toward the gangway, keeping their distance from Diego and the radiation. Isabella lost one of her heels as she was pulled across the deck. "*Aspetti!*" she cried out to Estevan.

Momentarily turning back, Estevan shouted, "We can't wait! Leave them behind!"

Ciccio was waiting at the pier to transport them to the private airport. Immediately after Estevan and Isabella boarded the SUV, Gabriel Picard and his crew boarded the *Sark*. Picard walked straight to the orchestra and instructed them privately to follow their previous orders regarding Diego Montemayor and his fiancée. Instead, with swift efficiency the orchestra surrounded Picard and, with the aid of Spanish authorities who had boarded the *Sark* with Andrea Bocelli, they handcuffed Picard and removed his holstered weapon. Retired Inspector Eduardo Sánchez, accompanied by some of the Spanish law enforcement agents, escorted Bocelli off the yacht. Picard looked in all directions and screamed at the top of his lungs, "What the devil is going on?" Turning back to the agents who were cuffing him, he said, "I order you to apprehend that man before he escapes." He tried to point at Diego, who was agonizing on the floor.

Of course, in the world of international espionage, as seventeen-year-old Minerva Epstein-Shelley would learn, the twists and turns of serial deception are never simple. Since Consuelo Cervantes and Max Kempball intercepted Gabriel Picard's private communications, they informed Interpol's secretary general that Picard was planning to murder Diego before bringing him to trial. Hidden behind doors in the yacht's saloon, Wagner, the secretary general, whispered to Consuelo, "Indeed, this event will be more 'climactic' than any of us thought."

Ram Edmunds, Consuelo Cervantes, and Marceline (Marc) Hugot came out from one of the fore cabins and disarmed the four-man crew who had arrived with Gabriel Picard. Consuelo and Marc accompanied the secretary general of Interpol, who had personally traveled to Palma, to confront Picard. "Your time has come, Gabriel," said Wagner, "but I truly am sorry that it had to end this way. The valuable service you offered Interpol will not be ignored."

Ram Edmunds ambled over to Diego Montemayor, who had crawled to the nearest seat on the deck and was retching violently. Diego appeared to be weeping. Medical personnel wearing full-body protective suits, goggles, gloves, and footwear approached Diego to examine him. They appeared to be asking him questions, and he kept shaking his head and repeating, "Too late…too late." Two other individuals in hazmat suits attended to the dropped vial that had spilled behind the bar. One other protected individual confiscated the two other polonium vials that had remained sealed.

"Unfortunately, Mr. Montemayor," said Ram Edmunds from a safe distance, "you will be charged in the United States with multiple counts of murder and crimes against humanity if you survive this…although it is highly unlikely that you will."

Turning to Ram Edmunds, Diego asked, "Yael…is she safe?… Where is she?"

Ram nodded, "Eliza Durazo is safe, Mr. Montemayor."

"Aren't you…the FBI agent, the…straight arrow…the one who worked with my father?" asked Diego in gasps and between moans.

"I most certainly am. And I'm proud to still be faithfully serving law enforcement of the United States of America," Ram said.

"Ha…" Diego could say no more as he experienced another wave of convulsions. Ram Edmunds walked away and instructed his international crew to attend to the most wanted international crime figure in the Western world. He signaled to Consuelo to allow Nate's family to board the *Sark*.

Upon boarding, Nate, Miró, Abraham, and Max immediately approached Eliza Durazo, who was being consoled inside the *Sark's* raised deck saloon. She was being examined by the medical personnel. Although shaken, Eliza seemed relieved that she had not been exposed to any radioactive poison. Upon seeing them, she embraced them and wept in Miró's arms. As she did so, she reached out to "Cousin Consuelo," who was standing at their side, smiling. Consuelo joined in the group hug.

Still being examined by the medical personnel in heavy protective suits, Diego caught a glimpse of the group hug inside the saloon. He weakly called out to Ram Edmunds, "Why is my Yael embracing the Shelleys?"

Ram responded, "Diego, your wife died in a fire seven years ago."

"You never fooled me," Diego said, smiling "And you're not about to fool me now. I know my Yael is…alive. Whatever you did to her… she will always love me." Diego coughed and expelled sputum into a covered metal bucket that the medical personnel handed him. "She is completely innocent…. She…" With labored breathing, Diego finished: "had nothing to do with this." At that point, the medical personnel forced Diego to put on a hazmat suit in case his clothing or body was contaminated with the radioactive effect of the polonium. They then took him away.

CHAPTER SIXTY

[Palma de Mallorca; March 2023]

Minerva Epstein-Shelley understood why she was not allowed to accompany the rest of the *Galatea* Force in their final mission. In her diary entry, which she faithfully filled each day, she reminded herself that any self-respecting adult should not involve an untrained almost-eighteen-year-old in such dangerous operations. What she did not know was that Ram Edmunds had, unbeknown to her, assigned seven Spanish law enforcement officials to protect Abraham's safe house, where she remained behind. They guarded the perimeter of the townhouse building until Nate, Miró, and the rest of the family arrived shortly before four in the morning.

When Miró arrived at the townhouse, she went directly to Minerva's bedroom. Minerva, of course, had not slept a wink. To pass the time, she streamed movies and messaged friends. Seeing her mom, Minerva tossed her cell phone on the comforter, jumped off the bed, and threw her arms around her. "Mom, thank God you're back! How's Dad…and Gramps and Uncle Max?"

"We're all safe—and mission accomplished," Miró said as she embraced her daughter. At that point—perhaps reaching the point of catharsis after so many years of repressed fears, terror, and emotional strain—Miró burst into tears. "For seven years we have not been able to provide real security for you and now that it's over, I can't bring myself to stop these tears from flowing…. Thank you for being so brave…and honorable…and supportive. You are a special young lady."

"Oh, Mom, I've learned so much from you and Dad. You've taught me well. And I thank God for such a wonderful family. And although Granma Miriam is no longer with us, her courage and strength have also...sustained me. When we were kidnapped, she reminded me, 'If you make the Most High your dwelling...he will command his angels concerning you.' I always keep that in mind."

"Isn't that from the Bible?" Miró asked.

"Yeah—when I spent time with them, Granma and Gramps would put me to sleep by reading me our favorite psalms. Her special reminder came from Psalm 91."

"I'm sorry that I didn't give you a good biblical foundation," Miró said. "I always leaned on my Catholic prayers, and as I grew up I gradually ignored those also."

"No worries, Mom. I've come to know Jesus in a special way, thanks to Gramps and Max. It's never too late.... Look at Dad—he had to go up Mount Zion to find him."

"Yes, your dad has undergone quite a transformation. I'm jealous. Since 'the Lord found him,' as he puts it, he has been more resolute and certain of his purpose in life. Although fearless and more courageous, at the same time he's more considerate, kinder, and gentler. If I loved him before, I love him more now."

"I'm so glad to have you as parents, Mom. Not to change the subject, but I do have a million questions."

"Of course," said Miró. "I'm sorry we could not include you in our final confrontation aboard the *Sark*, but you understand, don't you?"

Minerva nodded. "I do, but I still want to know. Where's Raquel... or maybe I should continue to refer to her as Eliza Durazo.... How is she?"

"As we feared, the polonium vials were aboard the *Sark*—"

Minerva gasped. "Oh, no—she isn't...Mom, is everyone okay?"

Miró again embraced her daughter to reassure her. "Yes, yes. We're all safe.... The one contaminated was Diego Montemayor. Estevan's plan was to kill Diego and Eliza with it. When Diego discovered that Estevan intended to poison him and his beloved, he leaped at Estevan to prevent him from opening the vial. Instead, Estevan dropped the radioactive poison and Diego inhaled it."

"So in effect, Diego saved Eliza…and the rest of you, for that matter."

With a tilt of her head, Miró said, "Well, we believe that Estevan and Isabella were about to pour the flavorless liquid in the two glasses of champagne—"

Minerva interrupted. "Which were meant for Diego and Eliza."

"Was Eliza close enough to also inhale the polonium? Will she be all right?" Minerva asked.

"The medical personnel who examined her moments after the fiasco don't think she was close enough to be endangered. We may not know for certain if she was contaminated until after forty-eight hours, but at this point we have every reason to believe that she was not affected by the polonium."

Sighing in relief, Minerva said, "Thank God."

"However," Miró added, "in addition to her physical health, please pray for her emotional well-being. I'm certain she will need some time to deal with the stress she endured."

Coffee in hand, Nate came upstairs and joined Minerva and her mom, who were now sitting on the bed. As Minerva hugged her dad, Nate said, "I'm sure none of us will be able to sleep. Let's debrief."

"Dad, this is not a 'debriefing'—but how about a good 'family talk,' okay? I got started asking Mom countless questions. Help her catch me up on all the details."

"Let's go downstairs," Nate said. "I need some fresh air."

For the next two hours Nate and Miró described the events and the many twists and turns that the night brought. They both confirmed that no one could have anticipated what came to pass. Yet looking back, they realized it all made sense. Although Ram Edmunds would be returning to the States, they explained to Minerva that he had asked them to remain in Palma de Mallorca for another "couple of weeks." Several meetings and much information-sharing would be required. In addition, Interpol had also requested that the family engage in a string of statements, depositions, and affidavits.

. . .

During the next sixteen days, Nate Shelley's family provided a total of forty-two *declaraciones testimoniales,* or depositions, to the judicial authorities in Spain and to Interpol affiliates. Although Interpol had an obligation to share all their data with French and Italian law enforcement and the judicial courts, the family was spared the need to testify before them.

On the seventeenth day after testimonials began, Nate's family was able to relax around the pool in Abraham's townhouse. They enjoyed the Mallorcan sun and drank lemonade. Max addressed the family and presented one special request. Since Max had never visited Europe before, he asked if he could treat them all to a short weekend trip to the Canary Islands, where the family's Iberian adventure had begun back in 2016.

"What a great idea, son!" said Abraham. "Once we fulfill all obligations to Interpol and Ram Edmunds, all of us will travel to the Canary archipelago at my expense. After that, you will be on your own to enjoy your much-deserved European vacation."

From their patio Nate heard a faint knock and said, "I think there's someone at the front door. I'll get it." He placed his lemonade on the bistro table and called out, *"¡Un momento, por favor!"*

"Excellent, Gramps," Minerva said, "I'd love to return to my favorite hotel in the world, the Hotel Santa Catalina in Las Palmas. I still remember their breakfast buffets...ooh, and that beautiful courtyard in the middle of the circular car entrance. I still remember trampling in the greenery and muddying my feet...and Granma chasing after me. I must have been a handful." Nodding in agreement, Miró noticed that Minerva's eyes watered as she remembered her beloved Granma.

"Yes, oddly enough, we have many pleasant memories of that hotel, despite the violent events that occurred there," said Miró.

"I've heard," said Max, smiling at his half-sister. "I look forward to the trip. As I recall, isn't that where Chief Inspector Sánchez arrested you and Nate for the murder of an American tourist?"

Leaning back in the lounger, Miró responded with a grin, "Yup, it most certainly was. It was also the place where Nate discovered the dead victim. Amazing how life has brought us through so many misadventures."

"Did I hear someone mention my name?" The retired inspector was standing at the glass sliding doors with Nate, who had received him at the front. "This time I am the bearer of good news. I just heard from the judicial system that all *declarantes* have been dismissed and that the collection of information is complete…for the time being."

"I presume the word *declarantes* refers to all of us who've provided testimony, yes?" Max asked.

Sánchez apologetically responded, "You are correct, Max. And as I understand, you would like to visit my beloved hometown, Las Palmas of the Canary Islands."

"We're all coming, Inspector," Minerva said.

"If that is the case," Sánchez said, "I insist on serving as your host. I am biased, of course, but I still believe the Canary Islands are the most beautiful in the world."

"You must admit that Mallorca is hard to beat," Max said.

The retired police inspector laughed. "That it is. No question."

. . .

[Las Palmas, Canary Islands; March 2023]

Within forty-eight hours the family. along with Eduardo Sánchez, made their exit from the Balearic Islands and flew eleven hours to reach the Canary Islands. To Max they seemed to be closer to the western coast of Africa than to Spain. Examining the map aboard the Iberian flight, Max asked no one in particular, "Are you sure that the Canaries are part of Spain?"

His dad sitting next to him explained, "Although the Canaries are approximately sixty miles from Morocco, they are an autonomous community of Spain—the southernmost—very much a part of the European Union."

Upon arrival at the Las Palmas Airport, retired inspector Eduardo

Sánchez took the role of "tourist guide." A former colleague who had formerly worked for Chief Inspector Sánchez and was now temporarily living in Sánchez's home while the inspector was away picked them up at the airport and transported Nate and his family to the Hotel Santa Catalina. He had called ahead to make their reservations. As he made the turn into the circular driveway to the hotel's front entrance, Minerva exclaimed, "Wow—I can't believe it! It looks exactly as I remember it. I've described it so many times in my diary that I've memorized every detail."

As the inspector's friend parked, two hotel attendants opened the rear doors on each side. Each one of them said in unison, "*Bienvenidos de nuevo*—welcome back." While the valets took care of the luggage, Sánchez bade goodbye and said he would return to join them for dinner. "First, however, I must go home to see if everything is in order."

To Nate's amazement, Manuel Montes, the hotel's general manager, greeted them at the door. Now graying at the temples, Montes was his usual self, hyperventilating and with both palms on his cheeks. As they approached him at the entrance, he said, almost shrieking, "I cannot believe it! I…I did not think we would see you again, Dr. Shelley…and Mrs…. no, no, Dr. Epstein-Shelley. Please forgive me, but I must embrace you." Montes proceeded not only to give Miró and Nate repeated hugs, but also to regale them with European kisses on both cheeks. Still blocking them at the front entrance, he announced, "Your presidential suite is prepared and two bottles—one *Bermejo* and one bottle of your favorite cava—are chilling." As if enraptured with the arrival of royalty, Montes did not realize that he was blocking the rest of the family from entering. With his gaze still fixed on Nate and Miró, Montes asked, "But where is the rest of the family?"

"Right behind you," quipped Abraham, who was smiling good naturedly. Startled, Montes almost jumped back, turned to face Abraham, and as he stumbled for words, begged for forgiveness. "Oh, Dr. Abraham…of course. How silly of me! Please excuse my insolence… and my bad manners. I should have known you were there. Welcome, Dr. Abraham. Welcome. Your suite is also ready."

Turning to Max, Montes grinned broadly and smoothed out his

hair. "And who might this movie star be? Welcome. I don't believe we've met. I am Manuel Montes, the Santa Catalina's general manager. I am at your service." Montes seemed to blink several times before smiling demurely and offering a limper-than-normal handshake.

"I am Max Kempball, Dr. Abraham Epstein's son…and Miró's brother."

"My, my—what a handsome addition to the family!" said Montes as he extended both hands to hold Max by his upper arms. "You're quite tall, aren't you?"

As Montes noticed the young lady who was standing at the curb of the circular driveway taking photos with her cellular phone, his mouth opened widely. Another shriek. "Oh…please…please do not tell me that young woman is little Minnie. She's so…so…how do you say it?…*todo una señorita.*"

"Indeed," Miró said. "Our eleven-year-old is nearly eighteen. She's grown up. Just a warning, Mr. Montes—she now goes by 'Minerva,'"

With hands modeling a prayerful expression, Montes said, "Ah, perfect. The name 'Minerva' suits her well." Scanning the entrance to the hotel and the entire external front portico, he turned to Abraham and exclaimed, "But where is Dr. Miriam…your wife?"

Acknowledging the family's hesitation, Montes almost whimpered, "Oh, no…did I ask a stupid question?…Is she all right?"

"She passed away a while back," Abraham stated. "She had a fond memory of you and your establishment, Mr. Montes."

Before Abraham even finished his statement, Montes had turned away from the group. He took out his handkerchief and wiped his eyes. The sensitive man seemed genuinely moved. In between sobs, he muttered, "She was such a beautiful and distinguished lady…a human being…with such a warm…and loving heart. When I saw her with her grandchild…it made me want a…family…of my own." Hand on his heart, he almost stumbled onto one of the cushioned seats of the patio bar. He slowly sat with knees together and away from the group. He fanned himself with a splayed right hand, saying, "Forgive me…. I just need a minute."

* * *

441

By the time each family member had settled in, Montes instructed his staff to advise them that he had arranged for dinner at the hotel's main dining area. Cocktails would be served at 8:45 and dinner would be served promptly at 9:15. Of course, dinner for the family and their guest, Inspector Eduardo Sánchez, would be "on the house."

In addition to a few simple tapas and pintxos, Bellinis were available for cocktails, as well as a full open bar. Nate and Miró's favorite aperitif, escargot, as well as *foie gras* was served. For dinner, paella Valenciana was available as well as salads and grilled fresh fish.

Uncharacteristically, Sánchez arrived late and explained that he had been on the phone with his old friend Archbishop José Gómez, or Pepe, as he knew him. He explained to the family that Diego Montemayor had asked for the archbishop to grant him absolution and to administer his last rites at the Mallorcan hospital.

"Did he agree?" Minerva asked.

"Indeed, he did," Sánchez said. "You must remember that the archbishop knew Yael and Diego Montemayor under very different circumstances. He never had any knowledge of their involvement in crime, until the very end, that is. Diego and Yael were well known community leaders and very generous donors to the Catholic charities."

"I would like to think that Diego Montemayor will have an opportunity to repent," said Nate. "I sincerely hope so."

"By the way," Sánchez added, "the archbishop mentioned something curious. He indicated that the hotel's general manager had reached out to him. Montes apparently told the archbishop that the Shelleys were in town and that he had something planned for you."

"I remember his fondness for 'special surprises,'" Miró said. "He pulled a good one on us the last time."

"Enlighten me," Max said. "What are you talking about?"

Nate jumped in: "It was Montes who planned our entire impromptu wedding. I wanted to have a simple civil ceremony here in Las Palmas, but he planned an elaborate affair within twenty-four or forty-eight hours."

Miró immediately said, "It was twenty-four hours, darling. Don't you remember?"

"I wonder what he's got up his sleeve this time," Abraham said. "We'll ask him tomorrow."

That evening the six enjoyed themselves thoroughly and even had time to drive around the island, take a walk along Nate's favorite beach, and drove by the torn-down hospital where Yael Montemayor had perished in the disastrous fire. Sánchez asked Max to sit in the front passenger seat. He served as driver, guide, and narrator for much of the events that may have been difficult for the rest of the family to describe. Each account from Sánchez brought bitter-sweet memories that included Miriam Epstein.

"Funny, Uncle Max, but driving around Las Palmas, it seems like Granma is still with us," Minerva said. "During that entire trip, I spent most of my time with Granma Miriam and Gramps."

CHAPTER SIXTY-ONE

[Las Palmas, Canary Islands; March 2023]

Max woke early, walked down one flight of stairs, and had coffee at the gloriously beautiful portico café. Behind him was *Carabela's*, the hotel's piano bar, which was closed to the public. Its wood and colorful drapery extended to the patio, where a pleasant eastern breeze greeted him. Max inhaled the sea air and basked in the early-morning sun.

Before Max could finish his first cup of espresso, someone approached him to serve his second cup. To Max's surprise, it was the general manager, Montes, holding a full metal carafe and taking on the role of waiter. "I thought it was you, Mr. Kempball. I trust your night was restful." Montes was wearing a double-breasted light-gray suit, a tasteful pale yellow paisley tie, and an aromatic peach-colored tropical flower as a boutonniere, a flower unknown to Max.

"Good morning, Mr. Montes. Yes, my night was relaxing, thank you. This climate is invigorating. Is it always like this?"

With a broad smile, Montes said, "Allow me to brag, but many people say the Canary Islands have the best climate in the world. And our establishment has gained notoriety since Brad Pitt called it his favorite hotel in the world."

"Did he?"

"By the way, whenever the family is ready, please inform them I will join you at the patio restaurant. There is a small surprise that I have," Manuel Montes announced.

"I'll let them know, Mr. Montes."

"In the meantime, can I get you anything?"

"No, no—I would just like to enjoy the view. It's breathtaking."

Standing perfectly still with his elbows close to his sides, Montes continued smiling, and locking his eyes with Max, said, "I was standing at the door…doing the same thing…admiring the beauty." Without another word, Manuel Montes turned around and returned to his office, taking small, deliberate steps.

At 7:45 Minerva came downstairs and discovered her Uncle Max asleep in the portico. He had dozed off with a smile on his face. She sat next to Max and made early entries on her diary while she drank her iced coffee. Sitting quietly until Max woke, Minerva noticed that Max's longish straight blond hair was blowing in his face. Startled, Max opened one eye. "How long have you been there?"

"Oh, just a few minutes. You looked so peaceful…"

"Is everyone awake?" Max asked.

"Mom was showering, and Dad is about to join us. I don't know about Gramps."

As Max yawned, he got up from the table and told Minerva, "Found out from the general manager that he'd like to join us for breakfast. He's got a surprise."

"It must be related to Inspector Sánchez's info he got from the archbishop. Montes needs to know the inspector let the cat out of the bag," Minerva smiled.

Just then Nate appeared at the door coming out from the main lobby onto the portico wearing an open yellow-and-blue, flowered button-down over a black T-shirt. He wore dark glasses, khakis, and white sneakers. A Chicago Cubs baseball cap was on his head. "Dad, why are you back to your surfer sleuth wardrobe?"

With a big smile Nate nodded, "I chose it because this is where I adopted my persona, which shall be retired after today. I'm fully comfortable leaving that role behind me and resuming my boring role as family man, psychotherapist, and priest of my home. No more sleuthing for me."

"Nate," Max said, "Montes wanted to join us for—"

"I just spoke to him," said Nate. "We're having breakfast at 10:00 in the patio restaurant."

While Minerva diligently wrote in her diary, Nate and Max walked around the hotel's gardens. Max was astounded at the botanical variety that seemed to blossom throughout the year. As they meandered throughout the vast parklike setting, Nate and Max took in the intoxicating fragrance of the reds, oranges, and pale yellows of the garden blooms. The walk opened Max's appetite. "Man, I'm ready for a hearty breakfast. This fresh air and breeze make me want to relocate to this paradise."

Nate took his iPhone to check the time. "We agreed to meet in the lobby at 9:45. It's time."

When Max walked into the enormous patio restaurant, he was impressed by the abundance of tropical plants and airiness of the glassed-in dome. The circular breakfast buffet dominated the center of the restaurant. Around the buffet sat the multiple offerings of cheeses, fresh and smoked fish, hard-boiled eggs, as well as an omelet station with a chef to prepare assortments of omelets and eggs benedict. Beyond the omelet station, the obligatory pastries and fresh fruits were also available. Inside the circular buffet presentation were tiered bouquets of flowers that adorned the spectacular centerpiece.

Ogling the buffet presentation, Max rubbed his hands in anticipation. As Nate removed his cap, he was approached by the female maître d'. "Your table is prepared. May I take you there?"

Montes was at the table to greet them. Miró, Abraham, and Minerva were already seated around the linen-covered circular table. Montes sat next to Miró, and he directed Max to the opposite seat next to him. After smoothing down his neatly coiffed hair, he sat and declared, "Unless you want to partake of the buffet, I've arranged to have individual choices to be prepared for each of us tableside. Any offering you'd like, I'm certain we can accommodate.... But first, we have the Shelleys' favorite champagne, the *Segura Viudas* Cava Brut, *Heredad Reserva*. Let us toast your arrival in Las Palmas."

Montes then addressed Nate and Miró. "May I assume that since Minerva is almost eighteen, she may be served some cava?"

Without waiting for a response from her parents, Minerva responded, "Thank you for your thoughtfulness, Mr. Montes. However, after having a few tastes of wine here when I was eleven, I contracted with my grandparents to refrain from having any alcohol until I turn eighteen, which will be in May."

"I respect your choice, Ms. Shelley. What would you like instead?" Montes asked.

"I will have mineral water—thank you."

After several toasts around the table, Miró and Minerva ordered the smoked salmon eggs benedict. The men placed their orders of omelets, fried eggs, and waffles. Max ordered an assortment of all three. Impressively, Montes ordered a health-conscious breakfast of yogurt, granola, and a tropical fruit drink.

While the family had final cups of coffee, Max accepted a fruit muffin to accompany his java. Montes finally announced, "Dr. Shelley has informed me that the archbishop…revealed that I am planning a surprise. When I learned three days ago that your family would visit…how do you say?…I want to celebrate—with several people."

Miró inquired, "Who exactly is involved, Mr. Montes?"

"The archbishop and now Inspector Sánchez. Of course, my staff and I…are planning a *renovación de votos*…. Dr. Abrám, please help me."

"Yes, a renewal of vows," Abraham said.

"That is very kind, Mr. Montes, but this is so unexpected," Nate said.

Montes said, "Please do not reject my gift…. When you return to your suite in a few minutes, Dr. Miró Shelley, you will have my seamstress and designer in your suite prepared to alter one of three dresses that I've selected for you. I believe that you were pleased with your wedding dress last time, no?"

"Very much so, Mr. Montes. You have very good taste," Miró said.

Montes added, "And since Inspector Sánchez arranged for a tour of the archipelago for the next two days, I invited several people to the celebration."

"But such extravagance…. I don't know what to say," Miró said.

"Nonsense, this time your friends in high places are taking care of such extravagance. I will explain to your husband later. For now, I beg you to accept."

Flushed, Miró objected. "But when, where…I'm unclear regarding details…"

"Let us plan on Saturday evening at 8:00. That will give you time to tour the islands. Why don't we celebrate here in our establishment—just like on your wedding day?" Montes asked. Again, assuming a prayerful posture, he added, "Please accept."

"Fine," said a flustered Miró, who clearly was uncomfortable with surprises.

For the next two days Inspector Sánchez arranged for the family's tour of the various islands in the archipelago. At Abraham's request, Sánchez included all the "touristy" stops for the sake of Max, who wanted to soak in the history as well as the ambiance of the Canaries. Max realized rapidly that the Canary Islands had its own character and culture. It was not the Spanish mainland, where you would find flamenco and bullfights. Instead, the seven islands boasted beautiful beaches, vegetation, and volcanic features and even a couple of national parks. Sánchez concentrated on the four largest islands, where it seemed to Max you could enjoy a perpetual springtime.

Max and the family also visited numerous colonial villages where the Spaniards had left their mark. In fact, Max was surprised to visit the church where Columbus last prayed before departing for the New World. "I learned that he'd sailed from the Spanish port of Palos in Andalucía. Was the history wrong?"

"No, it was not wrong, Max." Sánchez said. "After setting sail from Palos, his crew attempted to sabotage his ship, so he stopped in Las Palmas in the Canary Islands. After settling things, Columbus sailed to the New World."

Max joined his niece Minerva while she sunned and scuba dove on the island of Tenerife. Minerva consented to continue the tour only after Nate and Miró promised to return after the renewal of their vows on Saturday. Next, Sánchez took them on the obligatory trip to Lanzarrote, the northernmost island in the Canaries, where

Nate convinced Max to visit the vineyard where his favorite wine, *Bermejo Seco*, was produced.

Falling behind on their schedule, Inspector Sánchez was unable to return the family to the Hotel Santa Catalina on Friday evening as Montes expected. This caused great anxiety for the general manager. When Sánchez delivered Nate's family back on Saturday morning, he found Montes pacing up and down in his office. "I am sorry for delaying our arrival, Montes. I assure you everything will be fine."

"You don't understand, Inspector. The three-tiered cake is not ready. The baker, this horrible man who refuses to speak to me, can only say that he has had some setbacks.... Plus, the stringed quartet is missing their cellist, who apparently had a skydiving accident. They refuse to get a substitute. The tuxedo that I ordered for Dr. Shelley was damaged in the post, and my seamstress does not guarantee that it can be fixed. Worst of all, Dr. Shelley's good friends and colleagues, Drs. Luntz and Beech, have been detained. Their connecting flight from Madrid might be canceled." Manuel Montes, dejected and deflated, sat at his desk and pulled his hair in despair. He whimpered, "Everything is ruined."

"Montes, did you or did you not enlist my help?" asked the inspector.

Lip still quivering, Montes looked at Inspector Sánchez and merely nodded.

"Then trust me. Everything will be in order." Within forty-five minutes Eduardo Sánchez had made two telephone calls. First he communicated the predicament to his good friend Marceline (Marc) Hugot, who although back at the FBI's legal attaché's office in Madrid, planned to attend the celebration in Las Palmas. "Will you please contact two individuals who may be stranded at the Barajas Airport in Madrid? We need to ensure they get here in time for the celebration. I will text you their contact information."

"It so happens that the deputy director of the FBI, Ram Edmunds, will be using a private plane to transport us both from Madrid to Las Palmas. He flew in from Chicago this morning on a commercial flight. I'm certain we can find room for two more," said Marc.

"And by the way, do you know of any good bakers in your area?

We need a three-tiered wedding cake for the celebration. Is it too late for you to make that happen?"

"No bakers that I know, but my brother caters. Let me see what I can do."

Sánchez then called Max. "Listen—we need Consuelo Cervantes to do you a favor."

"Not sure I understand. What is it exactly that she needs to do for me?" Max asked.

Chuckling, Sánchez said, "Just lean on her to ask the secretary general to lend us the services of the string quartet, the one that plays for the Vienna Philharmonic. We need them for the celebration."

"Today's ceremony? Are you out of your mind?"

"Max, use your persuasive powers. You'd be surprised at your charming magnetism. You caught Consuelo's eye," Sánchez said in a mischievous manner as he ended the telephone conversation.

The retired inspector walked calmly back to Manuel Montes's office. He knocked on his locked door, but Montes said from within, "*Estoy muy ocupado.*"

The inspector told the despondent man to open the door. "Montes, *abre la puerta.*"

Looking completely disheveled, Montes came to the door. His eyes were red from weeping, and his tie was undone. There was liquor on his breath.

"Put the bottle away and know that you have support. Everything is under control. I've taken care of three of your four problems. I'll let you and your seamstress handle the fourth."

"What do you mean?" Montes asked.

"I mean that you need to find Nate Shelley a different tuxedo or an alternative. That can't be too difficult."

With both palms on his cheeks, Manuel Montes muttered, "How have you…are you certain…what if…" Montes hurried back to his desk, not really knowing why. He grabbed his pen, then fixed his tie in front of the full-length mirror behind his office door and combed his hair. He put on his suit jacket that was draped over his chair and asked, "Do you truly mean that is the only thing that is pending?"

"That's it. Now report back to me when that is done," said the inspector.

"*Sí, señor.*" Montes stood perfectly straight and saluted. Then, before leaving his office, he embraced Sánchez.

The string quartet arrived at exactly 7:30 p.m. They began to practice at 7:50. At 7:55 Ram Edmunds, Dr. Franz Lutz, and Dr. Arthur Beech walked into the lobby of the Hotel Santa Catalina. Ram addressed his new friend, Dr. Luntz: "What a grand hotel this is!"

"Yes, old chap—my good friend has extremely good taste. He stays here when he visits the Canaries." Ram could not help but admire Dr. Luntz's almost aristocratic demeanor. On his flight he had learned that Luntz and Beech were colleagues of Nate Shelley—both psychiatrists who had served in the World Psychiatric Organization for many years. Luntz was British and Beech was Canadian. Although both in their seventies, they looked energetic and full of vigor. Little did Ram know that Luntz, the distinguished, very proper Brit, was regarded in professional circles as a living legend, a giant in his profession. His work extended for several decades. He published innumerable publications and several bestsellers. His military posture and impeccable dress—aided by a silver goatee—were the epitome of distinction.

As for Beech, the beret-wearing rotund man who sported round, rimless glasses was also highly regarded more for his joyful and playful demeanor than his professional accomplishments. Nonetheless, Beech was remembered in his profession because of the significant publications in his youth.

Just then, the groom who was renewing his vows approached the trio standing in the elegant lobby. Nate wore a smart linen outfit that was reminiscent of his wedding attire, perfect clothing for a beach wedding. "What an amazing surprise to see you here!…my old friends Drs. Luntz and Beech. And Ram Edmunds, I did not know you would return to Europe so quickly. How in the world did you three connect?"

"Old boy, you would never guess. But the three of us have become good friends," said Dr. Luntz.

"Ahem…I beg your pardon. Am I being excluded from this new-found camaraderie?" asked Marceline (Marc) Hugot, as he walked in with two bakers following behind, gingerly balancing a three-tiered wedding cake that was on its way to the reception. Marc turned to Nate. "This came all the way from Madrid, in your honor."

As Marc led the bakers to the reception venue, Dr. Arthur Beech, stroking his white mustache, called out to Marc, "I will straighten out this group and inform them that thanks to you we did not miss our connection to Las Palmas!"

CHAPTER SIXTY-TWO

[Las Palmas, Canary Islands; April 2023]

Manuel Montes had decorated the banquet hall the same way that he had prepared it in 2016 for Nate and Miró's wedding. In honor of Abraham's heritage, a *chuppah*—the traditional Jewish canopy under which bride and groom say their vows—adorned the center of the hall. To the left and behind the *chuppah,* the string quartet was ready to begin. A long red carpet extended from the front door to the center. Five minutes before the arrival of the bride, Montes instructed Nate to stand at the front of the canopy, where he would await Miró to be walked down the aisle by her father, Abraham. Montes asked the best man, Max, to stand next to Nate. Marc Hugot stood by the door to be on the lookout for the bride's arrival. Montes fidgeted and combed down his hair one last time.

Finally, at ten minutes past 8:00 the bride, accompanied by her maid of honor, arrived. Marc alerted the string quartet to begin. They played "Canon in D," and Nate's heart raced just as much as it had the first time. As Marc opened the door, in marched the beautiful young maid of honor, who bore a remarkable resemblance to the bride. Deeply tanned and wearing her chestnut hair up, Minerva looked sensational. She wore a sky-blue dress that matched her eyes, the only physical feature she had inherited from her biological father. She smiled broadly at her "real dad," Nate, before sitting.

When Miró entered, Nate almost gasped because Miró looked more beautiful than she had the day of their wedding. Although it was a different dress, Miró had selected a beaded lace, mermaid-style gown like her wedding dress. The silver star-sequined skirt flared at the bottom, creating a sweep train. The low-cut back, adorned with a sash at the waist, exposed Miró's unblemished, tanned back. The subtle shimmer of the gossamer material captured every eye at the reception. Reminiscent of his wedding, Nate's eyes instantly watered.

As they stepped onto the *chuppah*, the same Jewish minister who had performed the wedding ceremony along with Archbishop José Gómez extended his Hebrew blessing. The Catholic ceremony followed, and when Miró said, "I do," Nate kissed his beloved bride. Montes noisily wept.

As the couple walked to the other side of the hall where the reception and elaborate dinner took place, Miró was surprised to see not only their old friends Drs. Luntz and Beech, but also Inspector Sánchez's former assistant, Sergeant Cobos, who had been promoted to deputy inspector. He extended his hand to shake Nate's, and immediately Nate remembered the hands that were as big as baseball mitts. Cobos had yet to learn a word of English, but he smiled and nodded with approval for Nate and the entire family. As Cobos moved on to the open bar, Inspector Sánchez approached Nate and handed him a note that his former best man, Carlos Lacroa, had sent the couple. In the note he apologized for not being able to attend since he was presently in Lisbon attending to some legal matters.

The *Galatea* Force was all there except for Eliza Durazo. She was addressing real estate matters back in Winnetka, matters that Commander Rob Rivers had called to her attention. It appeared that when law enforcement officials searched the principal building of Diego Montemayor's Winnetka estate, in Diego's personal records they discovered documents that clearly left the main house in the name of the twins—Pablo (Paul) and Mateo (Matt) Rosales. The trust also stated that if the twins superseded their mother in death, the ownership of the main house would revert to her and any of their heirs. Since the twins had no other designated heirs, Eliza—or Raquel Rosales—would remain as owner of the main house in the estate.

For several hours the group celebrated and enjoyed each other's company. Surprising to Minerva, Loni Peretz (the former Álana Rollo, her abductor) was present with her husband, Yosef Peretz. Before the end of the night, Loni asked Minerva for forgiveness, and to her surprise, not only did Minerva grant it, but she also offered a heartfelt embrace.

Max and Consuelo spent most of the time together. As she took her first sip of champagne, Miró commented to her daughter, "I would have never dreamt that there was any attraction between the two."

"Oh, Mom—I can't believe you missed all the clues. Couldn't you tell that whenever Max was around, Consuelo's hard edge disappeared? How many times did she smile during the day?"

"Not many—that's for sure," Miró said.

"I can guarantee that you saw her smile only when Uncle Max was around," Minerva said. "If you look at her tonight, do you see anything different?"

"Well, she certainly is wearing a knockout of a dress. She looks good, and she's smiling a lot," Miró said.

"What else?" asked Minerva. As she saw her mom struggling for an answer, she added, "Mom, she shaved her underarms."

"Aha...now I know who our next family sleuth will be," Miró said as she took her second sip and smiled.

The group consumed prodigious amounts of cava, *Bermejo Seco*, and *tempranillo*. In addition, they had assorted fruits, cheeses, tapas, and several portions of wedding cake. To everyone's surprise, at midnight, when the musicians had left, the group was still present, consuming the last tier of the wedding cake. "I must ask," said Ram Edmunds. "What divine ingredient is in this wedding cake?"

"I asked the same thing when I picked it up," said Marceline (Marc) Hugot. "When my brother allowed me a small taste, he told me it was a family secret. He shared it with me anyway. What he uses, unlike anyone else, is orange blossom water in the preparation. It gives his cakes a unique flavor that no one else seems to know about."

At Minerva's request, Dr. Luntz played the piano and the hotel general manager, Manuel Montes, an accomplished tenor, serenaded the group with various traditional classics. As he had done during

Nate and Miró's wedding, he sang "As Time Goes By," "It Had to Be You," and "The Way You Look Tonight."

Max and Consuelo were the first to hit the dance floor. Nate and Miró joined them, as well as Abraham, who danced with his grand-daughter Minerva. To everyone's surprise, Ram Edmunds took the microphone from the general manager and dedicated a song to the "newlyweds." When he started singing "Endless Love," Minerva ran up to him and joined him in a duet. It was such a beautiful rendition that Montes had to go off to a corner to sob in silence.

After the song, Minerva kept the microphone and asked Dr. Arthur Beech, "Would you please honor us with your special song? I don't think I can return to Chicago before hearing it." With a broad grin, Beech walked up, took off his beret, and keeping with his style, he performed a hilarious solo of "Do You Think I'm Sexy?"

The ceremony ended with a quartet. Arthur Beech, Ram Edmunds, Franz Luntz, and Manuel Montes sang Louis Armstrong's version of "What a Wonderful World."

. . .

[Chicago–Lyon–Palma; late April 2023]

Since Ram Edmunds had secured their round-trip airline tickets, Abraham and Minerva flew back to Chicago under their assumed names. Minerva took photos of her fake passport for the sake of pos-terity—since the FBI would reclaim it. She still could not fathom the notion that she had served as an "undercover agent" for an inter-national sting operation.

Nate and Miró flew back to Lyon, France, to prepare for an exit from Interpol. Before their departure, in an intimate formal ceremony held in Brussels, which involved a small number of Europol admin-istrators, the secretary general honored Nate with a commemorative "Medal of International Civic Contribution." Even Miró received a plaque for "Exemplary Dedication to the Elimination of Orga-nized Crime and Cybercrime." In a rare public address, the secretary general of Interpol, Jurgen Wagner, credited Nate and Miró Shelley for being the "key elements in the elimination of one of the world's most wanted criminals." Of course, consistent with Interpol's concern for discretion, few in the international media publicized the event.

The itinerary for Nate and Miró's return to the US was arranged and paid for by the general secretariat. Before leaving Europe, Nate Shelley made a last-minute change to their itinerary. Addressing his skeptical wife, he told Miró, "We need to make a stop in Mallorca. I know that Diego Montemayor's days are numbered, and there's something I need to say to him."

"What in the world needs to be said?" Miró asked. "Like Eliza, or Raquel Rosales, told me yesterday during her phone call, 'he can burn in hell for all I care.' I totally agree with her."

"Don't you see, Miró, he literally is burning from the inside out... one cell at a time? I don't think there can be a more excruciating death than death by radioactive poisoning. And there is no earthly punishment that he could have received from law enforcement that could match his self-imposed death. Remember that according to His Word, revenge belongs to the Lord."

"I will travel with you to Mallorca, but I refuse to see that monster face to face," Miró said.

It was a warm, humid day when Nate and Miró flew into the Palma Airport. They immediately drove to the hospital where Diego Montemayor was being treated and held under tight police security. As Nate walked into the guarded private room, Nate barely recognized the frail, pallid figure who was emaciated and broken. He was barely conscious, but Diego woke when he was informed that Dr. Nathaniel Shelley was there to see him. His eyes were lifeless, and he was intubated. Diego summoned an attending nurse to demand that his tubes be removed. He also asked that his hospital bed be raised so that he could be at the same level as his visitor.

"Why...are you here?" Diego Montemayor struggled to articulate each word.

Without biting his lip and without blinking, Nate said, "Your hatred toward me and my family—in a bizarre way—brought me to understand and accept my faith. So I am here out of duty. Now that I know God's mercy, I have come to understand that my God tells me that I should forgive you. I do so now."

"Archbishop Gómez has been here. I've been given absolution," Diego said.

"Have you repented of your sins?" Nate asked.

Still struggling, Diego responded, "He asked me the same thing… the archbishop. And I have…. He also gave me my last rites. I believe that I will walk through the gates of heaven."

"You will if you've accepted our Lord Jesus as your Lord and Savior. That's my belief." Before Nate turned around to leave, he noticed that Diego Montemayor wept and smiled.

As Nate walked up to the elevator, over the hospital's PA system came the emergency code of a "Code Blue," or *Código Azul en Sala 317*. Room 317 was the one Nate had just left. Three uniformed nurses and two physicians rushed into Diego's room. Ten minutes later, Miró walked out the elevator, looking for Nate. She found him at the end of the hallway. "What's the holdup, Nate?"

Before Nate could explain, the five medical staff members walked out and removed their latex gloves. The head physician said, "*Tiempo de defunción, 6:39.*"

Nate turned to Miró and asked, "Did he say that 6:39 p.m. was time of death?"

"Yup," Miró said. "Now we can go on with our lives."

. . .

[Chicago; May 2023]

On Saturday, May 13, Abraham Epstein hosted a special birthday party. "On this day," said Abraham, "we celebrate my granddaughter's eighteenth birthday. It is special because I feel that our lives have finally returned to normal. We are celebrating without the ominous threat of being hunted by one of the world's most dangerous criminals."

Among those present at the birthday party were Ram Edmunds,

who had flown in from DC with his wife, Claire, who had insisted that Laurie Martin, her husband's executive assistant, join them since she was a good family friend not only to the Edmunds family but also to the Shelley-Epstein household. Commander Rob Rivers of the 20th District of the Chicago PD was also there with his good friend Horace (Rosie) Rosenberg, star reporter from the *Chicago Tribune*. To everyone's delight, Raquel Rosales—who had resumed her identity after playing the role of Eliza Durazo—brought her sister-in-law Rosa María to the party. The newcomer to the group was Consuelo Cervantes, a visitor from Spain who had accompanied Max Kempball back to America. The tall, athletic blonde who spoke Spanish with a German accent demonstrated an even thicker accent when she spoke English, which forced Max to constantly ask Consuelo to repeat statements.

"Everyone, this is my guest from Toledo, Spain, Consuelo Cervantes," said Max. "Although she's on leave from Interpol, I'm hopeful that I can convince her to stay in Chicago…permanently."

A collective "Oooh" came spontaneously from the crowd. To those who knew Consuelo, a very uncharacteristic blushing appeared on her face. "Is there anything that the group needs to hear?" Abraham asked.

"Maybe later, after the birthday celebration is over," Max said.

Minerva, the birthday girl, also showed up with a guest. Although no longer "an item," as Abraham explained to the group, Cal Steele attended as Minerva's date. He was now proudly a student at West Point Academy and planning a career in the military. The couple remained good friends, but they both had decided that neither one was ready for solidifying next steps, so they were maintaining a long-distance friendship.

At Minerva's insistence, the party began with the cutting of the cake (prepared with orange blossom water) and the popping of Spanish cava, the family favorite *Segura Viudas Brut, Reserva Heredad*. Of course, plenty of *Bermejo Seco* and *Emilio Moro tempranillo* was available.

After the customary well wishes and opening of birthday gifts, Ram Edmunds led the group in singing "Happy Birthday" to Minerva.

Sitting around Abraham's enormous patio, Nate then led the group in singing his favorite Beatles song, "Here Comes the Sun." Max played the guitar, and the talented bass player, Rob Rivers, joined him.

At 11:00 that night the group gathered by the smokeless fire pit and listened to the Beatles and the rest of the *Abbey Road* album. Max, who had borrowed Rob's guitar, surprised everyone by serenading Consuelo with "She's So Heavy," and even Abraham, Nate, and Ram joined in to harmonize in the chorus. Turning to Raquel (Eliza Durazo), the whole group serenaded her with "Something," George Harrison's masterpiece.

"You, my dear," said Ram Edmunds, "played a perfect Eliza. This Pygmalion operation would not have succeeded without you. Cheers!"

"I do have a question," said Eliza. "Could someone tell me if Estevan and Isabella got completely away?"

"I'm afraid so," said Ram Edmunds. "Got away scot-free. My hunch is that they're in China. The CCP will protect them and shield them from any of our requests for extradition."

"So what will happen to the deputy secretary general of Interpol, Gabriel Picard?" Minerva asked.

Ram Edmunds responded: "In addition to aiding and abetting Estevan, he also protected Diego to a certain extent. The charges of child molestation were dropped a long time ago, but we believe that his involvement with the Pan Asian Shipping Enterprise will implicate him in child trafficking and other crimes against humanity. His demise will probably be in prison."

"What I'm unclear about," said Minerva, "is whether Estevan was Picard's plant in Diego Montemayor's organization."

Nate jumped in, "Ha! I asked Picard the same question…just as he was being led away by the authorities. Do you know what he said?"

"No, my love," said Miró. "How about sharing with the rest of us?"

Smiling, Nate said, "As he turned to look at me, Picard, who was already handcuffed, responded, 'What makes you think *I* was not *Estevan's* plant at Interpol'?"

"Whoa—wait a minute," said Max. "That puts a different spin on things. Are you saying that Estevan Chengfu, not Diego Montemayor, was running Diego's enormous criminal empire?"

"That's right, genius. That would make more sense," Consuelo said. "Thing is, Estevan, a high party official in China, eased into Diego's organization when Tío Dante and Diego parted ways. His efforts allowed Diego to consolidate his possessions and control multiple cartels. But Estevan never intended for Diego to truly assume full control of the entire cabal. Diego's organization was merely a 'wise investment' for Estevan."

"So," Max asked, "did Estevan want to eventually gain control of Diego's enterprise from the beginning?"

"Yes, we think so," Ram Edmunds said. "Posing as a mute, Estevan worked behind the scenes, and unbeknownst to Diego, infiltrated Interpol through his puppet, Gabriel Picard. It was a brilliant move on Estevan's part. He wanted Diego to see him as having limitations, a handicap, so he played the role of a mute. Having siblings who were truly deaf mutes, he had plenty of experience and the mastery of sign language."

"And," added Consuelo, "the mysterious voice recordings between Picard and his Chinese contact actually involved Estevan. We all confirmed that Estevan could speak perfectly well aboard the *Sark* when Isabella lost her shoes. Estevan cried out to Isabella, 'We can't wait! Leave them behind!' referring to her shoes…remember?"

"One more thing, Ram," asked Max. "I remember that you poohpoohed my suggestion that the former US President Archie Williams was Diego's handler. Was there any truth to that piece of information that the deceased Tío Dante shared with me?"

"I still refuse to believe that outrageous claim," Ram said. "However, during the secretary general's interrogation, Picard told his boss, 'If Estevan has his druthers, Archie will succeed you as secretary general…sooner than you think'. Until I see some proof, I refuse to believe such nonsense."

"I agree," Max said. "Archie probably wants to head the United Nations." A few around him chuckled in agreement.

Confused, Minerva looked around and exclaimed, "Would someone please explain all these connections! What does our former President Williams have to do with anything?"

"In a note left for your mom and dad," Ram said, "Tío Dante, Diego Montemayor's former associate and right-hand man, claimed that Diego Montemayor's 'handler' was former president Williams. A 'handler' is someone who—"

"Yes, Mr. Edmunds—I know the term 'handler,'" said Minerva. "If that's true, then who pulled the ex-president's strings?"

"Although Ram refuses to believe such a thing," Max said, jumping in, "according to that hypothesis, Estevan was not only Gabriel Picard's handler but also had Archie Williams under his control."

"So really, Estevan was running the whole show—according to that theory," Minerva said. "Wow—I have enough here to write a series of novels. I have a funny feeling, though, that I won't be allowed to publish this stuff, right?"

Ram Edmunds placed a hand on Minerva's shoulder, "I'm afraid not, young lady. I'm so sorry."

In a grandfatherly gesture, Abraham Epstein embraced Minerva. "Just think of it this way, *Mi'jita*—no one would believe a word of it."

THE END

ACKNOWLEDGMENTS

Pygmalion's Reckoning, the third novel of a trilogy, could not have been written without the love and support of my wife and best friend, Marty Kellam Vargas. As my first line of defense, she served as proofreader and content editor of my first drafts.

Of course, my talented editor and final proofreader, Jonathan Wright, rescued me from countless gaffes. Thank you for your masterful and meticulous editing.

In conducting research for this project, I consulted numerous books, journals, articles, and websites… too many to enumerate. A number of family members, friends, and colleagues served as beta readers of early drafts. My niece, Letty Leggett, provided valuable opinions and feedback, as did my good friends Miguel Conchas, Juan Sánchez, Dr. Tomás Coronado, Donato Martinez, and Dr. Mike Pérez. Also a good friend and future family member, Rob Roy, provided valuable support. My apologies if I've forgotten anyone else who kindly supported me.